Beyond
the Wood

Michael J Roueche

Beyond
the Wood

MICHAEL J. ROUECHE

Vesta House Publishing

Beyond the Wood

ISBN-10 0983756716
ISBN-13: 9780983756712

Cover design by Nick Zelinger, NZ Graphics
www.nzgraphics.com

by Vesta House Publishing
12783 Domingo Ct., Ste 400
Parker, Colorado, 80134
www.vestahousepublishing.com

*"Whom the dawn has seen proud,
evening has seen laid low."*

Thyestes, 613

*I*n contemplating the causes which may disturb our Union, it occurs as matter of serious concern, that any ground should have been furnished for characterizing parties by geographical discriminations—Northern and Southern, Atlantic and Western; whence designing men may endeavour to excite a belief, that there is a real difference of local interests and views. One of the expedients of Party to acquire influence, within particular districts, is to misrepresent the opinions and aims of other districts.—You cannot shield yourselves too much against the jealousies and heart burnings, which spring from these misrepresentations;—they tend to rend alien to each other those, who ought to be bound together by fraternal affection.

George Washington's Farewell Address, 1796

Prologue
Not Long Ago, Near Gainesville, Virginia

*R*eid Gragg scanned the open, rolling Virginia countryside that passed at 65 miles per hour. He had planned to make this trip for a long time, and now that he was so close, he felt the excitement of a small boy. He couldn't concentrate, and he fidgeted in his seat even as he drove. This was a sacred pilgrimage . . . something he had to do to set the world right . . . an epic task awaiting him alone.

He had put it off, then later tried to forget it. As much as he wanted to ignore it, however, it was always there waiting to be done. His adult life to this point had been unsettled. He had done poorly in school, lost a couple jobs, failed in romance. This trip would change all that. It would be a new start; the start he should have had long ago. It hung over him, unfulfilled and menacing, like a dark rain cloud that had to pass before skies cleared. He blamed his father for all this. His father had charged him to come to Manassas when he had given Reid the button.

Reid was a tall, thin man, in his mid-twenties. He'd never been to Virginia. He looked at the map that lay on the seat next to him, scanning it between quick looks at the road. The next exit was Gainesville and the Manassas National Battlefield Park.

His dad had visited the battlefield once, just before he married. It was one of his most cherished memories. Reid could remember the exact words his father used to describe it: "I saw Stonewall Jackson come out of the woods, ride his sorrel to a rise above the road. Watching. Just watching. I saw him race back. I heard him order his men forward. I heard the muskets of the Iron Brigade and saw their tall, distinctive black hats. I saw them in their first hour of greatness."

"Reid," he then would say. "I want you someday to take this button there. Before you set out on your life's journey, you must go back there. You've got to see Stonewall, too. My father sent me there. Now I'm sending you."

Reid had never been to a Civil War battlefield before, but he had read a few books and articles about the war, the Iron Brigade and the battle that took place on Brawner's Farm, between Gainesville and Groveton, the battle that opened Second Manassas. He had always wondered why the Civil War had such a following. It seemed a rather bloody, unneeded event to get everyone so excited, but his father always argued that the war was the focal point of America's past and future. The visions; the shortcomings; the unanswered questions of the American Revolution came into sharp focus in the Civil War. Much of what happened in the country after the war, from race relations, the government's role in people's lives, and the nation's role in the world, could only be understood by looking back at those four years of American tumult.

He told Reid the war was an earthquake of historic proportions, set up by shifting, conflicting rock formations beneath the grounds of culture. When pressure between the vision and reality of America in the North and the vision and reality of life in the South reached the breaking point, the cultural rift exploded to the surface, breaking the ground into fissures and then into a great abyss on the landscape. The surface had healed over the decades, but the rocks still shifted below the surface. Reid's father had come to believe the country, natives and immigrants alike, young and old—especially the young—had to come back to the Civil War . . . before they could move on.

This is it, Reid thought, as he pulled into the exit lane and eased on his brakes. The exit looped under the highway, and he followed it around at a comfortable speed and merged onto Virginia Route 29, formerly the old Warrenton Turnpike.

Shortly he saw something in the woods on the left, near the road. It looked like a monument. Could this be it? He didn't remember seeing a sign for the park, and just a few yards beyond the marker he saw a restaurant and a building that looked like an old gas station with heavy trucks parked behind it. He hoped this wasn't the battlefield: This couldn't be the battlefield. He continued driving.

He passed a brown park-like sign that mentioned "Stuart." He had arrived. He couldn't quite believe it. His radio was playing country music, and he reached over and turned it off. He thought of where he was and what had happened here. A feeling of reverence passed over him. He tried to make the feeling stronger by remembering the men's sacrifices. He had planned to go to the park visitor's center, but as he drove his eye caught sight of an old house, off to the left, distant from the highway on a small ridge. He drove through a wood that extended to both sides of the road and saw a narrow turnoff ahead on the left. He pulled into the driveway and followed it up a short hill to a parking lot. This was it! It had to be. The house. The wood. Just as he'd read. He parked the car and immediately got out, failing even to lock the door or take the keys.

Reid looked across the field. To his left lay the trees through which he'd just driven; to his right, a hilltop adorned with silenced, Civil-War-era cannons. In front, the land descended from the small parking lot into lowlands before rising again as a new, heavily wooded hill in the distance. The grass on most of the field was short, with a path worn still shorter. He followed the path to the lowlands in front, paying no heed to historical markers and information he passed along the way.

His thoughts flipped through dozens of random Civil War trivial facts—many his father had told him. Then his feeling of reverence vanished. He wondered why he was there celebrating such a bloody war that left 600,000 men dead and nearly as many disabled, but the thought didn't linger. Facts and figures again began running through his head. He reached an intersecting path that led toward the trees and followed it, crossing a dry creek bed, entering the wood. He wanted to get to the house, the orchard, the fence on the other side.

Reid's father had died one year ago to the day. Until he died, even during the months he spent in the nursing home, every time he saw Reid he had asked him expectantly, "Have you been there, yet?" or "Have you planned your trip?" He always seemed disappointed to hear that Reid still hadn't gone. Only once had he added, "You promised, you know. I promised my dad and went. I'm counting on you. I was hoping to talk to you about it." Reid was here now to settle with his father, and he had brought the button.

Abruptly, the pilgrim stopped. He was walking too fast. This was meant to be slow . . . thoughtful . . . profound. He looked around. Daylight filtered through a thousand trees, and Reid raised the button to look at it in the indirect sunlight. He had examined it countless times before. He looked at it now to set the final scene for what he hoped was his long-awaited spiritual journey of rebirth. It was an old brass-looking button with a raised image on the front. "Virginia" was embossed curving across the top, and in the center was stamped an image of the state symbol: a soldier with his foot upon the chest of a fallen enemy and the Virginia state motto, "Sic Semper Tyrannis." Reid remembered, "Thus always to tyrants."

He closed his hand over the button, lowered it and moved slowly onward. He noticed the small trees already turned red and yellow, and gazed upward at the under-side of the still green leaves of the larger trees. He listened to the sounds of nature, but noise from traffic on the highway distracted and irritated him. He heard movement ahead. It startled him, but he smiled in relief as he glimpsed a hint of rapidly moving brown bodies and large white tails. He heard birds flutter and chirp in the trees. He heard, then saw, several squirrels descend noisily from trees to the ground, then ascend the trees again. It was beginning to feel as it should for the experience he hoped awaited him.

When he came to the clearing, his hopes were dashed. He expected a house as it appeared in 1862, orchards with fruit and new, well-kept fences. Instead he found a few old fruit trees, no wooden fence, and a two-story house that could not have dated to the Civil War, but that was nonetheless in the late stages of decay. The house made of now-weather-darkened, rotting wood had no porch or stairs, leaving its doors strangely elevated above ground level. Its stone foundation was crumbling. Warning signs were posted on a six-foot-high, chain-link fence that enclosed the entire structure. And Reid again wondered why his father had been so insistent that he come.

For 20 minutes he walked the grounds, reading historical interpretive signs and exploring the site. He was ready to go home. There was nothing here for him. No Iron Brigade. No Stonewall. No secret. No magic to change his life or give it meaning. He studied one last time the interpretive sign that marked where the 19th Indiana infantry, his ancestor's regiment, had fought. He reread a quotation from the regiment's colonel, a Solomon Meredith, and closed his eyes trying to imagine what it must have been like. But the features of the land must have changed, and he couldn't bring the image to life.

"You're a Northerner, then?" a woman's voice said from behind him in a Southern accent.

Reid jumped slightly at the sound, and he looked around at a small woman with softly curling, shoulder-length blond hair standing just 15 feet behind him. She appeared to be about his age, wore blue jeans and hiking boots and carried a walking stick. She looked vaguely familiar, and Reid was immediately drawn to her. Her face was open, her eyes clear and strong. He noticed a long, pencil-lead-thin scar that ran across her right cheek. He tried to not stare at it, but his eyes rested on it as the only blemish on her otherwise perfect skin.

She laughed and said, "I'm sorry. I didn't mean to startle you."

"You didn't startle me."

"Oh, then you jump like that all the time," the woman said, laughing again.

"Well, maybe a bit."

"You interested in the 19th?" she asked, looking down at the interpretive sign he had been reading.

"I had an ancestor in the 19th Indiana."

"Tracing your ancestors then?"

"Something like that."

"And what have you discovered?"

"That a lot has changed. It's hard to imagine what really happened here."

"It is very different than it was."

"Your ancestors in the fight, too?"

"The Civil War? No, I didn't have ancestors in the war, but I feel close to it . . . to this battlefield in particular."

"You from around here?"

"From Virginia. I like to come here on special occasions."

"Oh? What's the occasion today?"

She smiled warmly at Reid and said, "Why . . . you're here, of course."

Her pleasantness put Reid at ease. He said, "So, you're a Southerner."

"Southern born, but I appreciate both sides. It's all over you know."

"The war?"

"Exactly. The war's over. It's all just history now, contrary to what you hear. Virginia's better off where she is, in the Union. I'm convinced of that . . . now. But it was hard to see that then, when there were so many voices and all of them loud . . . demanding."

Reid smiled. "You don't see it as the War of Northern Aggression, then?"

"Perhaps just a tad." She smiled. "It's a real paradox, the war. Not nation against nation or one nationality against another; just one powerful idea against another powerful idea and culture. Did you know that even as the states lined up on either side for the war, Congress was working on passing its originally intended 13th amendment. It would have protected slavery at the Federal level forever . . . would have left it entirely up to the individual states. The Federal government never would have been able to touch it. But its chances for success died; the Southern States weren't there to support it. Of course, the next version of the 13th amendment ended slavery. By going to war, the South succeeded in destroying its own way of life, weakening the argument for states' rights—the very things they wanted to protect. All for pride, perhaps. You know the South could never have succeeded."

"You don't think they could have won the war? You believe it was the Lost Cause and all that?"

"Not exactly. Perhaps they could have won the war. I don't know about that; lots of opinions both ways. But I must say . . . looking back on it now, it worked out alright in the end. But it sure was costly . . . so costly; and it still is." She almost whispered these last words, then raised her voice again and said, "And so unneeded. Those who called for the war. Those who caused the war killed all those men, all those men. I wonder if they'll have to pay for it; if they haven't already. It didn't have to be . . . the war that is. They should have stuck together and fought all they wanted to, but just kept it a verbal war. They should have fought the battles politically and left the ground to the farmers.

"Do you remember that Roman tragedy?" she continued. "The one where a man seeks revenge against a brother who's wronged him? He kills his brother's innocent sons; then feeds them to their unwitting father. The war was the same. It's as if for revenge, hate and pride, the politicians, the aristocrats fed the country on its own sons, and then and even now we all sit around and debate the justice of the cause; when the country ate its fair sons! There are wonderful stories of individual bravery, patriotism, tragedy and sacrifice—and they're all so romantic. They really are! But just below the surface, just barely conceivable by human conscience are clouded reflections of a country gorging itself on its own flesh. Its own children."

A little out of breath, she paused. "We just don't see it for what it was: a near national death." She hesitated. "Sure, some good came of the Civil War, but that good should have come without it! Arrogance and pride cost or ruined more than a million lives. Unlike today of course," she paused and smiled ironically. "In the United States of 1860, everyone focused on how the group they belonged to was different from some other group. Instead of finding what unified them, they took pleasure in what differentiated them: They were no longer one people with so much in common; they were Northerners; they were Southerners; they were slaveholders; they were abolitionists. And when they were so proud of the differences, it was easy for conspiring men to urge them on towards separation, hatred; towards the inferno."

She paused again, looking directly into Reid's eyes. "There must be a lesson for us in there somewhere. Yet, in spite of all that, we all seem to get caught up in it—to see it only as the romance of a lost age set amid the destruction of the pre-modern world. But I've digressed." She sighed. "Yes, to answer your question, there was a time when I believed it was a War of Northern Aggression, but that was a long time ago."

"You don't look old enough to have 'a long time ago.'"

"You flatter me," she said flatly.

Reid perceived she was offended by the statement, so he attempted to change the subject by interesting her in the button. He said, "I've got a button that came from this battlefield."

She looked at him without responding, looked at the ground, then at him again. "You know it's illegal to take historical artifacts from the park?"

He laughed. "Don't worry. This button was taken off the field in 1862. A few years I suspect before that law was passed." He extended his hand with the button, and she approached him to look at it.

"Your ancestor was a Southern soldier, then? Thought he was in the 19th?"

"He was in the 19th. He was a Southerner though. He was from Virginia, too. I don't know much about the button or for that matter about my ancestor. I only know it belonged to him . . . just thought he wore it on his uniform because he was from Virginia. I don't know what happened to him after the battle."

"That's not from a Yankee uniform; definitely a button from a Southern soldier."

"That's strange!"

"Not so unusual for a Virginian to be for the Union. Now everyone seems to think every Virginian, or for that matter that the whole South, wanted secession. It wasn't so clear . . . not then. You know there were several Virginians in the 19th and the Iron Brigade. I actually know quite a bit about Virginians in the 19th. What was your ancestor's name?"

"Henry Gragg."

A look of delight crossed the woman's features, "Hank Gragg . . . from Woodstock?"

"You know about him?"

"What hand of Providence has brought us together? I do know about him . . . quite a lot really. I may know the story of that button. Imagine: of all the people that could meet here today, a man who has a button and no story, and a woman who has a story but no button."

"You know about this button? That's odd."

"I think I do, and maybe it is odd. Would you like to hear about it . . . and about Hank Gragg? That's what he was called, you know."

"I would very much like to hear it. But how do you know about him? Are you a historian with the park?"

"Historian? Of sorts. I suppose, like you, I'm living history. I know it's not very comfortable, but sit down. Sit down right here in the grass. I'll tell you all you want to know."

She gracefully sat on the grass and patted the ground across from her. Reid slid to the ground at a comfortable distance from her. As he did, he was in a stupor. He could not conceive of this woman knowing about his ancestor and was angry his father had not told him more about Henry. If this woman, not even a relative, knew the story; then certainly, his father must have known it—or should have.

"You know," the woman began, "there would be no story to tell if Betsy hadn't rejected Hank . . . ."

Part One
Salted for the Fire

"Now let me keep my promise."

Thyestes, 507

Chapter 1
28 August 1862, Near Gainesville, Virginia

Oblivious to what awaited them, they were in high spirits. The troops of the 19th Indiana Regiment had just enjoyed a brief but welcome rest from their slow, often-interrupted, day-long march; and some, the lucky ones, savored the memory of freshly slaughtered and roasted ox. Others remembered only cutting strips of ox meat, raw and still warm, and chewing it as they formed again to march. The regiment was beyond Gainesville, Virginia, on the Warrenton Turnpike, making its way from Warrenton to Centreville where awaited, according to latest rumor, the long-sought enemy General Thomas J. "Stonewall" Jackson and his men. The Union soldiers could hear cannon to the rear, but paid little heed, marching happily in four columns, carrying their rifle muskets casually, visiting, singing.

Hank Gragg, 20 years old, slender and of average height, with dark, thick hair and penetrating blue eyes, was a volunteer in the 19th. He had grown up in Woodstock, Virginia, a hamlet in the northern end of the Shenandoah Valley, but he marched today with Union soldiers, and he had become one of them.

The 19th was brigaded with three regiments from Wisconsin. All four were comprised of men from the frontiers of the West, the only completely western bri-

gade in the East. The soldiers wore this identity as a
mark of distinction. They were frontiersmen and with
their unusual tall black hats were called the Black Hat
Brigade.

Hank was as content as he ever was now. He walked
silently enjoying the feeling of a full stomach and remembering the taste of the beef and the past year. He
joined the 19th in July 1861. After a few weeks of
training in Indiana, the regiment made its way by rail
to Washington, ready for a fight. Now, a year after
muster, the regiment and Hank still awaited their first
battle test and the accompanying hoped-for glory. The
Hoosiers had spent their early months in war preparation and their free moments wallowing in homesick-
ness and boredom. In Virginia, the regiment had skir-
mished with Rebels at Lewinsville and supported a
raid on the railroad at Frederick's Hall. Of late, it had
suffered under heavy artillery fire and been seasoned
by marching in the hot, heavy Virginia summer. But
these experiences were not full battle.

Hank, like his fellows, wearied waiting for battle,
but camp life came easily to him. He heard of soldiers
who grew so tired of army life—the picketing, the food,
the lice, the rain, the marching, the cold, the sickness,
the hunger, the drilling, the fighting—that they tried to
shoot off their own toes or fingers just to go home. He
heard of one soldier who shot off half his foot when he
was aiming for his big toe and of another volunteer
who got in a battle and hid behind a tree. During some
of the fiercest fighting, the soldier jumped up and
down, still behind the tree, waving his arms and legs,
hoping to be slightly wounded so he could go home a

still-living hero. Hank never considered such rash acts as he had no other place to go, and although he didn't consciously realize it, he liked camp life. He hadn't been sick as many others had during early weeks and months in the army, he enjoyed the company of the men around him, and most of the time he had enough to eat.

Hank did have difficult moments. Picket duty was particularly trying. During such duty, he was often overwhelmed with a feeling of futility before the dull face of the enemy. On one occasion, he was unable to move freely for hours because nearby Confederate pickets were particularly vigilant, so for entertainment he put his forage cap on the end of a stick that lay nearby and slowly raised it. Within seconds he heard two muskets discharged across the guarded fields and the hat danced on the stick. When he lowered the hat, he was disappointed to find only one ball had found its way through the target.

As he marched, he thought about the hole in his old cap. He still carried it with him in his knapsack . . . called it his "battle trophy." He planned to stop carrying it if he ever got a trophy from a full battle, but he wasn't sure he would ever see one.

Hank often wondered how he would fare in a real battle. Would he run? He remembered his rapid flight from Virginia three years earlier: Would he run from battle in fear as he had run then in despair. Many men, men he knew from the brigade, had run at Bull Run. Men from the Second Wisconsin, a Black Hat regiment that had fought at the battle of Bull Run, told how some officers ran from the enemy in the battle, and how, in the end, everyone had to run or be killed or captured. Hank wouldn't mind running if it was a general retreat. But to run alone! He couldn't abide the possibility. He already carried enough shame. But then, why would he run? He had nothing to run to; and it, even the shame, could all be over so quickly for him . . . on any field . . . on any day.

He had heard a few men in the regiment bragging during their first year of enlistment. They had promised great battle exploits, courageous acts, unimaginable heroics. Daniel Hume talked that way. Hume, a 20-year-old Indiana native, had joined their mess. They'd thought of excluding him because he was such a braggart and bully. Maybe they still would, but they hadn't yet. Hume had promised astounding feats. He was tall, broad and loud; often in brawls and arguments, always with men smaller than himself. Hank had never boasted of great valor: He harbored real doubts about his own mettle.

He marched now with a Union division comprising four brigades spread out over a mile. The Black Hats were second in line, marching as the sun descended over the thick, deep, green, summer Virginia countryside to the sounds of a regimental band somewhere in the brigade playing an unrecognizable tune.

"There's a Reb," one division soldier called out.

"Where?" another asked.

"On the hill. The horseman," the first indicated.

"He ain't Secesh. Looks like a farmer to me," the second said.

"No, no. He's a Reb all right," insisted the first.

"What he be doin'?" asked a third.

"Just scoutin'. Tryin' to figure out what we're doin'," the first responded.

"Hope he's luckier at that than us. Ain't no one in this army has the slightest idea where we're headin', or if we're comin' or goin'. Been marchin' for a month now . . . seems like . . . but we never get nowhere. We march here, then to over there, then to over there. We ain't never fightin', really fightin'. If we ever figure out who's runnin' this here army, we ought'o hang 'em higher than Haman," another added, as agreeing laughter broke out among those who heard him.

The horseman, on a distant ridge overlooking the pike was clearly agitated and rode back and forth along the flank of the passing column.

The second soldier concluded, "Ain't no difference if he's a Reb. What can one Johnny do? We could bring him down right where he rides. I could do it with one shot."

"You're right about that. At that distance, why even you could shoot him," said the third, laughing.

Abruptly, the rider turned and galloped from sight.

Within minutes, Hank heard cannon fire ahead. Cannon shells began bursting closer . . . in the trees near him. The 19th moved to the side of the road and into the protection of a small bank and trees north of the Pike. Hank moved to the trees and kept his gun at his side and his knapsack on his back as he lay down. He caught glimpses of a Black Hat regiment disappearing deep into the woods, and shortly he heard heavy musketry somewhere off in the same direction. Some of the men nearby spoke with great animation. He tried to hear what they were saying, but he couldn't concentrate on their words. The soldiers immediately around him were silent.

Seconds passed. Hank was anxious. They waited. The waiting was hard. Shells burst above them in the trees and behind them on the turnpike. The sound of musketry through the woods increased. He wished they would give the order to do something: Stand up . . . move forward . . . move backward . . . to battle . . . out of battle . . . just move. It was interminable. Panic slowly tightened its fingers around his throat. In agitation he rocked his head up and down as he lay waiting. He tried to calm himself by taking a deep breath. "No need to panic! No need to panic. Just lie here. Wait," he repeated slowly and continually in his mind. But the more he thought the words, the more he couldn't wait. He couldn't control his thoughts . . . his body. He wanted to spring to his feet and run. He lifted his head, looked . . . wild eyed . . . to the right . . . forward . . . to the left. He turned his head and desperately looked behind him . . . prone and huddled men and trees were in his way . . . everywhere he looked. He couldn't run . . . trapped! He had to run. He couldn't stay. Suddenly it was too much for him. Trying to rise and run, he lunged to the right . . . bumping hard into another prostrate soldier. The soldier barked, "Watch it," cursed and pushed Hank back. Hank fell prone again. The contact and aggression of the bump and shove felt good. It brought Hank up short. He rested his head on the earth, his face in the cool, moist dirt. His thoughts were slowing down. A warm sensation covered him . . . relief . . . cool sweat beaded on the back of his neck. He could wait. He began a silent dialogue with himself again: "Everything is going to be fine." His heart raced uncontrollably in relief. "It doesn't matter what happens to you. No need to panic. The only thing that matters is the glory . . . and the end. This is the hour!" He was strangely sleepy.

Battle sounds surged through the trees, growing in intensity. At last he heard the command, and with his comrades dropped knapsack and moved through the wood.

Chapter 2

28 August 1862, Brawner's Farm, Near Groveton, Virginia

As he made his way forward, Hank dodged trees that loomed suddenly near his path. He bent down to avoid low-hanging branches and once tripped over a rock protruding from the ground. Branches of small trees and brush grabbed at his shirt sleeves and pant legs. He couldn't see what was happening in the battle ahead or where they were going, but the sound swelled. Then . . . he was beyond the wood in the open and he saw the field.

The black-hatted Second Wisconsin stood 300 yards ahead silhouetted in the rapidly fading evening light on a small ridge, smoke obscuring them as they fired at will into the distance. Men in the Second were falling, some already on the ground, and others wandering aimlessly behind the line or stumbling back toward the trees. He heard encouragement from Solomon Meredith, "Long Sol," the regiment's six-foot, seven-inch tall, Quaker colonel: "Boys, don't forget that you are Hoosiers, and above all, remember the glorious flag of our country. Forward! Guide center! Double quick! March!" Hank moved forward, yelling at the top of his lungs with the other Hoosiers. He leaped a fence in the path. A house and orchard were ahead.

The officers dressed the line, all the while pushing the men forward nearly to the crest of the hill. There they were . . . Rebels . . . no more than 75 yards away, some crouching behind a fence, others near the farmhouse, and some among the trees in the orchard. Hank no longer felt the fear that so recently had almost driven him from his friends. He no longer wondered about valor or personal courage. He was no longer annoyed with braggart Hume.

Flame and smoke erupted from the Confederate line. Hank felt men fall . . . gasp . . . moan around him, but he didn't see them. He unconsciously took one step back, bumping the soldier behind him, then stepped forward again closing with those still in line, and returned the fire. The sound was deafening. He bit off the end of a cartridge, poured the powder into the muzzle, placed the bullet into the shaft, rammed it home, placed a cap on the nipple and fired again. His hands were shaking, his face already blackening from the powder. He could hear someone nearby cursing, but it seemed strangely distant. As he struggled to load and fire with his unsteady hands, he absentmindedly listened to the curses. It was George Dyer. Imagine that. George Dyer! Hank had never heard a profane word from George. George was a talker . . . constantly, and a prankster, but he never cussed. Now a new George Dyer was raving, blaspheming. Without breaking words into sentences for punctuation, he muttered one long phrase of profanity. Hank reloaded. Rammed. Primed. Fired. Reloading as fast as his shaking fingers could manage, he fired. He could hear Dyer's steady malediction. Men everywhere were yelling, cursing, cheering. Hank's eyes and throat burned from the smoke. He could see Rebels still there . . . partially hidden by the smoke and growing darkness . . . by fence . . . haystacks . . . fruit trees . . . house.

Hank took little time to load now, his fingers firming with experience. Men on both sides screamed. He heard someone command, "Fire low! You're firing above their heads. Aim low!" Hank aimed lower and fired. He reloaded. He fired low. He heard the hiss of the balls around him . . . sometimes fading . . . sometimes ending in an unexpected thud. One ball seemed to touch him . . . pulling at him as it passed. He felt no wound and without wondering kept at his task. For one brief moment, he imagined each hiss was potential death for him, but he couldn't hold the thought.

Inexplicably the Southerners were still there. Hank wondered why they weren't falling—but it didn't matter. Sometimes he thought he saw one drop, but before he was sure, another would seemingly sprout in his place. Hank dropped to one knee, kept loading and firing. The sound was enormous, but it was far away . . . disconnected from Hank and the others. The Rebs were close, too close; but they too were absurdly far away. He moved behind a tree and fired. Time ceased to move forward and refused to go backward. This work was done in one unending moment, between the click of the clock's second hand. Seventy-five yards away, he could see the Confederate dead, but still more were alive and shooting. He wondered who they were shooting at. He loaded and fired now with mechanical precision, taking better aim. His fingers were steady . . . his gaze firm. He fired low. He felt nothing for the men he faced. They were no longer human beings. This was target practice and the objects in the distance nothing more than targets used in last winter's camp.

Hank's musket fouled with powder. He couldn't ram another bullet down its blisteringly hot and now dirtied barrel. He threw it to the ground and grabbed an abandoned musket nearby that someone had kindly left for him. He loaded it and fired. Something fell in the distance. He saw hints of the gore around himself and among the Rebels—the "Secesh." He loaded and fired. Loaded and fired.

As time wore on, he became more aware of the battlefield. He saw a long row of Confederates. The Rebels came over the fence . . . came at him. Hank worked even more feverishly, loading and firing yet faster. The charge faltered. The Southerners fell back. Hank screamed with delight, and George blasphemed. The Confederates fired a volley into the Union men. Hank's consciousness drifted back to load, ram, prime, aim, fire. Load, fire. He was aware the general was near them . . . he liked being close to the general. Load, aim, fire. He stood erect, still behind a tree. Load, aim, fire. He heard more balls pass. Many above. He knew dead men lay around him. Load, aim, fire. He was beginning to feel warm and keenly alive. He liked the feeling. Load, aim, fire. Load, aim, fire. He felt cannon blasts from nearby, from the left; canister, small metallic balls packed into a thin cannon shell and released as flying screams through the air. Load, aim, fire. He saw the Confederate artillery. Someone stop that cannon! Load, aim, fire.

He heard an order to retreat, but didn't move from the line that kept up its hot action. Another call to retreat came, but still Hank and the others ignored it. A third call came, and they moved reluctantly . . . cautiously backward. The voices kept calling them to fall back, and Hank moved toward the voices, all the while watching and listening as Secesh fired more rapidly than ever. He moved over a fence, down a small swell and eventually to the edge of the woods. Load, aim, fire. He couldn't see them now . . . those Rebel soldiers. They were too far away and it was dark, leaving only small flashes in the distance. Flash. Concussion. He sighted a distant flash and fired. There were more flashes, more thunder, but it waned till it was no longer one long sound: just a pop here, a pop over there, then one nearby again.

Hank was tired. His throat was so dry he could barely force breath down it. He gasped for air. He was thirsty . . . desperately thirsty. With hands again shaking and unsure, he opened his canteen and poured the water into his mouth so fast it overflowed onto his cheeks, down his neck and onto his uniform. He emptied it with rapid, deep gulps that did little to quench his thirst. The men were beginning to talk among themselves. Hank didn't want to fire anymore. The word came: "Fix bayonets." Hank shoved his bayonet over the end of the still-blistering-hot barrel of the Springfield. He lowered his body to the ground and dozed.

When he awoke, Hank groggily glanced to his left, recognizing the faint shape of his friend George Dyer, the newly prodigious curser, sitting next to him. George, a short, thin youth with brown hair, dark brown eyes and no sign of a beard, heard him raise his head and said softly, "We seen it. We seen the elephant."

Hank was fully awake, fatigue instantly gone. "We've seen the elephant," Hank repeated. "But George . . . I don't ever want to see it again. Are Secesh still over there?"

"They is."

Hank listened for the peaceful night that should have followed the beautiful evening he'd witnessed earlier on the Pike, but moans met his ears from every direction, punctuated periodically by screams and musket fire. He had heard moans earlier, during the fighting, but they hadn't affected him then. They moved him now as they multiplied in volume and horror, penetrating his being. He shuddered but didn't comment on the sounds. "How bad were we hurt?" he heard himself ask.

"Lost a lot o' men. Don't s'pose even the general knows fer sure. They's countin' now. Men are goin' out to see if we can't bring some o' the wounded back. I ain't heared if we stay here." There was a pause, then George continued, "We gave it 'em, didn't we, Hank. I heared say it was the Stonewall Brigade, from that Shenandoah Valley of yours. We stood up to 'em pretty good, I reckon. And they's some of the best Secesh there is." He looked at Hank and asked, "You feelin' sick? You ain't wounded are you? Fer a few minutes, I thought you was dying . . . maybe already dead."

"Tired for sure . . . Virginians, you say?"

"That's right. Virginians. Say, looks like you won't need to be carryin' that old cap o' yours no more. Now that we done seen the real thing—the elephant. That battle . . . big thing . . . big thing. Sure is dark out here. Ain't no stars or moon tonight."

"Where have you hidden it, George?"

"Hidden what?"

"Your cursing. I never expected it." Hank laughed. "It was amazing! You may be the best in the regiment."

George sounded sheepish, "Fer a long while, didn't even think 'bout it . . . didn't even know it was me. Then I heared and knowed it was comin' from me . . . right from my own mouth. It just kept comin'. Don't know why. It just kept comin'."

Hank looked in George's direction and changed the subject to ease his friend's embarrassment. He'd never before seen his friend abashed, and it made him uncomfortable. "George, I didn't get a battle trophy," he said.

"What're you talkin' 'bout? You got memories. You was there. You fought like the rest of us. I seen you. You didn't run . . . I didn't run. Though there was a few times, specially when they pulled us back, just right at the end: I just wanted to throw down my gun and run . . . all the way back to Indiana and maybe all the way to Wisconsin. The boys in the Second telled me Wisconsin's a mighty fine state. Tonight, just fer a while, I was willin' to see Wisconsin fer myself. I'd like that better . . . least today, to stayin' here in your old Virginny."

"You didn't though, did you. You didn't run. That's what matters."

"That's all that matters, Hank. We did it. There ain't no battle trophy better than knowin' you was in the fight . . . fightin' real hard. Now you don't need no trophy!"

"But George, a memory's no trophy!" Hank protested light heartedly. "And I do need a battle trophy. But it's got to be something physical . . . something won . . . something taken from the men across the way." In the dark, Hank waved his unseen hand in the general direction of the Confederate position.

"Have you looked o'er your whole body? Maybe you caught yourself a ball and don't know it yet," George offered, laughing.

"A ball would be enough," Hank responded with a smile that George couldn't see, "and I doubt any of those army surgeons, least not while they're sober, could get a ball out of me so I could keep it. I'd probably just have to wear it inside for the rest of my life, always with me."

"You know you don't need to worry none 'bout the surgeons bein' sober. I ain't seen a surgeon sober yet in this here whole army. And we've been at this war fer what . . . more than a whole year now?"

"Sober or not, I don't have a ball inside or out of me. So that won't matter, and it won't do." Hank's voice turned earnest, "I need something I can hold . . . hold right in my hand. Something I can hold up and say 'I

got this! There! You can see it, touch it. I was there!"
He squeezed his hand into a tight fist.

"You got your musket. You fired at Secesh with that
gun. Though to be right honest, Hank, I ain't sure you
hit nothin'," George said chuckling quietly again.

"The musket won't do. My battle trophy: it has to
come from the Rebs. Regimental colors. Something
like that."

"We should'a taken some prisoners, then you could
have carted them 'round fer the rest of your whole life.
'Ma'am, it's a great honor to meet you. I'd like to show
you the battle trophies I brung home from the war.
Yes, ma'am. Here they is, ma'am . . . six Secesh
prisoners. Yes ma'am, it's a mite inconvenient to take
them 'round wherever I go, but fer the glory, ma'am . .
. the glory . . . you understand, one sacrifices.' Hank,
it's too late now to get you some o' them prisoners this
time. You should'a been thinkin' 'bout that earlier.
Course we never did get quite near enough today to
get their colors or nothin' else, other than that Secesh
scream and Southern balls."

Hank sat quietly.

George interrupted the lull. "Looks like more is
goin' out to look fer the wounded."

"I'm going to help."

"You go right on ahead and you volunteer, Hank
Gragg. I'll be right here savin' your spot when you gets
back."

"Come with me."

"I'm thinkin' I won't. That's a good way to get
yourself shot. Those Rebels 'cross the way, they's still
usin' real balls. They ain't just firing off no powder.

Maybe they'll 'blige and do that later tonight. I'm thinkin' I'll be awaitin' fer that. Yes, that's the thing to do. I'll wait here . . . right here till they's firing just powder."

"George, come with me. They're hardly shooting now. It's not nearly as dangerous as what you just did."

"Well, Hank, I'd just soon never do what I just done again. I'm hopin' we . . . none of us . . . you, too, Hank . . . none of us won't never have to again." George talked now as if to himself. "I'm pretty sure the war's gonna be over by 'morrow, 'bout this time."

"George, this war's not going to end anytime soon. We didn't run today, but neither did the boys on the other side. They stood in there. Come on, George," he said as he tugged on his arm, "we need to go look for our friends on the field."

"Hank . . . listen to that!" George resisted the tug. "Listen! Listen to all them noises 'round you." Both were silent, listening to the moans of the dying. "It might've been you, Hank. Or even worse, it might've been me."

"That's the very reason to go. You'd want me looking for you if you were out there."

George didn't respond but rose from the ground as Hank tugged again at his arm. Hank felt a hole in his friend's sleeve and said, "You tore your frock again I see."

"That ain't no tear, Hank. That's from a Minié ball . . . got lots of them holes . . . started counting them up but lost count."

Hank remembered the ball that passed close to him, and he reached down and felt the right side of his frock. He found a bullet hole. That close! He wondered if there were other holes. Why was he still alive?

George stooped to pick up his gun, and together they made their way to the detail. Within minutes they were with other volunteers combing the field where the two comrades had unaccountably survived for more than an hour. By lantern light they searched haphazardly among the figures that lay prostrate on the ground. Hank, only vaguely aware of the wounded during the commotion of battle, never dwelt on the wounds. Now searching among the injured soldiers in the weak lantern light, he focused on each new wound and was appalled. He had seen gore before. When the regiment had passed the Cedar Mountain battlefield, he saw and smelled bloated horse corpses. But he had not seen fresh human wounds among so many of his friends following a battle where he had fought and offered his body willingly to the barrels of enemy muskets. He saw his friends now . . . torn limbs . . . fresh blood. . . horrible smells. . . head wounds that left little of their once unique identities—they were all the same under the torn skin. Each new wound, repugnant to him, oddly attracted him. He was compelled to look at it, study it, understand it as best he could in the dim light. He pitied the few men they collected, especially those he had known before the battle.

The rescue crews improvised and carried the wounded from the field any way they could. They brought them back to the woods safe within Union lines where some of the wounded were taken to makeshift hospitals on the other side of the Warrenton Pike. The men labored moving farther and farther onto the field looking for the wounded. They moved closer and closer to the Confederate position. Their efforts did little to tidy the field, and Hank mused to himself that it had taken just two hours to make this mess, but it would take much longer, much, much longer, to clean up.

As Hank worked, he saw lanterns across the field among the Confederates and presumed they were bringing in their casualties as well. There was little rifle fire as both sides worked the gruesome task, and his mind began to wander.

Shortly, Hank leaned over to George who held a lantern and whispered, "This is where I get my battle trophy."

"What?" George demanded almost out loud. In his shock he swung the lantern widely.

"Hold the lantern still, man! Hold it still," someone said sternly. "I gotta see what I'm doing here. Hold it still, man!"

Hank was at George's ear and whispered, "Shhh! I'll be back. I'm slipping across the field. There has to be a dead soldier over there who wants to give me a trophy. We're so close. This may be my only battle, my only chance to prove I was here."

"You're gonna be someone else's trophy, Hank. Ain't no reason fer it. No reason . . . no reason fer it, Hank," George whispered back urgently.

With no further word and before George could object again, Hank slid onto his hands and knees, musket across his back, and quickly slipped into the darkness.

No one noticed Hank's absence but George, and he watched as Hank disappeared. He briefly followed with his eyes the path he imagined Hank would take and spoke softly to himself, "You can bring back some o' them prisoners if you want, but just make sure you come back, Hank! You come back, Hank!"

Chapter 3
28 August 1862, Brawner's Farm, Virginia

Hank crawled uncomfortably a few feet, but quickly realized if he stayed on his knees it would take too long to get across more than 100 yards to where the Confederates had fought. He was afraid, however, to stand and found himself shuffling across the broom-sedge field on his feet and hands, crouched low, musket still across his back. He tried to move silently, to keep his musket and canteen mute. His heart beat uncontrollably. He felt like standing up, dropping his gun, running up toward the Confederate line and grabbing the first piece of Rebel booty he touched and running back. He imagined it as a race—trying to beat the challenge of a Rebel Minié ball. Halfway across, winded, with legs aching from the unnatural crouch, he despaired. Why was he there? What had he done? Where were the Confederate pickets? He wished he hadn't come, but he couldn't will himself to retreat. He kept himself low, quiet, and watched carefully, feeling his way up and over the rise, avoiding the bodies, Union bodies he assumed, that lay randomly cluttering the field. He moved toward the Southern lamps, watching and listening for any clue that Confederate pickets were near.

To his horror, he began to take comfort in the awful groans of the wounded that, scattered across the entire field, grew louder between the lines where the armies had fought throughout the evening. It would be difficult to make out his muffled shuffling as he made his way across the field when so many were complaining of their final state in life, their voices sounding in such a range of pitches and from so many directions. When he thought he could go no farther and felt a compelling urge to fall to the ground for a short rest, he heard voices from Southern search parties . . . soft Virginia drawls like his own. He couldn't make out their words, but the voices encouraged him, beguiled him. He tottered on, getting ever closer to the enemy battle line. Precisely where that line began he didn't know. He had the impression, however, that he had slipped past any pickets, and he moved still carefully and as quickly as his cramped legs allowed until his hand hit something hard that groaned.

The groan brought Hank up short. "Careful," it said weakly. "It distresses me."

Hank held his breath, but the voice continued, slowly, deliberately, "I don't think you should move me. I'm not going to make it. Forget me . . . there must be others!"

Fire raced over Hank's body, but he didn't move. The man was silent, too, as if he never expected a response or had lapsed into unconsciousness. Hank had not thought this romp through to its possible endings, and he suddenly felt foolish. The Rebel had to be silent! Talking might attract Confederate pickets or rescue parties working close by. A troubling question circled in Hank's mind: Shouldn't he help this man? The impressions came fast. The soldier was alive. Hank couldn't kill him to keep him quiet. To have shot him earlier at 70 yards would have been war. To kill him now was something far meaner, if meaner were possible. To leave the wounded soldier would be to kill him, to stay beside him was perhaps suicide or certain capture.

Hank had long expected and unconsciously wanted to die in battle, but now with death threatening him directly, he quietly began to hope it could be put off indefinitely. He looked longingly back toward the lanterns still visible: small, pale yellow glows across the field. He saw one swinging freely and wondered if it was George. He put his hand gently on the man and found he had touched a shoulder. "Where are you hurt?" he asked softly.

Pulled from unconsciousness the man intoned, "Look to the others! The Yanks have . . . Water! Do you have water? So thirsty . . . My canteen!"

Hank had brought his canteen unthinkingly across the field, but had emptied it earlier in his vain attempt to quench his own insatiable thirst. Whispering, Hank asked kindly, "Where is your canteen?"

"Save yourself! Leave me! The Yanks may charge this position yet," the Southern drawl replied.

"Do you know where the canteen is?" Hank asked as he felt gently along the body of the fallen man whose uniform was soaked with perspiration.

As Hank gently searched the body for the canteen, his hands neared the man's midsection and he felt ragged flesh and a sticky, thickened gore. Hank quickly pulled his hands from the man and dragged them desperately across the ground trying to clean them, as if he feared it carried the contagion of death. He felt the field around him. A sword lay flat, half under the man. An officer! He quietly moved around the man's head and searched the other side. No canteen.

"I can't find your canteen. I don't have water for you."

"Oh," murmured the man. "It's all right. I'm so thirsty. Which regiment you from? You with the 5th? Ewell got hit . . . hit real bad . . . ." His words trailed off.

"We've got to get you away from the lines," Hank said. He would drag the man closer to the Confederate search parties, then Hank would feel free to run for safety. He crouched by the man's head and shoulder and began to lift him from the ground.

The man whimpered, then wailed in pain. Hank lowered him back slowly to the ground. "I can't move you, not by myself . . . I'll hurt you."

Breathing hard from the agony of the attempted move, the man answered, "I know. Save someone else!" In his pain he contradicted himself. "Just stay with me. Just for a while."

Hank swallowed hard and heard his own audible sigh. He could do nothing for this man. He should have felt free to move back to Union lines . . . to safety, but the officer's last words paralyzed him.

"Friend, where'd you get that hat? Haven't seen many of those in battle . . . except on those Yankees today. Sure made them look tall. Did you take it off a dead Yank? I bet you did. A trophy. Is that right?"

He had seen Hank's hat in the faint night light. Without hesitating Hank whispered agreement, "Yeah. Got it off a dead Yank; least he'll be dead soon."

"Good. Good. So we stormed their lines! I knew we would. Did we beat 'em . . . like down on the peninsula . . . like the valley? Did they run? I bet they ran, didn't they?"

He barely finished the sentence. As the word "valley" escaped from the man's parched lips, Hank felt kinship bud with this fallen neighbor. Hank had long ago imprisoned his feelings for home so he would no longer have to suffer, but they, now greased by the oil of sweet memories, slipped out through the bars of the hidden cell where he had locked them away. He craved seeing the valley and his family. With eyes focusing into the darkness, he remembered a day three years earlier . . . his last day in Virginia before the war.

Hank had long anticipated the day. He needed no preparation for it, no careful thought, for its only conceivable outcome was sure, and he saw that outcome with perfect clarity: His beloved Betsy . . .

Chapter 4
October 1859, Winchester, Virginia

He dismounted at the gate of the house and led his mare into the side yard. A tall, older, still-stocky, black man approached and greeted him with a pleasant smile. "Marster Hank . . . yuh're, uh, here again? Been a while to be sure, not like when yuh lived in town. Miss Betsy . . . she'll be glad to see yuh."

Hank handed the horse's reins to the slave, saying, "I hope so, William. I've got a surprise for her." He ended the statement emphatically, staring meaningfully at William.

"A surprise! She'll most certainly be happy to see yuh then." William continued speaking, clearly enjoying the chance to converse with Hank. "Yuh ride all the way from Woodstock this morning? That's a long ride!"

"I did. Stopped at my uncle's, cleaned up, then came right over."

"Yuh must'a started out 'fore sunup. Remember . . . I been to Woodstock! I know how far yuh come."

"I know," Hank said kindly.

"Went to bring yuh that note from Miss Betsy, when Marster Richman died. A long ride . . . got there just 'fore dark. Next day we come right back down to Winchester. What kind o' surprise yuh got for Miss Betsy anyways?"

Hank laughed. "So many questions from you, William, but I've got one of my own."

"Well . . . if yuh got a question, no point puttin' it off. Ask me right away. If I know the answer, I'll give it quick."

Hank laughed. "It's not that kind of question. If it were, I would ask you. So you'll just have to wait. It'll be a surprise for you, too. Now take good care of my horse."

William appeared offended. "Yuh don't need to tell me that. Yuh know I'll take real good care of her; always do. Then when yuh come out, yuh can tell me 'bout the surprise."

Hank laughed again. "I'll tell you. But you know it'll be too late. You'll already know. William, you know everything that goes on in that house."

"I do hear things. Ain't sayin' how. But I do know things." William smiled mischievously, then his expression darkened, and he cautioned, "Hank, Mistress Richman; she's home . . . with other folks, too."

As Hank sat beside the wounded Virginian in the dark of the battlefield, he remembered that he never responded to William's last comment, and William without saying more had led the horse toward the stable. Hank's mind traveled further back in time, and he remembered meeting William three years before leaving Virginia:

Samuel Richman, a tall, dark-haired man who carried himself elegantly, and Hank, 14 at the time, had ridden into the yard together, and William had come out to meet them.

"William," Samuel had said. "This is Master Henry Gragg. I want you to do everything you can to make him welcome. I want this to be his second home."

William had responded enthusiastically. "Yes, sir, Marster. I'll make him feel right at home. Don't yuh worry none. I'll take good care of him."

Over the years, William had been true to his pledge, treating Hank as a Richman family member, and William and Hank had developed an unlikely and mutually enjoyed friendship. On many subsequent visits to the Richman home, Hank spent time with William in the stable where they talked of horses, William's family, and what Hank was learning in school.

Hank's mind returned to memories of his last visit to Winchester:

As William had neared the stables, Hank had turned, stepping energetically toward the front lawn and porch.

The house was a large, two-story, wooden-frame structure. It floated in the middle of a green, well-manicured lawn completely contained within a white picket fence that rested on a stone foundation visible above the ground. The peak of the house's roof and its long sides ran from front to back so its shorter dimension faced the street. The roof extended unbroken beyond the front of the house, covering porches on both floors and resting on four thick Doric columns. A substantial, two-story wing protruded from each side of the main portion of the structure and ended in a brick chimney. Four taller chimneys rose from other parts of the home.

Hank, then 17 years old, had leaped up seven narrow steps to reach the porch and knocked firmly on the door. He waited anxiously, shifting his weight from one leg to the other, moving his hat from hand to hand, all the while looking down. He swiftly raised his head as the door opened.

"Good afternoon, Mrs. Richman. Is Miss Betsy at home?" the dark-haired, blue-eyed youth asked amiably. The Richmans' middle-aged house slave Rose stood slightly behind her mistress, apparently shunted at the last moment as Rebeka Richman moved to answer the door herself.

"Ah . . . it's you," Rebeka said with inadequately disguised disdain. "Good afternoon, Mr. Gragg. How unexpected! It's good of you to come. Betsy is at home . . . and you are most welcome to join her. But I warn you," she added in a confidential tone, "she is with several of her friends. The best people. I'm sure you understand." She paused, regarding his appearance, and smiled sweetly. "Yes . . . you have dressed well for the occasion . . . haven't you, Mr. Gragg? Put on your finest? I don't think I've ever seen you dressed well . . . so well. You look . . . you look splendid . . . distinguished . . . yes . . . almost distinguished. But with so many already here, are you sure you want to join them? I wouldn't want you to feel uncomfortable. If you wished . . . I wouldn't even give her the slightest clue you had been here. They'd never know."

Rebeka's hostile greeting saddened Hank. It contrasted sharply with the hospitality he had so often enjoyed at the Richman's.

Still deep in memory on the Virginia battlefield, Hank moved back further in time, to his introduction to Rebeka Richman:

On the day Hank met William, Samuel, Rebeka's husband, had brought Hank unannounced through a back door.

Upon seeing his wife, he spoke abruptly. "Rebeka, this is the young man I spoke of."

Rebeka was bent over looking at something on the dining room table and started at her husband's voice. Her surprise brought her to her erect posture, and she appeared shocked when she saw Hank.

Hank spoke first. "It's a great pleasure to meet you, Mrs. Richman. I've looked forward to this day."

"Hank. May I call you, Hank?" she had said, recovering her composure.

"Of course."

She studied him closely. "You look just like my husband when he was young. It's uncanny . . . really."

Hank didn't respond, and Samuel said nothing.

"Don't you think so, Samuel? He looks just like you, just as you did." She appeared fleetingly lost in thought. "I'm delighted to meet you, Hank. Samuel, my dear husband, has told me . . . told all of us . . . what you did. I have long wanted to thank you personally."

Hank was embarrassed and looked uncomfortable.

"I hope this won't be your only visit. Hopefully we'll see you often," she added.

"Rebeka, I've encouraged him to come as often as possible; told him he's always welcome here."

"And he always shall be. He will be like a son."

Hank's thoughts returned to his last day in pre-war Virginia:

Rebeka, by then recently widowed, was tall and full-bodied and looked younger than her 42 years. In spite of the fact her husband had died only a few months earlier, her attire and countenance gave no hint of mourning. She wore a simple blue dress, squared and laced at the neck with lace cuffs on the sleeves and a black cloth belt tied loosely at her waist. She didn't step back as she invited Hank in, but moved only her left hand in the direction of the parlor where Betsy and her guests conversed.

"Mrs. Richman," Hank responded with a faint smile to Rebeka's unfriendly greeting. "Thank you for your concern, but I appreciate even more your most gracious invitation. As you have extended it with such generosity, I could not disappoint you. I would be delighted to join Miss Richman and her guests."

Hank stepped forward angling toward the parlor, but Rebeka didn't clear the way. Instead, with subtle foot movements, hidden by her slightly shuffling skirt, she moved back, blocking his path, bumping hard into her house slave, Rose, who inadvertently grunted from the impact. Hank showed no sign of disappointment and with a quick step moved into the space Rebeka had just vacated. He extended his hat to the servant and said cheerfully, "Would you take my hat, Rose?"

"Yes, sir." Then looking at her mistress, she asked, "Shall I announce him, ma'am?"

"No," Rebeka said coldly. "I will announce him. I'll do it myself."

Hank followed Rebeka to the parlor. Rebeka passed through its door, stepping aside slowly, delaying Hank's entrance.

The parlor, spacious and elegant, basked in the afternoon light that poured through the tall windows along the side of the room. A grand piano forte stood in the front corner of the room and a fireplace adorned the back wall. Three young men and two young women sat on couches and chairs placed in a rectangle around the center of the room. Hank, taking in the parlor and people in a quick glance, began to feel the discomfort Rebeka had predicted. Glimpsing Betsy, Mrs. Richman's only offspring, inexplicably heightened his tension. She sat beside another young woman on one of the couches. Like her mother, she was not dressed in the black of mourning, but rather wore a long olive-green skirt and a salmon-colored, satin blouse topped with a white collar and a large pin at her neck. Her blond hair was pulled loosely back, partially covering her ears while some curls fell near her cheeks. A year younger than Hank, she had a small nose and a wide mouth; large, round, light-green eyes dominated her delicate features.

The moans from the battlefield momentarily interrupted Hank's thoughts of Betsy. But as he sat holding the dying man's head in his hands, still more memories

*. . . remembrances of other times with Betsy filled his
mind:*

*She hadn't been home on Hank's first visit to the
Richmans. She was visiting cousins in the Virginia
town of Martinsburg, north of Winchester. Later while
Hank was attending school in town, the Richmans had
invited him to visit for the weekend, and he first saw
her then. Hank had heard about Betsy from her parents and family servants, all of whom gave glowing
descriptions of her kindness, hospitality, intelligence
and beauty. Hank had assumed their descriptions over-
statement, but meeting her changed his opinion. Within months, they became close friends, frequently lock-
ing wits, debating the latest politics, and horseback
riding through the nearby countryside. As their friendship blossomed, Hank spent more time at the Richmans. He became an implicit member of the household, enjoying a close relationship with each member
of the family. To Samuel and Rebeka, he had become a
son; to Betsy he was the most important person in her
young life.*

*Betsy and Hank had been heartsick when he fin-
ished schooling in Winchester and returned to live
with his family in Woodstock; and to his family's consternation, he traveled as often as possible to Winchester to visit the Richmans.*

Hanks thoughts drifted again, to 1859:

Rebeka's voice had interrupted jovial and lively conversation in the parlor as she announced Hank: "Betsy,
my dear, an acquaintance has dropped by . . . most
unexpectedly."

Betsy rose and moved gracefully toward Hank as she said, "Hank! Oh, how wonderful: You've come. I'm so glad. I hoped you would. Please come in. Join us. We're hearing all the latest news from the Virginia Military Institute."

Betsy came to his side, slipped her arm through his and began escorting him to a chair. Her mother stopped them by speaking. "Mr. Gragg, I don't believe you know Betsy's friends and our guests. I present Hank Gragg, visiting from Woodstock . . . as I recall. Isn't that right Mr. Gragg?" She didn't wait for a response, "Mr. Gragg, this is Richard Lewis of the Lewis family here in town," she indicated a young man with sandy-colored, wavy hair. He arose and appeared to be about Hank's height with a similar build. She nodded to a second young man in the room, who also stood at the introduction, saying, "This is Robert Harris. No doubt you've heard of him." Robert had dark hair, a dark complexion, a noble air and was tall. She continued again without pausing for the young people to greet each other, so Hank merely exchanged nods with the two men who had risen to meet him. Rebeka then introduced the second young woman in the room. She also was tall; a brunette with a body hung on a heavy frame; kindly eyes were her best feature. "I present Marie Ann Allen." They already knew one another, and Hank and the young lady exchanged warm smiles.

"Mr. Gragg," Rebeka added with special emphasis, "this is Caleb Moore, a cadet from the Virginia Military Institute. He has kindly dropped by; from the Moores of Norfolk." Hank nodded at the tall, slender cadet in his meticulous VMI uniform. Mr. Moore stared at Hank barely acknowledging him.

"Come . . . come, Hank," Betsy said warmly. "Mr. Moore was just telling us of the strangest instructor at the Institute."

"Yes . . . I think you'll be interested in that, Mr. Gragg," Rebeka said speaking in a motherly tone.

"He sounds awful," Marie Ann commented, obviously eager to continue the discussion Hank had interrupted. Betsy guided Hank to a chair near the couch where she lighted. He was relieved to be near her. Rebeka moved in his shadow and sat in a chair behind him, leaving Hank with the gnawing feeling she was watching him closely.

"He's not as bad as I fear I've made him out to be," Mr. Moore confessed. "But truly he is a most awkward creature, the most awkward I've ever seen . . . perhaps ever born. I would think him made of wood, except that wood bends with more grace, and no piece of wood has feet that big." Those in the room laughed, except Hank who as yet didn't understand the conversation. Betsy glanced at Hank and smiled.

Mr. Moore continued, "He grew up in Western Virginia, and they must not know about humor out there. The major has no sense of humor—none. One of our favorite sayings, we use it all the time: 'Not meaning exactly what I say.' That's what 'Old Tom Fool' says whenever he tells you something not to be taken literally." The cadet shook his head. "He is as exacting in everything he does as he is clumsy in how he does it."

"Tell us another story about him," Marie Ann insisted. "The stories are so entertaining."

"Yes, do," encouraged Betsy warmly, she again glanced briefly at Hank and smiled.

"There's a story told that once years ago . . . oh, did I say he taught artillery? That's his military subject. It was during artillery drill one afternoon. It was scheduled till four, but the cadets had grown tired of it. They'd been working hard, and a rain storm came up from nowhere . . . a thunder storm. The good instructor wanted . . . no . . . he expected the drill to go on, right in the rain storm. So the cadets kept working at it. Can you imagine that," he looked directly at Marie Ann, "having to keep right on working with the rain coming down like it was, and with thunder?"

"I can't," Marie Ann whined. "How awful! How simply awful! They had to stay out through the whole storm? How could anyone expect that of you . . . of them? It's not humane. Was he punished for such cruelty? I hope they ignored him and got right out of the rain."

The cadet laughed, "Oh, Miss Allen. It's not as easy as that at the Institute. We must obey our superiors. It's a matter of respect and discipline. But in this case, the first chance they got, the boys skedaddled to a nearby barracks and protection. But not Old Tom! The major stayed out there by the gun, no cadets with him, no one to pull the cannons into place, no one to load them, no one to fire them—just the major. He probably kept on giving commands, then wondered why nothing happened." Laughter rolled through the room. "He stayed there . . . in the rain, the lightning, the thunder . . . right up to the stroke of four, the hour set for the end of the drill. Then did he run to get out of the rain?

No sir, not Old Tom. He marched off the field. No rain was going to get the best of Major Jackson."

Still uncomfortable, Hank tried to enter the conversation, but he did it clumsily. "Sounds like this Major Jackson was already wet; no point in running off the field at that point."

The cadet looked harshly at Hank, pursed his lips and began to respond, "Ah . . . Mr. . . . Mr. . . .?"

Betsy said quickly, "Hank Gragg."

"Oh yes, Mr. . . . Mr. Gragg. Mr. Gragg, are you an expert in artillery, perhaps? A graduate of the Military Institute or West Point?"

"Oh no, nothing of the sort," Hank responded, feigning politeness and humility. The cadet's arrogance annoyed him.

The cadet began his response. "Well then . . . ."

Hank interrupted. "But I know what it feels like to get wet in the rain."

His comment stirred quiet chuckles and nervous smiles, followed by a moment's awkward silence.

"My dear, Mr. Gragg," Betsy said in a playful tone, turning to look directly at him. "Haven't I been trying to get you out of the rain for years?" Everyone in the room, except Mr. Moore, laughed, grateful to be rescued from an increasingly uncomfortable situation.

"Yes," said Mr. Moore, cutting the mirth short as he had not finished his thought. "Old Tom is quite strange."

Betsy turned back to Mr. Moore and said, "He must have some becoming trait, or why would they let him teach at that wonderful school?"

"He must be good at something. But I've failed to find it." Mr. Moore said, this time laughing alone. "No, no, I only jest." He continued speaking, taking on a more serious attitude. "He's sincere, kind, devout; a Presbyterian and dedicated to teaching in the Sunday School—although they say he has taught slaves there. But he's a good man. I've heard he fought well with the artillery in the Mexican War. But he must have changed since then, maybe just got old. If the country should ever be in another war, you'll see many from the Institute prove their bravery on the field of glory. Just don't expect much from Old Tom, good soul that he is. Don't look for anything great from Major Thomas J. Jackson."

"Will there be war, then?" Marie Ann asked in a tone suggesting she didn't care whether there was war, pestilence or plagues as long as she could hear more from the mouth of the uniformed cadet.

Cadet Moore quickly took up her question, "I don't see how it's to be avoided. The North is always trying to force us to do their bidding. It's been going on as long as I can remember. I don't think loyal citizens of the South can put up with it much longer . . . I don't think Virginia will. They're trying to take away our rights. If they don't desist, you will see the day when we will have to rise as a people to defend our rights— the rights our fathers fought for. We'll have to! We, like our fathers, have a right to rebellion. We've got to defend the Revolution. Virginia, great leader that she is, must set the example now when our very freedoms are threatened. There may have to be a second Ameri- can revolution, but mind you, when war comes, responsibility for it will be on the heads of the people of the North. If they would leave us be, we would have no quarrel with them. If they continue to threaten and trample our rights: the rights of free men and free states, they will learn the lesson only men dedicated to liberty can teach."

Betsy queried, "Is slavery so important?"

Rose quietly entered the room as Mr. Moore answered, "Slavery? This isn't about slavery! It's about our freedom . . . our rights . . . liberty . . . the rights of our state. But Miss Richman, we have a right to slavery. You can read that for yourself in the Bible. Just last Sunday I heard an excellent sermon on that very point. It was something about we should keep our bondmen and bondmaids as inheritance for our children . . . that they'll be their possessions. And these slaves, they better remember to obey us . . . just as the Bible says." No one noticed Rose, and Mr. Moore continued, "When those infernal abolitionists come to take our slaves, they'll find us giving ourselves liberty and giving them death." Mr. Moore smiled, pleased with his adaptation of former Governor Patrick Henry's words. His voice rose, "But it's not slavery we would fight for. We would fight for our right to choose for ourselves. We can't have Massachusetts or Connecticut or New York or any other state, or all the Northern states together, or the Black Republicans—those abolitionists—telling us what we can and cannot do with our own property, our land, our chattel. We will defend our rights, as we should! It's as simple as that."

Mr. Harris entered the conversation with a quiet passion in his voice. "I'm not sure everyone . . . at least not in the valley . . . shares your opinion, Mr. Moore." He paused to let his words register. "I . . . for one . . . don't think there will be a war. Virginia's as loyal to the Union as Massachusetts, Connecticut or New York. We're not going to fight with anyone; it's just fire-eaters down south and rabble rousers in the tidewater always trying to get everyone excited—excited about nothing."

"Are you suggesting that I am either rabble or a rabble rouser, sir?" Mr. Moore said, rising indignantly from his seat.

"Please . . . I didn't mean to offend you or suggest you are anything but honorable. I merely don't believe there will be a war. And come what may . . . Virginia must stay in the Union. Those are my feelings, and the feelings I might add of almost everyone I know. Now please, sit down. I did not mean anything by it."

"Many at the Institute feel as you do," Cadet Moore said in a tone of disapproval. "But I must disagree. It won't take much to get everyone excited. Perhaps even you will find yourself one day fighting, fighting for our rights. We—none of us—can stand idly by . . . I tell you . . . and let them dictate what we can and cannot do. In your hearts, you know it's true."

Rose still stood by the door. Rebeka finally noticed and acknowledged her, saying impatiently, "What is it, Rose?"

"There's a message from Master Robert."

"Well, give it to me. How long have you had it? How was it delivered?"

"It just came, ma'am. Came by rider."

Rebeka quickly opened and read the note from her brother in Martinsburg. She dismissed Rose, and as soon as the servant left the room reported in a hushed voice: "It's news. Something's happened at Harpers Ferry. He's not sure what but seems to think it's some sort of slave uprising. Slaves killing their masters. He tells us to be careful with ours, not to let them act up. He'll write more when the situation becomes clear."

Cadet Moore rose to his feet as Rebeka finished the note. "An uprising? I knew these Northern fiends would make our slaves a threat to their own masters . . . to innocent women and children. The loose abolitionist tongues care little for order and the safety of our families. We've got to crush this rebellion fast. If this type of thing starts in one place, it follows to another, and leaps yet to another. We don't need a rebellion like the French, and we don't need any more Nat Turners." Cadet Moore clearly perceived himself to be the man to quell any rumored uprising. "I must leave. Could someone bring my horse?"

Betsy walked to the parlor door and called, "Rose, have William bring up Mr. Moore's horse."

"Yes, ma'am," Rose responded from the hall.

"Do you need to go . . . so soon?" Marie Ann asked. "Perhaps you should await more news. Perhaps it's just rumor."

"In times of emergency, we must not . . . we cannot wait. We must act and act decisively," he said pedantically with crisp diction, looking directly at Marie Ann. "I'd best be off. If I'm needed, it will be at the Institute. If we're called up," he paused, then with emphasis finished the thought, "we will give them the bayonet!" The three other men in the room suppressed smiles.

"We'll sorely miss you," Marie Ann responded with added softness in her eyes.

"It can't be helped." Mr. Moore said, ignoring her gaze and looking beyond her. He turned to Betsy, bowed low and asked, "May I give him your regards then, Miss Richman?"

"You may," she responded cordially. "Tell him I look forward to meeting him. He speaks of my reputation, but his precedes him as well, doing him great honor. Tell him to come and visit. And thank you, Mr. Moore, for bringing me his kind message. I am indebted to you for your service."

He smiled, nodded to Betsy and said, "The honor of delivering your answer is ample payment. You can trust me to relay your message faithfully." He paused to think, then added, "I know it will be received with as much warmth as it is given."

Hank didn't notice the exchange as he was engrossed in memories and thoughts of the business that brought him to the Richman house.

The cadet turned to Rebeka and said, "Please excuse my rudeness in leaving you so soon, Mrs. Richman, but I do believe you'll understand. It is, after all, duty."

"We understand completely. We're just grateful you were able to come," Rebeka said.

All arose, bid adieu to Mr. Moore and followed him to the front porch.

"I wonder what happened?" Betsy mused as the cadet rode from the house toward the street.

"And what it will mean," contributed Mr. Harris.

"I fear the cadet may be right: Before long we may have war," Mr. Lewis said. "But it doesn't seem possible, not today, not in Virginia."

"I hope for no war," Hank spoke softly.

"What? No war and no fame for Cadet Moore? The great call of duty . . . to protect our rights . . . our state . . . and whatever else . . . and you would hope it passes? It's selfishness, I tell you! Pure selfishness! That's what it is—selfishness," Mr. Lewis said smiling broadly at Hank.

Betsy, distracted by Cadet Moore's departure, didn't see the smile on Mr. Lewis' face and attempted to come to Hank's aid. "I'm sure Hank didn't mean to sound selfish."

Hank looked at her with the hint of a smile. "Perhaps it is just selfishness. But it doesn't matter." He spoke in a resigned tone. "We haven't yet got our calls to glory."

"Passions are just stirred up a bit right now. Such rumors make everyone nervous. You can't blame them. Even after all these years, they still remember Nat Turner," Mr. Harris said calmly.

Rebeka remarked, "No one needs to worry about ours. They're as happy as that sort can be; completely loyal. We take care . . . good care of them. They're like family, like our children."

Mr. Harris spoke again. "Without knowing what happened at Harpers Ferry, it's difficult to know what it's all about, and who needs to worry, and about what. Perhaps it's best to let it be for now . . . till we know something more."

"An excellent suggestion! I insist everyone abide by it while you're here this afternoon," Rebeka said firmly, but pleasantly.

Hank stepped awkwardly to Betsy's side and, in a hushed tone, said, "Betsy, may I speak with you . . . privately?"

She answered softly, gently touching his hand, "I can't with guests here. Perhaps later? Stay . . . visit with us today. Then come again tomorrow!" She paused. "I realize you have come such a long distance. But it must be tomorrow! I can give you all the time . . . attention . . . tomorrow."

Hank unconsciously raised his voice, "It's important that I speak with you today."

Misters Harris and Lewis lowered their eyes simultaneously to the ground. Rebeka frowned and watched her daughter's face closely. Marie Ann, sensing the difficulty, stepped in to help her friends. "Your mother and I can entertain these gentlemen inside while you visit, Betsy. Come, let us go in. But Hank, you mustn't keep her long."

Chapter 5
October 1859, Winchester, Virginia

*T*he party went in the house, leaving Betsy and Hank alone, and the couple moved closer together. Betsy spoke: "Hank, that was very strange. You are acting queer. You want to talk to me? About what?" She grasped his hand with both of hers and gazed at him with a remarkably more affectionate look than she had shown him in the parlor.

"I'm sorry if I've been rude, but I have to talk to you. It can't wait. I can't wait, not any longer."

Still holding his hand, she continued her kindly tone. "Can't wait? What can it be that you would offend my guests and, as usual, my mother?"

She had barely finished her question when Hank blurted out, "I want to marry you!"

She smiled. She desperately wanted to marry him, too, but she responded matter-of-factly, "I'm flattered, but this is not a new idea, Hank. You've mentioned it before. I've mentioned it before. Remember?" Teasing him she added, "You know there are others who want to marry me, and I received their proposals before yours. I am honor bound to consider theirs first. There are several interesting, no, they are appealing offers. Why . . . just today, that cadet brought word of someone who wants to meet me. Don't you think we should wait to see if he wants to marry me, too?" She looked down at his hand and squeezed it between hers.

Hank ignored her jests and affection, persisting in his purpose. "Betsy, I know I've talked about it before and that you've talked about it, but I've never asked you." He stopped speaking and looked directly into her eyes. "I'm asking now! Will you marry me?"

"Are you serious?" Betsy looked bewildered and considered him carefully. "You are!" She was irritated he pressed such a painful topic and said, "You know I can't answer that right now." She paused to think, then continued, "Why are you asking me now? And like this? You know my mother would never consent—not yet. She must consent! It's hard! It's hard for me, too. We're young; we can wait. You know she must consent, Hank."

"Betsy, she never will . . . not now. Everything has changed. You don't need her blessing. We'll never get it."

Anger welled up in her, and she let go of his hand, "No . . . no, I don't need her blessing. But I'd like it. I won't marry without it. It's important to me, and you know that." Her voice was no longer kind, and she looked sternly at Hank. "Why would you ask me to marry you now? I've already told you that Mama's set against it." As quickly as her anger rose, her tone softened. "Oh, Hank, I do love you, but to marry . . . we must wait. Don't you see that?"

She was silent momentarily, and her manner suggested a struggle of thought and emotion. Her voice was stern, "But I don't know today if I would marry you; not if you're so thoughtless as to put me in this

situation. I can't forget her feelings. I never would."
Her words came faster now and louder with each
phrase, "Why do you ask me today? What notion has
come into your mind? Why must you push this now . . .
this afternoon with my mother in the other room entertaining my guests?"

He showed no sign of disappointment and attempted
no answer to what he took as rhetorical questions. He
said simply, "We don't need to wait for your mother."
As an afterthought, he added, "I didn't know you
would have guests here today, or," he grinned, "that a
slave uprising would need to be put down. I ask you
only because it will make you happy."

His last statement pushed her too far; he saw it and
wished he had waited. Days earlier he had made his
decision to ask her, and he couldn't bring himself to
postpone the proposal even an hour longer. He had
ridden 30 miles, cleaned the travel off his face and
clothes and waited, patiently he felt, in her parlor. He
couldn't bring himself to put it off longer. It was too
important to him . . . to them both.

She responded firmly with an edge in her voice, "I'm
glad you know exactly what will bring me happiness.
Of course, I hope I am free to disagree. I don't appreciate your inconsiderate behavior this afternoon toward my mother, my guests or me. I will not speak to
you further on the subject . . . or any subject." She
turned her back on him and said, "Good day, Mr.
Gragg."

She pushed herself toward the door, swinging it
wide so it nearly collided with her mother who waited
in the shadow in the hall. Betsy stepped inside.

"What did he want? What did you say?" the mother whispered urgently, betraying a lack of confidence in what Betsy might have told him.

Without hesitation, before the door closed, Betsy answered, "He asked me to marry him. What foolishness!" The door slammed shut.

Through the closed door, Hank heard Rebeka repeat loudly enough to be audible in the parlor, "Asked you to marry him! That is foolish!" She laughed, "Who does he think he is? I hope that's the last we'll see of Mr. Gragg."

Hank still stood on the porch, staring at the door without seeing it. He didn't notice Betsy's brief look of tender concern as she moved to the parlor and glanced back at him through the door window.

He tried to understand what had just happened. He had pushed her too hard . . . too far . . . at the wrong time. He had never before heard Betsy embarrass anyone. She always soothed hurt feelings, made everyone comfortable. He remembered Samuel Richman and wondered what he would say: What counsel he would give? He remembered the relationship he'd enjoyed with Rebeka Richman; not long ago, he could have gone to her for comfort. His pleasant memories gave way to Rebeka's last words. He paraphrased them softly: "That is the last you'll see of Hank Gragg." Hank thought bitterly that his decision to ask Betsy today ensured that she never would marry him. There was no returning to Betsy now, but she was what he wanted most.

Hank descended dejectedly to the lawn and walked sluggishly toward the stable. He passed the rear of the house and heard a door open. His heart quickened, his hope returned, but he didn't dare to look back. A gentle voice called him, "Mr. Gragg!"

He turned to see Rose on the back porch holding his hat. His hope died anew, and he smiled sadly, retrieving the hat. As he took it, he saw sympathetic sorrow in the woman's expression. She smiled sensitively and said, "I thought you'd need this." She handed him the hat and fleetingly rested her hand on his hand.

Hank enjoyed the touch. "Thank you, Rose." He took the hat and walked toward the stable. William wasn't there. He probably already knew what had happened, and Hank was grateful he didn't have to face his friend. He found his saddle already cinched on his mare. William did know.

Hank left the stable and rode hard out of the yard. He was grateful the long ride home would give him time to think and grieve. As he rode, his regrets at being rejected by Betsy . . . in front of so many witnesses deepened into humiliation. He remembered a conversation he had with Samuel less than a year ago:

"Hank, what will you do when you're done here?"

"Go on . . . study somewhere else, I suppose."

"You won't go back to farming? Does your father know?"

"We've talked about it. John will be there working the farm. He doesn't need me."

"Well . . . we need you. Stay close."

Thoughts of the conversation were bitter to Hank. Why did Samuel Richman—his friend and second father—have to die? Hank's bitterness grew as he rode southward. Somewhere beyond Winchester, it became too much for him to bear and he had turned his horse westward, then northward. Waves of anger and humiliation welled up, covered him, then receded, each one driving him on farther, eventually beyond Virginia into Maryland. He was disgraced! He would never go back to Betsy. She would be sorry! He would never return to Winchester. Mrs. Richman, herself, would yearn for the day when Hank counted her as a friend. How ungrateful she was! His success would be his triumph . . . her humiliation. The farther he rode the greater his sense of embarrassment had grown. He could not go home, not to Woodstock, not even to his family. He couldn't face them and didn't want to see them. He wanted a new life. He wouldn't go back. There was nothing to go back for: He had lost Betsy. How could he have behaved so badly?

Chapter 6
28 August 1862, Brawner's Farm, Virginia

*H*ank's mind was pulled back to the battlefield by the wounded soldier's weak voice. "Take that hat off! One of the boys is likely to take you for one of those Yanks in the dark . . . sever the hat about at your neck," the Confederate said, beginning a laugh that mutated into a groan. Hank obediently removed the hat.

Sitting with the Rebel at that moment, Hank resigned himself to death or capture. He would wait for the officer's demise or rescue. If necessary, the rising sun would find him holding the head of this fallen but still-breathing soldier, even though that early light would also bring a Confederate capture party.

The officer was clearly glad to have company, and now awake, he sustained contact with Hank by talking. "This war won't last long. Marse Robert . . . Stonewall . . . they're going to send old Pope right back across that Potomac. I wouldn't be surprised if we're in Washington City . . . uh. . . ohhhhh . . . by Christmas. You and me . . . we'll have Christmas dinner in the White House . . . with our wives. Won't that be fine?"

"You comfortable?"

"No! Course not. We'll make Lincoln move out first . . . out of the house. Don't know . . . what we should do with him. We'll find something special." He emitted his laugh-groan again. Hank listened kindly, not judging words, man or cause. "That'll teach 'em to come into our country. Can't they just . . . leave us alone. We're not bothering them! Why do they have to come down . . . bother us? I just wish they hadn't come."

"Do you have family?" Hank asked, hoping to change the subject.

"A wife . . . a beautiful wife. I wrote a letter . . . in Staunton."

Hank sorrowed that the man was leaving something he loved, but the sorrow rapidly eroded to envy.

"In my pocket," the casualty continued. "Take it for me! To her . . . get it to her!"

"Your pocket? What's in your pocket?"

"The letter. I wrote . . . my wife. Take it to her!" the man said desperately.

"No . . . no. You wait till you can send it. You'll take it to her yourself."

"Don't torment me! I won't make it. I'm dying. You and I . . . we've seen it before. We know . . . won't be long . . . not long now."

Hank felt it was true and said, "Where's the letter? I'll get it to her."

"In person! Tell her I was . . . thinking . . . thinking of her."

"I can't promise that," Hank protested. "I go only where I'm sent."

"They're not sending you . . . where I'm going . . . not yet. You still have time. Go to Staunton! Promise! I'm . . . dying! Promise it! Pledge it upon my death . . . the death of a Virginian! You owe me that . . . at least."

The Southern soldier continued his argument, "Even a Yank . . . a Yank . . . would do the bidding of a dying man." In the dark, Hank couldn't see the subtle smile and flash of life in the officer's eyes.

The circumstance overpowered him. "I'll take it to her as soon . . . as I can," he said. The words came without conviction; he had no intention of delivering it.

"My coat . . . in my coat," the officer said with a voice suddenly raspy. "In my . . . pocket. Wrote it before . . . before the battle. Finished it . . . didn't have time . . . no time to send it . . . no time . . . no time. When I'm de . . . get it to her. Tell her . . . my last words . . . were of her. Make . . . uhhhh . . . make sure she's all right."

Hank didn't answer. He lowered the man's head carefully to the ground, moved around to the side of the body and fumbled tentatively in the dark for the buttons of the officer's wool coat. He gently opened each button, beginning at the top, one button falling off in his hand as he pulled at it. The soldier groaned long and low. Hank heard a gurgling sound in the casualty's throat; then all was silent. The officer was still and limp, his Rebel lips hushed. Hank sighed in relief and tore open the man's jacket. He felt clumsily for the letter, but the officer no longer felt pain. Hank quickly found paper, slightly wet, and pulled it from the jacket, stuffing it into his own trouser pocket.

He looked around fleetingly. He could see campfires far off, lanterns still on the field. He moved, crouching, toward a distant lantern. Hank didn't think of the dead Secesh soldier as he moved or of battle trophies. He felt only relief the man had died, freeing him to return to Union lines. All his faculties concentrated on getting past any pickets . . . to the lanterns . . . to friends and safety.

More often this time across the field, he bumped into other bodies. Most were silent; a few moaned. But he didn't stop. He tried not to hear them. How had he gotten across the field the first time without stumbling over so many bodies? There seemed to be more casualties on the ground . . . almost in a straight line along his path. Where had they come from? Just keep moving. Just keep moving. He was nearing the targeted lantern and could clearly see outlines in the light. He tripped over a rifle discarded among the dead. The lighted outlines moved abruptly at the sound of the rifle clatter as it spread across the field. A voice called out, "Who goes thar?" The accent was the same as the dead officer's and similar to Hank's own. Dread seized Hank: He had gone in the wrong direction.

"Who's thar?" the voice called out again, this time with more urgency. The figures in the light stood alert, facing Hank's direction. When no answer came, one raised a musket.

"Virginian," Hank called out hastily, from his rapidly drying mouth. The man slackened his rigid stance and lowered his gun at the response. "I'm wounded," Hank added.

"Where are you? We'll come to you."

Hank hastily surveyed the ground. Which direction was the Union line? How had he lost it? He stayed perfectly still, hoping they wouldn't be able to find him. The Confederates moved in his direction anyway. They would soon be close enough to see him clearly in their

lantern light. He was glad he had forgotten his hat . . .
at least they would be short that clue. In his anxiety he
considered for the briefest moment going over to the
Confederacy, not as a prisoner, but abandoning the
Union altogether. He was Virginian after all, as they
were. His memories, his love for the Old Dominion had
all come back to him as he kneeled by the suffering
Rebel. But abruptly he dismissed the thought: He was
not Secesh! They called out again. "Say something so
we can find you. Keep talking!"

Instinct directed Hank to run directly away from
them. But hadn't he come that way? Didn't the dead
officer lie in that direction? A thought blasted through
his mind: He had scrambled along the Confederate
line. He had bumped into so many soldiers sprawled
wounded and dead in a row because they had fought
and fallen there in rank. He looked to his right. It was
dark, and he was still on the Confederate battle line.

"Speak, man! Where is he?" the Confederate asked
his comrades. He called out to Hank, "What regiment
you from?"

Hank hesitated, breathed deeply, then leaped to his
feet, standing erect for the first time in over an hour,
and bellowed in his soft valley accent, "The 19th Indiana." He advanced across the field as fast as he could
run without falling in the dark. He heard confusion
behind and ahead of him . . . voices . . . but didn't listen to what they said. Then a fleck of light and the
sound of a fired musket. It was the race Hank had earlier imagined: Hank and Minié. But the Secesh soldiers
couldn't see him in the thick darkness, and he didn't

hear the ball cut the air. He heard voices nearby. Pickets? He blessed the night's profound darkness.

He ran with long but careful strides, his feet often landing on objects and bodies left on the field. He stumbled often, but each time miraculously regained his balance. Running felt good to Hank, and he ran harder hoping to increase the pleasure. He heard another small volley, but it was no closer. He was running down a slope . . . out of breath. He was going to win the race. He was descending the hill toward the woods and safety. Another shot! His right foot caught on something, and it brought him up short. He fell. Hands braced instinctively in his descent; his musket hit the ground; and his face followed. His chest fell on something soft, but a sharp blow stabbed at his right arm. For a moment he didn't move. He was hit? Was this his death: fear and flight and no glory? He rolled off the body on which he had fallen and felt his arm. It was cut, but not seemingly deep. He felt little pain. What had cut him? He reached out and found the blade of a bayonet angling up over the cold corpse. He felt for his musket and found instead a tall felt hat. At least he was going toward Union lines. He put on the hat. It was too big, but he left it on. His hands dredged the ground and found his musket; more slowly now, he made his way across the rest of the field.

Chapter 7
28 August 1862, Brawner's Wood, Near Groveton, Virginia

"*W*ho's out there?" someone called.

Hank relaxed at the sound of a Northern accent and responded, "Union . . . Indiana 19th. Private Gragg."

"You don't sound like no people I know that hail from Indiana. You better come in slow. You alone?"

"I'm alone," Hank responded.

"What you doing out there, anyway?"

"Went out with a search party, but got separated."

"Well, keep coming; come real slow."

Hank felt the picket close to him. The picket took Hank's Springfield and called out to some other hidden Yankee. "I got one. Claims he's ours, but he don't sound right. I'm taking him back. Keep a keen watch! It could be a trick."

No one answered.

The picket prodded Hank through the trees, till they came to a fire where he could see him better. Hank's face was wet with blood, blood had splattered his uniform, blood was dripping from a torn sleeve, and below, his hand bloodied where it ran. Hank could see the picket. He didn't know him; wasn't from the brigade. The picket's interrogation continued, "If you're from Indiana, how come you sound like those folks fir-ing on us?"

"I'm from Virginia . . . but with the Union."

"Your hat ain't right. How come you're wearing a Wisconsin Second? You said you was from the 19th?"

"Lost my hat . . . grabbed this one on the field today."

"How'd you get wounded?"

"Fell on something."

"During the battle? The battle's been winding down for a while now. How come it's still bleeding? How come you're coming in just now? Let me take a look at it."

He tugged at Hank's sleeve and pulled it up over what now appeared to be the deep but short cut in Hank's forearm.

Hank said, "It happened after the battle. I tripped in the dark."

The blood dripped freely from the wound, and the picket suggested, "You should get that taken care of 'fore you bleed to death . . . already enough folks dead."

"Gragg! Gragg! Where you been?" a deep, rich, powerful voice boomed from the darkness outside the light of the fire. Its unique timbre was familiar; it was the voice of Nathaniel Andersson, a 23-year-old whom Hank had met the day they both mustered into the ar-my. Nathaniel loved to sing, and men would gather around their fire at night to hear his voice accompa-nied by a well-worn guitar.

The picket asked, "You know this man?"

Nathaniel moved into the fire's glow. He was tall, one of the tallest in the Regiment, although much shorter than Long Sol. Nathaniel, with George Dyer, Daniel Hume and Charlie O'Neal, was Hank's mess mate.

Nathaniel was kind, gentle, open and exceedingly patient. He spoke, "I know him, least I think I do. It's a mite hard to tell with his face all covered with blood like 'tis and his tiny little head hidin' under that big hat. Reckon that hat's a couple sizes too big for you, Hank. Two of your heads could fit in it without stretchin' it a bit. Where'd you get bloodied like that? George said you was fine; now it looks like you're 'bout dead. You ain't dead are you, Hank?" Nathaniel smiled widely, clearly relieved to have happened upon him.

Hank wiped one hand across his face. He was covered with blood. He thought about the past hour. The blood on his face wasn't from the Confederate. It must have been from the Union soldier he had fallen on.

"I'm fine . . . just got a small cut. I tripped and fell; got some blood on my face. My arm got scratched. Nothing to worry about."

"You better get that taken care of," the picket admonished returning Hank's musket, then disappeared into the dark beyond the lighted circle of the fire.

Nathaniel approached Hank. "I just got back from takin' a wounded boy up to the surgeons. Let me show you where they got a hospital set up, not too far . . . across the road's all. We'll get that arm looked at."

"Where's our regiment?"

"'Bout the same place where the battle ended, along the trees. Most people are gettin' some sleep right now, while they can. I can take you there, but let's take care o' that arm first."

"My arm's fine."

"I ain't so sure 'bout that. Looks to be bleedin' a good bit. Let me take you up to the hospital."

Hank acquiesced and walked with Nathaniel to the Pike and toward Gainesville, through the confusion of foot, horse and ambulance traffic crowding the road. They followed a narrow path that turned to the left, and Nathaniel and Hank trailed several ambulances to a small house serving as the evening's hospital. As they walked, they continued their conversation.

"You ain't gonna like the hospital, Hank. Lot o' people injured."

"That's why they need the hospital, Nat."

"They been doin' a lot o' operations there," Nathaniel said meaningfully.

Taking the cue, Hank asked, "What kind of operations?"

"Cuttin' off a lot o' arms, legs . . . that kind o' thing."

They walked along silently for a while. Hank considered Nathaniel's explanation and responded in a flat tone, "I hope they don't take off my arm."

Nathaniel laughed. "I think there's more chance they'll take your good arm than that one that's doin' the bleedin'."

They walked along silently again.

"Guess we showed 'em today," Nathaniel said, breaking the silence.

"Guess we did."

"Think they'll attack tomorrow? I heard tell the whole Union army's comin', so we may do the attackin'. They'll be down tomorrow . . . gonna go right after old Jackson himself . . . the whole Union army."

"I hope so. Finish the old man right now before Lee gets here. We fought good today. I think they fought just as good. Lots of husbands and sons on both sides won't be going home after this one."

"I reckon you're right. But Secesh deserve such. You know that! If they hadn't tried to break up the Union— they don't got no right to do that—we wouldn't be here. We'd be workin' back on the farm . . . bringin' in the crops. No we wouldn't," he said, abruptly correcting himself. "Right now, we'd be in bed . . . sleepin'. That would feel good. Wouldn't that feel good, Hank? Wouldn't that feel good: in bed sleepin'?"

They were nearing the hastily arranged hospital, and Hank understood why Nathaniel had told him about the arms. There was considerable commotion and wounded men lay scattered on the ground around the small house. Some were squirming, some were quite still . . . a few moaned. Hank felt dizzy. There were candles and torches in the yard around a house. People were passing in every direction with litters. In the dark, it was impossible for Hank to tell who had already seen the doctor and who still waited. He could see a makeshift operating table in the house and a doctor working on an unconscious patient . . . sawing, seemingly no more concerned than if his patient were a tree fallen in a forest. By the side of the house, in the faint light escaping from the house's gore, Hank could see freed, independent arms lay stacked amid similarly severed legs. He was feeling the effects of lost blood: A fog of nausea rolled over his senses, and he stumbled a bit. He bent over and vomited. His arm throbbed and burned, and he felt exhausted. He gripped his arm tightly for the first time, hoping to stop the pain. He rose from vomiting and shivered from a chill.

"You sick, Hank? Maybe you been losing blood now for a while. We should'a patched you up right then."

"I'll be fine. It's nothing, Nat. Just give me a moment here." He continued after a brief pause. "Is there a tree around here to lean on . . . just for a while? I'm not feeling too good. If I can just rest."

Nathaniel found a tree trunk with space between two other soldiers and guided Hank there. "You rest here. I'll see if I can get someone to look at you."

"Hey what about me? I need help," said one of the two soldiers resting beside Hank. "I've been here a long time," he continued. "Get the surgeons to come over and see me . . . fix my arm. I'm bad hurt. I was in the fightin', too. Tell them to come help me," his voice choked with sobs. "Tell them to come. I don't have anyone lookin' after me."

The soldier on Hank's other side was strangely still and quiet.

Hank sat silently, too, fatigued, dazed and dizzy. He dozed only to be awakened by the sobs of the man on his right side. As he awoke, he felt as if he were falling. His legs twitched. His head pitched forward. The soldier on the left was silent. Hank dozed again. Nathaniel's voice awakened him next. "Hank it ain't no use. Ain't no doctors 'round that can help. They're all busy . . . real busy. I grabbed this bowl; filled it with water. Maybe we can just wash some o' the blood off your arm and wrap this bandage 'round it . . . stop it from bleedin' more. You can wash off your face. You got blood on your face, Hank."

Hank didn't answer, but with Nathaniel's aid worked to get his jacket off. The man on his right babbled on, "Don't forget me! I've been here a long time . . . a real long time. Help me."

Hank pulled up his own shirt sleeve and took a handful of water from the bowl and washed the injured arm. It hurt and stung, but not as much as he'd expected. After he rinsed it several times, he held it out, keeping pressure on it. Nathaniel wrapped a cloth around it and tied the cloth tight against his arm. Hank then took both hands, rinsed them in the water and washed at his face. With no mirror and minimal light it was impossible to know if his face was getting cleaner or just smeared. After rinsing at his face, he got up. He felt better, but still slightly dizzy. The man on his right kept up a constant dialogue and wailing, begging Hank and Nathaniel for help. They ignored him as best they could until Hank finished cleaning up.

As Hank stood, he turned slowly, cautiously, to the man and asked, "Where are you injured?" He suddenly felt faint again.

The man said, "It's my right arm . . . my arm. Can you help me?"

Hank stepped carefully over the man. As he leaned forward to look at the arm, he wavered. Nausea swept over him. In the dim light, he saw, stepped back, turned away. He felt drained and nausea doubled him over again. Nearly severed above the elbow the man's arm hung, it seemed to Hank, by the literal thinness of the man's skin. Someone had crudely bandaged the stump, but hadn't finished the job, leaving for the surgeons the torn arm dangling through the wrapping;

strips of human meat; raw and still warm. Memories of dinner afflicted him, and with his own loss of blood, Hank couldn't deal with more.

Hank raised himself, and Nathaniel whispered, "It's for the surgeons. There's nothin' we can do."

With no further word between them, they walked away with Hank exhausted, leaning heavily on Nathaniel. They could still hear the soldier crying, calling after them, "Don't leave me! Won't somebody help? My arm. It's bad hurt."

Chapter 8
Not Long Ago, Near Gainesville, Virginia

As Reid Gragg sat upon the coarse grass, he was having trouble dealing with the story the young woman was telling him. It totally engrossed him, but how could this woman, this stranger, sitting so close to him seem to hold answers to so many of his questions? It wasn't possible. He wanted to know more about her, but held back his questions because he desperately wanted to hear the rest of the story.

She continued, "Before I tell you more of his, no their, story, let me give you a little more background on Henry Thomas Gragg." She smiled wistfully as she said his name. "Hank, as he was called by everyone but his mother, was born in the Shenandoah Valley of Virginia. His Gragg ancestors came from Scotland, where they'd been part of the Macgregor clan. They lost a power struggle with the Campbells, I think, so they had to move on, first to Ireland and eventually to the Colonies. They, like many Scotch-Irish, settled in the Shenandoah Valley. Over the years, many immigrants migrated up the valley . . . which by the way is south. Remember that. In the Shenandoah Valley, up is south."

"It's probably because the direction of migration was north to south," interjected Reid without any prompting, and he regretted his comment as soon as he said it.

"That's possible. Though I think it's because as you move south, up the Valley, the elevation rises and the Shenandoah River starts at those higher elevations and flows north or down the valley. But back to the story: Several from Hank's family fought in the Revolution. There were no Tories in the Gragg family. Hank was born in 1840 and grew up in Woodstock, a small town up the valley from Winchester about 30 miles or so. It's right at the base of the Massanutten Mountain that would become so important to Stonewall Jackson during the Civil War. Hank's father was prosperous like many in the valley, but he wasn't among the socially elite. The Shenandoah, in the first days of the war, before its production capability was destroyed, was able to feed the entire Confederate Army in Virginia. Before the war, the valley folks were doing pretty well. Did you know any of this?"

"None of it, not the stuff about the valley. But keep going," Reid said almost impatiently.

She returned to Hank's story: She told Reid that Hank, after his rejection by Betsy initially fled to Maryland and tried to make a life there. It was difficult to find work, and he succumbed to scratching out a living as a farm laborer—a humble lifestyle he had never before imagined. He found he could barely survive on his minimal wages, and he was ever discouraged by the contrast between his deteriorating lot and the memory of his family's comfortable circumstances. He did

eventually overcome his despair, anger and humiliation at Betsy's unexpected rejection. But by then, he
knew a new humiliation. He was disgusted to think he
had abandoned his family, and he nursed a sense of
personal failure. He couldn't even care for his own
needs and comforts. Nonetheless, he didn't completely
give up hope. Within a year, that hope pushed him
westward to Ohio where he found work once again as
a laborer. His life in the Buckeye-state mirrored his
humbling experience in Maryland, and within a few
months, discouragement pushed him still farther west.
He crossed into Indiana to work again on someone
else's land.

She explained that there were many men who went
west as paupers and worked the fields for others.
Some graduated to land ownership and climbed to af-
fluence and social respectability. Hank was no less
able than such men, probably far more able than some,
and definitely better educated than most, but he felt
no ambition. At some point in his westward trek, he
accepted his poverty as just punishment for abandoning, without a word, his family. What had he done? He
tried not to think about it. But in his increasingly troubled mind, it seemed wrong to want more than he had
after what he had done to them.

Several times he sat down to write his father of
what had happened, what he had done, what he
lacked. Perhaps his father would send money, clothes,
food, whatever he needed . . . or invite him home. But
Hank couldn't bring himself to write, deciding it would
be wrong to post such a letter before he had felt the
full weight of punishment. In his darkest moments, he

doubted his father would even answer. His father had never made a mistake. Hank was convinced of that and knew his father wouldn't understand or accept what Hank had done. Hank had nothing now, except to continue the day-to-day, meager existence of the farm laborer.

As national tension grew before the war, Hank took little notice. When fellow laborers spoke of the 1860 election, he would close his eyes in apathy to a discussion that years earlier would have excited his hottest passions. He never spoke the names of presidential candidates Abraham Lincoln, Stephen Douglas, John Breckinridge or John Bell and would have been hard pressed to remember their party affiliations or political views. He didn't follow the news in South Carolina, although he heard about the surrender of Fort Sumter and South Carolina's secession. For weeks after Virginia seceded, Hank didn't know his family was in Confederate territory.

The war found a willing Hoosier recruit in Hank Gragg. He had left his family, lost the woman he loved and failed even to earn a comfortable keep. He was suffering, and although he never consciously thought it, he wanted that suffering to end. He wanted an honorable death sentence and joined the army expecting that sentence to be carried out on some distant field in the height of battle—his final punishment . . . and glory . . . in one decisive act of passion.

Reid let his mind wander into the story the woman told. He hadn't expected all this. His head drifted, and he stared blankly over open field. He was beginning to see it all. The woman smiled, noticing that he had stopped listening to her. She watched him and let him wander, saying nothing. After several minutes—once she was sure he was ready to listen again—she continued her story:

Hank felt the burden of his cowardice. His poverty on a succession of farms and later his physical hardship as a soldier matured him slowly until he could see his mistake. But recognition brought him no closer to healing his self-inflicted wounds. He was sure his family despised him, and that it was forever impossible to go back. Hank tried not to think about home and family. After joining the army, he had written many letters for fellow Hoosiers, but he addressed each one to a comrade's wife and children, parents or the hopefully faithful girl back in Indiana. Not one letter from his hand was directed south of the Mason-Dixon Line to the Gragg family of Woodstock.

Ultimately he was able to hide his parents, brothers, sisters, former friends, and Virginia acquaintances in some inner crevasse. Early in his days of despair, he would find himself creeping into those memories, but he hated the anger, the discouragement, the frustration that always followed. Over time he steeled himself against visiting there. Layers of dust and cobwebs covered the memories, and he had no desire to disturb this environment of disuse. Hank had sealed off nearly all feelings beyond those of the current day and the current moment. For him the world included only his regiment, especially his closest companions—his mess, the handful of men with whom he ate and slept.

The young woman explained to Reid that the Black Hat Brigade's general at Hank's first battle was a career soldier, John Gibbon. When appointed brigadier general, he brought a discipline the brigade hadn't known before, and the men had a difficult transition. Drills became the order of the day, and some of the men didn't like the new general or the drills.

Gibbon also gave them special hats. Instead of the usual forage caps with their upside-down, tea-cup shape and short bill, he gave them the tall Hardee hat—the hat used by army regulars . . . the career army. It took its name from a man, now a Confederate general, who was a member of the recommending committee before the war. The black felt hat was six inches high with a brim all the way around. Many soldiers raised one side of the brim and fastened it to the side of the hat with a brass eagle. Attached to the front of the hat were the brass trumpet symbol of the infantry and a letter showing to which company a soldier belonged. A light-blue cord ending in a tassel wrapped around the base of the crown of the hat. The final touch was an ostrich feather placed on the flat side of the brim.

General Gibbon ordered the men to wear formal army frocks and white leggings. Hank, she explained, didn't find the leggings as important as the general did, quickly lost them and actively joined the rest of the Indiana regiment in refusing to wear them. Gibbon, frustrated by the recalcitrance of the 19th, overcame their resistance only by threatening violence and following up the threat with a feigned cannonading of their camp that had Hank, and the rest of the 19th, prostrate with faces pressed hard against the ground and thereafter much more willing to wear the leggings.

Some other troops laughed at the western men because of their uniform, some saying they looked like a "bandbox brigade," but the name that stuck was "The Black Hat Brigade." The westerners got so they were proud of their hats and eventually began to like this General Gibbon who was making soldiers of them. Hank liked the hat from the beginning and took the drilling in stride, never resenting it or the general. To him, the most-of-the-time ample food more than compensated for the discipline and discomforts that went with soldiering.

The woman continued her monologue: During that first year, the Black Hats saw many runaway slaves. The slaves brought news to the brigade that angered some. These contraband assured the soldiers that the Union was fighting the war to free them. Some of the western soldiers didn't like the idea. They figured they joined the army to save the union and few had good feelings for the slaves. The contraband talk didn't bother Hank. He had, unlike many of the westerners, personally known and been close to slaves. He had witnessed the peculiar institution first hand before the war and enjoyed thinking the war would end slavery as it would also destroy a way of life he believed was no longer available to him.

She described Hank's reckless search for a battle trophy and how sitting with his wounded Confederate comrade had opened to Hank his memories of family, friends and state. She also explained that Hank's first battle over the years had been called the battle of

Gainesville, Groveton, or just part of Second Manassas or Second Bull Run, and most recently Brawner's Farm.

Reid interrupted the story to ask, "What happened to the girl?"

"What girl?"

"The one who refused to marry him."

"Betsy?"

Chapter 9
March 1861, Winchester, Virginia

*E*ighteen months after Hank left Virginia, Marie Ann Allen sat with Betsy in the same parlor where Hank had last seen them. They were alone, relaxed and happy.

"Betsy, he's going to make a wonderful husband. I should be envious."

"You? Jealous? Why? Don't you still have hopes of a certain young man in Lexington?"

Marie Ann's eyes brightened, "Oh, I do! And my cadet writes the most wonderful letters and promises a visit as soon as he stands for examination."

"I'd like to see him, too. He did me a great service. Do you remember . . . that first message?"

"The day John Brown attacked Harpers Ferry! My dear Caleb! I hope he'll come soon."

"He was right about war," Betsy said reflectively.

"I got a letter from a friend in South Carolina. She says the whole world is turned upside down in Charleston and it won't be long before something happens . . . something big. She writes everyone, or at least nearly everyone, in the entire city wants secession. They're mad for it. It's just a matter of time."

Betsy shook her head. "Everyone? Seems inconceivable, yet I hear more and more people talk of leaving

the Union here, too. It's changed in the last six
months. It's different than it was just . . . even a month
ago. It's all changing so fast. Does Caleb still look forward to war as much as he did?"

"Caleb doesn't want war, just freedom from tyranny.
He hopes to do his part. He's going to be a great hero.
I just know it."

"Doesn't that frighten you?"

"Frighten? Why should any of us be frightened? We
will quickly show any who seek to take our rights that
God and courage are on our side. With those allies,
how can we fail? Foes will run from battle when our
soldiers of Christ appear before them in their glory
and splendor. What's your betrothed think?" Marie
Ann asked, redirecting the discussion.

"It's strange: We haven't discussed war or politics
much. He did say it would be unwise for Virginia to
secede, regardless of what other states do. We have
much to lose. Marie Ann, he doesn't even believe we
have the right to secede, thinks the Union was meant
to be perpetual. If there's war, he thinks it will last a
long time."

"You don't need to fret over that. I've heard from so
many that it will be short . . . very short . . . the war. It
can't be long. We have much to protect . . . much to
gain. Our liberties are worth the greatest sacrifice, but
we'll have to make few. The people of the North aren't
going to send their sons down here to be slaughtered
on the altar of that king of fools, Lincoln. But if they
do, we'll whip them before breakfast and send them
home to their mothers for dinner."

"I hope you're right. I quake to think it won't come quite so easily . . . that it will be a long, drawn-out war."

"Would you, then, have us give in to coercion?"

"Coercion? I'm not sure of that, but I'm afraid we haven't thought out the costs."

"My dear Betsy, how you worry about nothing. The cost of any war will be borne by the North. The war will be over by breakfast. I'm sure of that. I only hope my handsome cadet will be able to get in that early morning fight. He is so wild to show his bravery. Betsy, he is brave . . . fearless! I can just feel it. You should read his letters, courage drips from the ink of each word. I have little worry for Caleb Moore."

"You must feel some anxiety for him? I would think some will die if there's war."

"A few . . . perhaps. Protecting our liberties is worth it! Caleb will be ready for the fight. You forget, he's almost graduated from the Institute. He'll have the finest military education Virginia can give."

"I hope your cadet will be safe."

"What of you? Would you rather have your betrothed stay home at such a moment, when men of honor are responding to the state's crisis? Wouldn't you want him to be with the army?"

"I certainly hope he doesn't join. He doesn't have the military education that will protect your kind cadet. My handsome young man would be lost on the battlefield, and I forever tormented if he joins. Marie Ann," she said, her face brightening, "if this war of yours will be over by breakfast . . . I'll make sure he sleeps very late that morning."

Both women laughed.

"I don't think you appreciate how brave he will be," said Marie Ann, still smiling. "He is after all Virginian! He'll be one of the first on the battlefield. With the rest of our men, he'll return with laurels on his head."

"Perhaps," Betsy said with resignation.

"Betsy, what will you do if war breaks out? Will you hurry your wedding?"

"I would want to . . . but we haven't discussed it."

"And you?"

With her eyes clear and excited, Marie Ann responded, "I will tell Caleb to come at once for we must be married." She giggled at the thought.

Betsy smiled but at that moment remembered a young man she had once loved and that she still loved. He was gone now, and she never knew what happened to him. He was just gone. She would have married him. If she were honest, she'd admit to Marie Ann, right now, that she still wished she was marrying Hank Gragg. If it were him, she wouldn't wait another day, nor an instant longer. She'd marry him right now. But she couldn't. He was gone . . . dead by some silent, unknown calamity. Hank Gragg: she remembered at that moment laughing with him as they raced their horses across an open field. She had won the race that day, and he pulled his horse along side of hers and from his saddle had held out his hand. She had reached out for it, and both had stopped laughing as their hands touched. She had drunk in his penetrating blue-eyed gaze, her eyes wide open, allowing him entry into the depths of her feelings and mind.

A little more than a month later, just after Fort Sumter surrendered and Virginia seceded, Betsy married.

Chapter 10
29 August 1862, Manassas Junction, Virginia

*F*rom the makeshift hospital, Hank and Nathaniel hiked back to their regiment in Brawner's Woods, arriving about one in the morning, in time for orders to retreat. The Black Hat Brigade—Hank, Nat and George included—retreated during the night. Their long, painful, night-time march took them toward Manassas, and Nat and George took turns supporting Hank so he could keep up with the regiment . . . so he wouldn't fall into Confederate hands. Once they got to the railroad tracks of Manassas Junction, they collapsed and rested well beyond sunup.

When they awoke, Hank, George Dyer, Daniel Hume, Nathaniel Andersson and Charlie O'Neal, the five mess-mates, sat together near the railroad tracks. Four of the mess-mates had naturally drawn together a year earlier, while Daniel had joined them recently. He had been uninvited, but nonetheless latched on to them, and they let him.

The friends revived after their brief rest and began to eat just-distributed rations. Less than 18 hours had passed since their last rations. But to each man, those hours had been interminable . . . a week . . . a month . . . a lifetime of pain, memories and experience stuffed into one evening, night and morning. They now ignored the guns firing continuously at a distance. They were used to the sound, didn't mind it as long as they weren't ordered back into the fray. They never once considered that other men at that moment were living the ordeal they experienced: the shells and balls, the Rebel yell, the throat-choking, eye-burning smoke.

They were still grimy and blackened from the battle. Hank had blood on his clothes and bits of blood on his face, arms, and hands where he hadn't succeeded in rinsing it off. His arm ached, and he was still fatigued, but he didn't complain. A fresh bandage covered the wound under the torn sleeves of his frock and shirt. Hank sat by his knapsack, and as the men chatted, he pulled a clean shirt from it and began taking off the torn and soiled clothes.

"Well, Mr. Hume," George Dyer began, looking at Daniel, who upon hearing his name became uncomfortable and fidgety. The braggart had seemed to Hank uncharacteristically bashful. He hadn't joined the conversation around the fire, but sat quietly and attentively listening to everything said by the others. Hank thought he looked frightened now, and he understood why. George had a well-developed ability to find a man's open wound, and it was clear he had discovered Daniel's. George was about to poke and prod.

"Been lookin' forward to hearin' stories of heroic deeds that you done on the battlefield," George said. "'Specially since you always said you was goin' to be a hero. Haf to say I ain't heared 'bout you from no other regiments. In my figurin', you ought'o be famous as Stonewall Jackson right 'bout now. The name Daniel

Hume ought'o be on the lips o' every soldier in this here army, and on the lips o' the girls back home—you bein' so brave and all. So how come, Daniel, I ain't heared no stories yet? Are you just that humble? I know 'bout Nat's heroics. Just standin' up on that line, head stickin' up 'bove everybody else, that takes courage. I know 'bout Hank. We was together. Charlie was with us the whole time. So Danny boy, how come I ain't heared nothin' 'bout you? I'm sure you got a story that you been awantin' to tell. It's as good a time as what's ever gonna come to tell that story."

Daniel was anxious to respond. The muscles in his face contracted unnaturally and twitched. The words burst from his mouth, "If you'd been on the line where I was standin', you wouldn't be so cocky, George. Men on both sides of me . . . good Union boys . . . was mowed down like the Secesh was usin' a scythe to cut 'em with, like they was the grass on that field." He waved his hand toward a nearby field. "I'm willin' to admit, I got separated from you fellas. Goin' through the trees, I got lost from the battle line some ways, and the army's better for it. You can be sure of that, the army's better for it. When I realized what'd happened, I trekked right through those trees and brush; came out in the middle of that battle. There was a hole in the line where I come out of the woods. It was the Sixth. They'd lost a lot o' men. So they can tell you what I done. And they will tell you if you ask 'em. It's worth hearin', George. It's worth hearin'. . . be sure o' that. They needed me right there in the line, so I just stepped up and fired. No hesitatin'. They needed me, and I just stepped up and plugged the line. I'm tellin' you the line would've crumbled right then . . . right there, but for me pluggin' it the way I done. I wasn't there but a few minutes when men, not just a few, mind you, but a lot of 'em fell on both sides of me. I was almost by myself, but I didn't move. Not me. I didn't move, but I just couldn't—fight as hard as I could—hold the line by myself. Not all by myself. It was too much, even for me. They was retreatin' all 'round: I mean the Union boys. So I had to retreat with the survivors and wounded. One boy was wounded real bad. I he'ped him back up to the hospital. Just like you, Nat, he'pin' Hank. I knowed Hank 'preciated it, didn't you Hank? So did this boy."

Hank didn't respond, and Daniel didn't wait for a response. "When I got to the hospital, they needed my he'p with the wounded. There were so many wounded. I wanted to get back to the line, but the surgeons . . . they told me the best thing was for me to stay and he'p 'em. There was lots and lots o' wounded. They needed he'p. They needed my he'p."

The other four men tried to hide their smiles, but Daniel ignored them and kept talking. "They said lots would want to get back to the fightin', and they wouldn't blame me if I went. But they told me the brave thing to do . . . the thing of courage . . . was for me to stay with them at the hospital and he'p the other soldiers. I was so brave, George. I was real brave. They called me a hero: all the surgeons, they said that . . . about me."

The other men in the mess let out full-belly laughs. Men along the railroad tracks looked at the five men; a few wandered over.

"What's going on?" some who came asked.

George answered them, "We just been hearin' 'bout the courage o' one o' our brave soldiers here. He done leaved the glory of fightin' to the rest of us, while he was doin' the brave thing: skulkin' back o' the line. 'Lots and lots o' wounded.' He's mighty brave to stay back helpin' all them wounded. I could never have done nothin' like that. And that's the truth."

Hume's bulky frame was trembling with anger, but George spoke again. "Why you're all cowards." He pointed accusing fingers sequentially at Hank, Charlie and Nathaniel. "You was out there in that field with all them balls avoidin' you. You was probably duckin' a mite out there. I want you to know every time you ducked, one o' them balls carried right on over and went after them brave soldiers ahidin' back o' the lines at the hospital, 'mong all the wounded. Next time, you just stand up and take them balls. I'll have no one riskin' the life of brave Danny Hume. Danny Hume, our man o' courage." He shook his head in mock disgust still pointing his finger at his friends. "You ought'o be ashamed o' yourselves."

It looked as if Hume would attack George, but a small crowd had gathered, laughter coursing through it as the visitors perceived the joke. Daniel held back his anger, rose on his mammoth feet, kicked dirt at George and pushed his way through the amused, gathering crowd. As he retreated, Dyer called after him, "He helped lots and lots o' wounded."

When Nathaniel had overcome his laughter, he said, "That was a bit mean, don't you think, George?"

"Deserved it. Skulkin' like he done. Then he come up with a story like that one, that he held the line by himself. That's mighty brave, Nat. I ain't heared nothin' 'bout the Sixth retreatin'. I heared they wasn't even near the woods. There was only one that was retreatin', our good friend Daniel Hume. He plays us for the fool. Nat, we ain't no fools. I ain't eatin' no more with him, not with no coward like him." The crowd that had gathered slowly dispersed.

George was silent for a time, then a new topic entered his mind, and he said, "Not all of us run to the rear. Some snuck out on that battlefield after the fightin' was all done, and we hain't heared 'bout it. What happened out there, Hank. You come back all bloody and wounded." He looked straight at Hank. "D'you get that battle trophy you was lookin' fer?"

Hank had removed his soiled and torn shirt and replaced it. As George questioned him, he remembered the letter. Ignoring his remaining mess-mates, he pulled the blood stained letter from his pant pocket. As he pulled it out, something fell to the ground. Mildly startled, he reached to pick it up. His fingers found a brass button from a Virginian's uniform. He looked at it, quickly remembering it had come off the Confederate officer as he had searched the soldier's body for the letter. He must have inadvertently held on to it.

Seizing his good fortune, he held out the button in his right hand with a playful, self-satisfied look on his face. "Here's my battle trophy, boys! A button off a Secesh uniform, an officer's uniform."

"A button?" George asked incredulously. "You risked the whole life that God give you going out on that battlefield in the dark of the night, running the pickets, fer a trophy, and you brung back a button. That ain't no trophy, Hank. And it sure ain't spoils. It's . . . it's . . . it's . . . what's that word? Trifle . . . a trifle. Hank you done got yourself a trifle! That ain't no trophy."

The mess-mates, including Hank, laughed. He then waited for the laughter to fade before responding, "But George, it's my own personal trifle, and I'm the only one that's got one. None of you have this Rebel button or anything like it." He then continued, more serious now, "George, you want to hear what happened last night?"

Hank told them the story, and as he did they listened, mesmerized. When Hank was finished, George asked, "What's you gonna do with that letter now you got it?"

"I guess at some point, I'll try to get it to the man's wife."

"Ain't that like talkin' to the enemy, Hank? What you think, Charlie . . . Nat? One of us wants to talk to the enemy. That ain't right."

Hank responded seriously, "I don't think so, George. You know that some of our pickets talk and trade newspapers, tobacco and coffee with Southern pickets. It's happening more and more all the time. I think that's more like talking to the enemy than my forwarding a man's last letter to his wife."

"Hank, don't you want to read it and find out 'bout that man?" asked Nathaniel.

Hank thought. He would have liked to have read the letter and knew he had to read it to figure out to whom to send it. But in some incomprehensible way he felt a personal affiliation, a brotherhood, with the Confederate officer. He wanted to read it alone; the man was due his respect. He doubted his friends would feel the dignity of the soldier. To them, he was a dead Reb. To Hank, he was long minutes of shared fear, pain and suffering—a perception rapidly ascending in retrospect. He was bound inexplicably to the dead Virginian. Nonetheless, egged on by his mess, he opened the envelope, pulled out the letter and scanned it briefly, silently.

"Read it fer us, Hank!" George directed.

Hank continued to look at the letter. The writing was neat and easily legible, each letter well formed. Portions of the page were bloodstained, but not enough to make the letter illegible. He looked at the envelope. There was no address, but a Virginia Battle Flag and accompanying verse adorned it.

"Here's something for you boys. It's verse on the envelope."

He read:

All fair sons of blessed Virginia,
answer your nation's urgent call,
Fight for home and for your family,
and for liberties dear to all.
Forward quickly, courage, honor,
Stand before the foeman tall,
Array yourself for battle's glory,
watch the cursed vandal fall.

George was the first to comment, with a spark of mockery in his voice, "Cursed Vandals is we, then? How d'you like bein' one of them Vandals, Charlie? I always thought your people was from Ireland. Now I

find you ain't Irish, just one o' them Vandals from . . .
from . . . Hank, where does Vandals live?"

Hank ignored the question.

"George, those Secesh are fightin' for our side," Nathaniel unexpectedly interjected.

"What figurin' give you that, Nat?" George asked,
looking perplexed.

"What was the line 'bout the nation, Hank?"

Hank read again, "Answer your nation's urgent
call."

George laughed, "You're right, Nat. I see what
you're sayin'. Since there's only one nation, it's mighty
clear to me they wanna fight fer that nation. Ain't that
the Union? They's fightin' fer the Union and don't
know it. They should'a just told us. We'd 'bliged 'em.
Charlie, next time when we're afightin' 'em, instead o'
shootin' 'em, just call 'em over . . . 'splain the way
things is to 'em. Invite 'em to join us."

"I'll do it, George. I'll do it," an animated Charlie responded. "Then when they come over," he said with a
vicious snarl, "I won't go wastin' no balls on 'em, I'll
give 'em the bayonet. That'll teach 'em to leave the
Union. When I've given them the cold steel, they won't
be leaving it no more. They'll be resting forever under
sacred Union sod. And I'll still have all my 'munition so
I can go down to Carolina and shoot down those man-
gy dogs that started this whole thing." Without stopping even long enough to breathe, Charlie continued,
"Read the letter Hank! What's the letter say?"

With distant battle sounds still audible, Hank began
to read aloud the pen and ink letter. The men were
attentive, eager to hear the last words a doomed of-

ficer would write to his beloved. As Hank read, each
man visualized the recipient as beautiful in just the
way he imagined his own perfect woman, and each of
them grew homesick for her.

Hank read, *28th of August 1862.*

Nathaniel interrupted, "That's the morning of the
battle . . . just yesterday morning . . . the very day he
died."

Hank read on.

My dearest love,

*I sit under a tree to write you a few words. I haven't
much to write but of my great affection for you. I told
you of our victory at Cedar Mountain and we have not
fought in other battles since then. So I have no battle
news to tell, no glorious new gain made by the wondrous Stonewall Brigade. They're calling us that everywhere now. It gives me pride to be in it, to be a
member of Jackson's foot cavalry, as we reckon ourselves. We can march just about as fast as Stuart's
cavalry can ride, and we can fight a lot better than the
cavalry, too. We're resting today. Many boys are playing cards. I'm not playing because I know how you feel
about cards. I think we wait for the enemy to come.
Right now I have a few moments to write to you. We
have been well fed of late, and, just in time, too. I was
getting very hungry. We ate this time, courtesy of old
Abe and that Yankee general Pope, no relation I don't
believe to that Papist in Rome. We raided Manassas
Junction, found many train cars of food and supplies.
We ate to our heart's content all the good things in life.
We had lobster. It was wonderful. There was plenty of
cake, candy and nuts. I even enjoyed two oranges and*

took a lemon for the road. There was some fine whis-
key there, courtesy of Genl Pope, and he left me a
pocket-full of cigars. I'm enjoying one right now. The
hard part of the whole thing was burning what the
men couldn't eat or load in their knapsacks. We had to
do it though, so the Yanks couldn't have it. What a
smell that fire created! As I write this letter, I think I
can still smell bacon cooking at Manassas.

Ellie, I am ever grateful to you for your loving kind-
ness in sending me that package. The food was so
good and I needed the new shirt. The food made me
wish I was home with you and you were eating right
beside me. I'm wearing the shirt for the first time to-
day, and even the Colonel said I look like a new man in
it.

Hope all is well in Staunton and that our dear
friends take good care of you. I think me the luckiest
man in the world to be married to the most beautiful
girl in all of Virginia.

George interrupted, "Now he ain't got no life atall."

Nat added reflecting, "Makes you think. It can all be
gone with just one charge, one ball, a little bit o' canister. I don't want to write no letters like that. It's too . .
. too . . . unnatural."

Hank ignored his friends and read on, silently to
himself.

Charlie interrupted his progress, saying, "Don't go
on without us! Keep reading, Hank."

Hank returned to where he had left off and read.

I can't imagine life without you, Ellie. Be true. My
heart will always be true to you. Remember that night
when I swore I'd never love another. It's true. I could

never love another the way I love you. When I come home, I hope we have many children. Once we drive this Union army out of Virginia as we drove them out of the valley, I will come home and we can begin where so soon we had to leave off. We will be very happy. I am eager to come to you. I shall write to you again soon. In the meantime, I leave you in the hands of our Father in Heaven.

Faithfully,
Your ever loving husband
Captain Thaddeus Henderson
5th Virginia
The Stonewall Brigade. CSA
Written near Manassas.

The silence that followed the reading was broken by George Dyer, "Well . . . ain't that sad after all."

"It is. Can't imagine how sad she'll be to find he's dead . . . seemed to want to live just for her," Nat commented in his resonant voice, caught up in the romance of the moment. "And all that talk 'bout returnin' home to her."

George responded quickly, "That ain't what's sad, Nat. It's sad cuz you got a woman that lost her husband . . . a beautiful wida lady there. What's her name? Ellie? The problem the way I figure is Ellie's a Reb wida. So we can't even go marry her ourselves. It's a waste, a real sad waste o' all that beauty." He laughed and added, "Only Yankee widas ought'o be pretty."

Charlie joined him laughing and said, "You don't know she's pretty, George. You got one dead soldier who's saying she's pretty. Nobody else is saying nothin'. Maybe he's embarrassed she's so ugly. Maybe he joined Jackson just to get away from her." George and Charlie shared another hearty laugh.

Nat looked slightly confused, and Hank ignored the comments, still lost in personal thoughts of the letter, the dying soldier and his promise to deliver the missive. Unlike the moment when he feigned the promise, Hank now wanted to personally deliver the letter to the widow.

As the men finished their rations, a fresh column of Union soldiers passed. Hank's mess-mates went to cheer the passing troops, leaving him alone with his thoughts and the letter. He took pen and paper from his knapsack. It was the pen he used to write letters dictated by other soldiers. For the first time in his year in the infantry, he wrote a letter of his own, a letter to the widow. He finished it and a thought passed through his mind that he didn't put on paper: "I pray I was not the one who felled your valiant husband."

He put his letter in the envelope with the Confederate soldier's letter and put the envelope into his pocket. Hank also made a copy of the captain's letter. He took out Federal coins, gold and silver, that he had saved from his pay months earlier and placed them with the letters. Then he picked up the button. He looked at it closely . . . the words . . . the image. He closed his left hand around it and squeezed it tightly, then slipped it, his newly won trophy, into the same pocket.

Chapter 11
September 1862, Upton's Hill, Virginia

After Second Bull Run, the 19th Indiana plodded to Washington with the rest of the Northern army. In spite of fighting stubbornly, the Federal troops had lost. The commanding general had misused the army, and many of the soldiers knew it. This battle, however, was different from First Bull Run: It hadn't been a rout; the army wasn't disgraced.

The 19th Indiana and the rest of the Black Hats in particular had proved themselves in battle. Following their courageous battle against Jackson, they had fought again credibly two days later and eventually were called on to guard the army's rear, allowing it to retreat in order and safety to the protection of the forts and massive guns around Washington. But after it was all over and heads were counted, Daniel Hume wasn't with the 19th. The mess-mates never saw him again, and he was officially listed as a casualty—missing in action.

At the end of its retreat, the 19th encamped at Upton's Hill, Virginia. They quickly created an organized tent town where men camped by company along neatly laid out streets that boasted small ditches to catch water and rain and direct it from camp. From Upton's Hill, the men could see the capitol in one direction and in the other they were convinced they could see the banners of Lee's army, reminding them they were still in the Old Dominion, a land where many residents, Southern and Union loyalists, had abandoned houses and farms.

One young Southern sympathizer still in the area was a black-haired, brown-eyed, skinny girl named Nellie. She looked to be nine or 10 years old. Dressed in tatters and with a dirt-smudged face, she walked on bare feet caked in mud and covered with dust. Mercilessly she harangued the soldiers of the 19th Indiana as they marched into their camp. The boys took her badgering well, promising to bring Bobby Lee to meet her personally after they captured him. "You'll never catch him! He'll catch you!" she replied, hands defiantly on hips.

The next afternoon Nellie was again in camp, arguing with soldiers brave enough to take her on. Many tried but, to the delight of all witnesses, she always won by describing to them wondrous things Stonewall Jackson had done to soldiers at First Manassas, in the valley and at Second Manassas. She didn't flinch a bit when she accused them of being some of the very men her hero had so thoroughly trounced. The men looked around nervously when she started pointing her finger.

Hank thought Nellie might be the answer to his dilemma. She might be the first link in sending the Confederate captain's letter to Staunton. He lay on his bedroll in his half of the dog tent, two halves of a canvas tent buttoning together at the top.

He quickly scribbled a short note:

I have a letter that I must get to a woman in Staunton, Virginia. It was written by her husband, a Confederate captain, before he died. He asked me to get it to her. Can you help me? If so, please send your daughter to see me tomorrow and I will give her the letter.

He decided it was safer not to sign the letter, relying instead on the young girl's ability to recognize him.

Beyond his view, he could still hear her telling the soldiers what she thought of them. Hank smiled and slipped out of the tent. He approached the little Rebel mid-sentence in her diatribe. Abruptly he said, "Give this note to your ma. It warns her about what we do with little Secesh girls who like Lee and Jackson."

The child looked frightened. Hank stuffed the note into her hand, and with both of his hands held out, he swung them outwardly as if he were swatting at a fly. "Now, shoo. Give that note to your mama, and take a good look at me. Remember what the soldiers look like that'll vanquish this Jackson fella you've been bragging about. There'll be no more Jackson lovers in this camp." The young girl backed away from Hank, tripping as she moved backwards, then turned and ran from the camp . . . paper clutched tightly in her hand.

Reaction around Hank was mixed: Some men laughed at his treatment of the miniature Rebel; some murmured their disappointment at having their entertainment so suddenly ended; some, silent, gave him glances of disgust for his treatment of Nellie.

The next day was painfully slow for Hank. As he went about the camp routine, he kept watch for the child. Every laugh attracted him, thinking someone might be laughing at the girl, but each laugh was a disappointment. Whenever he saw a crowd, he joined it hoping to see her, but no crowd gathered around a Jackson worshiper. By sunset, Hank was beside himself, and to avoid despair he adjusted his expectations: It was possible she would come the next day.

The following day likewise passed without Nellie appearing in camp. Hank made a long mental list of possible reasons: He might have scared her—he definitely had scared her. She might have dropped the note. Perhaps her parents didn't know how to read or were frightened for their daughter. They might have suspected a trap to catch Rebel sympathizers. The sentries might have kept her out of camp. As he bedded the second night, Hank knew he wouldn't be able to send the letter by Nellie and didn't want to send it formally across the lines. There was no one else and no other method he could trust: He would have to take the letter to Staunton himself.

Hank never considered his actions disloyal to the Union, but knew others would. As a native Virginian, he felt particularly vulnerable to being branded a Southern spy or traitor. He couldn't jeopardize his position in the army by mentioning the letter again to anyone. He would have to find a way to get a furlough and make his way to Staunton. While his decision disquieted him, he felt an overall sense of relief. He had made the decision, and he fell soundly asleep.

Late on September 6, the Black Hat Brigade began its next movement. The men marched through the dark, empty streets of the capital city, Washington, with its unfinished capitol dome, into Maryland. In the coming days, they advanced to the town of Frederick and beyond. In heavy fighting, they pushed through South Mountain, clearing away the Georgians and Alabamians stationed to hold them back at Turner's Gap, and eventually joined McClellan and the bulk of the Army of the Potomac.

Chapter 12

17 September 1862, Near Antietam Creek, Maryland

*D*uring the afternoon, the regiment proceeded south in columns toward the Maryland town of Sharpsburg. Confederate skirmishers popped up to slow the advance and someone, somewhere, late in the evening, decided not to continue. The Black Hats, with the rest of the Union's First Corps, lay down in columns, their lines parallel to the road. They tried to sleep, ready for the morrow. Hank lay down on the wet ground, wrapped in his gum blanket and with loaded rifle musket at his side.

Suffering in a cold drizzle and fog, knowing battle was at hand, Hank slept fitfully. This pre-battle experience was different from the surprise of Gainesville and Jackson's men—there had been no time to worry then. At South Mountain, they marched against a foe fighting only to delay the brigade. This time would be different. Hank knew he would wake early the next morning to fight an opponent who was waiting for him, not willing to retreat. He knew it, could feel it: They would be the first Northern troops put into battle. The thought unnerved him.

In the fine rain that fell, he had time to think, but his thoughts drifted from glory, the Union cause, his regiment and friends, and death . . . to his commitment to deliver the letter. He imagined his reception in Staunton. They would welcome him warmly. He envisioned the widow, young and dependent—dependent upon him—and her friends and family welcoming him as a now-recognized, long-lost son. They would know of his great sacrifices, the monumental odds he had overcome, all to deliver, in person, news of the saintly Captain Henderson. He heard the widow's family confide in him that they were grateful he had come, that she needed a strong shoulder to lean on.

He drifted toward sleep with pleasant, peaceful thoughts of such heroism only to be bothered by images that surfaced slowly between wakefulness and sleep. He saw unfamiliar faces of individual Southern soldiers in battle line, features fixed with determination—bodies lean, hard and flexed—ready to loose their power and fury. He saw himself, the sole Union soldier on the field, yelling ferociously, charging the unmoving Rebel line. Without warning, his voice was swallowed up in a fiendish scream arising from the Confederates . . . a cry of pent-up . . . now unleashed violence. The Southern soldiers ran toward him . . . flanked him . . . surrounded him . . . overwhelmed him in an instant. He tried to surrender, to give up, but they couldn't or wouldn't hear him. It was no use. There was no hope. Again and again, he died. He awoke with a sudden start and accumulated drizzle dripping as cold drops onto his face from his blanket.

He stared into the darkness around him, drifting again toward slumber. He thought of the countless hordes of Confederate soldiers just ahead that lay on their own wet bedrolls, sleeping intermittently like him. Then his mind was adrift again. Each of those soldiers wanted to stop him from crossing the Potomac River, stop him from getting to the Shenandoah Valley. Each soldier had been ordered by Lee himself to stop Union Private Hank Gragg, make sure he never saw the widow, was never welcomed, never praised by her appreciative family. Lee had ordered them to shoot him, "Kill him! He has no homeland or kinsmen . . . a traitor . . . only death for a traitor." He awoke. He heard periodic picket fire and sat up, looking around in the dark and breathing heavily.

The landscape was similar to the Shenandoah Valley that lay just a few miles south. In the night, he couldn't see the mountains, but knew they were there.

As dark receded, drizzle stopped and troubled dreams ended. The 19th was awakened, and by 5:30 Hank found himself in column advancing over large rolling hills in patchy fog. He was wet and uncomfortable; but well used to the feeling, he didn't dwell on it. Sunlight diffused over the fields, and he was pleased with the impression that the fog might burn off entirely. It was going to be a beautiful day after all, and that promise lifted his spirits.

Hank expected at any time to see Confederates in a line waiting just for him, just as he had imagined it. The cannonading from both sides and the picket fire ahead attested to a coming battle, but he kept hoping that he had misread their message, that they spoke only as cover for a Confederate retreat.

The column paused in a grove of trees to form battle lines and marched on. They approached a farmhouse and outbuildings, and Hank wondered about its occupants and what his family was doing at that moment. Would he live to find out? Would he be alive a day from now . . . this evening . . . in an hour? Would he live long enough to finish the thought or would a sniper's accurate aim bring him down in mid-notion. He laughed inside as he completed the thought. He had survived. He was a survivor. Hank Gragg no longer wanted to die in battle.

He listened to the increasing din of battle ahead. Other Black Hats were already engaged in heavy fighting in the farmer's cornfield, and the action dashed his dim hopes that the enemy was retreating. The Confederates were there still, just ahead of him. Artillery and musket fire echoed among the disordered-wave-like hills. The 19th was ordered to lie down, then deployed across the road pushing Secesh skirmishers south into woods and toward Sharpsburg. The skirmishers fell back, joining the Confederate front as the 19th pushed persistently forward, deeper toward and into the trees.

Hank could hear cannon and muskets across the pike. An internal fire warmed his face. He fired his Springfield and advanced, seeing only the Confederates ahead as they melted before the pickets and the 19th's wrath.

It was light work, yet Hank quickly lost track of time. He didn't know if he'd been fighting for hours or just a few minutes. The regiment pushed the Confederates backward. He felt strength pulse through his body. The day belonged to the Union. A victory won. Secesh were retreating, not quite on the run, but the 19th was pushing them back. The regiment moved still deeper in the trees. Then Hank heard it, beyond the trees, that unearthly and inhuman sound: the Rebel yell, a sound now ever in his mind, embedded as subconscious fear.

The screaming Confederates charged the Black Hat regiments that were fighting—desperately fighting—in the cornfield across the pike. The 19th, seeing the charge, pushed to the road and uphill into the enemy's flank, into the cornfield, breaking the Southern charge. Hank and the others kept pushing, but a new line of Secesh appeared, opening a shattering fire into the charging Hoosiers. Along the enemy battle line, he could see the gray and butternut soldiers clearly, even in the smoke of the battlefield. He fired into the new foes, but the enemy, fixed and powerful, maintained crushing pressure. The 19th wavered. Balls buzzed around Hank . . . thick . . . frightening . . . screeching like fighting cats. He felt as if a physical force pulled him back from the Confederate rifles. He retreated over a fence, slowly moving backward, resisting at each step the pull to the rear. The fight became vicious.

Out of the corner of his eye, he saw the regimental color bearer fall and a new man pick up the colors only to fall. He was near the colors now . . . they were falling again. Should he pick them up, wave the standard, rally the boys? But some other distantly familiar boy-soldier was there hoisting them momentarily until he too fell upon the body-covered ground. Hank felt a deep sorrow, but he was still firing . . . the fight pushing away thoughts of colors and sorrow. His friends, the men of the 19th, fell as they moved toward shelter. Hank felt himself pulled again as if by a rope back down the hill, over and behind a sheltering rock formation. Shielded from further devastation and the heat of the fire, Hank saw the liquid 19th solidify . . . much smaller than at dawn. The regiment fired into the Confederates. Hank was exhausted, yet it was still early. He wanted to crawl onto the field ahead, lie down on the grass amidst the bodies and sleep. Were those dead bodies? Did it matter?

Well before 9 o'clock, Hank had completed a lifetime's destruction, and he let his musket cool. After a short wait, he and the remaining men of the 19th moved back toward where they had begun. Small duties occupied them for the remainder of the day, and when they were done, the regiment bivouacked near their campsite of the previous night.

At some moment during the day, after the killing, as he moved from the battlefield, Hank had seen Nathaniel towering above the men around him. He was relieved to see his friend.

"Have you seen George?" he queried Nathaniel. "George is fine. We was side by side the whole time. He's here somewhere."

"And Charlie?"

Nathaniel became thoughtful. He lowered his rich voice and said, "I saw him grab the colors."

Hank didn't respond. He remembered and understood now that he too had seen Charlie grab the colors. He had seen it all, but in the fever of fight he hadn't understood it. Charlie, not Hank, had plucked up the fallen colors. Charlie, not Hank, had waved them defiantly at the Confederates. How long had Charlie held them? Not long, not long at all. Did someone else grab the colors from Charlie's faltering fingers and wave them boldly? Hank was not as close to Charlie as he had been to Nathaniel and George, but he was still fond of him. And as Hank remembered what had happened, guilt crushed him. His chest was heavy and breathing seemed a chore; pushing out the rib cage to let air fill his chest was no longer natural and involuntary, but took conscious effort. Why hadn't he grabbed the colors?

Nathaniel looked with concern at Hank, "You all right?"

Hank didn't respond, and Nathaniel let it pass.

Thinking back on the day now, Hank wondered what they had accomplished. He would have been content to have stayed behind, to have had the entire 19th stay behind, just spend the morning setting up camp. The result would have been far more satisfying. He would have had more sleep, more food, more coffee, and more friends. It wouldn't have mattered if they weren't able to brew the coffee, he would have willingly munched on the beans if it could have only been different. He thought grimly of the harvest Maryland and Virginia farmers reaped on their fields that autumn. An enemy had crept in unnoticed and sown not tares but hatred, and it had blossomed and fruited prodigiously. Listening to the distant racket of guns and muskets, it was clear to Hank: nothing had changed. There were still tens of thousands of Confederate soldiers between him and the Potomac. Once again, his mind wandered: Those soldiers were just as committed to thwart his journey south as they had been throughout his restless night. Had the battle . . . Charlie's death . . . meant anything? He wasn't sure he even knew who won.

Chapter 13

*Late September 1862, Near Antietam Creek,
Maryland*

After Antietam, Hank wasn't the young man who had fled Virginia and come back as a raw volunteer soldier. He had seen the dead and dying, the brave and the coward, the leader and the lost on battlefields in Virginia and Maryland. The sight of wounds and the dead no longer repelled nor attracted him. He was desensitized to the swelling, gaseous, blackened and bursting corpses of men, horses and cows—cows slaughtered indiscriminately among dying men near the cornfield.

Yet, Hank felt a new, almost paralyzing dread of battle. He thought it odd that before his first battle, less than four weeks earlier, he couldn't wait to get into the fight. If he could see the elephant . . . just once . . . he would no longer fear it. He had seen it now three times. Instead of finding comfort and confidence in familiarity, he now feared profoundly the elephant's roar and panicked charges, the pounding under its feet of all who slipped to the ground short of safety or those who ran too slowly to escape its terrorizing momentum. He was tormented by the thought of its by-man-sharpened tusks swinging erratically, goring those who dared stand up to it.

He didn't know why he feared battle now: Perhaps it was because he'd seen so many die around him, dread in their eyes and suffering on their lips. . . or the smell after the battles that nearly overcame him . . . or the dead men. Perhaps he had been worn down by the sheer magnitude of the effort required . . . the ferocity he had felt and now loathed . . . the sense-numbing noise and commotion. Or perhaps battles now forebode he would never complete his personal business in Staunton. Or most likely of all, somewhere deep within, Hank was keeping a tally along with the great god of battlefield odds and knew that one day on some future battlefield that timeless pagan deity would nod at him as if to say, "You are chosen." In response a Minié ball—with Hank's likeness etched shadow-like into its casing—would be tucked snugly into a bed of powder deep within the bowels of a musket, and a caring, loved and lovable human eye would see that god's nod, sight the chosen and, with slightly held breath and best intentions for all involved, squeeze gently the trigger. Concussion . . . fire . . . smoke . . . now incense . . . a worthy offering to the war god. A rapidly spinning bullet would testify that it was time for Hank to lay down his musket. Perhaps it was all these things. He didn't know why, but he now lived in dread of the elephant.

In the days that followed Antietam, Hank labored on burial details. He watched soldiers and civilians collect battle souvenirs: shreds of uniforms, equipment, weapon pieces, all strewn on the ground. How easy it was now to pick up such trinkets. But they seemed so ephemeral, so insignificant. Lasting meaning survived only in spent struggle and courage that scattered them across the fields. Hank was ashamed, remembering his cavalier expedition for a captain's button: stumbling, tripping over the bodies of dead and dying men who had abandoned their life blood for duty. He had won what in his naiveté he called his trophy of war, but what had now become his souvenir of carnage . . . a reminder of his folly. He had dishonored the dead and the living. At Antietam, he didn't pick up souvenirs off the field. Nonetheless, neither did he part with Captain Henderson's button, keeping it always in his pant pocket.

Antietam's aftermath was morbid. The three remaining mess-mates found Charlie's body already swelling and darkened. He had fallen precisely where Nat and Hank had remembered, fattened hands rigid as if still grasping the colors. The three young men bore their friend's body to a long trench dug for the dead of the 19th and gently placed Charlie in the communal grave. As they stepped back to look at him, Hank envisaged the body as his own. It might, maybe should have been him! He felt the weight on his chest again, his breathing accelerated, he couldn't get enough air. He was saved only when distracted by George's partially successful attempt to read a scripture from the New Testament he always carried and a prayer offered by Nathaniel. The three friends covered Charlie's body with dirt and marked the spot with a headboard into which had been carved his name, company and regiment. They were silent walking back to camp.

As the army waited near Antietam Creek, Hank's longing to get to Staunton grew. In peacetime, it would have been an easy trip. He could have crossed the Potomac by bridge just a few miles from Sharpsburg, traveling 130 miles up the valley by foot, horse, wagon, buggy or on the regularly scheduled stage coaches that traveled the macadamized Valley Turnpike from Winchester to Staunton. But these were not normal times: The Confederate Army had re-crossed the Potomac as it retreated from Maryland, and was now quartered in the northern Shenandoah Valley. But as daunting as the Confederate army appeared to Hank, his first challenge was to convince the Federals to give him leave to go behind enemy lines.

"George, how can I do this?" he asked his friend, forgetting his resolve not to mention the captain's letter to anyone again. "I've got to deliver this letter. It's making me mad with worry."

George had forgotten Hank's Confederate letter and asked, "What letter?"

"The letter from the Confederate captain."

"You still carryin' that thing 'round with you?"

Hank had by this time dismissed memories that he originally had no intention of ever delivering the letter. He responded, "I'm honor bound to get it to her."

"Why? Just ask to have it sent across the lines. Then ferget it! I think you Virginians is so full of that chivalry everyone talks 'bout . . . makes a man sick. All the boys from Virginia that I seen, all have the same crazy notions. None of you thinks right. You know that don't you, Hank Gragg." He stopped to catch his breath. "It ain't right! You don't know what makes sense. It don't do you no good. You gotta ferget what you told that Reb. If it was you dead out there on the field, do you think he'd be takin' a letter to Indiana fer you? He'd be sayin' that's one more Yank that ain't gonna bother us no more. Why just at this battle here, he would be tellin' his fella Rebs, 'Did you see who wasn't shootin' at us this time? Why that boy from Indiana that we kilt at Manassas. I knowed then we should'a kilt more of 'em. Then we wouldn't be havin' this here fight no more.' Hank, he wouldn't be worryin' 'bout your wife . . . or kids . . . or your horse . . . or nothin' else. He'd be mighty glad you was dead. He'd be hopin' the rest of us would up and die real soon, even me. Hank, here you are getting yourself all excited 'bout a dead Reb. I think somethin's wrong with you. I declare 'fore Abe Lincoln himself it be the truth." He paused to think, then continued his harangue. "I can say more, Hank, if it's helpin' you see you're wrong. Why I ought'o go tell the General . . . go right on up . . . just walk right into his tent and say, 'We got ourselves a boy from Virginia that wants to go see a wida lady in Staunton.' You think he's gonna say, 'What's he waitin' fer? Why ain't he got that letter to her yet?' He's not gonna even think them thoughts, Hank. He's gonna say words like them here, 'Hang the boy. Shoot the traitor.' He ain't gonna say what you wants to hear. You ever been hanged, Hank? I ain't, but I don't think it's a good feelin' havin' that tightness all 'round your throat like that."

Hank responded, "All your talk is nice, but I still have to get to Staunton. I'm bound, honor bound. You can say all you want to me, to the general, to Abe himself. You can hang me yourself—it's not going to change what I have to do."

"Tell me 'bout honor, Hank. Where you seen honor this whole past month? D'you see that cornfield and those woods? That's our buddies out there: Charlie and a whole lot more. It must be honor that makes them bodies bloat up like that, like Charlie done? Did you see them horses all swelled up and burstin'? The smell, worse than them hogs back home. Course the men, they smell worse than them horses. Did you hear it out on the field? Them men howlin' all night? They ain't wolves, Hank. They's men, but they's ahowlin' anyway cuz o' the pain. I tell you, Hank, there's only one honor what means somethin' now. The honor of gettin' the fightin' done so we go home. Whippin' Se-cesh, humblin' 'em. Then when we conquer 'em, then you set your eyes on Staunton. Then you go see your pretty little wida lady. You can marry her, don't make no difference then. Why you can raise two dozen little Jeff Davises, it don't matter. With you as their papa, Hank, they's bound to be as ugly as old Jeff." George paused again. "It don't matter once we done what we got to do. Hank, anything short o' doing that ain't hon-or, just pride—foolish pride. Just like that pride that got us in this here war in the first place. Everyone's so proud. Think they know best—both sides was proud. You know what the Bible says 'bout pride? It says 'pride comes 'fore the fall.' We's a mite more humble now than when this here war started, I think, Hank. I know them Secesh, when we be done with 'em, they's gonna be mighty humble. If it ain't so, another war'll just come along and make 'em humble. Ferget your

pride, Hank! Just be grateful for what you got and
where you are in life. That's the medicine for pride . . .
just the thing . . . that's the cure if there is one. Let go
o' this foolish talk, Hank. It ain't gonna make no difference to the wida lady." George closed his eyes briefly.
When he opened them again, he stared off into space.
He continued speaking, "Hank! Hank!" He spoke with
a new urgency. "I can see her. I see her right now. I'll
tell you what I see. It's . . . it's this: Right now . . . this
very moment . . . she . . . why it's the little wida. She's
asittin' in her pretty parlor . . . she's apinin' fer you,
Hank. Just sittin' there in her pretty parlor and apinin'
fer you. No! Oh, no, Hank! That ain't it! She's asittin'
there in her parlor all right. But she ain't doin' no pin-
in'." George opened his eyes wider. "Why, Hank . . . oh
no! It can't be! Hank, she's sittin' there with five, maybe six men right there in that parlor, and they's each
acourtin' her. Right now, Hank! It's a terrible thing.
Hank! Hank! She's choosin' right now, Hank, right
now, what one of 'em is gonna take her to wife. Hank,
they's all Secesh generals! She's choosin' right now
what one o' them is gonna be her husband. Hank,
Hank, oh Hank, you're too late! You are too late! She's
already chosen the one with the big whiskers. I am
sorry, Hank. But I gotta tell you this." George shook
his head in mock sorrow.

Hank shook his own head, but in disgust at George's
humor. Nonetheless, he responded sincerely, "Maybe
it is pride that makes me want to go, George, but not
the same pride that gave us this war."

George's voice was high pitched now. "Oh, so now
there's two prides, Hank? Two prides: one pride comes

'fore the fall . . . the other comes 'fore Staunton. Is that what you're thinkin' the Bible says, Hank?"

"George, I'm growing tired of this."

"You're growin' tired of your own conscience. Wantin' a Rebel lady when you're afightin' fer the Union. You know it's wrong, wrong as Judas."

"I'm not pining for the Captain's wife."

"It's some unholy feeling, Hank."

Hank could see he would never win the argument, and tried a new tactic, "Pride or not, George, how can I get there?"

"Why don't you just ask fer one of them furloughs, if all you're doin' is the right thing?" George asked sarcastically.

Hank sat quietly. Why not, he wondered. After all, the army didn't seem to be going anywhere anytime soon.

Nat approached as George finished his last suggestion. Nat said, "Don't go holdin' out for no furlough, Hank. They ain't givin' 'em."

Chapter 14
Late September 1862, Near Antietam Creek, Maryland

*H*ank carefully considered his options: A furlough? Just flank the pickets and disappear for a week or two? He grew increasingly restless as the army idled at Sharpsburg.

He woke one morning with the decision made, and he immediately wrote a letter. He tried to imitate a woman's hand as he wrote:

Beverly, Virginia

September 21, 1862

Dear Beloved Brother Hank,

I have learned that you have joined the Federal army. My heart overflows with joy to receive such glad tidings for I thought I alone in our family was for the Union. I felt alone. It became so unbearable for me at home among those rebellious souls that I fled, as you did. I am staying with a friend, a loyal union family, in Beverly and plan to move North in a month or two. I left the valley just after Lee's defeat at Sharpsburg and heard news that may be very important to the army. I don't know how to get it to you safely for I can trust no one else. Fly to me dear brother. Spare no effort to get here as soon as you can. I don't give you an address,

but know you can find me when you get here. But hur-
ry as I believe it will be of value to your good general
and our noble cause.
May God bless you.
Ever your devoted sister,
Corny Gragg

When he finished writing, he held up the letter to examine it. The effort disappointed him. He hadn't adequately disguised his handwriting. He copied the forged missive, this time widening the letters, making them rounder with more flourishes. He analyzed his new effort, concluding that at least it no longer looked like his handwriting. He folded the forged letter and placed it in a plain white envelope. He addressed it to Private Henry Gragg, 19th Indiana, Federal Army. He sealed the envelope with wax, and dropped it on the ground around the fire pit. He picked it up and dusted it off, but was not yet pleased with its level of dirtiness. He dropped it again; this time it landed on one of its corners damaging the envelope before settling flat on the ground. He picked it up a second time and dusted it off just as he noticed George approaching.

"What's you got there, Hank?" George asked.

"I don't know. Looks like a letter. That soldier," Hank pointed vaguely off to the right, "just gave it to me. Asked if I knew Hank Gragg. I said I was him, so he gave me this envelope."

"What soldier?"

"That soldier," Hank said again pointing and this time looking off in the same vague direction he had indicated initially. Hank looked surprised and said, "I don't know. He was just here."

George squinted, looking in the direction Hank suggested. "It's lookin' like he's gone now. Read it yet?"

"No . . . just got it. When he handed it to me, I accidentally dropped it. You came up just then," Hank concluded. He hoped George had not seen him drop the letter twice into the dirt. Hank brushed the envelope off again. The soiled result pleased him, and he opened it at once. He read the letter aloud. He paused periodically as he read trying to appear as if he were moved to hear from his sister. He said, "A Union girl! I never imagined it. This is wonderful! I'm so glad she's gone with us." For George's benefit, he ignored the feigned request for a visit and emphasized his sister's Union affiliation.

"Hank, you're missin' the whole point o' the letter. You gotta go see her."

"It's no use, George. They're never going to give me a furlough."

"I ain't talkin' 'bout no furlough. You got a special job to do. You're like one o' them spies."

"Special job?"

"You gotta find out what your sister knows. It's mighty important, I s'pect . . . to have her write like that to you. You can't wait a moment. You gotta go see the lieutenant. He'll wanna send you right out."

At George's constant urging Hank made his way to talk with the lieutenant. Hank explained that he was from Virginia and that his sister had sent him a letter promising important information. The lieutenant, also frustrated to be encamped idly across the Potomac from the enemy, didn't need much convincing. If he could bring information to the general that would ben-

efit the Union, the lieutenant's career just might benefit from the results. The lieutenant went on Hank's behalf to the company captain. The captain was less convinced, but didn't think there was much risk in letting
Hank go, even with the greatly reduced number of bat-
tle-fit men in his company. The captain recommended
through channels to the general that Hank be allowed
to go, and the general acted upon the recommenda-
tion.

Before noon Hank was wearing a set of clothes
which could barely pass as a Confederate uniform,
confiscated at some earlier time from a Southern prisoner or casualty. He had a pass to get through the
lines and across the river, information on the location
of Confederate pickets and his parole as a Southern
soldier sent home to await exchange.

In the flurry of preparation Hank had taken the time
to carefully and secretly sew a hidden, sealed pocket
inside his trousers behind his thigh. Inside the pocket,
he secured the original and copy of Captain Henderson's letter and the coins Hank had set aside for the
widow. The coins were held tight and flat behind the
letters in the pocket so they didn't jingle as he walked
and weren't easily visible.

As he slipped from camp and approached the last of
the Union pickets, he chuckled to himself. So many
others had connived unsuccessfully for furloughs. It
had been so easy and fast for him. Proud of his ingenuity, he set out for Staunton.

Chapter 15
1 October 1862, Northern Virginia

Once over the river, he avoided well-traveled roads, instead traversing fields and forests. He carried Nathaniel's cherished but never-used compass, but didn't need it as he navigated by the mountains. A Confederate bedroll hung over his left shoulder and rested against his right hip. He carried a captured Enfield rifle musket, cartridge box and percussion caps, canteen, cup and haversack with hardtack, dried apples, salted pork and coffee. He knew some might question his musket, but he preferred to travel with both a musket and parole rather than depend solely on the forged paper. He thought the whole idea of an honor-based parole system nonsense. After all, he had just lied to get out of camp, wore stolen clothes and held a fake parole. He remembered that in his distant past honesty had been important to him, and he wondered what he had done to lose that conviction.

As Hank walked across browned, harvested, rolling fields, he began to relax and let his mind wonder aimlessly. He considered the widow. What would she be like? In mental vignettes, he imagined her as girls he had known. He saw her as Lucinda Wertzel whom he had known all his life. She was his age and had attended a girls school in Winchester. She was tall, with a dark complexion and dark hair, weak chin, high fore-head and large nose. She was an excellent dancer and could move quickly and elegantly in any undertaking, but she couldn't carry on a conversation. He chuckled. The widow would not, could not, be like Lucinda.

Ellie McFadden? Red hair, but no temper to go with it. She, too, was from a Woodstock family. Her face was a pale white, colored only with patches of freckles on and around her petite nose. Small features and del-icate hands suggested frailty to Hank's mind. He en-joyed being around Ellie. She was thoughtful, kind and listened with utmost attention to anything Hank said. Perhaps the widow would be like Ellie. He liked that idea. He would be her strength in difficult times.

His thoughts passed to Betsy Richman. He refused quarter to most of the images of Betsy that came, but couldn't stop the memory of a stroll they had taken one Sunday afternoon in Winchester:

"Hank, I listened to the Rector this morning," Betsy had said. *"But I don't see things exactly as I heard them."*

"That's precisely what I would have expected, pre-cisely why I'm afraid to be seen with you." Hank chuckled. *"Have you ever agreed with the Rector? What did he say this time that was so clearly wrong?"*

"Sin."

"Sin is wrong? You're right."

She laughed. "No . . . no."

"Are you claiming then that sin's not wrong?"

"I'm deciding what sin is."

Hank looked severely at her. "The Reverend will be glad to hear you now determine sin. He won't have to ask for divine guidance any more or read the Bible. It will save him much time. He can just ask you. It will be much quicker. But, can you tell me, Betsy, have you made the list of sins shorter?

She smiled. "The list is the same. I'm not adding or subtracting."

"How disappointing. I'd hoped you'd define sin around my frailties. It would be much easier." Hank felt a pang of guilt pass through him as he began to feel blasphemous.

"Perhaps for a few days it would seem easier." she said in a serious tone. "But not over a lifetime."

"So what are you doing with sin then, if you're not easing my burden?"

"I've been trying to figure out what sin is, what it means, what its essence is. What makes something a sin . . . and something else not a sin. And I think I have the answer." She looked at Hank with a tentative glance and continued, "I've decided sin is anything that can't be perpetuated forever."

"What?" Hank said, clearly perplexed.

"I think sin is any of those things that can't be continued forever. That when we sin we are basically doing something that leads to the downfall of humanity . . . or to the destruction of the world. A little sin being a small step, a big sin being a larger step toward the end of humanity. Sin isn't some arbitrary rule that outlaws something for God's pleasure . . . only for his pleasure. We are his pleasure. Sin and its consequences are like the sun coming up or going down . . . or the grass

growing after it rains. It's a normal process. When you do something that the Bible . . . God . . . has said is a sin, you are doing something that takes the world one step closer to disorder and destruction. When you do something that's not a sin, you are taking a step to keep it alive, making it better."

"Destruction of the world? Is that even possible? Sounds to me like Miss Richman has become a blasphemer. Sin not determined at God's pleasure? Say no more or I will have to turn you over to—what do you call him?—the Right Reverend Bishop. Just by listening to you I think I'm losing my soul, and you an Episcopalian. Even a Presbyterian can't listen to this kind of talk."

She ignored him and continued her musings, "God tells us what sin is to help us . . . to save us as individuals . . . as a people . . . as a whole world. But they are sins independent of his telling us they are. They are in and of themselves wrong. Let me show you with an example. What is a sin that you can think of?"

"How about one of the 10 commandments?"

"Which one?

"How about coveting? How about coveting a man's farm."

"Oh, that's good." Her face brightened. "Think about how that extends forever."

"I don't understand."

"What is the natural outcome of coveting someone's farm?"

"I suppose eventually you do something to get it."

"What could you do?"

"Buy the farm."

"*You don't have the money. Or perhaps a good question is: What would you be willing to do to get the money if you want the farm bad enough? Or if the farmer doesn't want to sell it? How else could you get it?*"

"*Steal the farm through some swindle . . . or . . . I suppose you could kill the owner.*"

"*Exactly! Remember King David? He coveted another man's wife and had the man killed just to have her. Sin and all its ramifications bring ruin and destruction to individuals, then to societies. If sin were to run its full course it would destroy the world . . . if that were possible. God is not arbitrary. He understands where happiness lies . . . where destruction lies. He warns us, all of us, so we can find happiness. But it even goes further. I think he asks us to do only those things that don't destroy his creation . . . those things that perpetuate and beautify his creation.*"

"*You can't destroy the world. I can't even imagine that. That's nonsense. You, Betsy have simply become a lunatic, and that just by going to church this morning. Besides, what of animals and plants? We kill them to eat and survive. Wouldn't that then be a sin? That kills part of his creation. But we'd starve if we didn't eat them, and that would destroy his creation, too. Betsy, I've seen you eat lots of beef.*"

For a moment, a craving for beef interrupted Hank's thoughts of Betsy.

"*If you look at the world only through the eyes we have now,*" she responded, "*you would think that kill-*

ing cows destroys creation. But if we kill only what we need to maintain life and God's creation. Animals have a role to feed us and be our work helpers. We have responsibility for them—to use them carefully and protect God's creation."

"I think," Hank began with a thoughtful frown on his face, "that you really have lost your senses. I'm not even sure I understand what you just said." He smiled. "And since I don't understand it, I don't have to turn you in for blasphemy."

Not willing to have the conversation shift to another topic, Betsy said, "Here's another example: War—what do you think, Hank—is it a sin?"

"I'm not sure I want another example, but it's your sermon. You go ahead: Ask the questions, but only if you answer them, too. It's ever more easy that way."

"Yes, I will do that. Thank you for the cooperation, Hank Gragg." He lowered his head in a bow as she continued, "Is war sin? Yes . . . and no. For those whose covetousness, or pride, or vanity, or hate, in short those whose sins contribute to the war or keep it going, they bear great responsibility. It is sin for them. War is brought about by every little and big sin, all added up over time. They just accumulate till they burst into war's violence and destruction. But for the person who goes to war only to preserve freedom . . . to protect his family and friends . . . with the most noble intentions, it's not a sin. It can't be sin. It becomes an effort to protect God's creation and the liberty with which we are endowed."

"But aren't we all covetous or vain or proud or sin-ful? Then aren't we all responsible for war? At least according to your idea."

She stopped, turned to face him, smiled and said, "That's the first interesting thing you've said to me all day."

Hank's thoughts of Betsy stopped abruptly, and he questioned his own motives for being in the war. Had his actions attributed to it? Was his involvement sin? It might be. He didn't join the army in the beginning to save the Union or free slaves, just to eat . . . and die. Would Betsy have thought it a sin?

Chapter 16
1 October 1862, Northern Virginia

*H*e saw the woman as he cleared the top of a steep rolling hill. He was hiking in the general direction of Front Royal, still lost in thoughts of the soon-to-be-seen widow. The woman stood behind a large boulder that rested at the hilltop and brandished a shotgun at her shoulder. By the time he saw her, it was too late.

She was small and appeared old, with large gray and white patches in her dark brown hair and deeply ridged, leathered skin. She spoke with a harsh, thin, high-pitched voice, "Johnny, yuh stay right where yuh is. Yuh ain't agunna take another step. Yuh hear me? Yuh've taken 'nough o' our food. Yuh ain't gettin' nothin' more. Yuh hear me?" She paused to catch her breath, then shifted her tone to mockery: "The proper thing for a gentleman such as yuh'self is to turn right 'round and march back the same way yuh come. And don't go thinking yuh can outsmart me. I ain't like them fancy city lady's yuh's use to. And don't yuh worry none 'bout this here gun. I know how to use it, and I'm awantin' to show yuh just how good. I do know how to use it, Johnny. Yuh boys have stolen so much from us that I's willin' to shoot yuh just for being Secesh. Ole Jeff Davis ain't sendin' yuh to steal, and he ain't never acomin' out here to see what done happened to his soldier boys. When yuh's shot and buried, my maker, he gunna give me one o' them larger mansions in the heavens . . . just 'cause I shot yuh. So yuh just put down yor musket, yor cartridges, right where yuh stand."

Hank was astounded at how comprehensive her speech was and had the impression she'd given it before. He slowly crouched, carefully laying the Enfield and cartridge box on the ground.

"Now yuh just turn right 'round, march on back to yor regiment. Don't come stealin' no more on my land, or I'll call my man out here. He'll know what to do with yuh. Now, git! Go on! Git!"

Hank was willing to leave, but not without his rifle. He said, "I'll catch it when I get back if I don't have my gun."

"'Tain't no concern o' mine. Be assured o' that. Yuh most likely is a deserter anyways. Yuh ain't thinkin' o' gonin' back. Ain't no matter then. With deserters, they shoots yuh if yuh got yor gun or if yuh ain't got yor gun, won't make no difference for yuh."

"I'm not a deserter. I was a prisoner . . . taken at Antietam battle. Just released, paroled on the field. I'm going home to family in Woodstock to wait for exchange."

"Antietam?"

"Sharpsburg! The battle down at Sharpsburg. You haven't heard of that battle? It was a pretty little thing. We gave those Yanks a real scare. They're so afraid of us now, they don't want to fight again. It wouldn't surprise me if Lincoln himself doesn't come and surrender right to Marse Lee." Hank worried he was talking too much and overstating his loyalty, but he didn't know what else to do under the circumstances and continued talking. "I was fighting near Antietam Creek. Fighting so hard I couldn't retreat, so the Yanks got me."

"Humph. I just as well believe yuh as believe that all them Northern generals takes orders from ole Jeff Davis. More likely story is yuh was runnin' so hard from the battle that yuh was confused . . . run right into the Yanks what took yuh prisoner. Sharpsburg? Humph. I could o' whipped McClellan myself if I had all the Secesh soldiers what's been walkin' 'round my . . . our farm over the last month. Yuh's all good for nothin'." She quickly changed the subject, "My, but yuh's goin' the long way to Woodstock . . . ain't yuh? Why ain't yuh heading toward the Valley Turnpike? I'll tell yuh why! Yuh's one of them deserters. Y'all have the same guilty look on yor thin, bony faces. Ain't hardly any young men now what has courage . . . all cowards . . . every one of yuh. I should shoot yuh right now and save yor general the work."

"Please don't. I'm not a deserter," Hank pled half-heartedly, uncomfortable because he felt momentarily as if he were deserting the army. "I'm not here to steal from you. I'm just going home to wait . . . wait till I can fight Yanks again."

She stood rigid and still. He hadn't convinced her, but at least she hadn't driven him farther from his gun.

"How'd yuh get caught?"

"The Yanks came charging hard and took our position. A lot of the boys got killed. I was surrounded and shot one of them, but another hit me with his gun in the gut . . . doubled me over. Then they grabbed me. I can show you the bruise." Hank began to pull up his shirt, as if he had a bruise to show.

"I don't believe nary a word of it. Yuh's a deserter or somethin' worse, out here maraudin' . . . stealin' horses from those yuh think is helpless women and children. Yuh chose the wrong one this time. I ain't so helpless. Got my man right here on the place, and we's doin' fine. We knows how to make runaway Rebs leave our land 'lone.

"I give you my solemn promise, I will not steal from you."

"Yuh do talk though, don't yuh. But yuh knows yuh gave a promise most solemn like to the Rebs when yuh joined up; now yuh's runnin' from 'em."

It occurred to Hank that she might be a Northern sympathizer from her emphatic use of the words "Reb" and "Secesh".

"Sounds like you don't like our Southern Confederacy."

"Scalawags . . . all of yuh. Desertin' your army comes easy for yuh when yuh already deserted yor country."

Hank could see from her sudden change of expression that she hadn't meant to divulge her allegiance. He pressed his advantage. "You were right."

"'Bout what?" She looked startled.

"Everything I've told you's a lie."

"Don't need to go tellin' me none o' that," she said, laughing loudly. "I already knowed. Don't wanna hear no more 'bout nothin'. Yuh just better turn yuh'self 'round and wander back down the hill to where yuh come from. Yuh's a deserter. I was right, weren't I?

"I'm a Union soldier."

The woman guffawed. "A Yank! Yuh must be desperate tellin' a story like that to a woman in Virginny. Yuh must wanna get yuh'self hanged, and I myself got a lot o' trees what can be used just for the honor. Course all that ain't necessary 'cause I can shoot yuh down faster than yuh can say John Brown's body." He could see he had raised her curiosity. She continued, "What's a Yank doin' in what looks kind o' like Secesh clothes, course they ain't got much uniform. I heard all the Secesh was stealin' Yankee uniforms, not t'other way 'round. Yuh one of them spies? Yuh must be one of them dumb spies the North has. That's why they don't never win no battles 'round here."

"We won at Sharpsburg."

"That ain't what I been readin' in the newspaper what I've seen. Said our Virginny boys did fine up in Maryland."

"Where's Bobby Lee right now?"

"Somewhere's 'round these parts. Is that what yuh was sent to find out?"

"If Bobby and the whole Rebel army are here, then they retreated from Sharpsburg. They retreated . . . because we won."

"Well, the army up this way tells it a mite different."

Hank pressed again: "Will you help me?"

She hesitated, clearly wondering if he was trying to trap her. "I ain't 'bout to help no Yankee, and I don't want no stragglers tearin' up the place. Yuh can tell yor general that for me. So yuh better just march off

the way yuh come and go be a spy somewheres else. I
got to say . . . to be honest with yuh . . . yuh really
don't look like no spy . . . more like a plain, ole deserter to me. I ought to know one when I sees one 'cause I
sees a lot o' 'em."

"Can I take my musket?"

"Yuh leave yor musket right where it's asittin'. I'll
make sure it's safe. Come back for it after the war if
yor still livin'. . . . whatever side yuh's really on." As she
spoke, the sound of loping horses reached the pair.
Hank could see five horsemen coming toward them.
The woman took a step back and to the side so she
could keep one eye on Hank and still see the riders as
they approached. Hank saw for the first time a house
and outbuildings not far from where they stood. He
had wandered too close to the woman's house. She
must have felt compelled to confront him.

The approaching riders didn't appear to be Confederate cavalry and wore no uniform. Whatever they
were, Hank was sure they weren't sympathetic to
Northern interests. He felt a twinge of foolishness at
revealing his Northern allegiance to this woman. One
word from her and he would be bound for a Richmond
prison or strung up on the nearest tree. He remembered his musket and cartridge box and tried to move
toward the woman and riders, away from the gun. She,
for her part, was distracted by the riders. He walked
right past her, holding his hands in the air. She let him
go. He moved to put the boulder between himself and
the musket.

Hank could see the riders clearly now. All of them
were young men in their late teens and early to middle

twenties; one with a full beard, another with whiskers down his cheeks. Three were cleanly shaved. They wore slouch hats and farmers clothes. The bearded rider spoke in a distinctively high and nasal voice. "Naomi, what have you caught there?"

The voice was peculiar and Hank thought he had heard it before . . . but he couldn't quite remember where.

The woman spoke. "Got myself a deserter. Yuh've come up just right, boys."

"A deserter?" The man responded pleasantly. Hank could feel his shoulders loosen. She was keeping his secret.

"Which brigade you from, boy?" the man asked. His mount was perfectly still while the others pranced nervously under the hands of their riders.

"I'm with Hood. We were with Jackson in Maryland." Hank replied.

Another of the riders spoke, "Hood? Ain't his men Texans? You're a long way from home. What's you doin' wanderin' around down here?"

Hank turned to face the man who asked the question. "I'm with Hood and some are Texas boys, but my family's from Woodstock. I was captured at Sharpsburg."

"Sharpsburg . . . and just escaped?" the bearded rider asked.

"I wish I'd escaped and could return to my regiment." The last phrase sounded phony, and Hank wished he could take it back. "But I can't. I was paroled. Here. I've got the papers."

The bearded partisan ignored Hank's offer to show him his parole papers, and Hank continued, "The Union colonel gave us field paroles . . . told us to go home and await exchange."

"How many Southerners with you?" the bearded man asked moving his horse closer to Hank.

"When I was captured? Just five. I'm just working my way up now to Woodstock."

The bearded rider eyed Hank suspiciously.

"Woodstock?" a third rider asked rhetorically. "What's your name?"

Hank didn't hesitate to answer, but his heart accelerated and his throat tightened. "Hank Gragg."

"Hank Gragg!" the third rider exclaimed. "From Woodstock? I didn't know any Graggs were with Stonewall no more. Not since that one at Manassas . . . what was his name . . . David . . . Daniel . . . ."

Hank didn't hear the rest of the soldier's words. His mind froze, then raced through memories. Daniel, his younger brother, would be 16, but Hank remembered him as a 13 year old. What had happened to Daniel? He tried not to think of it, but nonetheless, grief dismayed him. He wanted to fall to his knees, bury his face in his hands and scream. Daniel might have been on the same field Hank had crossed in the dark. Hank might have bumped into him as he searched for his foolish button. Daniel might have been one of the groans he ignored. Hank might have been the one . . . the one who shot him. The rapid-fire thoughts made Hank inwardly shiver, but he stood outwardly stoic.

The third rider, Hank judged him to be no more than 17 years old, eyed him curiously. He had been speak-

ing continuously and only now realized Hank had not
heard what he said. "Lots of men dying . . . just part of
war. Can't worry about it. Just be happy you're alive.
That's the way we think. Do what it takes to stay
alive."

Thoughts of his family flooded Hank's mind. He
wondered about his sisters and parents. But Daniel
gone? It wasn't possible. He didn't believe it . . .
wouldn't believe it. It couldn't be true. They were mistaken. Daniel was too young, too good to die . . . to be
a soldier. Hank again noticed the woman. She was agitated. Her eyes watched him closely. He wanted to
reassure her that he would not now reveal her Northern sentiments just as she had not revealed his Yankee
allegiance. Hank was relieved the riders didn't seem to
take her seriously and focused their attention solely on
him.

Hank didn't know what to do or say, so he stood silently.

The bearded one still watched Hank suspiciously
and said directly, "Can we take you back to your regiment? D'you lose your musket?"

"They took it from me," Hank said in a stern voice
never taking his eyes off Naomi.

"No wonder you could take him on all by you'self,
Naomi. He didn't have no gun," the third rider said
snickering.

"I can't go back to the regiment till I'm exchanged,"
Hank said directly to the bearded rider.

"You're paroled? You were captured?" the bearded
rider asked Hank again as if he had not already explained his situation.

"At Sharpsburg. Got paroled this morning."

The bearded rider was visibly uncomfortable with Hank's answer and asked if Hank had papers. Hank took the parole from his pant pocket and handed it up to the rider, taking the opportunity of moving farther away from the rifle that lay just out of the riders' vision.

The partisan looked at it and peered over the paper asking, "How many brothers you got, Gragg?"

"I go by Hank," he responded, trying to establish rapport with the man.

The rider repeated the question, measuring his words carefully, "How many brothers you got, Gragg?"

"Just two . . . John and Daniel."

"As I recall there were three Graggs. Two dead . . . the one at Manassas. That other brother . . . didn't know him . . . died I think before the war . . . near as I can recollect. Who does that make you? Lazarus raised from the dead?" He didn't wait for an answer. He looked for the first time at Naomi. She met his gaze calmly as he said, "Naomi, you done good this time."

Naomi lowered her shotgun, and the bearded rider chirped commands in his peculiar voice to one of the other men: "Madison, tie his hands!"

Hank tried to respond to the rider's question about who he was, but the jury's verdict was in, and the judge was no longer listening. Hank looked at Naomi. She watched, without expression, as Madison, a sullen-looking, bulky man in his mid-twenties who had yet to speak, roughly pulled Hank's hands behind his back and tied them there.

"Naomi," the bearded rider said. "We'll be staying the night . . . down by the creek. You got food for us? Why don't you go cook up something tasty for us."

The bearded partisan rode his mount to the side of the second man, and they conferred privately in quiet tones. When the discussion ended, the man galloped away, and the bearded man watched.

Chapter 17
1 October 1862, Northern Virginia

*T*he remaining men dismounted and, taking Hank with them, descended the hill on foot to a small creek. Madison walked behind Hank, his hand weighing heavily on the captive's wrists.

The men tied their horses and made camp, each one quickly pitching a dog tent. They seemed to know by practice where to place them. One of the men cleared a fire pit of old debris, added new wood and started a fire. Madison pushed Hank toward a nearby tree, ordered him to sit, untied his wrists, pulled his arms backward around the trunk, fastened them there, and left him alone.

As the warm fall afternoon cooled into evening, Hank was chilled. The other four men sat around the fire talking in hushed tones. Hank didn't care what they said, but he did envy their fire's warmth. His shoulders ached, he shivered. Inconspicuously he pulled the rope as tight as possible against the trunk and raised and lowered his arms and hands along the bark of the tree, hoping to wear the rope down with friction or to cut it on some sharp trunk protrusion. He held little hope for success, but it was the only scheme he had.

Hank considered his circumstances as he worked to wear away the rope. These men might contact John. John was unpredictable. John himself might shoot Hank on the spot—an outcome as likely as being freed by him. Daniel, he remembered, had been different. Even as a small boy, he was sober and serious, a hard worker, quiet and shy. Daniel would have freed Hank. The two younger brothers, Hank and Daniel, had always been close. But Hank was anxious about John. They had often fought, argued, especially after Hank moved to his uncle's Winchester home to go to school. John thought Hank too independent and not concerned with family needs.

In response to his growing anxiety, Hank unwittingly quickened his efforts to cut the rope. He thought again of Daniel. Had Daniel been on that farmer's field, perhaps lying next to Captain Henderson? If he had found Daniel that night, not Captain Henderson, Hank would have quit the war . . . the Union . . . to take Daniel home. Daniel was his mother's favorite child. If he were dead, she would be suffering. He yearned to go home.

Working on the rope fatigued Hank's muscles; he was still cold and increasingly hungry. They had been in camp for hours. One of the men had been sent to Naomi's and had brought back supper. The partisans had eaten, joked and jostled with one another, but no one had acknowledged Hank since tying him to the tree.

"Mr. Gragg," he heard Naomi say softly from beside him.

He looked up. In her partially illuminated face, he saw none of the bravado he had witnessed earlier in the afternoon.

"I brought yuh somethin' to eat."

"Naomi," called the bearded rider. "What you doin' over there?"

"Givin' this poor boy some supper. I know as well as I'm standin' here ain't none o' yuh shared nothin' with 'im. Yuh talk 'bout helpin' the South, and here yuh got yuh'self a good Southern soldier tied up like he's yor prisoner."

"Deserter! That's what he is . . . just like you said. He knows more than he's tellin'. We'll get it out o' him, when we're ready. Then we may just leave him there to starve to death, then rot. Or maybe we'll shoot him. That'll be the end of it."

"But he give yuh papers. He's paroled."

"That don't mean nothin'. He's forged 'em . . . the papers. Found out a name from the valley and forged 'em. Get away from him, woman! He don't need no food to be hanged . . . or shot."

"Least let him relieve hisself."

"Why bother? He won't notice nothin' in the mornin'. If he needs to bad . . . let him just do it right where he sits. You knew he was a deserter when you nabbed him. Naomi, don't go losin' your nerve. You're always losin' your nerve."

"I'm gunna feed 'im. Do as yuh like with 'im, but he's gunna be fed long as he's on my land. Why don't yuh turn him over to the army? Let them deal with 'im."

"Not this boy! He thought he could trick us. 'I'm paroled,' he said. He'll learn you can't do that, not with us anyway."

Naomi grunted and sat beside Hank. She carried a tray with food on it, but Hank didn't notice it. He was straining to see her clearly in the dark. The fire light now faintly silhouetted her head. "Mr. Gragg, yuh eat this up." She spoon fed him the food and information. "I can't do much to help yuh escape. They'd know it was me. Yuh'll have to escape on yor own. I'd help if I could, but others depends on me. I gotta stay here." She then began a warning, "This one's a bad one. Take what he says like he means it. I think yuh's dead right here on this tree if yuh ain't gone 'fore sunrise. He's mean."

"You've been kind to me, Miss Naomi. Thank you."

"Oh," she responded, pleasurable embarrassment in her voice, "I ain't no Miss. I'm married." Her voice turned suddenly sad. "Husband's run off. Said he was gunna fight, but I think he just run off, left me to run the place." She spoke softly to Hank so the partisans couldn't hear as the men returned to their conversation. "Lookin' forward to this ole war endin' and everyone goin' home. Don't know that he'll ever come home to me. He don't write none, never did, not since the day he left. Maybe he's dead. I like to make myself think he's agunna come back; don't even know what regiment he's fightin' with . . . don't even know what side he's on. I really don't think he's fightin' atall: He's too old. When this is all over, yuh go home to yor family. Yuh mind what I' tellin' yuh. Yuh go home to yor family. Where is yor family? Up North somewheres I reckon."

"I don't have a family," Hank said, falling back into the role that had grown comfortable. "I am a Union soldier, and I take it you're for the Union, too. Perhaps someday we'll meet just to celebrate the Union victory." Hank spoke in the same soft tones Naomi had adopted.

"I'd like that. A lot o' folks what I see would like that day . . . freedom. Lot's o' folks just want to be free . . . do 'bout anything for it," Naomi said reflectively. "Not all the Rebs as bad as them. Fact is, they ain't even real Rebs, just thieves ridin' up and down the valley stealin' what good folk has, scaring folks to death and killin'. They were thieves before the war . . . still are. Secesh as far as what I know, some is good boys. But," she shook her head, "I don't see no good ones, not out here. Only the stragglers . . . deserters. Some of 'em is scary, like him over there. I know some mighty fine men what's fightin' with the South . . . and a few what's fighin' with the North. But I don't see 'em down this way."

She spoke in a louder voice, "There . . . now yuh's finished. Good luck, Mr. Gragg . . . or whatever yor name is. Yuh won't see me back here no more." She lowered her voice and spoke quickly, "They're beginnin' to drink now. It'll get a mite dangerous for a spell, then they'll tucker out. Yor musket's on the hill where you dropped it." She raised her voice again to be heard at the campfire, "I feel sorry for yuh, but don't know what to do to help yuh. These faithful Southerners, if they's thinkin' yuh should die, yuh has to die. Ain't no point in arguin' 'bout it. But I hope yuh's full when yuh go, so 'tain't nobody what says I lack for hospi'lty."

He couldn't see her face as she moved to get up and was startled when she stumbled. She fell forward toward Hank and the tree and dropped her tray and dishes. "Oh, my . . . my," she said in an unexpectedly loud tone. Her hand fell hard against the tree just above Hank's hand as she stumbled, and she swiftly brought it down over his hand. Her hand rested on the ends of his fingers, and she slid something slender beneath his fingers and into his palm.

"What're you doin' over there, Naomi?" the bearded man called, laughing. "Don't go killin' our catch till we're done with 'im. You be careful over there." The tone of the voice changed. "Naomi, come on over and talk with us a bit. You been takin' good care of that deserter. Come on over here, sit a while."

"I gotta get these plates on back to the house," she said nervously. She hurriedly gathered the dishes and scurried into the dark. The men around the campfire laughed at her apparent fright. Hank wondered if her fear was real. He was grateful for the risk she had taken and remembered her words of caution.

The partisans were, as she predicted, growing louder now. "Maybe we should go on up and see her a bit later," said one.

"We should. She's taken real good care o' our prisoner and ain't taken 'nough care o' us," added another.

"Later, then," chimed in Madison.

The bearded rider expelled a long, shrill laugh that echoed quickly off the nearby hills. "Boys, she's a bit old."

Hank was alert. He no longer worked to wear away the rope, but held Naomi's small knife under his hand and wrist. It was peculiar that they hadn't tied him better. Was his entire plight, Naomi included, a trap? An attempted escape—a reason to shoot him? Regardless, he would not put her in jeopardy by cutting the rope before the partisans fell asleep. If he cut it now, and they discovered it, they would take it out on Naomi—disgusting. Better to sacrifice himself than to let that happen.

Eventually, two of the men, including the bearded rider, went off to bed. Two others stayed at the fire, talking and drinking incessantly. After what seemed to be hours, one of them stood up, unsteady on his feet, and said, "You take the first watch! I'll relieve you." He staggered, stumbling across the fire, spreading sparks in all directions as he made his way to his tent.

The remaining man sat with his back to Hank and his face to the fire. Hank watched him closely. He could see his head bob forward intermittently. He was falling asleep. Hank waited for the moment when he would be out. The man's head bobbed forward . . . backward . . . then far forward . . . then backward in a jerk. The guard, it looked like Madison, jumped to his feet, awakened by his own nod. He turned, tripped and lurched toward Hank. Madison's face was in shadows of night, and Hank couldn't see his expression, and he waited nervously for a clue to the partisan's mood. The man said in slurred speech, "I'm gunna make sure you're tied up good and snug." Madison disappeared behind the tree and tugged on the rope. "Stand up!" he commanded as he pulled the rope up the side of the tree. He jerked on the rope again as Hank tried to stand.

"Quiet out there," someone yelled from a tent.

"You heard 'im, keep quiet," Madison said loudly as he jerked hard again on the rope. Hank was crouched and rising when the third tug came. It caught his hand between the rope and the tree and wrenched the knife from his grasp.

Hank held his breath as the knife fell. It seemed long minutes before he heard it land softly. Madison was busy behind the tree doing something with a branch, Hank's arms, and the rope. He made enough noise that he didn't seem to notice the gentle tap of the knife as it hit the ground. Hank groaned inside. The knife had fallen softly, but his hands were now three feet above it as it lay in the open. His escape had been foiled, and now evidence of Naomi's involvement lay unreachable on the ground. By morning, the knife and her complicity would be unmistakable to all.

Hank was standing now, and he could feel Madison's hand on his hand as the partisan fumbled at untying the knot. Madison said nothing. Hank felt the pressure ease around his swollen, numb wrist and realized his hand was free, but he didn't move it. He could hear Madison doing something with the rope behind the tree. He then felt his hand again on his wrist and smelled the rider's alcohol-laden breath. He was retying the hand. Madison must have looped the rope around a branch higher up the tree so Hank

couldn't sit down. He was forcing him to stand all
night. Madison released Hank's wrist and the rope,
patting it as he tottered backward. "There," he said.
"Now you stay right there."

Madison moved to a nearby tree and sat down,
slumping over and snoring rhythmically at once. Hank
shifted his arms to see how much freedom he had. The
retied knot on his wrist was loose. Hank smiled. He
quietly and easily slipped his hand out of the clumsy
knot and moved around the tree, collecting the rope in
his hands as he went. He didn't stop to untie his other
hand, but immediately crouched searching the ground,
feeling the earth for the knife. He found it and slipped
it into his pants. He untied his hand, placed the rope
over his shoulder and seized his bedroll and knapsack
which Madison had tossed nearby.

He made his way carefully to the horses, untied
each and tied three of them together. Hank took the
saddle of the bearded rider and cinched it as quietly as
possible on the bearded man's horse. He worked nervously as periodically he heard the partisans roll over,
grunt or snore. The horses made noise as well, adding
their snorts and heavy breathing to the sounds from
the tents. Each noise sent shock waves the full length
of his body. But no one awoke, and Hank led the horses up the hill to search for his musket.

He moved cautiously, suspecting a trap. At anytime
now, he expected one of the men to pop out from behind a rock, laugh lustily and lead him back down to
the tree he had just abandoned. The evening's events
would culminate in an impromptu firing squad arranged for Hank's benefit, with Naomi at its head.

Besides the Enfield, Hank had lost one thing in his brief Virginia sojourn. The bearded rider still had his parole. Without it, Hank needed the musket. Still holding the horses, Hank dragged his foot in the area where he expected to find his musket. The horses shifted nervously. He dragged his foot faster in desperation. He heard something . . . a voice . . . far off. He didn't move, but the horses jostled one another. He dragged his foot again and heard the voice anew. He didn't stop searching for the gun this time. He heard commotion in the camp below. Someone was yelling. He heard running. He had to go. He hit something with his foot. Holding the horse reins in his left hand, he reached down with his right. It was his Enfield, with cartridge box beside it. The raiders were coming up the hill fast . . . yelling. He grabbed the musket and threw the cartridge-box strap over his neck, jumped into the saddle and kicked the sides of the horse. Holding the musket and the horse's reins in his left hand, and the leads for the other three horses in his right, Hank felt as if he were carrying one too many plates and would drop them all. But the horses seemed to easily follow his horse's lead, and he miraculously held on to reins and musket as he loped across Naomi's farm.

In the distance he could still hear men yelling, and he wondered if Naomi watched from her window. He heard firing behind him, but he didn't hear the hiss of the balls.

He rode hard for 15 minutes. When he felt out of immediate danger, he dismounted, checked the saddle and secured his musket. As he remounted, he heard

horses coming from the other direction. He led his
horses into a small thicket by the road and waited.
Two riders passed, and Hank thought he recognized
the posture of his brother John. His brother? He felt an
urge to call out, but held back. As John's sounds receded in the direction of Naomi's farm, Hank quietly
moved to the road, continuing his trip to Staunton. He
smiled to himself. He had expected to make this trip on
foot, but thanks to his new-found friends, he was traveling on horseback, with four horses to choose from.
How neighborly!

Hank took back roads that soldiers or irregulars
were unlikely to guard. It was relatively easy to make
his way through the valley with Confederates in control. Perhaps the partisans would have been more ac-
tive and aggressive along these roads if the Federals
occupied the valley.

He planned to ride through Powell's Fort Valley, a
narrow valley that ran behind Massanutten Mountain.
It would be less traveled than either the Valley Turnpike on the mountain's western side or the roads in
Luray Valley on Massanutten's eastern side. Hank had
heard that Jackson had used Massanutten Mountain
and the valleys on either side to defeat three different
Union armies. He hoped he could use the mountain in
his own battle to get safely to Staunton . . . and back.
He knew the mountain well, but wished he still had his
parole papers.

Hank wondered if John was a partisan. Was he on
his way to join them? He tried to imagine John's
thoughts when the bearded man showed him the parole. John would have asked for a description and

wondered if his associates had captured a ghost—that would explain why they hadn't been able to hold him. At least they would describe Hank as a Confederate so if John mentioned the incident to his family, his father wouldn't have to be ashamed, knowing his son was a Union soldier.

As dawn approached, Hank let three of the horses go and rode hard to get near the mountain before full light. Once he reached the mountain, it would be easy to hide as he traveled south. But he wouldn't make it before sunup, and he was becoming recklessly sleepy. His judgment was declining with each passing minute. He needed his wits about him, he needed sleep.

Chapter 18
2 October 1862, North of the Massanutten Mountain, Virginia

As the first morning gray appeared above the Blue Ridge, Hank happened upon a large stand of trees off the road and headed toward them. When he was deep in the still-green woods, he laid out bedding and collapsed on it, examining his condition. Thoughts of the last 24 hours entertained him. He had forged a letter from his sister, crossed into Confederate territory, nearly been hung or shot, seen one brother at a distance, lost another. It was happening so fast.

The morning sky was already visible in patches through the trees and the air was unusually dry. He lay on his bedroll, looking up at the canopy of leaves and bits of heaven. There were hints of fall color in the smaller trees, and he listened to the rustle of a light breeze as it blew through the copse. He drew air in deeply—the air of freedom. He hadn't thought about it yesterday, but he was free from military control and commands now. He remembered Naomi's words about people wanting freedom. He was one, and for now he wanted to use that liberty to lie perfectly still. Perhaps if he lay quietly the war would pass by, perhaps end the killing and maiming, the loneliness, the heartbreak, the tragedy. Perhaps he could close his eyes and be back at his father's house waiting to be called to the fields. He thought about Naomi, the bearded rider, the widow, John, Daniel and himself—neighbors, family embroiled in self-annihilation. He wondered about his parents and sisters. He remembered nostalgically the last time he had seen Daniel:

It had been early morning and Daniel had been on the front porch of their father's home. He watched as Hank mounted his horse for his last ride to Betsy's. Daniel didn't know but probably guessed where Hank was going. The two brothers had planned a bear-hunting expedition to the Blue Ridge Mountains. They were to set out in three days, and Daniel had been particularly excited. Daniel never actually hunted, but loved any excuse to disappear into the mountains. Instead of a gun, Daniel always took along paper and pencil and sketched whatever he saw. Hank tried to imagine the sketch Daniel would have made of him butchering bear, but he couldn't bring it into focus.

Daniel was always watching, noticing. That morning three years ago, he had watched Hank with particular care. As Hank mounted the horse, Daniel said to him, "Hank, let's go hunting today . . . no reason to wait till later. We can leave within the hour."

Hank called over his shoulder, "Not today."

Daniel had called after Hank as the older brother turned his horse and trotted from the house, "Hank, let's go today, right now."

Hank had called out without looking back, "Later, Daniel, later."

Hank hadn't before recalled this scene, but remembered it vividly and sadly now. A vague emptiness enveloped his chest. He closed his eyes to rest, to muzzle his soul's reproach. He was exhausted and fell quickly into a silent sleep.

When Hank began rousing himself it was afternoon. He awoke slowly. The sun was bright and warm where it made its way through the trees to touch his skin and clothes in splotches of light. He was groggy. At first he couldn't remember where he was. He smelled a nearby fire and cooking meat. Had they distributed meat rations? Had he slept through it? Had he missed it? He quickly opened his eyes, shading them with his hand.

"Feeling rested?" he heard a familiar but unexpected voice ask.

Hank sat bolt upright and reached for the gun at his side.

"It's not there. I've got it," said the voice belonging to his brother John. "I didn't want you to shoot me accidentally when you woke up."

Hank looked at John, hoping for a hint of his brother's intentions.

"You sure made a fool of Cole last night. But that's not hard to do," John said laughing. "And I'm a bit confused myself."

Hank looked around. He remembered the day before, his escape, his flight. His camp had not been as far in the woods as he thought. He could vaguely see the road, so someone from the road could have seen him. John may have seen him or the horse or may have followed his trail from the road. Hank was angry with himself for being detected. He couldn't tell how long John had been there, but he had started a fire and was cooking a rabbit over the flame. Hank sat up on his bedroll and said as calmly as he could, "Was Cole the one with the beard?"

"That's Cole. Completely mad. He would kill his own mother if he felt the impulse. Some people down in Bunker Hill claim he did kill his mother, but I don't know that for sure. He is a thief and murderer, though. I'm convinced of that. This war just gives him more opportunity to kill and steal. And I think you've made it to the top of his list to be killed. It's probably best not to go near him again, Hank."

"I didn't try to go near him the first time. Aren't you part of his little band?"

John laughed. "No! Where'd that idea come from?"

"Then how'd you know where I was last night?"

"One of Cole's boys told me. It's better to be friends with a madman, you know, than to worry about where he is all the time. So I do know them. I happened to see them yesterday in Berryville. When you showed up claiming to be kin, Cole sent one to fetch me. He wanted to know if I wanted to shoot the boy claiming to be my dead brother. He didn't believe your story. But you probably knew that." John waited briefly, then added, "Neither did I. I didn't believe your story."

The tension in Hank's face increased, and he said suspiciously, "You came mighty fast."

John laughed. "Wouldn't you, if someone claimed to see your long-lost brother? Cole's men are a bunch of half wits, and a three-quarters wit like Cole . . . even if he's mad trumps the others. They just fall right in file behind him. But Hank, I'm still nearly a full wit, and I didn't come to shoot you. Besides I didn't believe it was you . . . came just in case."

Hank ignored his last comment. "How come you aren't in the army? I heard the South was conscripting everybody."

"The South? Interesting way to put it. We've conscripted just about everyone . . . at least in the Valley . . . except for those who hide out whenever conscription officers come around. I am in the army . . . cavalry. I was with Turner Ashby till he was shot. Unfortunately, I was shot not too long after that, and I've been recuperating ever since. I'll be fighting again soon." He changed the topic abruptly, and his voice became pointed: "Where have you been, Hank?"

Hank didn't answer, and John looked over his head into the trees beyond. John spoke again, more softy than before, "There was a lot of grief at home. Nothing was ever the same. Ma never stopped grieving. Daniel, he changed . . . stopped drawing. No one could figure out what happened to you."

Guilt and the previous evening's emptiness clutched Hank.

John spoke, "It was like he stopped caring. He went off to join the army quick as he could when the war broke out. Ran away to do it. He was too young, you know. But he was so big they didn't ask questions . . . just took him." John stared blankly past Hank. "A member of the Stonewall Brigade. He fought in a bunch of battles, some here in the valley, down by Richmond, a couple at Manassas. He's dead."

There! It was confirmed: He was dead. The full weight of Daniel's death descended on Hank. His eyes moistened and reddened. He feared sobbing in front of his brother, but the pain was heavy.

John continued, seemingly without feeling, "They said he was skin and bones at the end, like all the infantry—sometimes he didn't even have shoes. Ma tried to send him shoes when she could get them, but all that walking they did wore out even good shoes. Can you picture Daniel without shoes? He died in that first night battle at Manassas. They buried him right on the field." A hint of emotion entered his voice for the first time, "I wish he hadn't gone. He didn't have to, not then, not yet. He was so young." He continued to stare past Hank. "You were his hero you know, especially after you went away to school. He didn't want to be like me . . . not interested in the farm. He wanted to be like you. He was always so excited to have you come home." He paused again. "So what happened to you?"

Again John waited, but not long enough for an answer. "We thought you were dead. Searched the whole lower valley for you. We learned you went to see Samuel Richman's daughter, but couldn't figure out where you went from there. We heard something about you asking her to marry . . . that she'd said no. We thought you were dead, that you'd been killed or fallen in the river and drowned or something. We searched for a month for your body."

Hank felt humiliation greater than any he had ever imagined, but his grief at news of Daniel's death and at his mother's sorrow was the stronger emotion. He wanted to cry. He wanted to confess everything, every detail of his actions since he left home, but he could only muster, "I ran."

"Ran?" Hank could hear rising anger in his brother's voice.

"I loved her . . . Betsy Richman. I thought she felt the same way. I had wanted to marry her for so long. I thought she wanted to marry me. That was the way it was going to be. I loved her family, I loved her, they loved me. She had to marry me. Then her father died. And it all changed . . . changed so quickly. Don't even know what happened . . . really . . . or why. Her mother welcomed me one day . . . the next she hated me. Maybe she was angry that I didn't save her husband again. When Betsy said she wouldn't marry me, my whole world crumbled right then. Where was I to go? What was I to do?"

"All this because some silly girl wouldn't marry you!" John yelled the last sentence at Hank. Then he lowered his voice. "Hank, you always were a bit head-strong, independent. It was hard to get you to do what the family needed. But I never expected . . . never . . . that you would do anything like that . . . not to us. The war came along and destroyed a lot, but your family . . . our family was devastated long before the first bullet was fired. You destroyed it, Hank."

Hank had never imagined or even considered the impact of his behavior on his family. He had seen only what it had done to himself. He had never confronted what he had done to them—never perceived the pain they must have felt. Guided by John's brutal frankness, complete sorrow descended on Hank and silent tears finally slid down his cheeks. John watched with disgust on his features. For the first time, Hank sensed what each member of his family must have experienced when he ran. The thought of being at home no longer comforted him.

Hank looked up and saw abhorrence in John's expression. Hank began, as if begging. "I was humiliated. I couldn't face them laughing at me. I'd lost her. Everyone knew it. I just rode . . . rode away. My only thought was get away, to get away. Then when I was away, I couldn't bring myself to come home. I was so ashamed."

"Couldn't you write?"

"I was afraid to write. Thought you, thought Pa wouldn't want to hear from me. I couldn't come home and have the family repudiate me, too."

"It's been three years, Hank! Where have you been hiding?"

Hank answered, "I went to Maryland, then Ohio, then on to Indiana. Worked on several farms. Couldn't ever make much. Life was hard, so I joined the army when the war came along. Thought it would be easier."

"How'd you get back to the valley and join without us hearing? Or did you join somewhere else? You must have in all those months run into someone you knew from the valley."

"It's not exactly like that." Hank looked at the ground and spoke tentatively, "I joined the 19th Indiana."

John's eyes opened wide, his lips opened in a subtle grin. "The 19th Indiana? Didn't know we had regiments from Indiana."

Hank looked up and with a slight feeling of pride, "You don't. It's Union, part of the Black Hat Brigade."

John stood motionless and quiet, still showing the slight suggestion of a smile.

Hank told him about working on farms, his failures, joining the army, his war experiences and his loneliness. He told about Captain Henderson's letter and said he was going to deliver it to the widow if John would let him. He half expected John to shoot him on the spot, but John listened with growing interest.

At the last sentiment, John grimaced, "Why 'If I let you?'"

Hank responded, "John, you have the better of me. I'm fully prepared to accept my punishment. I'm a traitor, betrayed the family, Virginia."

John let him finish. "You may have betrayed Virginia. But there are plenty who have gone both ways in this war. I've chosen my side, as did Daniel. You've chosen the other. I know some families—a lot of families—are split by the war. Brothers hating brothers—it's almost trite. But I'm not going to hate you . . . or harm you. I decided a long time ago that as hard as it was, and as much as I hate the Yankee cause, Abe Lincoln, and the way they have invaded our country, I was not going to let this war divide our family more, not if I could help it. I'm not going to hate you . . . or Corny . . . or anyone else. I've seen some people in families where they hate each other more than they hate enemy armies. There's no sense in that. It's not right. One boy I know captured his brother and turned him in. He's rotting in prison somewhere right now waiting to be exchanged. I couldn't do that. It appears you have done some pretty stupid things, but I've done a few myself." He chuckled, then quietly added, "I think if Pa were younger and had his way, he might be in the 19th Indiana with you."

Hank looked at John, mercurial John. Relief swept over him as he realized he was not in physical danger. For the first time, John approached Hank. Hank noticed his limp, but said nothing about it and stood up to meet him. John extended his hand to Hank. Hank took and shook it warmly. John pulled him closer, and they hugged.

When they released their grips, John spoke, "Come on over and get something to eat. You've been sleeping the day away. You've become mighty lazy since joining the Yanks. But from what I hear, all Yankees are lazy."

The two brothers shared the meat and valley gossip, but oddly, John didn't offer reports on the rest of the family, and odder still, Hank felt uncomfortable asking for family news. Eventually, John asked, "Will you stop at home? You should. They'll want to see you . . . to know you're alive. They'll want to know what happened. With this war, it might be their only chance to see you again." He cautioned, "But you better watch out for Cole. He'll try to find you. He has a knack for killing foes. If he finds you, he will kill you. You made him look a fool, he won't forget that."

"What happened to Naomi?"

"Naomi? Who's Naomi?"

"Naomi, the woman who lives where Cole and his men slept last night."

"I don't know. What difference does that make anyway? She must have left her house sometime last
night. It must have been before you escaped. Cole
fetched me, but when I got there you were gone. I
didn't see any woman. Now, dear brother, you'd better
be on your way. If I could track you so easily, others
can, too. I don't know if Cole is a great tracking hound,
but he is surely a tenacious bull dog. Once he gets his
teeth on you, he'll hold you."

Without another word, Hank packed his bedroll,
saddled his horse and mounted. John handed him a
pistol and said, "On horseback, perhaps this will work
better for you than a musket."

Hank took the pistol and proffered bullets, tucking
the pistol into his belt. He gave his musket to John and
removed his cartridge box from around his neck, toss-
ing it to his brother as well. He said, "A pistol will be
better. If only I had my parole, too."

"Oh, I almost forgot. I've got your papers . . . took
them from Cole. You may still find it handy before
you've finished your fool's errand." He grinned. "Fool's
errand it is, too, Hank. You ought to just forget it and
head back to Maryland while you can." He handed the
parole to Hank who stuffed it in his pant pocket. John
watched him.

Hank looked directly into John's face.

John smiled sadly at Hank.

Hank kicked the sides of his horse and headed south
toward the mountain.

John called out to him, "God be with you, Hank."
And Hank waved in return. The older brother watched

him as Hank rode toward the road and the south. He watched until he disappeared from view.

Hank rode throughout the afternoon and evening and well into the night. He didn't want to stop again until he reached Massanutten Mountain. He gave Front Royal and its Confederate forces a wide berth and rode into Powell's Fort Valley. He was in greater danger as he rode than he had been since leaving Sharpsburg, but he didn't worry about the dangers, not anymore. Feelings for his family fully engrossed him. Why had he run from the Shenandoah in the first place? It all seemed so long ago and so unimportant on this cold, early fall night. Before rolling out his bedroll, Hank rode up the eastern side of the mountain away from road and path. He was going to make sure no one was near and that no one would take him by surprise again. The next time that happened . . . . He couldn't bring himself to finish the thought.

For the next several days, Hank carefully journeyed on back roads and fields and through woods. He had time to think, and he split his thoughts evenly between the good widow and his family. He thought about every member of his family—the harm he had done to each— becoming increasingly depressed. When he could bear no more sorrow, he would unconsciously shift his thoughts to his fantasy of Mrs. Henderson and their soon-to-come fateful rendezvous. With little further difficulty, he made his way to Staunton.

Chapter 19
October 1862, Staunton, Virginia

*H*e arrived north of Staunton early in the afternoon. It was a cool autumn day with white, soft clouds that blew rapidly across the rich, blue sky. Surges of excitement and energy pulsed through him as a cool breeze fanned his face. He had made it! Shortly he would present the letter to Mrs. Henderson. He would stay if she invited him. He had already decided that. For how long would he be willing to stay? He found a forest near the town and slipped into it with his horse. He sat down, took off his pants, and cut away the inner pocket he had sewn behind his thigh. He removed Captain Henderson's letter, its copy, and the coins. Both letters were badly bent and soiled but still legible. He tucked the letters in a pant pocket with the money, put his trousers back on and walked out of the woods and into Staunton.

It had been a long time since he visited Staunton, and he had forgotten its steep hills and streets. There were countless Confederate soldiers in the town, especially near the train station where he guessed they awaited passage to Richmond. Many of the soldiers were wounded. He also passed Union soldiers held under guard at the court house. Hank pitied them, suspecting they too waited for transportation to Richmond. He was uncomfortable among so many soldiers, fearing he might meet someone who knew him or who would see through his charade. He discreetly avoided the crowds.

As he walked his horse through Staunton's streets, he feigned casualness. He began to feel dirty, noting for the first time the thick coat of dust on his clothes and hands left by rapid travel in an especially dry month. He felt uncomfortably conspicuous and quickly asked several people along the street for directions to the captain's home.

"Promisin' young man," responded an older, stout gentleman that stood outside a storefront. "He had a promisin' life ahead of him. With his businesses and influence, nothin' he couldn't have done. Very sad. Cut down, just like so many others. We've lost a lot. I imagine Mrs. Henderson's real sad 'bout it. Beautiful couple, and now she's alone."

"Where is his house?" Hank asked again, trying to get the gentlemen to answer his question.

"Ah . . . yes, yes. His house. I saw you come from that direction. You probably passed it on the way into town. You go on straight out of town 'bout a half mile. It will be on the left. It's a large, beautiful red brick house. White picket fence around the yard. Small balcony and porch on the front. You'll know it. Say . . . it looks like you rode hard to get here. You might want to clean yourself up before you meet her . . . a lady like that. Please give Mrs. Henderson my regards. Mr. Porter. Tell her Mr. Porter gives his regards. That's me. If she needs anything, my establishment is open to assist her. I do feel for Mrs. Henderson . . . such a lovely la-

dy. She is so beautiful! Haven't seen her for such a
long time. Hope she's well. And how is General Lee?
And Tom Jackson? Have you seen him? Stonewall's
doin' a great work. He's from the valley . . . met him
once. He taught artillery at the Virginia Military Institute up in Lexington before the war, other things, too.
He was a brilliant professor . . . a favorite. To my way
of thinkin', VMI's the best military school in the world.
I know others think West Point is better, but not me.
West Point may be older, but that doesn't make it better. Stonewall was a leading citizen up there in Lexington, and he's a mighty soldier of the Cross now. He's
done all right by us . . . made us proud. If you see the
generals, you let them know we're praying for them . .
. especially Stonewall. Now don't forget, you tell Mrs.
Henderson my establishment is open to serve her. Anything she needs . . . just anything."

As quickly as possible Hank extricated himself from
conversation with Mr. Porter and retraced his steps
toward the edge of town. He remembered seeing the
house. It was massive, and there had been a servant
on the front porch. He hurried now, eager to conclude
the business. He wanted to shed the responsibility and
burden . . . and begin his romance with the widow. In
his rush, he forgot his dusty condition and Mr. Porter's
advice.

Within 15 minutes he approached the house. The
lawn had been freshly cut, and the smell of paint lin-
gered around the porch. No slaves were in sight now.
Hank leaped up the three steps to the front porch and
knocked boldly on the door. Presently he heard a faint
noise from inside. The door opened slowly, and a tall,

elderly black man stood imposingly, blocking entry to Hank.

The man, for his part, saw a young man dressed in worn and soiled clothes, with dirty face and hands and greasy hair. "Sir?" he asked in greeting.

"I am here to see Mrs. Henderson. Is she at home?" Hank asked formally.

"She is not at home," the servant responded stiffly.

"Do you expect her soon? I have come a long way. I have a letter I am to give to her." To prove his business, Hank held out the letter.

"She does not live here now."

"Where can I find her?"

"She is unavailable. If you give me the letter, I will have it sent to her."

"I am to give it to her personally," Hank said, persisting.

The man, a long-time house slave for the Hendersons, had been trained over the years by three generations of Hendersons. He would never allow such a filthy fellow into the house, particularly to see a female member of the household. The slave, loyal to his departed masters, said, "I will see that she gets your letter." The slave reached for the letter.

Hank pulled it back. Should he just leave it with the servant? How could he be sure this slave would get it to Mrs. Henderson? Each promising sign for the North in the war made the slaves in Virginia a bit more unreliable, a larger risk for their masters and mistresses. Hank had placed money in the letter, nearly half of his $13 a month pay. That surely would tempt a slave. But Hank had no other option. Delivering it to her home and this slave appeared as close to delivering it to her personally as he could get.

Hank was crestfallen. He had for so long looked forward to seeing her . . . hearing her voice . . . looking into her eyes . . . taking her into his arms. He had traveled so far, risked so much, and for what? He now knew he carried no news for her. From Mr. Porter's comments it was clear that Mrs. Henderson and the rest of Staunton knew her husband was dead. Hank's hoped for romance with her was not to be; he wouldn't even meet her. The trip was for naught, and he was angry.

In frustration, he decided to leave the copy of the captain's letter he had made and the money with the house slave. Hank would, someday after the war, in more prosperous times, if he survived—a possibility he now doubted after what he had seen at Antietam— deliver the blood-stained letter personally. He looked at the slave and said condescendingly, "Since I cannot deliver it to Mrs. Henderson in person, I would like to seal the envelope. Bring me a candle or sealing wax. It must be sealed!"

The slave replied that he would bring it and disappeared into the house, closing and bolting the door behind him.

While he was gone, Hank removed the copied letter and the money and placed them with his note into a plain white but soiled envelope he had addressed earlier. When the servant returned, Hank closed and sealed the envelope with wax and gave it to the slave who quickly disappeared, again securing the door.

As Hank walked back toward the road, it dawned on him that considerable open and cultivated land surrounded the stately home and yard. The woman was undeniably wealthy. He felt foolish for putting money in the envelope and imagined her laughing at him.

Chapter 20
October 1862, Staunton, Virginia

Mrs. Thaddeus Henderson sat alone in the large room, tawny afternoon light filtering through the two tall windows at her back. She was in deep mourning, wearing a floor-length black dress adorned with crape, loose sleeves and buttons up the front to the collar that was tight around her delicate neck. She wasn't crying, but sorrow marked her young and pretty face. Her eyes stared into the distance. Her head leaned slightly forward, and she let thoughts wash over her without control and direction. She had not known him long, nor for that matter as well as she would have liked. He was a handsome man: tall, robust, ever proper, the product of generations of the finest Virginia breeding. His wealth had been cultivated over those generations and ties of friendship reached the highest levels of society. Two years ago friends in the national government had lived in Washington City, to the northeast. Today such friends lived only in Richmond; there were no acknowledged friends in the North.

When she heard of his death, she considered going back to her childhood home, but thought better of the idea and moved to town to be with her husband's cousin. The cousin would appreciate the company.

Married as the war started, the cousin also had sent
her young husband to fight, but he was still alive. Her
cousin's husband had been in both battles at Manassas, had marched and fought in the valley and on the
Peninsula, and traveled with the army north to the
border of Virginia. From Berryville he had written that
he, like many others, had refused to cross the Potomac
with the rest of the army. He had no intention of invading the North. He assured his wife he was fighting only
to protect his home, family and Virginia. He didn't believe it proper to take the war beyond the Confederacy's boundaries. When the Southern army crossed the
Potomac, it became the aggressor. It was no longer
faultless. He wrote that he only hoped God would not
punish the South for this wickedness. The cousin
couldn't understand her husband's thinking and wondered aloud why God would want to punish his nation,
the Confederacy. However, she was secretly grateful
her husband had stayed behind. By remaining in Virginia, he had missed the terrible battle at Sharpsburg
that had filled Staunton, including one room on the
main floor of her home, with wounded soldiers. Many
valley men died at Sharpsburg, and while she wanted
the Confederacy to win the war, she did not want to be
a widow like Mrs. Henderson. She pitied Mrs. Henderson. For herself, she looked forward to the war's end
when her husband would be back, when all would be
as it was before. Mrs. Henderson understood all this.

The two women often spoke of their feelings about
the war, about slavery, about their husbands. Mrs.
Henderson held that slavery wouldn't survive the war
no matter its outcome. Her cousin disagreed doggedly,

believing the war wasn't about slavery. It was about protecting rights and being true to the principles of '76. The cousin could not conceive that Lincoln's heinous proclamation on slavery, published after Sharpsburg, would make any difference. When England and France came to the aid of the South, the North would have to give up their ignoble cause. England—especially England—needed the south's cotton. It wouldn't be long now before these European powers joined with the Confederacy. The cousin had heard news from a woman who had a husband who had spoken to a friend who knew someone in Richmond. That someone had told the friend, who then told the husband, who told his wife, who had told her that cotton reserves were desperately low in England. England would have to come to the aid of the South soon or there would be an uprising among her working class. The Confederate government had already sent ministers to England and France who were negotiating recognition. To be sure, it would come any day now. It would all then be over for Lincoln and for all those corrupt abolitionists . . . when England joined the Southern Cause.

Northerners, the cousin always said, couldn't appreciate what a blessing slavery was to the slaves: It ennobled them. The Northerners didn't live among the slaves, didn't know that slaves were a lazy lot, needed constant supervision, constant work; and that they would be idle and worthless, even wicked, without their masters. Masters were as necessary for slaves as parents were for children.

The South had a right to slavery. There was no denying that. Surely it was God who had given slaves to the Southerners as a blessing to master and especially to slave. In these tirades, she always quoted the Bible, "'Servants, obey in all things your masters according to the flesh; not with eyeservice, as menpleasers; but in singleness of heart, fearing God: And whatsoever ye do, do it heartily . . . for ye serve the Lord Christ.'"

"Remember," she would say after citing the scripture, "our slaves are to serve us as they would Christ; by serving us, they serve Christ. It was his will that they labor, and labor hard to make their calling and election sure." Then she would quote another verse, "'Let as many servants as are under the yoke count their own masters worthy of all honour, that the name of God and [his] doctrine be not blasphemed.'" There! It was clear: Slavery was part of Christianity. It's doctrine. There could be no Christianity without slavery. It was blasphemy to deny it. Didn't Abraham have slaves? And the Israelites? God gave masters to the slaves that those masters could raise up the child-like slaves just as Christ, the great Master, had raised up free men.

The cousin expected Mrs. Henderson to understand all of this. After all, Mrs. Henderson's family owned slaves, and the widow herself had inherited slaves from her husband. Mrs. Henderson was sure, however, that she could find no scripture claiming slavery was necessary or good. She didn't believe the oft-quoted verses from the Old and New Testaments encouraged slavery . . . just made it better where people chose, perhaps in wickedness to have it. She couldn't believe slaves were better off under masters than on their own. She always answered the cousin by quoting scripture back to her, "Masters, give unto [your] servants that which is just and equal; knowing that ye also have a Master in heaven." She would then subtly suggest that not all Southern masters treated their slaves justly and with equality. Mrs. Henderson knew, she had seen it with her own eyes, that some masters—she hoped only a few—were brutal to their slaves and to their own families. Perhaps it was all of the same thing. To Mrs. Henderson, trying to control someone else—slave or family—didn't seem likely to bring happiness to anyone . . . or raise anyone up. She even toyed at times with the idea that slavery was a sin, and it made her queasy knowing that she might be in sin.

Mrs. Henderson was not thinking today about their discussions of the war or slavery or her cousin. She was thinking about her husband, killed early in the fighting of Second Manassas . . . shot on a farm near a place called Gainesville. She had learned of his death from a letter the cousin's husband had sent several weeks earlier. He wrote that Captain Henderson died bravely, quickly and without suffering. The captain's men spoke highly of his courage and leadership. They loved and respected him. Even the Colonel praised him ardently. The cousin's husband went on to write that Captain Henderson spoke often of his wife, always carried a daguerreotype of her. All who saw it were impressed by her character and beauty. He was sorry to have to write of his death. He would rather tell her in person, but that wasn't possible.

The cousin had buried the captain where he had fallen, but kept his sword and the picture and would bring them to her when he could get home. He also, strangely enough, had found a Yankee hat near her husband's body and kept that as well. It was not the common soldier's hat, but tall and black, and he couldn't imagine how it got there. He closed by saying the war was going well, that they had whipped the Union boys for a second time at Manassas. It couldn't last much longer. The people of the North would not continue to sacrifice their sons and husbands in such a villainous cause.

Now Mrs. Henderson sat in the sunlight thinking how she didn't really want her husband's sword and didn't care about a Yankee hat, as unusual as it might be. All that mattered was her husband; and he was gone.

Chapter 21
October 1862, Staunton, Virginia

"*M*a'am?" Mrs. Henderson was diverted from her thoughts as she became aware that a bronzed-complexioned house slave, Ruth, a member of the cousin's household since birth, had come in and stood beside her.

"Yes? What is it, Ruth?"

"A letter's come for yuh."

"From whom?"

"John, from yor place, brung it up. Says a man with dirt all over hisself come to de house and ask for yuh. When yuh wasn't there, he look sad and say he come a long, long way to see yuh. John says yuh ain't staying there no more. De man then give this to ole John, and de man go away. Somet'in' real heavy in it, ma'am—coins or somet'in.'"

Mrs. Henderson took the letter in her hand. It was heavy, and she recognized the weight and shape of coins. The plain envelope was addressed: Mrs. Thaddeus Henderson. She thought the handwriting perhaps familiar, but it was definitely not from her cousin's husband.

"Ruth told me you got a letter," her cousin said, sweeping into the room and sitting in a chair that faced Mrs. Henderson.

"One's just been delivered."

"From your family?"

"I don't think so. It was delivered to my house."

"Have you opened it yet?"

Mrs. Henderson laughed. They were both desperate for news of family and friends. "I just got it. I'm opening it as fast as I can. It's sealed with fresh wax."

The cousin alternated her stare between the letter and Mrs. Henderson as if waiting to see which would speak first.

Mrs. Henderson carefully opened the letter and poured out the coins in her hand. She laughed and said incredulously, "It's money."

"Coins! Who would send you coins?"

She looked up at her cousin and asked, "How long has it been since you've seen gold or silver coins?"

Her cousin didn't answer, still eager to know the details in the letter.

Mrs. Henderson read the date and salutation out loud.

Near Manassas, Virginia
August 29, 1862
Mrs. Thaddeus Henderson at Staunton, Virginia
Dear Mrs. Henderson,

"It doesn't sound like someone you know," the cousin commented.

"Not someone I know intimately."

She continued reading.

I write to you with bad tidings. Perhaps you have already heard the news, but I believe I have details that will be important to you.

She commented that it was a strange beginning to a letter and read on.

First, I want to tell you that I am a union soldier from Virginia, having grown up in the lower end of the valley.

"A Yankee?" the cousin squealed. "What's a Yankee writing to you for? Doesn't he know your husband was killed by Yankees. This is just one more way for them to hurt us . . . and from the valley. He's a traitor."

Mrs. Henderson looked across at the cousin and waited until she had finished, then read again.

While in a farmer's field near Manassas last night and after a terrible battle, I came upon your husband who had been grievously hurt.

An audible breath escaped her lips. The cousin said nothing.

I tried to move him to where he could receive help, but he was so weak and in such pain that I could not move him, being alone at the time. I regret to inform you that he died on that field. I was with him for his last minutes. His last thoughts and words were of you. He was concerned that you would be all right. He also spoke of how much he loved you. You cannot imagine the pain I feel at writing you of this tragedy. While your husband and I fought in different armies for conflicting causes, I hope you will not consider me your enemy, nor hate me for the allegiance I owe.

"How can you consider him anything but your enemy? He killed your husband . . . betrayed Virginia. He mocks you with this letter. My husband has already told you he didn't suffer. Now this Yankee writes to hurt you . . . to lie to you! Don't read any more! Burn it! Throw that dirty . . . blood money in the street. It's nothing but the thirty pieces of silver. He's a Judas. He once again betrays our Lord."

Mrs. Henderson listened to the cousin stunned by her words and the letter. She had pondered a thousand times what his last moments must have been like. She'd wondered if he thought of her . . . asked herself if she would think of him or another in her last moments. She had loved him. Yes, she had loved him, hadn't she married him. But he didn't consume her thoughts, even after his death. She looked toward her cousin, but her eyes focused beyond in a penetrating, thoughtful stare. She said nothing and briefly considered reading the rest of the letter to herself. But she liked hearing the words, so she continued to read aloud.

In your husband's final minutes, I felt a kinship and respect for a man who would die so honorably on the field of battle. I know that it will be difficult to live as a widow, so I'm enclosing a little money to help you during this hard time. I wish I had more to send, but I am but a poor private. I hope you can use these coins in Staunton.

The cousin was visibly irate. "Who does he think he's writing to? How dare he write to you at all. He's a scurrilous traitor from the valley. He dares to send you a handful of coins . . . the ignorant Yankee!" She spoke the last phrase with venom.

Mrs. Henderson wanted to smile at the cousin. She was enjoying the letter and now was enjoying the cousin's consternation. The simple naiveté of the young man had touched her. His kindness affected her. She hesitated to read more out loud, but couldn't stop herself. "There's still more. Let me read on."

There is one last item of business of which I must write. In his final moments your husband made me promise that I would deliver to you a letter that he had written.

"I cannot believe it! I cannot believe it!" the cousin yelled, and she cursed the soldier. "Your husband would never have asked a favor of a Yankee. He is a liar!"

Mrs. Henderson leaned slowly back in her chair, amazed. She had never heard this soft-spoken cousin raise her voice and never imagined her capable of profanity. She thought of the Yankee hat found near her husband's body. Mrs. Henderson responded compassionately. "Perhaps he was unable at that point to tell if someone was a Yankee or a patriot."

"My cousin would be able to tell by the smell!"

Mrs. Henderson hesitated to continue. She sat silently, no longer enjoying her cousin's frustration.

In a low, accusing tone the cousin continued. She spoke in a slow cadence, emphasizing each word for the benefit of this woman who had angered her and who had degraded her own husband and disregarded the Confederacy: "I would think that if you had ever loved my cousin," she paused, "or if you love your country now, you would not read another word of that shameful letter. You would spit on it. Grind it into the ground with your heel. My cousin would never cavort with the enemy. I'm not so sure right now," she paused to cut more deeply, "if I could say the same for his wife."

Mrs. Henderson could see the cousin's fury in her blood-flushed face. She could feel a similar anger welling up in her, and she responded in the same low tone, likewise emphasizing each word: "I believe you are wrong to speak to me in such a manner. I am the widow here. I am the one who has sacrificed her husband—my husband—for the South. Your husband lives," then she added maliciously, "and probably will if he continues to run from battles as he did from Sharpsburg. Don't worry! He will live to comfort his delicate flower once again." She now spoke with determination, "Let me not mince words. I will not be spoken to in the manner you have used. I will not stay in this house one day longer. But while I am here, I will read my mail. I will do with my mail what I wish. I will not be spoken to as if I am your slave, and I will not be accused of being a traitor to country . . . or husband."

The cousin's eyes were open wide. The anger was passing; the hurt waxing. Half-swallowed, convulsive sobs began to shake her, till she was unable to control them, and she ran from the room. Mrs. Henderson could hear her climb the stairs, and she regretted losing her temper and hurting the cousin's feelings. As she sat, a strange guilt crept into the room. Was she loyal?

She elevated the letter again to reading height and read, "*He . . .*" She had lost the context of the letter, and she tried to remember who "he" was. Then she remembered it was a letter about her husband. She started the sentence again.

He insisted that I deliver it in person, although I don't believe he understood at that moment how difficult it would be to do so. He did not realize that I was a Union soldier. But I have made that pledge and intend to fulfill it.

Was it the Yankee then who delivered the letter? Why hadn't he stayed? Perhaps he was afraid. It certainly would be dangerous for a Union soldier in Staunton. She continued reading.

To keep my pledge I will copy the letter that your husband has written to you. I will send the copy with this letter to you. How, I do not know, but I will find a way. I will hold the original letter until I can deliver it personally to you, although that may be many days from now. I know you would like to have the letter, but to maintain my honor, I must do it this way. Forgive me.

She wondered why he needed to be forgiven. He had shown kindness to her and to her husband as he lay dying. Was he the man who killed Thaddeus? He would have, even if he didn't, she reminded herself. Her cousin was right. She should be angry, and the sorrow of losing her husband and anger that someone had killed him depressed her. Why would anyone want to kill him? He always had been kind and generous. She sat and cried quietly, carefully folding up the soldier's letter and slipping it back into the envelope. She read her husband's letter. She read it several times . . . crying all the while. She sat for a long time.

She heard a soft noise from the doorway to the hall. She turned her face to the door. Mrs. Henderson had spent her emotions, leaving her face wet from tears, but she was no longer crying. The cousin stood there, shoulders stooped, head bowed respectfully, her skirt filling the doorway. She spoke softly in a pleading tone, "I am sorry! Can you ever forgive a foolish cousin who loves you so much? Can you forgive me?"

Mrs. Henderson smiled tenderly. "I'm sorry," she said and began to cry again. "It was unkind of me. What I said of your husband was not true. I should never have said it."

"Oh, my darling." The cousin rushed to Mrs. Henderson's side, knelt beside her, and they embraced. "No, forgive me. Please forgive me!" They held each other, the cousin squeezing Mrs. Henderson tightly and rocking the two of them backward and forward. "We need each other," she said. "You mustn't move away. You mustn't leave. You mustn't! We need each other. You must stay. You must."

They sat together quietly as the afternoon sunlight settled to dusk. Their confrontation had exhausted both of them, and Mrs. Henderson eventually excused herself to take a short evening nap. When she got to her room, she again opened the letters and read them, first her husband's, then the soldier's. As she read both, she felt no anger at the Union soldier. He had been kind and was attempting to keep his commitment to her husband. She read the last lines again.

I know you would like to have the letter . . .

He was right. She would like to have the original letter . . . a last gift from her husband.

. . . but to maintain my honor, I must do it this way. Forgive me. Yours faithfully, Private Henry Gragg, 19th Indiana Infantry Regiment, US Army.

A shiver traveled the length of her spine. Henry Gragg? She hadn't seen that before. She wasn't sleepy anymore. It could not be him. Not Henry Gragg! At least not the same Henry Gragg! She pictured her Hank Gragg on the porch of her mother's house, pleading that she marry him. She wanted to marry him . . . marry him that day . . . but it wasn't the right time. They had to wait. She remembered his persistence . . . her anger . . . her words. Even as she left him there standing on the porch, she thought she would make it right with him later on. But she never saw him again. He never came back, and she never had the chance to show how much she loved him. She remembered how happy her mother had been when the former Miss Richman had abruptly, and without thinking, rejected Hank. She remembered how her father had loved him.

Even after her marriage, Mrs. Henderson had often wondered what happened to Hank. She had often wished to speak to him, to apologize to him, to tell him what she was doing and what she was thinking. But he had disappeared . . . completely. She had heard his family, whom oddly enough she had never met, feared he had died. They searched for his body for months, but he was gone without a trace, but not without regret. Those who knew him in the valley mourned him. How many of those same men now, unknowingly, wanted to kill him? For his turn, he willfully sought to destroy his former neighbors?

Thoughts of him enveloped her. Where had he gone? Why had he gone? Why would he fight against the valley? She felt a happiness, a hope long absent from her life. Was it him? Was he alive? It was him! The handwriting—the words—they were undoubtedly his. An old guilt weighed on her. Her pride and her anger, they drove him away. She had silently mourned Hank Gragg when he had disappeared; had never stopped mourning him. She could only mourn him silently, however, as her mother hated him so, and then she had married Thaddeus.

How did Hank know it was her; that she was Betsy Richman? He must have heard about the marriage. But he couldn't know who she was. She had met Thaddeus after Hank disappeared. On the day Hank proposed, she had received her first message from Thaddeus, delivered by the cadet from the VMI. Hank could not have known that she was Thaddeus' wife or that she lived in Staunton or that Thaddeus' pet name for her was Ellie. He didn't know. Hank had written his letter, sent his money to the widow Ellie Henderson of Staunton, not to the former Betsy Richman of Winchester.

Without warning her heart quickened with excitement. She hadn't felt this way since courting. Hank was in Staunton or at least had been within the last several hours! Where was he now? If only she could find him. He couldn't have gone far. She thought of ordering up a horse. She would search for him. But it was dark, she wouldn't find him tonight. She would have to wait till morning. In the morning she would search the roads leading North; she would find him. Then what? She couldn't bring him here. He wasn't merely Hank Gragg, Valley boy. He was Private Hank Gragg of some company of some regiment of some brigade of some division of some army of the unwelcome invading hordes. She imagined introducing him to her cousin: "Emily, I'd like you to meet Hank Gragg, a friend of mine from Woodstock. Yes! He's one of the boys that was shooting at our husbands at Manassas. Yes! He probably killed my husband. Yes! He's a fine example of a traitor. Yes! I love him. Yes! I betray my husband's memory with this love. Yes! Yes! Yes! Everything you yelled at me was true." She lowered her head and cried softly again, but just for a moment. Her thoughts rebounded in a different direction: She would go with him. She would leave all and walk beside him to the North. She would follow him from battle to battle just to be near him. A camp follower, she would cook for him, do his laundry, sew his uniform. She would comfort him as she had failed to do in Winchester. She would be a Yankee. Even as she dreamed of darning socks, she knew it was impossible as searching for him would increase the likelihood of his capture. She had to let him go on his own.

Supper was a quiet affair. Both she and her cousin, Emily, retired early, each silently hoping for the sun to rise quickly on a new and better day. Both slept fitfully and were up early, still hoping for a happier day than their last. Emily hoped Betsy would not still be angry with her. Betsy hoped she would have the courage to order up the carriage or that Hank would inexplicably sense her presence and come to Emily's front door. The cousins met at breakfast, Emily watching closely for signs of forgiveness while Betsy suffered mental and emotional confusion. In one minute of exhilaration, she determined to order up the carriage. The next minute saw her plunge into gloom, resigning herself to do nothing. He was so close, and she tortured herself as she constantly watched the clock mark the morning's passing. In the end, she never did order the carriage.

The cousin saw evidence of the battle waged in Betsy's mind and interpreted it as proof of Betsy's still brooding anger. Each time Emily brought up a topic, it met silence or a distantly polite response. The cousin's heart ached. Betsy's heart ached. They sat across from each other, each in pain, each oblivious to the suffering of the other or its cause.

Chapter 22

October 1862, Staunton, Virginia

After delivering the letter to Mrs. Henderson's home, Hank returned to the hilly town, riding unwittingly past Emily's front door. Within a few blocks of her house, he sold Cole's horse. He had determined that riding that particular mare toward the Potomac, while much quicker than other travel options, would present an obstacle larger than the entire Confederate army. He had the impression that the self-appointed partisan, Cole, was combing the northern end of the valley searching for his lost horse, and for Hank. Hank felt safer parting with the horse, and selling it would give him more than enough money for transportation down the valley.

Hank was increasingly distressed over his failure to meet the widow. He had been so close. He was angry at the servant for not revealing her whereabouts, angry at the widow for not being there, angry at himself for being so willing to give the captain's letter to a slave. He felt foolish. To dispel his dark mood, Hank walked Staunton's streets. As he strolled, he grew comfortable moving among the Confederates. Recklessly, he greeted several soldiers, chatting with a few, all the while cursing them in his mind. His anger was unabated. He passed the Union soldiers still held on the courthouse lawn. He heard guards barking instructions to them . . . commanding them. The arrogance of the Confederates! He hated that most. They needed to learn a lesson; Hank wanted to teach it. They had no right to command Union soldiers! The Union soldiers had done nothing. It was Secesh that started it all and who kept it going. His anger crystallized into a passion to help the prisoners. He would free them—at least some of them. The widow . . . the slave . . . the Confederacy . . . they would know then that Hank Gragg and the Union weren't to be trifled with.

During the afternoon, Hank learned that a stage coach traveled North on the Valley Pike the next morning and arranged travel on it. He took a room at the hotel from which the coach would leave, ate dinner and paid to have his clothes brushed. As he waited for his clothes, he cleaned up and napped briefly, but his still-smoldering anger awoke him with thoughts of the captive Union soldiers: They were still at the behest of Rebels. Alone in the room, he sat on a bed staring blankly at the wall. His thoughts came slowly. The harder he concentrated, the fewer ideas surfaced. At the moment he gave up hope, an idea came. It wasn't much . . . just a beginning, but he had to do something. He wrote out a note.

When his clothes returned, he was off. He again walked the streets of the town, staying near the train station, waiting, hesitating to put his plan into action. Then he saw it. A careless soldier laid his musket against a building wall so he could gesticulate widely while telling some amusing anecdote to his comrades.

His comrades seemed fully engrossed in his antics. Hank drew a deep breath . . . exhaled. In spite of the conviction that he would surely be caught, he walked quickly between the story-telling soldier and the wall against which the gun lay. As he passed, he deftly lifted the musket.

He didn't look back, but listened as long as he could to the Confederate soldiers' conversation. He barely breathed as he walked. At one point he heard a voice raised behind him, and he closed his eyes in terror. Someone had seen him! But the voice lowered again. Surely someone could see his legs shake. He could hardly walk they trembled so violently. No one paid heed to him or his legs. He walked on, resisting a desperate urge to run. He continued on the same street for two blocks, then turned left. As he rounded the corner, he carelessly glanced back at the still-talking soldier. He could see him only faintly now, but there was no ruckus, no commotion. The soldier hadn't missed his musket. Hank sighed and a smile flashed across his lips. They were as stupid as they were rebellious. He had completed the first phase—he had a musket.

He immediately marched with an official, martial air toward the courthouse. His legs still quivered. He could see the guards at the gate of the wrought iron fence that surrounded the courthouse. Additional guards were stationed at frequent intervals around the fence's perimeter. The Union soldiers lounged as best they could inside the enclosure.

Nervous, Hank had a strong, but brief, impulse to walk by . . . pass the courtyard. But anger and determination won out. He walked directly to the corporal of the guard that stood at the courtyard gate. Hank saluted crisply, and the corporal returned the salute indifferently.

Hank said firmly, "Corporal, I have orders to take 20 prisoners."

"Twenty prisoners? You . . . private?" the corporal responded condescendingly.

"Yes, 20 prisoners."

"Where are your orders? Let me see your orders," the Corporal demanded. "Who are they from?"

"The colonel."

"What colonel?" the Corporal asked disdainfully.

"It's in the orders." Hank handed him the paper he had written in his hotel room.

"What colonel is this?" the guard asked squinting at the messy signature. Hank didn't answer. "This doesn't look official."

"The colonel's staff was assessing damage on the railroad. He used what he had with him."

"Damage? Who is this colonel?"

When Hank didn't answer, the corporal said with less arrogance, "This says you're to take 20 prisoners with you and two guards."

"That's right!"

The Rebel looked skeptically at Hank. Hank stared defiantly back into the corporal's eyes. It took Hank's total concentration to maintain his gaze. Hank wanted to shift on his feet, to look away, to get more comfortable, but he resisted the desire and stood erect, unflinching.

The corporal spoke with less force. "We are to stay here. Keep the prisoners here. We'll put them on the train tomorrow. We can't give you guards! We're short as it is."

"The Colonel needs the 20 prisoners for work on the railroad . . . immediately. Union cavalry damaged the track between here and Gordonsville. Nothing serious, but it must be repaired immediately. We drove off the Yanks, but the damage was done. He needs 20 men to do it. He wants Union prisoners to fix the track. Better to use these prisoners than his soldiers for that kind of work."

The corporal chuckled. "I can see that."

Hank could see the man was beginning to let down his guard.

"Can this wait till morning? I'll report it to the captain. He can give you the men you need and all the guards you want. You're not going to work them tonight anyway? It'll be dark soon."

"The orders are specific! The colonel hopes to have the men in place, ready to work at first light."

"Makes sense, but I don't have authority to detail two of our boys to you." The corporal spoke now in a soft conversational tone.

"What shall I tell the colonel? As you can see, I can't take responsibility for guarding 20 soldiers . . . not by myself, with just a musket and pistol. Three would be barely enough. I will have to report to the colonel that you would not comply with the order." Hank spoke loudly and looked hard into the face of the corporal. The corporal gazed at the ground.

"What colonel is it?" he mumbled.

"It's on the order! I've told you! You can see it for yourself! Colonel Johnston! It's perfectly clear! He directed me here personally. He would have sent others . . . an officer, but they were all inspecting the track, getting ready for the repairs. These repairs are vital. Richmond is adamant! The repairs must be made immediately!"

This was the critical moment. Hank could see the corporal's mind working. Was he buying the bluff? Could this Yankee private intimidate a Rebel corporal? Hank inadvertently held his breath.

The corporal said softly, "Colonel Johnston, huh? This order doesn't say when the prisoners will return."

Bully! Hank had won. He wanted to laugh, but maintained his composure, and said sternly, "The prisoners will not be returned. After the work's done, they'll march to Gordonsville. They'll board the train there. They're going to Belle Island, aren't they . . . or are they to be exchanged?"

"I don't know. They're on their way to Richmond tomorrow. That's all I know. Two men?"

"That's correct, I will need two of your guards. We will send them back tomorrow morning. Or we can send them back as soon as we get to our camp."

"They'll be back tomorrow, then, you say?"

"Tomorrow morning."

"Garrett," the guard barked at a nearby soldier who had listened to the entire exchange. "Count out 20 prisoners. . . ."

Hank spoke again, "The colonel indicated he wanted the 20 strongest prisoners for the work."

The corporal spoke in a commanding voice again, "Garrett, make sure they're all healthy, from the big ones."

"Are you sure, sir?"

The corporal turned his wrath on the private. "Don't question me, Garrett! Just count out the men. Count them out now!"

"Yes, sir," Garrett responded. He called two guards to him to assist, and the three of them disappeared among the prisoners in the courtyard.

Hank stood still, saying no more. His legs began to tremble again, and he felt an urgent desire to run . . . to forget these prisoners . . . to get to safety. The corporal looked briefly at Hank, shook his head and turned to look for Garrett among the prisoners. For the 10 minutes it took Garrett to collect the 20 prisoners, neither the corporal nor Hank said anything, seeming to ignore one another.

Garrett led out a line of 20 men. The corporal, Hank, Garrett and the two guards surrounded the 20 prisoners, and Hank ordered them into columns of four, warned them that they would be shot if they tried to escape, and reminded them that even if they did escape, the area was far from Union lines with many Confederate forces in the vicinity. They would never make it to safety if they tried to escape. Garrett and one of the other guards were assigned to go with Hank, and the small procession finally moved north, away from the courtyard.

Garrett marched on the left of the procession, the other Confederate on the right. Hank followed behind the Union soldiers and carefully watched the two guards, sizing them up. Hank had hoped for small guards. That attribute didn't fit Garrett who was of medium height with a powerful build. It would be difficult to restrain him. Hank already knew Garrett was savvy. It was clear Garrett thought the corporal wrong to release the prisoners, and he questioned Hank's authority. As they marched in the thickening darkness, Garrett looked alert. The second guard was small and seemed little interested in where he was going or why. The prisoners were animated. Marching from the courthouse, the column climbed a steep hill, heading in the direction of the Valley Turnpike.

Within a few blocks, Garrett had become worried that the prisoners would try to escape as it became darker. Confused by the direction of the march, he called a halt and carefully came back to Hank to discuss the situation. Hank was short with him, responding that they could easily keep the prisoners under control until they got outside the town. Perhaps Garrett wasn't up to the task, he suggested.

"We need more guards in the dark!" Garrett said.

Hank responded with displeasure in his voice. "I am carrying out my orders. I'd hoped the corporal would have given me men I could count on."

Hank's tone didn't intimidate Garrett. He persisted, questioning the northward march.

"North?" Hank responded genuinely confused.

"We're marching north! You don't know we are marching north! What kind of imbecile are you. This is inane: a private commandeering Union prisoners. I thought we were going to the railroad tracks . . . to the east."

Hank wanted to hit him, but any commotion among the guards and the prisoners would take off on their own and that would be disastrous for the lot of them. He had to keep the situation under control. "Of course," Hank said in a relaxed tone, trying to defuse Garrett's impatience. "Your confusion's understandable . . . very understandable."

Garrett waited for further enlightenment, but Hank was silent, trying to think of a viable explanation. Garrett demanded, "Are you going to explain it to me? Why are we going north? If you don't, I'll turn these prisoners right around and take them back to the corporal. You can explain it to him . . . and the captain."

Hank looked at him and said firmly, "Those are my orders. We turn east outside town. It will be clear to you once we get outside of town. If all is as planned, we may be able to release you at that point. I didn't want to mention it earlier. When we get north of the city, it will be clear . . . and much easier to control the prisoners . . . fewer interruptions. It will be obvious to you when we get north of the city."

Garrett was not ready to give up, "You expect additional guards north of town?"

Hank was brusque in his response, "We are at risk here. I've been patient with you long enough. We must be on our way. Yes," Hank liked Garrett's idea, "we will have new guards somewhere north of the city."

Garrett returned hesitantly to his position on the left of the prisoners and the party moved forward at a quicker pace. It marched out of town, past its outskirts and past a tollhouse on the turnpike. Hank could see

Garrett's head in the moonlight looking anxiously forward, watching for replacement guards.

When the soldiers were well beyond the tollgate, Hank halted them and commanded they sit on the ground. It was dark, though the moon was bright enough to cast shadows. He called out to the prisoners, "We're making some changes here. I'm expecting a change of the guard shortly. New ones . . . more guards. We'll wait here. Any man who attempts to escape while we wait will be shot."

Hank called to the second guard, cautioning him to watch the prisoners closely. Hank approached Garrett.

"Do you have a pistol?" Hank asked in an urgent whisper as he approached.

"No."

"Oh, I had hoped you had. I'm a bit nervous. We should have already met our men. I don't know what's happened. Another gun would have come in handy. There are just too many prisoners."

Garrett was angry. Hank could hear it in his voice: "We should march them back to town. We can't control them out here in the dark. There are too many of them . . . and too few of us. They could easily overwhelm us or slip away one by one."

"Perhaps you're right." Hank was silent for a moment, then answered definitively, "Garrett, you are right! We can't go farther under these circumstances. Guards were to meet us. They aren't here. They can't expect us to go on. We'll turn around."

Garrett didn't say more. He waited for instructions from Hank. Hank was busily devising his next move. Beyond writing the note, stealing the musket and rescuing the prisoners from the courtyard, he had never developed a plan. He said, "Let's turn the prisoners around. You watch them . . . most carefully. I'll let the other guard know what we plan to do."

"At last," Garrett said with clear relief in his voice.

Even while sitting, the prisoners were showing energy and talking in murmurs. This was their opportunity to escape. Hank walked around the prisoners. He could feel an escape coming. They couldn't revolt . . . not now . . . not before he had everything in hand. Just a few more minutes. An escape would put him and the prisoners at greater risk. He stopped to explain the new plan to the second guard. As an apparent afterthought, he added, "Oh, do you have a pistol?"

"No."

"That's too bad. I had hoped we would have more weapons." Relieved the guards only weapons were their rifle muskets, Hank ordered the prisoners to stand and face about. They rose noisily, complaining.

Hank stepped close to the guard and raised his own pistol, shoving it gently into the guard's side. He smiled, although in the dark the guard couldn't see it. "Put down your musket! Don't make a sound."

With the commotion of the men rising to their feet, Garrett couldn't hear or see what Hank had done.

The guard nervously lowered his musket to the ground. The closest prisoners could see what had happened and word spread quickly among the prisoners. To Hank's consternation, they quickly quieted, waiting to see what the change would bring.

Without a word, Hank pulled a prisoner from the line and roughly moved the guard into his place. The prisoner took the former position of the guard.

Garret was increasingly nervous. He was especially attentive. He had noticed the prisoners' change in demeanor, had heard the shuffle as Hank had shoved the guard among the prisoners.

The prisoners were beginning to understand Hank's intentions and attempted to cover his actions with the hum of conversation.

Hank moved quickly behind the prisoners and approached Garrett. Hank still carried the pistol in his hand and Garrett caught a glimpse of it in the moonlight. Garrett shifted his musket to point at Hank.

"What's happening?" Garrett called to Hank.

Hank answered cheerfully, "It's a changing of the guard . . . I promised you. They're here, Garrett . . . the new guards. I don't want to shoot you, but I will if I have to. Lay your musket on the ground."

Garrett stood rigidly. "I'm not putting my gun down. I can shoot you as easily as you can shoot me."

"Put it on the ground, Garrett! I'll have to shoot you. I don't want to do that. Even if you shoot me, you'll be dead. If not by me, than by one of these other patriots. You can't want to die like that."

Garrett slowly, haltingly, lowered the rifle to the ground, and Hank directed two of the prisoners to pick up his gun and hold him. As the two Union soldiers moved toward Garrett, he broke into a run. He was off the turnpike quickly and well across an adjacent field. The two soldiers ran after him. A third Union soldier followed. The remaining former prisoners were silent.

They forced the remaining Confederate onto the ground and held him at bayonet point with his own musket. Every man listened for clues of the chase. Each of them realized their chances for a successful escape dimmed if Garrett escaped and alerted Confederate authorities. The minutes went by slowly with no sign of Garrett or the three Union soldiers.

Hank had planned to return to Staunton that night and catch the stage on which he'd already reserved a seat. He intended to give much of the money he'd made off Cole's horse to the escapees to help them get to Union lines. However, if Garrett escaped . . . or alerted the neighborhood, he wouldn't be able to go back to Staunton. He would have to travel with these soldiers, and there would be little hope for any of them.

Long minutes passed: five, 10. The soldiers began talking among themselves. Hank could hear them. They were questioning why they waited, talked of making a run for it, every man for himself. Hank pictured a Confederate manhunt tracking down all 21 of them. "Hurry! Hurry! Bring him back," he said under his breath.

The murmuring was getting too loud and Hank ordered the men to be silent. They quieted . . . just briefly. Soon they were talking as loudly as before.

Hank was ready to give up. If these men ran, he would have to run, too. At least he had money. Nearly 15 minutes passed.

"What's that?" one of the former prisoners called out.

"Shhh," Hank commanded.

The men listened intensely. It was a rustle from the field beside the road. It grew louder. Two Union soldiers emerged from the field, carrying an apparently unconscious Garrett. The third soldier followed them onto the pike. A collective exhale greeted the returning men.

Hank became animated. He led the group off the road and into a field. He outlined his plan to the soldiers, directing them to travel west into the Allegheny Mountains. He gave them charge of the two Confederates and captured muskets, divided his money among them and bid them good-bye.

There was no officer among the men, so they elected a leader. To Hank's consternation, the new leader refused to accept Hank's plan, deciding instead to march audaciously down the Valley Turnpike. He directed two of the men to don the Confederate uniforms of the two guards. Hank argued against their plan: It would be much safer if they made their way through the mountains to the west. He pointed out that none of them would fit into the smaller guard's clothes. But his arguments didn't sway the men.

One of the men quickly stripped Garrett who lay, still unconscious, on the ground. A second Union man, whose shirt and pants were nondescript, took the hat and accouterments from the second guard. The men worked quickly and were soon in order to march. Two former prisoners held the stocky Garrett, now sloppily dressed in Federal attire, between them. The men warmly thanked Hank, quickly bid him adieu and began their long march down the valley's main thoroughfare.

Hank watched them march till they were out of sight. He couldn't believe what he'd done, and relief overpowered him now that it was over. He was a hero . . . a tired hero. He staggered back to Staunton and his hotel room where he collapsed for a good night's sleep.

Chapter 23
October 1862, Staunton, Virginia

At the last possible moment the next morning, Hank boarded the stage coach. He was particularly cautious, avoiding being seen by anyone as he took the few steps from the hotel to the stage. The day was beautiful, and he was tempted to ride on the top of the coach to enjoy the fall weather. But anonymity seemed the wise course, and he elected instead to ride in the obscurity of the inside compartment. Two boys did ride on top of the coach, and when he entered the coach itself, Hank found three other passengers already there. All three men seemed to be traveling north, having completed their respective business in Staunton. There was ample room for the four inside passengers. Hank had seen as many as 12 people ride inside such coaches before the war and was grateful there were few passengers for this portion of the trip.

He immediately sat in the open corner seat in the coach's right front, leaning his head against the side of the vehicle and closing his eyes. The flaps of the coach windows were open, having been rolled up, and as the stage pulled away from the hotel, the cool breeze flowed freely across the interior. Hank listened to the clatter of the horse shoes against the macadamized road surface.

While the sounds of the horses lulled him, he involuntarily eavesdropped on the conversation of his three traveling companions. The three men seemed to know each other and conversed freely about transactions of cotton, salt, sugar and coffee. Hank didn't listen carefully with the vague feeling they were speculators. He found it interesting they would talk so openly of the money they were making on shortages in the South. He relaxed. These were not men who would challenge his credentials. Even if they did find out his Union-loyal identity, it was more likely they would ask him to smuggle goods across the lines than turn him over to Confederate authorities. He fell asleep.

After a while, Hank awoke, opened his eyes and watched the passing terrain. He hoped the army was still in Sharpsburg and wondered what George and Nathaniel were doing. He tried to imagine what the widow was doing at that moment, but couldn't remember what he had decided she looked like and fell asleep again. When he awoke it was to the laughter of his three fellow travelers, and with his eyes still closed, he listened to their conversation.

The man across from Hank was speaking. ". . . plenty to choose from now, and if the war goes on much longer, I think you'll be able to have any one you want in the entire state. Why already in Staunton—and the same is true in nearly any town in the valley—such a selection . . . quite a handful are available. They're all in need . . . either of money or affection. It's easy pickin's now for the right offer. Wouldn't you agree, Ben?"

The man next to Hank responded, so Hank presumed him to be Ben. "Yes, there's no doubt. If I were in your shoes, I would take a good look around and find just the right one. I wouldn't choose one that comes too cheap or easy. There are a select few that come with money—and lots of it—money that could be yours. Those are the ones I'd choose from. I personally, would court one in Staunton, met her before her husband died. She has everything you could want."

Hank perked up at this conversation that he found much more interesting than salt and sugar, but kept his eyes closed, hoping not to interfere with the conversation flow.

Ben continued. "Why she was barely married. There are no children. Her husband—his will—left her everything . . . everything! Amazing really! Must have had great faith in the girl. He left her everything, free and simple. She got his entire estate when he died, and she can do with it what she likes . . . every bit of it. Unwise if you ask me. Women need to be protected. Money needs to be protected. She's got land . . . slaves . . . money. If a man worked it just right, it would all come with her to the holy state of matrimony; it would all be his in the law, if he worked it just right. What more could an honorable gentleman want?"

Under normal circumstances, Hank would have taken offense at the way these travelers discussed this woman, whoever she was, but he was so ravenously drawing a mental image of his own widow that it never occurred to him to take offense.

The first traveler was speaking again, "Lothario, may I call you that?" The three men laughed again. "Lothario, you have but to ask and the fruit of that tree will fall gently into your palm."

The third passenger, the man Hank presumed to be
Lothario, responded reflectively. "I've never met her,
but I have heard that she is a lovely woman. Money as
well then. That's an attractive thought. An attractive
woman."

Ben said, "I don't believe you'll find a better girl. I
can't imagine she'll grieve for long. She got married
just before he went to the war. No wonder they have
no children. How bad can she feel? Wait a month, and
she'll be available for courting on the sly . . . at least
for the right man. Six months . . . a year . . . she can be
yours. I'm sure she looks elegant in black. Wouldn't
you expect so, Matthew?"

The first man who had spoken as Hank awakened,
Matthew, answered in mock lofty tones, "She is divine.
An angel set here on earth to tempt mankind. You cannot but see her," he lowered his voice to a conspirato-
rial aside, "and know of her money and connections,"
he raised his voice again to his lofty tones "without
wanting to share sacred marital bliss with her."

The three men laughed.

"Yes," Ben continued, "she may be the blessing of a
lifetime."

Matthew added speaking directly to Lothario, "If I
were not a married man, you'd have to fight me for
her."

"Me, too," Ben said looking at the third traveler.
"But our bad luck is your good fortune. If things were
different, we could make it difficult for you. We'd be
sitting right at her ear whispering just a bit about how
many hearts you've broken, how much money you have
extracted from each broken heart. Why, I'd even tell

her in how many towns you're no longer welcome . . . but still wanted! But my dear friend, you don't have to worry about us. And here's my best counsel for you: Wait a week or two; not much longer. Start calling on her. Make an offer to assist her in any way. Visit her often. How often should he visit her at the beginning, Matthew?"

"Every fortnight in the beginning would be good. Not too much. You don't want her to suspect anything. Don't give her many gifts, but do look for clues . . . clues about what she needs, what she wants. Arrange it for her. Just a thoughtful new friend in a most diffi-cult time . . . ."

Ben cut in. "Yes, just a thoughtful new friend. You've heard of her husband's bravery, want to ensure that the wife of a hero of our revolution . . . ."

Matthew interrupted, "Yes. Yes. Do use the word revolution. They all like that. You're just there to honor a nation's hero."

Ben added, "Whatever you do, don't comment on her beauty for the first four or five visits."

"Nor on her money," Matthew contributed, and the trio laughed again.

Hank had finished dreaming about his widow and was growing weary of the cynicism of his fellow trav-elers. He opened his eyes, hoping they would end the discussion.

Matthew, a red-haired, balding man with a happy, open face, saw his eyes open and said, "Ah, at last . . . our young hero awakens. You are a soldier, are you not?"

Hank looked at him and nodded politely.

"Just as we thought. Ben said you were probably just with our General Jackson," he tilted his head as to make an aside, "perhaps wounded . . . now returning to the front. Could that be it? What sacrifices you young men make."

Hank considered the three coach riders. Each appeared to be in his mid to late twenties, the same age as many of the men in Hank's regiment and just slightly older than Hank. He was angry at being called "young man" by them, but he attempted to hide his aversion as he responded with his parole story. "I'm paroled. Going home."

"Paroled? You were a prisoner, then? That must have been horrible," Ben, with thick, dark hair, bushy eyebrows and brown eyes, interjected in a forced voice. "But you are well? We want our brave young men to be taken care of."

"As well as can be expected."

"I understand we've had some terrible fighting, but you boys stand up to the invaders like the brigands they are, like the paladins you are. You make our young nation proud."

Hank simply responded, "Thank you."

"No," Matthew was speaking again. "It is we, the citizens of our young nation, that are grateful. The flower of our youth sacrificing for such a noble cause. How can we show our gratitude? We—the three of us—are anxious to get in the fray . . . as they say. But instead they leave us to travel this valley working hard to supply the army with what you soldiers—and others—need. It's so little that we do compared to your great sacrifice. I only wish . . . I wish there was more we could do."

Hank laughed inside at how true the man's statement was if his speculating was considered from Hank's Union position. He responded respectfully. "You do a great service to our effort. May the Lord continue to bless you as you work for our great army . . . nation . . . and cause."

Matthew nodded his head, lips pressed tightly together. "Your prayers, young man, are most welcome."

Lothario, seemingly taller than his companions, with blond hair, blue, penetrating eyes, and a neatly trimmed beard, had listened silently to the farcical exchanges and now waded into the conversation, "And where are you from?"

"Down valley."

"Have family there?"

"Yes."

"And I'll bet," Matthew chimed in, "I'll just bet that you've got other brothers serving in the war. Ben, I can tell these things. This is a family making real sacrifices for the cause."

Hank thought the joke old. But they clearly didn't expect him to be able to tell farce from reality, so he responded as enthusiastically as he could, "Several brothers."

"And you're the oldest, aren't you? I can always tell these things, Ben . . . I can always tell these things," Matthew said.

With a straight face Hank responded, "I am most sorry, sir. You are mistaken this time. I'm not the oldest. My older brother . . . he's a mite older than I am.

Born before me, you understand . . . but only a few years earlier."

"Yes." Matthew continued the charade, rubbing his chin with his forefinger and thumb, "Yes, that would make him older than you. You are correct."

Hank spoke up again, more eagerly than before, "Yes, I am sorry that I have had to disagree with you on that point. But don't be upset with yourself. I am pleased to say that you are right . . . in one way."

"In which way is that, my boy?"

"My younger brother . . . he ain't as old as I am. I was born before he was. So of the two of us, I am the oldest. You were right all along." Saying "ain't" felt unnatural to Hank, but he thought they would expect him to use it.

The three men could hardly contain their merriment at Hank's apparent stupidity, but dared not respond for fear of laughing. All three looked out their respective windows, lips quivering, holding back smiles.

They rode along silently for a while until Ben could control himself. "So young man, have you killed many Yanks?"

Hank, suppressing his own smile, responded, "Haven't killed any Yanks, not yet . . . least none I know of. Some of the boys in my regiment say with my shooting, it's more likely I've been killing Confederate soldiers. I asked them how many, but they couldn't tell me for sure. With all those muskets going off at once, it's real hard to see who you shot and who the man next to you shot. And when I've been in a battle, it wasn't just me and the man next to me . . . there's been a whole row of men. So it gets real hard to figure out who you shot.

Course, you can always tell who gets shot. That's easy! Them that gets shot get wounds . . . big wounds . . . little wounds. It don't matter what size, if they get shot, they all get wounds."

"That, young man, clears up something I've wondered about for many years. Let me be sure I understand: You say they get wounds when they've been shot? So simple. Marvelous! Just so simple. Ben, there's the answer . . . the answer to that most perplexing question," Matthew said.

Hank asked, "What perplexing question?"

"That difficult question of how does one know when someone is shot. You've answered most directly . . . most directly. You are marvelous."

Hank blurted out, "Another way to tell is when they're shooting at us, if the boy next to you goes down, you know he's the one that got shot. Course if you go down, maybe you don't know that you got shot . . . 'cause sometimes you're dead. If you're not dead, then you know you've been the one shot. So it's a lot easier telling who got shot on our side than who shot someone on the other side. I know you're going to ask me how I know all this . . . who taught me. You may not believe this, but I figured it out by myself—didn't need no one to tell me all this."

The three men were astonished. It was beyond their wildest dreams that they could have this much fun. Hank was even more stupid than they had believed possible, even for a soldier.

Ben commented, "With brave men like you, it shouldn't take long to win our independence. I bet you do just what your general tells you to do."

"I do. But sometimes that lieutenant . . . Oh! He tells me to go places that aren't very nice. I'm sorry, but I just can't obey those orders!"

"Are you speaking," Matthew said in a low, resonant voice, "of the place of eternal damnation?"

Hank looked surprised, letting his jaw drop and his eyes widen, "You must know my lieutenant! That is exactly the place he wants me to go. Course he doesn't call it that. He has a special word for it, comes right out of the Bible."

"Soldier, I do believe we know your lieutenant!" Matthew said.

"I thought you did," Hank responded with a sheepish smile.

"What's his name?" Ben asked.

Hank gave his lieutenant's name.

"This is amazing! We do know him! Don't we gentlemen?" Ben said. "What does he look like?"

Hank described him in precise, boring and long-drawn out detail, leaving out only the color of his uniform.

The three men looked at Hank in amazement. Hank imagined that each one was now busy considering how they could use a simple-minded soldier like this one in their business ventures.

Hank, bored with the game, leaned his head back and looked out the window. Each passenger was left to his own thoughts, but before conversation could resume, the coach arrived at an inn.

After quick refreshment, the passengers reentered the coach. The three men had worked out a plan to take advantage of this simple-minded soldier. Matthew started the explanation, "Private, there are other ways to help your country besides fighting."

Hank looked at him with humble anticipation, waiting for the coming revelation, then decided he no longer wanted to entertain his traveling companions. He spoke in the most innocent tone he could muster. "I know there are many ways to help the country, but none is better than fighting. And don't try to tell me anything's better. You can't fool me, I'm too smart for that. I know you men are probably on the way, right now, to the front to volunteer. I knew you were brave men the way you were talking with so much courage— the way you took such an interest in a lowly soldier such as myself. I welcome you to the ranks. I'll take you right to my lieutenant. Especially since you already know him. He'll know what to do with the likes of you," he paused and noted the nervous glances the men gave to one another. "Before you know it, you'll be right up there with the Minié balls flying around your heads. I can tell you're the brave sort . . . knew it right away. With you among the Confederate ranks, we'll rout the enemy within the month."

The men were uncomfortable. Hank now appeared mad as well as stupid, and madness frightened them. None of them responded, and they left Hank to soliloquize: "We'll be in Harrisonburg soon. Don't you worry. There'll be someone from the army there. I'll find a way for you to join. I won't leave your sides . . . not till you're all mustered in. You're going to love the army. We can even mess together!"

As Hank finished his sentence, he glanced out the window and saw his rescued Union soldiers resting at

the side of the road. He smiled to think they had made
it that far on the turnpike. He said a silent prayer asking that they get to safety, but didn't think to include
himself in the prayer.

In the meantime, Ben had decided to cool off Hank's
ardor a bit before they reached Harrisonburg. "Soldier."

"Yes, sir!" Hank barked back.

"Yes . . . yes," Ben said, nervously looking at his two
companions before venturing further. "Unfortunately, I
wish I could enlist, but I'm not fit to fight. I've . . . I've
tried before. They just won't let me join. I have to help
the cause in other ways."

"That don't make no sense to me. Why Robert How-
ard—he's in my regiment—he snuck past the doctors . .
. got enlisted. A good soldier, too . . . he was."

"He was?"

"He was a real good soldier, right up to our very
first battle."

"What happened at the first battle?" Matthew asked
having been drawn into the story.

"Robert didn't turn out too brave . . . not at the beginning. He tried to run away, but that lieutenant of
ours, he hit him right over the head with the hilt of his
sword. Ohheee! The blood come out. You should've
seen it—it come out all in a rush. It was everywhere . .
. just like someone shot him with a ball. Oh that Robert, he fell down grabbing his head. I saw it all, every
bit of it. The sword, the blood, the falling, but then I
had to charge. I heard he was whimpering the whole
time the rest of us were charging that infernal enemy.
The Doc—he tries hard—did his best to help him after

the battle. He did pretty much stop the blood, but there was a big gash on Robert's head. You should have seen it . . . a big gash. Old Robert, he was mighty strange after that. Couldn't even remember his name some of the time. But the Doc sure fixed his courage. He was the bravest man in the regiment from then on . . . well, for a while . . . at least. He sure was brave. Right at the next battle he charged the enemy like the devil. They say he was the first one to fall. He didn't ever retreat after that. That's a true story. All this happened right here in this valley. So you can see you can do a lot of fighting for the country no matter what the doctors say. With the right lieutenant to motivate you, like ours did with Robert, you can be real brave . . . just like Robert. Even if those old saw-bones say you can't fight, they don't know. If Robert can fight . . . just about anyone can fight. I'm sure you can join and help the Confederate cause just as much as me . . . or Robert. My lieutenant's going to like you men. You'll be some of his favorites. And don't you worry none, I'll be there with you. We'll mess together. We'll be friends! We'll mess together!"

Lothario, tired of Hank's idiotic prattle, spoke up, anger in his voice and eyes, and with clenched fists at his sides, "That's an interesting story, young man. I think you will do well to take Robert's example and be the first to charge the Yanks next time you see them. We'll know then whether you're brave or not."

Hank responded in an earnest, plaintive tone, "Oh, sir, I intend to get to the Yanks as fast as I can. You can be sure of that. You can count on me to do just that. I was just hoping I could take the three of you with me."

Lothario responded, "I won't be going with you, but I'll be glad to help you along the way anytime I can."

Matthew seeing their acquaintance's anger, refrained from teasing Hank further and said, "Don't worry about our soldier here. I do believe he will meet up with his destiny real soon. No need to worry about that."

Lothario's face was red. He glared menacingly at Hank and said, "He may as well meet his destiny here . . . now."

Lothario's quick, intense anger amazed Hank, and he wondered what exactly he had said that so infuriated the man. Hank felt a sudden hatred for him, an emotion he hadn't felt for a long time.

Ben spoke to soothe his friend. "Have you worked out your plan for our widow?"

The question distracted Lothario, and he rested the back of his head against the coach wall, smiled and said, While the two of you talked incessantly, I came up with a plan."

When the coach arrived at Harrisonburg, Hank's three traveling companions ignored him, disappearing quickly into the streets. Hank was glad to see them go and took pleasure in the hope he would never see them again.

Hank had decided to visit his family. He intended to ride the coach all the way to Woodstock, but elected to rest overnight at Harrisonburg. He needed another day to prepare himself to see them. However, once off the stage, he became bored and regretted the decision to delay his travel. He was so close—just 30 miles from Woodstock . . . from home. All at once, he wanted to get there as soon as possible.

Chapter 24
October 1862, Harrisonburg, Virginia

*H*ank passed the late afternoon and evening walking Harrisonburg streets.

"Wasn't it Mr. Craig?"

Hank had been walking, looking at the ground ahead of him, thinking about seeing his family again when he heard the words, and they startled him. He halted, looking toward the questioner. He knew him, but couldn't place him. He struggled to remember. "I do know you from somewhere, don't I?" Hank responded, slightly nervous at being recognized.

"Yes, we met several years ago . . . before the war. I remember it distinctly."

Hank still couldn't recall who he was. He stared hard at the soldier who addressed him trying to remember. He was a Confederate officer, abnormally thin, with light hair that curled slightly. He sported a mustache, and one arm rested across his chest in a sling. He was noticeably pale and sat on a bench in front of an inn. He did not rise to meet Hank.

"We met at the Richman's . . . in Winchester." The soldier smiled pleasantly at Hank. "I'll never forget that day . . . or that braggart from the VMI. Do you remember him? Quite entertaining, really."

Hank could feel muscles in his shoulders tighten and rise with stress, and he consciously tried to lower them. This officer was about to test Hank's role as a Confederate soldier to the limit. The risk of being discovered so engrossed his mind that Hank forgot his humiliation of that afternoon in Winchester. His mind was busy cautioning him, warning him to affect nonchalance. "Oh, yes. It's actually Gragg . . . Hank Gragg. But I'm sorry, I've forgotten your name."

"Gragg? That's right . . . Hank Gragg. I'm Richard Lewis. I'm delighted to see someone . . . anyone . . . who I knew before this war began." He stopped, laughed softly, and said, "As I recall the day, neither you nor I ever expected a war or that we'd be in it, or that Virginia would ever secede. Now, here we are . . . proven wrong. We were naive, Hank. Naive."

"You're injured, Captain."

"Don't call me captain, Hank! My pleasure is in seeing someone who knows me as something other than captain . . . or soldier. I relish such moments . . . every moment before this madness began. They have each become precious to me."

"I will call you Richard then."

"Good. That will suit me."

"But you are wounded."

"I am, but this is nothing to worry about. Shot at Sharpsburg, been recuperating in Winchester for several weeks. I'm well enough to travel now, so they put me in a coach and they're sending me to Richmond. I got worn out on the ride from Winchester . . . just from Winchester. So I've put off the rest of the trip, waiting for the next coach. I'm going to Staunton tomorrow, then by train to Richmond."

"Shot in the arm?"

"Shoulder actually . . . still hurts, but they've given me pills to take. When it gets too bad, I take them. They make everything seem just a little bit better." They were both silent, but eventually the captain forced the conversation along. "Neither of us, I don't believe, ever expected to be in the Confederacy . . . at least not on that day at dear, sweet Betsy's."

Hank smiled at the irony of the statement.

"Sit down for a little while?" the captain said.

Hank said as calmly as he could, "I'd like that."

"You going to Richmond, too?"

"Me? No, I'm going the other direction . . . home."

"Home? Winchester?"

"Woodstock."

"You're close then."

"I'll be there tomorrow."

"Hank, you in the Second Infantry?"

Hank felt a familiar tightness in his throat. "No, I'm with Hood."

"You were at Sharpsburg then, too?"

"We were both there."

"That was a fierce battle, wasn't it? Never saw anything like it. For a while I thought those Yankees were going to whip us, but you boys came on just in the nick of time. Otherwise, I think our lines would have broken." He chuckled softly. "They'd already broken. Only you stepping up at that moment saved us . . . and me . . . from annihilation. As it was, I was left on the field and wasn't picked up till the next morning. If it weren't for you . . . and the rest of Hood's men, I'd be a prisoner somewhere up north . . . or worse."

"I was captured."

"You, captured?"

"In one of our retreats, I was overtaken. Death or capture were the choices."

"You chose correctly, Hank. You chose correctly. But how then do you come to sit on this bench with me . . . south of any Northern prison camp I've heard about? Did you escape? I've heard of such things. Or were you already exchanged?"

"I was lucky, I guess. I was captured with just a small group of men. The Union officer didn't want to deal with us. They kept us around a few days, and then they gave me my parole; told me to go home till I was exchanged. So that's what I'm doing. Hope to be exchanged soon."

"I've heard of men who think they can't accept a parole, not the brave thing to do. They have to go to prison to await exchange. It's the only honorable way. But that's foolishness." Richard breathed heavily, clearly worn out by so much conversation.

At that moment 18 Federal soldiers guarded by two Confederate guards marched into sight.

Richard watched the procession. "It would be easy to escape under such circumstances, with just two guards. But they don't. Just look at them . . . marching orderly along. It leaves one with the impression that Northern soldiers just don't have the will that could ever defeat the Confederacy. But . . . you and I know differently, Hank. We were at Sharpsburg. We saw those men in the black hats. We saw them charge and fall, charge and fall . . . charge and fall. They were our match, Hank. They were our match that day."

The column of prisoners passed in front of Hank and Richard and one of the guards saluted the two men.

Richard called out to them, "Careful with those Yanks, better keep them under control. Shouldn't they be shackled?"

To Richard's and Hank's surprise, one of the prisoners yelled back, "We're just a bunch of pussy cats. No need to shackle us."

One of the guards yelled in an unnaturally heavy Southern accent for the prisoner to be silent.

Hank wondered what had happened to Garrett and the other Rebel guard.

Richard laughed, "If only you and I had faced that group in Maryland . . . I'd still have my shoulder . . . and you, you would still be with your regiment." He paused and the conversation lagged for several minutes. Richard broke the silence, "Hank . . . she got married, you know."

"Who?"

"Who'd she marry?"

"No, who got married?"

"Oh, I thought you'd know who I was talking about. Betsy got married. Betsy Richman, she got married." Richard was clearly at ease.

Hank felt an instant and deep sorrow at the news. He wanted to know the details: Who had she married? When? Why? Where was she now? But to save face he responded, sounding as disinterested as possible, "I didn't know that. Hope she's well."

"Don't think she is. Husband's dead. She's a widow. Lost her father . . . now her husband. Course that crazy mother of hers, she never even let Betsy mourn her father's death. That was strange . . . scandalous in Winchester for a while. But all of that's forgotten now."

Hank wanted to ask what Betsy was doing and how he could see her, but he only said, "That's too bad."

"Wasn't Betsy fond of you? Didn't you ask her to marry you? You didn't ask her mother; and the mother wouldn't approve? I hope I'm not offending you by all this talk. It's all blurry just now . . . not that any of it matters now. Not now. Nothing matters any more. We're losing everything, Hank."

"Certainly not the war," Hank responded simply, not having the liberty to take offense at the Captain's remarks.

"Not yet. We're not losing the war yet, but everything else. My slaves are gone. My house burned down. My mother's dead. They were refugees . . . my mother and father, and she died in Richmond. Father's still there, ailing now, too. My brothers are in the army . . . likely to die any day.

Hank responded, "Well at least the Yankees haven't occupied too much of the valley."

"They've occupied enough for me . . . seized my home. That's all that matters to me. They've taken my home: destroyed it. They'll take yours before it's over, Hank Gragg. They'll take it all."

Hank's mood was progressively deteriorating in Richard's company. He wanted to get away from him.

Both men watched the column of Union prisoners disappear and said nothing. Richard shifted in his seat, moaning softly. He slipped gently into sleep, and Hank quietly slid from the bench and walked to his hotel room.

Chapter 25
October 1862, Woodstock, Virginia

*T*he stage dropped Hank near his father's house, where he walked the short remaining distance to the farm. As he drew closer to the large, white farmhouse, his apprehension peaked. He hadn't slept well the night before, knowing he was coming home. Would they greet him with open arms . . . or reject him? He expected the latter.

From the road, he could see the two-story house and outbuildings. They appeared as they had when he left, seemingly untouched by the war. The garden in back still boasted fresh vegetables and the fields to the north of the house had been reaped. Not all the fields in sight had been planted, and Hank could see some crops had been destroyed before harvest. As he gazed at his childhood home, a wave of emotions threatened rational thought and controlled feelings. He sorrowed at Daniel's death. Daniel wouldn't greet him from the porch where three long years earlier he had futilely called Hank back. Hank expected his sisters to be there along with his mother and father—those whom he had caused the greatest sorrow and who, for all he knew, still thought him dead.

One sister—he couldn't tell which—worked feverishly at something on the porch, while two dogs chased each other not far from the house. Hank stepped off the road, and the sister, looking up, saw him. She stopped her rapid arm motion and watched him as he approached. The dogs seeing him began barking. They were charging, but slowed their pace and barked more aggressively as they closed the distance. He called them by name, and they responded, barking less. The dogs reached him and began smelling his pants and shoes, becoming increasingly animated. He leaned down, petting one at a time as he walked.

He was nearing the house now, and the girl somehow recognized him. She leaped across the porch toward the front door yelling, "Ma! Ma! It's Hank! It's Hank . . . Ma!" She hurried into the house, and Hank, before long, saw a silhouetted head appear briefly at a second story window. His sister returned quickly, running out the front door, down the steps, stopping at the bottom step. He now recognized her. It was Lucinda . . . Lucy . . . the youngest. She had changed since he had last seen her, and Hank was impressed with how much she had grown. Lucy watched him, still calling for their mother to come see Hank.

Hank wondered where Corny and his father were. He wanted to see them all now. He had forgotten that Corny was supposed to give him information for the Union army. If he had remembered it wouldn't have mattered. He didn't care about the Union army at that moment . . . not about Abraham Lincoln . . . saving the Union . . . ending slavery . . . fighting for the men of his regiment and brigade. He was briefly happier again than he had ever thought possible. In that moment, he forgot his fear. He was reborn a young boy—little Henry Gragg—son of a prosperous Woodstock farmer and his wife, with two sisters and two brothers. For just that minute, he was at home, he had never left, never traveled, never met Samuel Richman, never gone to Winchester, never met Betsy. He savored each remaining step to the house. Lucy waited at the porch for him as if tethered to it. She didn't seem to know what to make of Hank's sudden return, although he could see excitement in her features and her rapid, nervous movements as she shuffled back and forth on the bottom porch step.

As Hank reached Lucinda and put his arms around her, the door opened and Hank's mother, Margaret Gragg, emerged. Without hesitation, the short, stout woman with a round face and plain features descended the stairs and wrapped her arms around both of her children. No one said a word. Hank could see tears on his mother's face as he looked down at her and could hear his sister's soft cries. They hugged for a long time.

As the embrace ended, Lucy, who was 13 years old, began scolding him as if he were late for dinner, "Hank, where have you been? We've looked all over for you!"

Hank responded, his voice unsure, "I know you have."

His mother spoke her first words. "Henry, we're so glad you're home . . . that you're alive! Your father will be glad to see you."

"You are so dirty, Hank," Lucy continued her scolding. "Don't you ever bathe. Look at your clothes. It looks like you've been wearing them for a month of Sundays."

She continued chattering, asking question after question. Her queries were the same as those on their mother's mind: "Where have you been? Why didn't you write and tell us you were all right? Have you heard about the war? That looks like John's pistol." But his mother saved Hank from having to answer with a simple, "Of course he's heard about the war. He's a soldier. Give him a chance to clean up. Then he can answer you."

She turned to Hank. "You're hungry!" She held his hand tightly. "Why don't you clean up a bit. While you're doing that, we'll get you something to eat." She reached out and held Hank again. He felt as if he was an infant, and he nestled in his mother's embrace. The moment was strange to him, unnatural, so different than his life among soldiers and death. He lowered his head to her shoulder and sobbed uncontrollably.

Hank cleaned up quickly. Lucy brought him some of his own clothes, and he dressed in his old bedroom. He thought it odd that they had kept his room as it was when he left, that they still had his old clothes, and that they still fit. But in his eagerness to get downstairs, he didn't dwell on those thoughts.

When he came to the kitchen, both Lucy and his mother noted how much he had changed. His face was suntanned . . . hair creeping back from his forehead. As they examined him, Hank noticed for the first time how his mother had changed. She looked much older, heavier. Her dark hair had thick threads of white and her face deep creases. He wondered if he erroneously remembered her as young or had she aged so much since he left. Lucy, energetic, prattled continually. She was forward in her words, but shyness seemed to physically hold her back.

His mother invited him to sit at the table where a homemade meal waited for him. He couldn't believe his eyes: Fresh garden vegetables, white bread, soup, apple pie. He ate heartily while his mother and sister sat silently on either side taking pleasure in watching him.

As he ate, the front door opened and closed. Neither Lucy nor Margaret glanced or moved toward the hall. They remained totally transfixed on Hank as if he would disappear if they turned their heads even briefly. Hank turned his face toward the hall as his father came into the kitchen. His father stopped, stared— disbelief in his eyes. "Hank?"

Lucy answered for Hank. "Pa, it's Hank! He's come back!"

Still stunned Robert Gragg asked absentmindedly, "From where?" He was a tall, broad man, with thick brown hair cut short, and he moved to the table, lifted Hank from his seated position, hugged him tightly. "Oh, Hank. Are you an apparition? Are you real? Are you really here?" His father didn't cry, but the scene brought new tears to both mother and sister.

"Hank," his father said in a wavering voice. For a long time, the father held his son, then abruptly released his grip and stepped away. He said, "We all want to know where you've been." He spoke the sentence with deference not accusation. "But we have some things to tell you first." Hank's father took a seat at the other end of the rectangular table from Hank, while his mother and sister remained close on either side of the returned son. Hank was grateful to his father for allowing him to put off his confession for a little longer. As was his custom, his father was direct: "Hank, Daniel's dead." He spoke as if he were reading off a list of products to buy at the general store.

"I know."

"Cornelia's married."

"Corny married?"

"Last year. Married a boy from Beverly and moved up there. She's living there with his family now. He's union. They think it's safer up there for them. He joined the army. He was in western Virginia last we heard."

Hank couldn't believe it and laughed aloud.

His father looked at him strangely but said nothing.

"Pa, I have to tell you some things." He was ready. Over the next hour and a half, Hank recounted the last three years of his life. They listened with rapt attention, often expressing remorse that he hadn't come home—he would have always been welcome. They told him he should have just come home when he confessed his mortification at his awkward proposal to Betsy and her rejection, when he described his suffering as a farm laborer, when he recounted his joining the army. They laughed together only when he explained how he persuaded the army to send him to get information from his sister in Beverly.

"Hank, did you know Pa's for the Union?" Lucy eventually blurted out.

"Shhh. You're not to talk like that," her mother cautioned.

"Ma," Lucy complained, "Hank's Union, too. It's all right to tell him. He's family."

Her father rescued her. "You can tell Hank. But don't talk about that with anyone else, including John."

"John won't tell," the girl retorted.

"I know, but it upsets him," her father answered.

"There are others who are for the Union around here, Pa. You know that."

"There are, but it's best not to talk about it. There's already enough trouble between neighbors. The Laws, do you remember them, Hank? They had to go North. He was Union, and they kept on him. Destroyed his crops. Burned his barn. That was enough for him. He took his family to Ohio. Only reason we're left alone is because we have sons in the Confederate army. Everyone just assumes we're Southern sympathizers, and we just keep quiet about it."

"Who destroyed your crops then?" Hank asked.

"It doesn't matter what side you're on, Hank. When either army . . . or just cavalry comes through, they're like locust, destroying everything in their way. Doesn't matter what side they're on . . . or you're on . . . the result is the same."

Hank stayed at Woodstock two days. Both mornings he awoke in his own bed. It was so comfortable, so unreal. He would lay motionless, afraid to even shift his legs, afraid it was only a dream, afraid that at any moment rain would drip on his greasy, blackened face and awaken him to a camp of dirty, smelly soldiers and smoldering fires. Both nights he suffered a recurring dream about Antietam. Each time he woke from it, he found himself holding his breath, near tears. He would quickly remember where he was, take comfort in the thought, wrap his arms tighter around his pillow . . . drift off again.

In the dream, Hank marched with George Dyer at his side:

They heard skirmishers on their right. The lieutenant colonel ordered them to clear the skirmishers and the regiment responded, wheeling right and firing into the foe. The Rebs would fire back until all firing would in an instant stop. The Northern troops would be sitting on the same ground . . . cooking. Hank would start coffee and a vaguely familiar voice would call to him, "Someone's looking for you, Gragg." Skirmishers would start shooting again from their hiding place behind a rock ledge. Daniel, his brother, would appear as a 13 year old, seated across from him, wearing his farm clothes and ask him, "What are you doing here?"

Hank would respond, "Fighting Secesh. We're going to whip them."

Daniel's dress would become that of a Confederate general, and he would say, "Will you whip me, too?"

Hank would respond quickly, "Not you Daniel, not you." Daniel would be gone . . . breakfast over . . . and Hank would find himself charging the skirmishers. The skirmishers would flee. A Confederate general would fall in the retreat. Defying time and place, Hank would be in that moment over the fallen general. Looking down he would see in the uniform a boy's face, Dan-

iel's face, looking up with eyes glazed . . . dead. Daniel's pale, post-death lips would move and speak, "You whipped me, Hank."

Hank would turn to look for George. He would see a Union private dying on the field. Hank would be at his side. It was George, dead, his eyes staring into the sky. Hank would hear George's voice, but his lips wouldn't move, "You best join 'em Hank. They're your people. You never was one o' us . . . always one o' them."

Hank would instantly be on that farm near Gainesville . . . holding the button he had taken from Captain Henderson. The battle would be raging and Hank would walk between the lines without harm. He would look for Daniel, for Daniel's body, but not find it.

Then Hank would awaken. He tried not to think of the dream during the day.

Early the third morning, the day Hank left, Robert took him aside and told him how proud he was that Hank fought for the Union. As his father spoke, guilt lifted from Hank's shoulders.

Chapter 26

October 1862, Northern Shenandoah Valley,
Virginia

*S*hortly thereafter Hank departed for Sharpsburg on foot, with haversack filled with food from his mother. Robert offered Hank a horse to get back to Union lines, but Hank declined saying he would be fine on foot. Over the protests of his father, Hank also left behind John's pistol. Hank walked back roads and through rolling fields. The beautiful countryside regenerated his love for the valley, and he hoped to come home . . . here . . . when the war was over. He enjoyed his time alone, reliving priceless moments of the past two weeks. He was reconciled with the world and reconciliation brought a new sense of freedom. Freedom. It tasted good. He had seen his family, and they still loved him. He had delivered a copy of the letter to the widow. He hadn't met her, but it didn't matter for the moment because he had family again. All was well. If he were killed now, he would be square with the world, but life was pleasing, so promising, and he desperately wanted to live.

But still topping the list as his most important reason for living was the woman. He didn't know her, had only heard from Mr. Porter how beautiful she was and might not ever see her. But that didn't keep him from a rapidly growing infatuation for her. She must be beautiful, charming. The captain had written it. Mr. Porter had verified it. He only wished he knew her—that she knew him—that he at least had seen her in Staunton. He never dwelt on the thought it might be easier to love an imagined woman than to love an existent being who thought and acted according to her own will.

Hank hoped the war would end soon; no more loss of life in the valley, no more Daniels . . . please. He remembered his many friends in the valley. But Hank was no longer a Shenandoah Valley boy. He had seen the push of the nation and its people westward and had witnessed regions and people beyond Virginia's borders. He was still a Southerner, but there was more to him than that sole attribute.

He had become a Union man. The states, rebelling and loyal, belonged united. He was going to do what he could to make sure they stayed together. Born with a Virginia pedigree, he now thought of himself as American, but "American" and "Virginian" could no longer be separated.

He felt himself in fraternity with other Virginians who had chosen the Union. As he walked across the fields under a cool October sun, he considered such men. Old Winfield Scott, the great Mexican War hero, had directed Union forces in the early days of the current struggle. Hank deemed himself a friend of General Scott.

He thought about a general in the West—George Thomas. From aristocratic tidewater Virginia, Thomas

had chosen the Union. Hank had heard that Thomas'
men loved and respected him, claiming for him the
demeanor of General George Washington. Like
Washington, General Thomas had chosen the Union
over states' rights. Common soldier Hank Gragg felt a
newly developed affinity with General Thomas . . . and
with General Washington.

He thought of other men, closer to him, who had
Virginian roots, yet fought for the North. Isaac May,
who left Virginia as a young man to migrate to
Indiana—a major in the 19th until his death shortly
after Second Bull Run; General Reno of the 9th Corps
who died at South Mountain; and Captain Williams of
Company K. They all had Virginia blood and Northern
allegiance.

As he mentally manufactured these bonds with
Union men of Virginia, his mind unconsciously edited
his own memories to fit his newly born philosophy.
Now he understood: he had chosen to fight for the
Union and to free the slaves from the beginning. It was
a conscious choice, and his father was proud of that
choice. Hadn't he left Virginia in 1859 because he had
seen the rebellion coming? Surely that was the case.
Hadn't he left on the very day he heard of John
Brown's raid?

Hank also remembered Naomi. He was fond of the
woman. He relived in his mind her kindness in feeding
him and helping him escape. Naomi's nurturing act at
that moment of crisis had created a familial bond in
Hank's mind. He now felt he had known her his entire
life, that at some point she had been his mother, a

beloved aunt, a grandmother. She, too, was for the Union, and he wanted to see her again.

The sound of horse hooves pounding at a distance on the road caught Hank's attention. Why were they running the horses so hard? He ran to get as close as he could and hid at a hilltop that overlooked the road. Peering over the hill, he saw two horsemen pass, riding hard, periodically looking backward. They were clearly evading someone. Within seconds three more horsemen appeared. His stomach knotted. It was Cole. Why had he left John's pistol behind? Why didn't he take his father's horse? He'd be in Maryland by now. He knew the answers: Long-carried burdens had been relieved, and he could no longer fathom that he was still in danger, but he had been mistaken. Cole and his men rode by quickly.

With the danger passed, Hank renewed his trek and began thinking of excuses he could use to explain not seeing Corny. He could say she was dead. That was it. She was dead, died before he got to Beverly. Of what? Childbirth? That would leave a husband for whom they could search. The shakes? Probably weren't swamps near Beverly. Measles? Consumption? The Virginia quickstep? None of them would do. Smallpox! Smallpox would be a good way for her to die. Even with the vaccine, many were dying of it. They'd never verify it. If they tried they would never find a Cornelia Gragg in Beverly. Smallpox was common enough and sympathetic people would hesitate to probe because of his sorrow. It was a safe story. He would use it. Hank again felt guilt for his deception. He was tired of lying and wished he had never begun. He looked forward to a time when he could stop—hopefully soon.

Fully engrossed in thought, Hank was startled by a familiar and frightening voice. "Well, Madison, looks like we once again got ourselves a Gragg."

Hank stopped, his eyes closed, and he shook his head slowly in small, barely visible movements. They had conquered him.

"Mr. Gragg. May I call you that, sir? We thought we'd lost you, and now here you are, come right back to us. Different clothes, same boy and without our horses—horses you stole. Looks like a deserter to me now more than ever dressed in those farmer clothes. Don't you think, Madison?"

"A horse thief and spy," answered Madison. "He's come to find out what we's doing and report it to the Yanks. He's on his way right now to Washington to tell ole Abe."

Madison's words and Cole's voice provoked an unexpected vivid memory. Horse thief?

It was night. Hank, 14 at the time, rode carefully along the turnpike on his way to Winchester. The next week he was returning to school there. His parents had begged him to wait till morning to leave, but Hank had insisted on leaving that evening. As he rode, he heard commotion ahead on the turnpike. He cautiously sped his horse, and its hooves clattered on the roadway. Ahead, it sounded like a struggle, the noise growing louder, till he heard a man call out. "Leave him! Someone's coming! I've got his horse!" Horse thief! He remembered the voice now . . . oddly high and nasal . . . Cole's voice. It had been Cole that night. Cole and another man. They'd badly beaten a traveler on the road, perhaps intending to kill him for his money. They'd already taken his horse, but Hank interrupted the attack. He had saved Samuel Richman. He still remembered riding that night, Samuel leaning heavily against his back. Hank had worried he would fall and rode cautiously, slowly. He intended to take him to Winchester, but soon was convinced he had to do something to help the man immediately. When he saw the pole at the tollhouse lowered across the road, he decided he would count on the hospitality of the tollhouse family to care for the man. The tollgate keeper and his wife responded quickly and summoned a doctor. Cole was the horse thief! He had attacked Samuel!

Hank turned slowly to see Cole, Madison and a third rider on horseback not 10 yards from him. They must have seen his head silhouetted above the ridge and circled back silently to see who it was. Hank felt an urge to run and responding to it moved as fast as he could across the clearing. He had no idea where he was going, but it was his only chance to survive. The men laughed behind him. Eventually voices talking and horses in pursuit joined the laughter. As the horses approached, he heard Cole call to his friends, "Shall we shoot his leg?"

A shot was fired. Hank felt it pass close to his left leg. He ran faster. The men still laughed. Again the horses were running. He heard another shot and the whine of the bullet near him. Hank ran now like a wild animal, arms waving in all directions as he exerted every possible movement to speed his run. He heard a third shot . . . anticipated pain, but none came. He kept running. He was winded and on the verge of collapse when he felt a blow to the back of his head as one of the riders hit him as he rode by. Hank tumbled to the ground. He tried to rise to run again, this time in the opposite direction, but a blow came quickly to his back. He fell again face down, and slowly rolled over. He looked up at the riders from where he sprawled. His head ached. They were still laughing.

Cole spoke mockingly, "I sent your brother after you, but he never come back. I suspect he never found you. So we're lucky to have you again so we can hold a big reunion. Course we ain't gunna call no pretended brother this time. You're not gunna escape this time. You won't be alive come nightfall. Traitor or spy, Gragg or not, you are a horse thief . . . and a dead man."

"Why don't we just shoot him here?" Madison asked. "It'd be much easier."

"Easier, but not as fun," Cole responded with a wide grin across his bearded face. "We'll take him to the mountain. We'll hang him there, listen to him choke, squeeze life out of 'im. Madison, you ride with 'im!"

Seconds later, with hands again tied, Hank was behind Madison in his saddle. The horsemen were talking among themselves, settling arrangements before riding off. No one spoke to Hank. The running and the blows to the head and back had worn him out, and he was limp in the saddle, leaning forward to rest on Madison. The horses in unison bounded forward, and Hank, dizzied by the rapid acceleration, tightened his legs against the sides of the horse to maintain his balance.

Cole split from Madison and the other rider. Hank, Madison and the third rider headed southwest across the field until they met a road that went due south. They rode fast without speaking. After a few minutes, they turned onto another road. Hank knew the road. They were heading for Massanutten.

Eventually they slowed, turned off the road and headed into the forest up the side of the mountain. They climbed for 20 minutes before stopping in a camp hidden from below by trees and a rocky ledge. No one was there, but a fire still smoldered. Several tents were pitched. Wooden crates were placed around the camp, apparently serving as storage units, seats and tables. Madison dismounted and pulled Hank roughly from the horse. It occurred to Hank that this lair was safe from detection by either army.

The third rider rode off when Hank's feet touched the ground, and Madison led Hank to a tree. He tied him firmly to the trunk without saying a word. Hank's wrists were already hurting, and he couldn't take the silence any more. "Haven't we been through this before," he said flippantly.

Madison responded gruffly, "The end'll be different this time."

"What? Do you think Cole's going to get killed this time?"

Madison responded, "Cole's not dying. You is."

"Has anyone ever told you that you have a wit . . . a way with words?"

Madison moved quickly until he was close to Hank. He swung an open hand across Hank's face as he sputtered savagely, "Shut up!" Madison, saying no more, walked across the camp and lay down in one of the tents.

Hank was angry. His face hurt where Madison had slapped him, and he complained to himself of his plight. It wasn't fair to go through this again. He already escaped once. Why should they tie him up again? He'd already won this game. Bring on the next game, but don't ask him to play the same one over. Hank was at a loss, expecting Cole at any moment. The sound of a horse approaching with celerity made him nervous. He tried to turn his head toward the sound, but couldn't. He waited to see who it was. He jerked at the rope frantically, now frightened. The horse was close now. He pulled harder on the rope till it cut into his arm, and he strained his neck to see who it was. It was Cole, and Hank's heart sank.

Cole rode hard into the camp, stopped the horse with a powerful pull on the reins, and dismounted. He moved hastily to where Madison lay sleeping and shoved him hard with his foot. "Wake up, fool!"

Hank could not see or hear Madison's response, but within minutes the two men were standing side by side 20 yards from Hank. Cole carried a rifle, and he called out to Hank, "We're gunna take target practice, Mr. Gragg. Care to join us? What am I saying? Oh, course, you'll join us . . . just as you are."

Hank shifted his feet nervously.

Cole continued his monologue, "Did you think we were gunna use you for the target? Don't be foolish!

One shot would end the practice for us. No, you're not our target. That tree . . . the one you're tied to is the target."

Madison laughed.

Cole explained the simple rules, "If we shoot and hit the target, you're safe. Better pray we hit the target. Madison's gunna take the first shot. He's not real accurate, so that should make everything a little more excitin'. What do you think, Mr. Gragg?"

Hank was silent.

"Take your shot, Madison!"

Hank closed his eyes. He expected a bullet to hit an extremity at any time and stiffened for the blow. He heard the shot. The ball sailed by the tree and Hank. Hank opened his eyes.

"Madison! You missed it! You missed the tree completely." He then called to Hank, "I told you Madison couldn't shoot. Let's see if I can do better."

Hank watched as Madison handed the musket to Cole. Cole loaded the musket deliberately . . . slowly biting off the cartridge . . . slowly pouring powder into the barrel. Hank could see him put the bullet into the top of the barrel and saw him ram it down on top of the powder. Hank watched as he replaced the ramrod, pulled the hammer back and placed the cap. Everything was silent. This was not the glorious death Hank had imagined . . . to be killed like this . . . for nothing. Hank's heart beat furiously. Cole primed the musket and pulled it to his shoulder. Madison stood next to Cole, but Cole shouted to him, "Madison! Tell me when to fire!"

Madison said slowly, "Are you ready? Take aim! Fire!"

Hank kept his eyes on Cole. He saw him, as if up close, put his finger on the trigger . . . slide his finger up and down slightly. Hank stopped breathing. He could see the finger firm and tighten against the trigger, then pull it back. Instantly, Hank felt a thud in the tree. He had the feeling it was just above his head, but couldn't tell. Hank was wet from sweat and his body went limp.

"Madison, I think I out-shot you. That was a pretty good shot. Let's see if you can come that close. Try to hit right where I hit . . . just above his head. Now remember, like I'm always telling you, aim low . . . aim low."

Madison slowly loaded the musket, raised it, but didn't fire. Hank was shaking . . . totally exhausted. He didn't watch this time. He closed his eyes and prayed.

Cole saw his eyes close and called out, "I hope you're prayin'. With Madison shootin', you'll need that."

Hank heard the rifle fire, then a second shot. He opened his eyes, puzzled. Madison lay slumped forward on the ground, apparently dead. Cole stood petrified. Another shot rang out, and it brought Cole back to full awareness. He fled on foot through the trees as fast as he could run.

Hank craned his neck to see where the shot had come from and who had fired it. Exhaustion overpowered him, his hands shook behind the tree and he felt like crying. Finally he saw something up the hill in front of him. His heart sank: It was a butternut uniform. A second Confederate uniform followed the first . . . then a blue uniform came down the hill. It wasn't possible. It was the Union prisoners freed in Staunton. He could feel himself losing consciousness.

When he awakened, a canteen of water was at his lips and one of the former prisoners was saying in a heavy New England accent, "Drink this up."

Hank, still bewildered, sat up and looked around. Cole was nowhere to be seen, and the former prisoners were searching the camp for food and munitions. When the leader of the group saw he was conscious, he smiled and came to him. "Looks like we're even now. But we need your help to get out of here."

"Where did you come from?" Hank asked weakly.

"We've been hiding in these hills for several days. I figured the farther north we got the more suspicious we looked. Figured they've probably found the guards' bodies by now and are looking for us. If we kept going, someone was going to catch us. We just don't know the area . . . ran out of ideas. We were just waiting for a chance, and you came along . . . again. We were just up the hill when the gun fire attracted us. We saw what was happening, figured we ought to repay your kindness."

"Thank you."

"Our pleasure . . . but that's enough talk. How do we get north?"

Chapter 27
October 1862, Somewhere Northeast of Winchester, Virginia

*H*ank approached the house cautiously and looked around its exterior. It seemed empty. He climbed the small porch, making for the front door. As he extended his hand toward the doorknob he heard behind him the hammer of a rifle pulled back. He stood still. There was silence. He didn't move but imagined he could see the rifle.

"Why don't yuh back off the porch there?" said a familiar harsh, thin, high voice. "Let's see what we got here."

Hank backed up slowly and said, "Naomi. It's me. Don't you remember? I've come to thank you for helping me escape."

"Escape? Yuh don't look like no one I ever helped escape." the voice said in surprise. "Helped yuh escape? From who?" She showed no sign of recognition, but as he slowly descended the steps of the porch and turned to face her, she broke out in a wide grin. "Well if it ain't Johnny Reb. Or is it Billy Yank? Or is yuh Billy Yank all dressed up like Johnny? Or is yuh Johnny fightin' for Billy? I'm not sure what yuh is. I'm not sure yuh know what yuh is." With the last few sentences, her voice softened to the voice she had used when he was tied to the tree. She didn't wait for an answer, but continued, "I see yuh got away from them demons. Looks like yuh's doin' well for yuh'self." Naomi, in spite of the warmer tone, did not lower her rifle. It was a Springfield rifle musket, not the shotgun that had greeted him the first time.

"I am well and hope you are. I was worried about you when I left in such a hurry."

"Don't yuh go worryin' 'bout me. I been takin' care o' myself a long time now. Yuh's the one what needs worryin' 'bout. I know those men that was after yuh. One o' 'em's been after yuh ever since. Comes by here every few days to see if yuh's 'round here. He's gittin' to be a nuisance. He's a devil. Always comin' here, gittin' in my way. Can't do no good work with him always 'round."

"Naomi, thanks for saving me that night."

Naomi lowered the gun and grinned. "That slip yuh give 'em," she chuckled, "that was something. Worth helpin' yuh just for that. What's yor name again?"

"Hank Gragg."

"That's right. I remember. Well, Hank, what yuh doin'?"

"What do you mean?"

"Are yuh Reb or Union? And why yuh wanderin' 'round farms out here? Specially after the last time when you near got yuh'self kilt."

"Have you got a lot of time?"

"Sure, I got time. Do yuh with ole Cole still out there wanderin' 'round? But it's fine if yuh stay. We can visit a bit. Come on in. I'll put on a pot o' coffee, and yuh tell me 'bout it. I got real coffee!"

Hank explained his adventures to Naomi, and she listened. She periodically interrupted him with a comment or question. When he was done, she said, "Hank, that's a story to tell. Yuh's mad. Don't know there's nothin' yuh could do or say what would change my mind 'bout that. Yuh's mad!"

"I'm beginning to agree with you, Naomi. But what can I do? I've already lost my senses. It's too late to do anything else."

"Then yuh got to go wherever yor madness takes yuh. I might even be willin' to help yuh in yor delusions."

Hank laughed.

"Hank, yuh better get over the river as soon as yuh can with them men yuh got with yuh. There's many Confederate folks 'bout and scouts and pickets. Yuh's far north now and so far from any town, a wanderin' Confederate like yuh . . . and a whole group o' Yank prisoners—look mighty unusual. Yuh have to make it on yor own. But I can help yuh with something else," Naomi said with a playful look in her eye.

"With what?"

"You gunna write more letters to yor lonely widow?"

"I hadn't really thought about that." The possibility of ongoing correspondence with Mrs. Henderson had never occurred to him. As Naomi asked the question, he craved writing to her and dreamed she would answer. He answered, "But I would like to write to her again."

"Every time yuh write one o' them letters, yuh gunna deliver it yuh'self?"

Hank laughed. "Doesn't sound promising, does it?"

"No, Hank it don't." She waited a minute then softly said, "I can get 'em delivered for yuh."

"How?"

"I got family, cousins, in Maryland, just 'cross the river. Yuh get the letter to them . . . addressed to me. They'll get the letter to me. Then I can send it on to yor widow friend. Course it's gittin' hard to get envelopes and paper 'round here, but I can find it. But don't go addressin' the letter on the inside to the widow by name . . . yuh can't go signin' the letter. Yuh gotta tell her that up front. Yuh gunna have to trust me. Course yuh know I'm gunna read them letters," she added mischievously. "If that don't bother yuh none, send 'em just that way."

Hank listened. "I can do that. But why would you do this for me?"

"I like romance, specially when the cause is lost like yors and the kind widow lady's. Not a chance in this world or beyond the two of yuh will ever meet, so I'll do something to help it 'long. Wish someone would'a done that with my husband . . . helped keep us together, but no one done nothin' to help me. If I can help yuh with the ole widow lady, I'd be proud."

"You're as mad as I am," Hank said with a smile.

"I's been a mite crazy for a bit longer than yuh . . . that be the honest truth. Yuh's just new to it. Everybody knows 'round here I'm crazy, so ain't no one gunna bother me now 'bout it."

"What if you're caught?"

"Caught?" She laughed. "Doin' what? Readin' a love letter? That sure ain't gunna get me hung, 'less the South's a whole bunch more worse than I think. They all will think it's sweet havin' yuh writin' love words to an ole lady like myself. But all this talk can wait till after the war. Yuh best get yor friends 'cross the river."

Naomi rose from the table, then had another thought. "Hank, 'fore you go, write out a letter to the lady and sign it with your own name and tell her what yuh's intendin' to do, and I'll go on and send it. That'll be easy 'cause it won't be crossin' no Federal lines right now."

With that guidance, Naomi produced pen and paper and Hank wrote,

October 1862

Dear Mrs. Henderson,

I hope this letter finds you well. I am sending it through a friend, Naomi Callister. I would like to write to you from time to time to make sure you're well. It is the least that I can do for your husband. I will be unable to address you by name in future letters or sign them. Naomi has agreed to get the letters to you and she says she can get any to me that you write. Just send the letters to her, but you must not sign your name or mention mine. I would be honored to receive letters from you. Why I do this I do not know. I know I have not met you, but hope you will not consider this suggestion too forward. I was sorry that you were not home when I delivered your husband's letter. I carry the original copy and intend to deliver it to you in person when that is possible. If you do not want me to deliver it to you, you can write that, too, and I will understand.

Your devoted servant,

Hank Gragg

Hank finished the letter, folded it as its own envelope and sealed it with wax Naomi provided. He addressed it and handed it to Naomi. She looked disappointed, but took the letter and disappeared into another room. When she came back she was complaining to herself . . . mumbling that she had hoped to read it, but she would have to wait for later letters. She told Hank that since she didn't get to read the first one, later letters should be even more romantic than he had planned. Hank laughed and assured her he would make them as romantic as he dared. Hank stayed with Naomi until after sunset when he slid into the woods where the escaping Union soldiers awaited his return.

Naomi told Hank where Confederate pickets were posted, and he easily avoided them. Hank led the escaping soldiers in the direction of Sharpsburg and sent them quickly to the Union pickets. He realized it would be difficult to explain why he was in Staunton when he was supposed to be in Beverly, so before parting from the soldiers he committed them to secrecy regarding his help in their escape. He waited two hours after the men cleared the Union pickets before approaching the pickets himself.

It was early morning when he arrived, and the pickets nervously questioned him. They sent him to headquarters, but members of the general's staff could find no record of his assignment. The staff, enthralled by the unexpected arrival of escaped Union soldiers from Staunton, had little interest in Hank and directed him to his company commander. The captain vaguely remembered something of the orders and vouched for

Hank. But the captain and a lieutenant were busy speculating on how the union men had escaped, and the captain never asked Hank for a report of what he'd learned. In the end, Hank went back to his mess without debriefing.

Back with the 19th, Hank regaled Nathaniel and George with stories of his adventures, never mentioning the escaped prisoners or that his escapades took place going to Staunton and not Beverly. They in turn described seeing President Lincoln near Sharpsburg soon after Hank had left and reported that the Black Hats had a new moniker: the Iron Brigade.

Salted for the Fire: Epilogue

Not Long Ago, On Brawner's Farm at Manassas National Battlefield Park, Virginia

"My third great grandfather did all that?" Reid asked, interrupting the flow of the story.

"He did. Amazing isn't it . . . an amazing man."

"How do you know about it? Is there a book or something where I can read all this?"

The woman laughed, "I'm not sure there's a book about Hank, but I'm sure you could dig out some of the information if you researched hard enough. You probably have family papers somewhere."

"Then how do you know it?"

"I suppose it's as if I've lived it, or at least parts of it. Heard the stories so many times in my family. It's so real to me. I could never forget it. It's part of me. I even remember trying to make a family tradition of Hank Gragg. I brought my son out here once . . . told him the story. I wanted him to know what happened here, so it wouldn't be forgotten. It can't be forgotten—not by anyone—or we'll risk losing all we gained."

"Why my ancestor? Why is he so important to you?"

"I don't have an ancestor in this battle. You have to latch onto someone if you want to feel the drama, the significance of the day. Simply, I latched on to Hank Gragg. His story's memorable—and eventually it became my story—as if it were the story of my family."

Reid looked at her carefully and thought for a minute. He was confused. He had concluded the woman reminded him of someone he knew, and he was trying to remember who it was. He was comfortable with her because of that general feeling of previous acquaintance. He broke the silence, "So that's the story of the button?"

"That's how he got the button," she said definitively. "But there's much more to the story." She paused briefly then continued, "You're lucky to have a family connection like this. I think your ancestors, where your family has been, what they've done, who they are . . . it's all a part of you. You may think it sounds crazy, but I think they actually care about you just as you care about Hank. Something of family endures over generations. Maybe it's just the desire to know where we fit in . . . but I think it's something more, much more."

She continued, "We have to understand where we come from, what we've been given . . . before we can decide where we must go."

Part Two

A Widow's Might

*"O count it wrong to harm even
a wicked brother."*
                    Thyestes, 219

Chapter 1
November 1862, Staunton, Virginia

*I*t was early afternoon and Captain Henderson's cousin, Emily, sat in the parlor with Lucius Walthrope, lately of Lexington. He was a wonderfully handsome man with straight, blond hair and blue eyes. He wore a short, full beard and dressed elegantly. Emily was speaking. "Mr. Walthrope, you have been so kind to us. I know I speak for my cousin when I say your visits have been most appreciated in her grief. Losing her husband has been difficult for her. She has not taken it well. I know it's been difficult. I'm so close to her . . . I can see it. Why . . . knowing you were here for her these last few weeks has even comforted me. I worry about her so."

Walthrope responded, "I assure you, it is only what any gentleman would do under the circumstances. She has suffered terribly . . . and her husband, a national hero. I owe her this esteem."

"We all do! Just don't let her hear that. She gets angry at times when I speak of such things. She's confused and doesn't know her anger disguises grief. We do owe the captain . . . and all the others much. Many people have already forgotten his sacrifice—perhaps her anger stems from that. For myself, I can't understand how they can forget such an honorable man . . .

such a hero. Mr. Walthrope, that makes your friend-ship all the more important to her. It's hard for her to be cut off from her mother. She worries much about her; the news she gets from that quarter is not the same as seeing her mother in person. She did receive a letter from the lower valley yesterday . . . seemed to brighten her spirits. She is, at this very moment, re-sponding to it. She hasn't been so happy in a fortnight as when she read that letter."

"And who was the letter from that it would make her so happy? From her mother?" Walthrope asked. He had shown an exceeding but tasteful interest in the widow. He had met Emily at the home of an influential family, the Smiths, during an evening's entertainment. Confederate officers, women of the highest social rank, gentlemen from the finest families of Staunton and many other parts of Virginia and the South had been there. Mrs. Smith graciously introduced him to Emily, who for her part invited him to her home where he met the mourning Mrs. Henderson. He was solici-tous, indicating he had known her husband well . . . that he had the greatest admiration for him. Walthrope assured Mrs. Henderson that he was at her disposal for anything she might need. He told her the war was difficult for everyone, but especially for those who had sacrificed so much. He hoped she would call on him for any assistance she might need, after all, he had known the captain before the war. He had been an intimate business friend and had great respect for him. He ex-plained that he sold wool to the Henderson Woolen factory before the war . . . that he continued to sell wool to the factory.

The exceedingly successful woolen factory was only one of the establishments owned by the dwindling Henderson family. The captain had been the last of his line. With the death of his father and mother, the factory and other business concerns had come completely into his promising hands. Betsy now owned all of them because of the captain's precise and unusual will. She never wanted the responsibilities he left her, but had worked hard since her husband joined the army to understand the businesses, which included the woolen factory, two flour mills and a large, prosperous farm. Since his death, she had immersed herself, to the consternation of the respective superintendents, in conquering the details of each enterprise.

The Confederate government oversaw operations at the woolen factory and had since early in the war. It gave her little leeway as to whom she could sell wool, limiting her transactions to the government and long-time customers. She also had little say in prices charged or the color of the wool material—gray was now the factory's specialty.

She did have more influence in operations inside the factory and had gone as far as to suggest changes in the way it operated. Stokes, the factory superintendent had resisted her suggestions, and she had eventually threatened to replace him. The specter of shell and ball helped him see the advantages of Mrs. Henderson's suggestions: He would be forced to join the army if he lost the factory position. Within weeks of implementing the changes, he saw dramatic improvements in the cost and quality of cloth produced.

Once he saw how successful the changes had been, Stokes let it be mentioned by a few friends that he had suggested the changes to Mrs. Henderson . . . who was after all new to the business . . . and to Staunton. His friends assured everyone in their social circle that he had been contemplating such changes for a long time. Regrettably, as long as Mr. Henderson—who clearly had not understood the business—directed the operation, Stokes had not deemed it appropriate to suggest them. The Henderson widow needed assistance in her overwhelming burdens of ownership, so Stokes felt an obligation to undertake his long-planned improvements. They would help the bereaved widow, and more importantly would aid the war effort. His friends reported that Mrs. Henderson wanted the factory left as her husband had operated it, but that Stokes insisted on making the changes. Her resistance, everyone felt, was understandable. She was in mourning after all and so young. She couldn't be expected to accept such progressive changes or understand why they were needed.

Stokes' friends assured everyone that he was kind to the grieving widow. They let it be known that she liked to come to the factory in her mourning just to be near where her husband had worked. She was admirably dedicated to her husband's memory. Stokes himself said he didn't mind listening to her constant chatter about her husband, but hoped her visits wouldn't interfere with the business. His friends insisted the good fellow was vital to the war effort, that he didn't want to be impatient or resort to asking her not to come to the factory anymore. Stokes' friends and, soon thereafter, everyone agreed that Stokes would have to stop her visits if her grieving interfered anymore with his efforts to serve . . . to save the Confederacy. In the end a good portion of the community was convinced that Mr. Stokes was a patriot and most understanding of the young, struggling widow's plight.

Such a reputation gave the superintendent a security in his position he'd never had before. He wholeheartedly believed there would be a great public outcry if she fired him and that the government would never allow him to be removed. He thought he might even be able to ask for a significant raise since his improvements had worked so well . . . and the town was now so well aware of it.

Mrs. Henderson saw and knew much of this. It angered her and weakened her ability to deal with him. However he had made the requested changes so she sensed it better to leave him alone for a time.

Since his introduction to Mrs. Henderson just two weeks earlier, Lucius Walthrope had found a dozen reasons to visit the Henderson home. During those visits, he illustrated his business acumen through a myriad of stories. He appeared to be a man who could get things done . . . at a profit. He assured her she could rely on his expertise at any time. For a week now, he had been a constant dinner guest, and Mrs. Henderson plied him with questions about the woolen industry and factories. They laughed together at rumors of how poorly made the Union uniforms were and the shoddy material used. The widow expressed concern about how it was getting harder to find enough sources for wool. She told him of her worries about the shortage of Confederate uniforms. She said she wanted to produce more, but there were so many limitations.

He agreed it was a national tragedy that the Confederacy—that Virginia—couldn't clothe its soldiers and suggested several of his ideas might help in the factory . . . if she were interested. She was, and he had outlined possible improvements. Some she liked, some she didn't think would work. But she quickly began to think that Mr. Walthrope was a man who could help her; he might be just the person to put in charge of the factory, someone between herself and Stokes. Then she wouldn't have to deal directly with Stokes, and Stokes, to his satisfaction, wouldn't have to deal with her. She had the impression that Walthrope would intimidate Stokes just as Thaddeus had. The arrangement would offer other advantages as well. It would give her more time to focus on her mills and farm. It was against this backdrop that Emily and Walthrope discussed the letter Betsy received and from whom it came.

Emily answered Walthrope's question, "The letter came from a woman. I believe her name is Naomi. When Betsy got the letter she seemed a bit confused. After reading it, she was elated. She said Naomi was an old family friend to whom she was deeply indebted."

Walthrope smiled mischievously at Emily and said, "Ah, not a rival for her attention, then?"

"Mr. Walthrope!" she giggled. Regaining her composure, she said, "You ought to be ashamed of yourself. It's too soon." Then she added, "But let me say, I do not believe anyone holds a higher place in her affections than you do for all the kindness you have shown her. And I'm sure her husband—my dear cousin—would approve of your attention . . . perhaps of your intentions as well."

"You misunderstand me . . . and flatter me, my dear. I am her faithful servant and only hope I can help her through this sad time. I would be untruthful if I did not tell you—most confidentially—I find her a beautiful, charming woman. But that only makes my mission of mercy that much more pleasurable."

"Then you would do it only out of duty if she were not the most lovely creature in the South?"

"I do it only out of duty and appreciation now . . . but she makes the duty so enjoyable. But I do believe that you do an injustice to someone very close to both of us."

"Injustice!" Emily, convinced that she was Betsy's staunchest supporter, looked crushed.

"Yes, I believe you do."

The cousin's voice rose in indignation, "I would never . . . . "

"But you already have," Walthrope spoke smoothly. "Didn't you say she is the most lovely creature in the South?"

"I did, but that is no . . . ."

"I thought you did. My dear," he leaned toward Emily as if he was to make an intimate private confession. "She is not only the most beautiful creature in the

South, but the two of you—you and your cousin—are the most delightful creatures in both countries: North and South."

Emily's expression moved quickly from indignation to embarrassment mingled with delight. "Mr. Walthrope! Wonderful Mr. Walthrope . . . ."

Before she could finish her thought, the hall door flew open and Betsy came through it. Her black dress was the only part of her appearance not full of life and color. "Ah, Mr. Walthrope, I didn't know you were here," she said breezily.

"I have just but arrived."

"It's good you're here. I know my most cherished cousin and our dear hostess has made you feel at home."

"Of course she has. She has been charming as always. If she were not already married, I would be tempted to propose to her at this very minute."

Emily giggled, and Betsy smiled.

"I understand you have received a letter from an old friend," Walthrope said, probing.

"I have. All is well with her and those who pertain to her. I've just this hour finished responding. It is so good to hear from old friends. Don't you like to hear from old friends, Mr. Walthrope?"

"Mrs. Henderson, I do. It's such a relief, with such awful things continually reported by the papers, to hear that all is well with friends . . . that they remain constant in their feelings for you."

"Precisely! You put the matter in just the right words, Mr. Walthrope. It is no wonder that you are such a welcome guest in my cousin's home. And I have just settled on a proposal for you . . . one that will keep you even closer."

The cousin glanced meaningfully at Walthrope, raising her eyebrows and pursing her lips.

Walthrope attempted to ignore Emily's look and responded quickly and directly to Betsy. "Oh, I cannot marry you . . . though it would be an honor." The cousin tittered again and exchanged glances with him.

Betsy looked seriously first at Emily, then at Walthrope, and said sternly, "Mr. Walthrope, I am a widow! My husband died less than three months ago. Please don't jest about such things."

Walthrope, with a chastened look, responded, "Mrs. Henderson, I assure you I meant no harm. You know I have the greatest respect for your husband . . . for you." He lowered his head as if bowing, "You know I would do nothing to bring the slightest dishonor upon this house. Please forgive me my frivolity."

"No! No! Betsy dear, I have put Mr. Walthrope in such a position through my silly prattle before you came in. Oh, don't hold our dear guest responsible for attempting to dishonor you when I have caused it."

Betsy didn't respond to either protest immediately. She had made her point out of a widow's duty, not from any deep sense of being dishonored, and she wondered what to say. "Oh . . . I know neither of you meant anything by it. Let's imagine it never happened."

Emily and Walthrope looked reassuringly at each other; the guest was particularly pleased to have planted the thought of marriage in Betsy's mind.

Betsy continued, "Mr. Walthrope, would you supervise the woolen factory for me? You understand the business so well. I believe it would be easier for Stokes to listen to you than it is for the poor man to listen to me. I have given this matter serious reflection and can think of no better way to fulfill my responsibility to care for the factory than to have you superintend it for me."

Mr. Walthrope responded with little surprise or concern, almost matter-of-factly, "I'll do it if that's what you desire. I've told you: I'm here to serve you. I'll do whatever's needed to support you."

"That's wonderful! Good! Then it's settled."

"What about the mills?" he quickly asked in an anxious tone.

Betsy looked startled. "What do you mean?"

"Would you like me to oversee the mills as well? I would be delighted to serve you in that way."

Betsy was thoughtful. "No . . . I don't think that's necessary. I can handle them for now."

"I didn't mean to suggest . . . forgive me. I only . . . I only want you to know how willing I am to help you. I believe that Mr. Stokes and I will get along famously. I suggested the mills only so that you knew that I am ready to assist you in any way. Your burden is great and I wish only to lighten your load."

"Thank you. You are most kind . . . but I believe the factory will be enough. I can manage the rest."

"Oh, I know you can. Just be assured the factory will be taken care of then."

"It's settled," said Betsy, nodding her head to Walthrope.

Betsy seated herself across from Walthrope and said, "We'll meet here every day at two o'clock for dinner . . . at least in the beginning. We can address any problems then. I'll visit the factory with you once a week." She was direct but pleasant. "Oh, what have I done. We've failed to discuss your wages. How can you commit to such a position without knowing the salary? I am sorry. What will be your salary?"

"Salary? Don't worry about it. We can arrange that later. Just helping you in your time of need, supporting our cause—those are compensation enough."

Betsy looked concerned. "We can't ignore your pay. We must address it now. You have your own work to consider. It will suffer from lack of attention. You will improve the factory so it can produce better clothes . . . faster; you must be compensated fairly!" She hastily suggested an irresistibly attractive wage. The offer stunned Walthrope and Emily. There would be little profit for her at current production levels if she paid him what she offered. Walthrope took her generosity as indication of her personal interest in him. It was a large step toward the aisle where he hoped to see the two of them joined as man and wife in a commonly shared near future. The eyes of the new superintendent and Emily met fleetingly. They shared a common understanding.

"I can't take that much. I will take half . . . no a quarter of that . . . and that's more than enough. And you won't even have to visit the factory . . . or worry about it. I'll take care of everything," Walthrope blurted out.

Emily knew from his response that all would fall into place just as she had hoped for her cousin, and she sighed as she often did when reading romantic novels.

Chapter 2

*November 1862, Near Fredericksburg,
Virginia*

"*H*ank," George said, "Somethin' strange . . . real strange happened."

"What might that be?"

"You got yourself a letter. They called your name right out. Don't remember you gettin' a letter 'fore, Hank. Course you got that letter from your sister once. As I recollect though, that letter didn't come through no mails."

Hank, who huddled near the fire stoking it to keep it hot, felt a thrill that startled him, but tried to show no emotion. She wrote! No. It was impossible—too far fetched. The letter must be from his parents or his sister Corny who probably found him through their parents. He said, "It's probably from a family I met at Beverly. They were kind to me while I was there." He grimaced slightly as he found himself telling another lie.

"You sure are a strange one, Hank Gragg. You're the only one that I know that don't get all excited when he gets a letter. The rest of us run 'round camp like we were little children 'bout to get whupped. Not Hank Gragg. You just go right on a stirrin' ashes. You're a strange one."

Hank rose and stepped away from the fire and moved a step or two closer to George. He calmly held out his hand. "Here, I'll take it." If it was from her, he knew it would be full of venom and hatred.

"Hank, I ain't got it. They ain't 'bout to give it me. You gotta get it yourself, and I'd hurry if I was you."

Without another word, Hank hurdled the fire and ran to retrieve the letter. George eyed him curiously as he ran.

Hank returned quickly with an envelope in hand and sat down by the fire, again. George, now likewise situated by the fire, watched him without saying a word. Hank looked for a long time at the envelope.

"Looks like a woman's gentle hand," George offered, although he was too far away to see the handwriting.

The penmanship was rough and primitive, but that added to Hank's excitement as he expected that Naomi had addressed it. It was clear Naomi didn't have much schooling, and he didn't expect her to have refined handwriting. He remembered being surprised she could read and write at all. He examined the envelope closely for any clues before opening it. It was addressed to Private Henry Gragg, 19th Indiana, Army of the Potomac.

"Ain't you gonna open it, Hank?" George asked, still watching him with utmost interest.

"Yeah . . . of course. I'll open it. I'm just not in any hurry. I kind of like this feeling," he said honestly.

Out of the corner of his eye, he could see George smile. George said, "Sort a like when you gets a gift. You don't know to tear it open real fast to see what's you got . . . or wait and feel all excited. Is that it,

Hank? I'm thinkin' you should tear it open real fast. It's mighty clear to me, you ain't never got no love letter since you joined up with the infantry. You don't know the pleasure of openin' a letter . . . hearin' the warm words a sweetheart wrote to you."

"George, you never got a love letter in your life! When did you suddenly get all this knowledge?"

"Never mind what you say, Hank Gragg. I've got myself lots of love letters since I joined up. Some of 'em the kind that makes your mouth water. Hank, I get 'em all the time." He paused, and Hank looked up at him with lips pressed together, silently protesting. George saw the look and quickly added, "Course I always find out later they ain't fer me—they was fer someone else. Still the thrill of gettin', then readin' 'em is worth it all. Hank, here, pass it on over to me. I'll do the openin' fer you. I'll let you know if it's one of them fine love letters or not." Hank ignored the extended hand. "Open it, Hank . . . 'fore you find out it's fer Nathaniel."

Hank shook his head in response to the nonsense his friend had been spewing. He looked down at the letter. He was afraid to open it, felt he should read it in the privacy of his tent. But he appreciated not being alone, even if it meant putting up with George's harassment. Hank faltered. This letter held the key to his happiness.

"Want me that I should open it, Hank?" George offered again.

"No . . . no. I'll open it," he responded, still lost in his thoughts.

George smiled, rose to his feet, patted his friend on his shoulder and walked from the fire, leaving Hank to himself and his letter. Hank didn't notice George's departure and shifted his position by the fire. He slowly opened the envelope.

Inside he found another envelope; this one addressed to Naomi Callister. He couldn't believe it. She had written him a letter and sent it to Naomi, just as he had suggested. He focused on his next worry. She surely had written asking him—maybe threatening him—to never write again. He didn't want to open it. He sat staring at the second envelope. It was already opened; Naomi had read it. He smiled at the thought. He enjoyed the moment. As long as he didn't read it, he still could believe the widow wanted to correspond. Opening the letter might . . . .

Finally he shook off his fear, slowly opened the second envelope, pulled out the letter. He began to read.

Staunton, Virginia

November 1, 1862

Dear friend,

I shall call you that as you have indicated that I should not mention your name or mine.

Hank was rising from dread to shock: She was being gracious. He read on:

I like the sound of that salutation and think it well earned after what you have done. I received your letter and cannot express how disappointed I was that I did not meet you and that I did not receive it from your hand. I would like to have heard directly from your lips of my husband's last moments and thanked you personally for your kindness. The thoughts of your service to my husband are treasures to me. I cannot express the gratitude felt for what you did. I am currently living in town with a cousin and fear that my servant did not recognize how important you and your errand were. Had he known, he surely would have sent you to see me. For that misunderstanding I feel deep remorse. I have warm sentiments for you and feel as if I already know you well.

I take no offense at your suggestion that we correspond and would be honored to exchange letters with such a noble man.

You must understand, nonetheless, that I am a loyal citizen of Virginia and of the Confederate States and cannot be swayed. I'm employed doing all I can to free our state from the invading Union forces, which unfortunately includes you. I am proud of our men who have sacrificed so much as soldiers to free Virginia. I hope you will not take offense at my forthrightness, but I do not want our friendship to be based on anything but a true understanding of our respective positions. A friendship such as you propose is difficult under all circumstances for it is difficult to find in life a friend with whom you can share intimate thoughts and feelings. Under our circumstances, such a friendship is particularly challenging. I see in your words and kindness that while you have chosen a path that is abominable to me, you have done it in sincerity. I accept your friendship and believe that it can endure in spite of the differences between your loyalties and mine. Please write as often as you can, and I will respond to each letter. Do not ask me to question my loyalties, and I

*will not ask you to question yours. May this cruel war
be over quickly that we may meet face to face.*

"Your most grateful friend"

When he had finished the letter, Hank's first instincts were to wonder if Naomi had forged the letter—the tone was too personal, too intimate, too
friendly. But Naomi wouldn't and probably couldn't
write such a letter. He gazed beyond the fire. He could
not believe Mrs. Henderson had written it. It was impossible that she should respond as she did. He had
dreamed she would. But even encamped across the
river from Fredericksburg in the misery and hunger of
an early cold spell, he could distinguish between his
dreams and reality.

For a long time Hank had been convinced that by
springtime every scenario he had dreamed involving
the widow would be buried beneath a volcanic creep of
despair—not crushed by a sudden, hard word from the
widow—but smothered instead slowly, incrementally
by volcanic debris creeping over his hope, until after
waiting for months—waiting in vain for word—the mol-
ten material would melt and bury the last of his expectations of affection. He never honestly believed she
would write. He expected that some morning he would
simply wake up to the fact that she would never respond. He could accept that; it would give him time to
gradually, gently adapt to the truth. There would be no
crisis. His hope would just slowly be submerged and
cease to exist.

As he opened the envelope, he held to his conviction
of the futility of his hope, frightened that it would end
so soon, so brutally. It was clear he would find a formal

response to his letter. She would say she wanted nothing to do with a Yankee. But the letter hadn't said that.
It had repeated—if it were possible—the very words of
his dream, quoted verbatim from his thoughts. He felt
just for a moment that he already knew her. Such
things did not—could not—happen, certainly not to
Henry Gragg from Woodstock.

George's voice pulled Hank from drowning in a
whirlpool of his own thoughts. "Hank, read the letter
yet?"

"I did," he said in a restrained voice without looking
at his friend. His voice changed as he looked up, and it
sounded like an entreaty. "But George, I can't believe
it!"

"Who sent it?"

"The widow."

"The wida! What wida?"

"The widow. Don't you remember? The wife of the
man who died in our first battle. The man who wrote a
letter to his wife. The woman I wrote to."

"You wrote her . . . the wida? You didn't tell me
'bout that. I told you to ferget her. You h'ain't talked
'bout her. I thought you'd fergot her, just like I told
you."

Both men sat silently thinking until George asked,
"Then you sent her husband's letter?"

"Yes."

"How d'you do it? When d'you send it?"

"I took it to her," Hank said now gazing straight
across the fire with unblinking eyes.

"You took it to her?" George responded, incredu-
lous.

"I took it to her when I was supposed to be in Beverly seeing my sister."

"You never went to Beverly." George confessed, "I kind o' 'spected you wasn't goin' to Beverly when you left: I figured the letter was a fraud. I saw you that day trying to get the letter all dirty like. I thought it weren't real. But I never thought you was goin' to see the wida—I should'a. Thought you was just takin' a furlough the only way you could think of, just wanted to get away from Nat fer a few days. I wouldn't'a blamed you. I'm always wantin' to get away from Nat. But don't go worryin', I never said nothin' 'bout it . . . not to no one. When you come back, I fergot all 'bout the letter." George paused to think. "Hank, you had yourself a good plan. You just didn't stay away long enough. I don't think I would'a ever come back." He sat thoughtfully, then added, "Your sister ain't dead, then?"

"She's not dead."

"Probably don't even live in Beverly."

"No, she does live in Beverly. But I didn't know that when I left. She married a Union man up there, but I had no idea."

George looked at Hank silently for a moment, then his head rolled back, and he howled with laughter. Regaining his composure quickly, he said, "That's a wonderful yarn. You gone and seen her? What's she like? Everything you dreamed?"

"I never got to see her."

"You went all the way up to . . . where was it? Lexington?"

"Staunton."

"You went all the way to Staunton and never seen her."

"Never got to see her . . . but she wrote me a letter!"

"You never seen her and you're gettin' yourself excited 'bout gettin' a letter? Hank, somethin' ain't right. Don't you see what's agoin' on here. She must be ugly . . . maybe mighty ugly. Else why'd she write a plain Yankee private. If she was pretty, there'd be a thousand Johnnies just awaitin' to marry her. Is she Union?"

"Secesh, through and through."

"Then she's ugly! She's ugly . . . and real poor. She done wants your pay, your $13 a month. . . real Union money. That's a fortune fer one of them Secesh widas. That's it, Hank! The wida, she don't have no husband to provide fer her no more. She's writin' to get your money! Did she ask fer your money?"

Hank winced at the mention of money as he remembered the coins he had included in his letter to a woman who seemed to own a plantation. "George, it isn't like that. I think she's rich."

"Rich! Then Hank, she's ugly. Otherwise it don't make no sense."

George's point bothered Hank. It had been somewhere just below his conscious mind and it bobbed quickly when George suggested it. Why would this woman, beautiful and wealthy, write back? Something was amiss. He couldn't quite figure out what it was. George was still talking, "Why didn't you see her, Hank?"

"The servants didn't let me."

George chortled, "Well, Henry Gragg, that's the best reason I ever heard fer endin' slavery. Them Southern slaves is gettin' in the way of your romance. Did you ask the slave if she was pretty?"

"George," Hank shook his head in disgust, as was his usual practice when talking to George. He remembered Mr. Porter saying she was beautiful, and he took comfort in that witness. With animation he said, "George, she wrote to me! I never believed she would actually write, thought she'd ignore my letter. She wrote to me! She wants to keep writing to me!"

"Hank! Wake up!" George came around the fire and slapped him playfully on the cheek, "Wake up, Hank. This is just one of them dreams. You're gonna wake up soon, find it's all been one of them dreams. I ain't even here with you, Hank. I'm home in Indiana. This is just your dream."

Hank laughed. "You can't wake me up from this one, George, not this time. You may be right; it may all be a dream. But if it is . . . I refuse to wake."

"You better get to writin' then. You don't want her to be the last Confederate wida that ain't got a letter from her Union lover. She might find some other fool 'stead o' you." George laughed again. "I think I'll go lookin' fer Nat and tell him about our Lothario . . . or is it Romeo, I can never remember which done what?" George wandered down the company street.

A small burst of anger ran through Hank's body as George's final comments took him back to the last time he had heard the name Lothario. It was on the stage to Harrisonburg. He remembered with particular hatred that man . . . Lothario. He had sensed a bitterness and coarseness in him. That was a man Hank would like to meet on the battlefield someday, but he doubted Lothario would ever see a battlefield.

Hank pushed away the hatred he felt and pulled his haversack near him, searching it for paper and pen. Having secured both, he sat back down to write a letter.

Across from Fredericksburg, Virginia
December 1862
Dear friend,

I received your letter today with the greatest of pleasure. My heart is full, knowing that you would like to write to me and to maintain a friendship. I too wish we had been able to meet in Staunton while I was there. I hope to have the great honor someday of meeting you in person so I may give you my regards.

We are camped across from Fredericksburg. It seems like the entire Confederate Army is camped across the Rappahannock River on some hills. We haven't received word on exactly what we will be doing here, and the opposing army has sent us no message on what they plan to do, so we're left in the dark, as usual. But dear friend, mark my words as someone who's been in a few big battles, I have the feeling that a great one will be fought here. Don't be surprised if you hear of a battle sometime soon somewhere near Fredericksburg. Perhaps this one will be the battle that will end this bloody war. I acknowledge that you have chosen to be loyal to the Confederacy. I will not try to change your allegiance. I will however pray for this conflict to be over so that we can meet. I wonder what it would have been like if we had been friends before this war. I have given it much thought and hope to settle again in Virginia, in the valley, after the war.

I have not told you about my family. I have family that lives in Woodstock. A sister, brother and my parents live there. One sister married and moved to Beverly. One brother died early on at Second Bull Run. He was in the Southern army. Perhaps he knew your husband.

It is difficult for me to write to you, because I don't know what to say. So please do not be insulted by anything I write. The food here is not very good, and for the first time really, there is not nearly enough of it. It's getting cold now and everyone suffers from that. But it can't be helped. We have a new general. We sure liked our old general, McClellan. Our new general has bushy hair that comes way down his cheeks. His name is Burnside. I saw him pass once. It was strange, but he wasn't cheered as he rode by like McClellan. I didn't feel much like cheering him either. Maybe that will change after he wins a battle or two. Burnside is the one that sent us here to Fredericksburg.

That is all that I can write now. Please write back soon. You don't know how happy it made me to get your letter.

Ever your friend

Chapter 3
December 1862, Staunton, Virginia

"*O*h, it's wonderful! General Lee has led us to victory again! The war will be over well before the call of another December. Next year will bring peace . . . peace and liberty," Emily said.

She sat amidst ample food at the well-set cherry-wood table. Dining with her in the spacious room were Betsy, Lucius Walthrope, and Mrs. Robertson, a long-time friend of Emily's family and refugee of late from Northern Virginia.

Walthrope piped up, "You can be sure of that! It was a great slaughter. Yankees just kept charging across an open field right up to our guns. Longstreet's men fired down on them . . . annihilated them. Fifteen thousand Yanks in all . . . not a bad day for the Confederacy. We cannot help but win this war. As you always say, Emily: 'It is our destiny and God's will.'"

Emily responded quickly and indignantly. "Longstreet? I heard it was Jackson. Jackson again. Lee and Jackson who won this victory. Why speak of Longstreet?"

Distracted, Betsy didn't listen to the two converse. She was experiencing new emotions. Stories from the battle at Fredericksburg had thrilled her. The Army of Northern Virginia had punished the Army of the Potomac, but for the first time worry and fear tempered her elation in victory. Love for the Confederacy was no longer her sole emotion. Hank had been at Fredericksburg. She had received and pored over the short letter he had written from there. She imagined he was among the thousands wounded—or worse—dead on the battlefield. Some said many wounded Union soldiers had lain on the battlefield's frozen ground overnight, many dying in their weakened states. She imagined Hank sprawled on a crusty-snow covered ground, murmuring softly, "Help" . . . calling feebly her name. It was ludicrous even as she thought it, but she pictured the entire Northern army nearby—close enough to save him—denying him succor. She hated Yankees! But he was different. She knew him. He was kind and warm. She enjoyed being with him . . . loved him. Betsy now had redoubled interest in the war, but equal yet opposing forces were tearing her in twain. Her sympathies lay with both armies, and she was constantly terrified. She could lose both the war and the man. She could lose Hank on any day, and the Confederacy in the end.

Betsy had not waited for details of the battle before writing and posting a letter to Hank. The minute she heard rumors of the battle and of the capture of the Union General Burnside, she had written to him. Rumors turned out better than the final outcome as the general had not been captured. Nonetheless, Fredericksburg was a clear Southern victory. Betsy only hoped Hank survived the slaughter and was alive to read her letter. Then something softly suggested that he was alive . . . alive but blind—blinded by some errant shrapnel. Blind! It insinuated that in some Union hospital a steward read her words to him. She could accept that. They could endure it together. He then could come to her; she would care for him: safe in her arms . . . safe from war . . . and guns . . . and men.

"Betsy," Emily's voice burst through her imaginings, "Do you think the war can last much longer?"

"I'm not sure it can, and I hope it won't," she answered without thinking.

Taking her response as a lack of interest in the topic, Walthrope changed it. "We got more wool in this morning. But there are fewer and fewer sheep in the valley. They're nearly all gone: stolen or killed for food or sold. It's fortunate we get any wool. Blockade runners will never be able to make up the shortfall. It's getting harder and harder to get wool, and it can only get worse."

The new topic brought Betsy back to the conversation, but she sounded depressed as she spoke. "How can we keep up the production? Too little wool . . . too few men. Thank goodness for the women, or we'd have to close the factory doors completely. It's hard to find men to work in the factory, the farm, the mills. We've lost so many to the army. Even with exceptions for our factory operatives, we can't keep enough men. The farm, it's even worse. So big and there aren't even enough men to harvest the wheat and corn now."

Walthrope spoke optimistically, "Mrs. Henderson, you've got to stop worrying about the factory. When will you . . ."

Betsy laughed, interrupting his comment. "You always seem to find a way to make it work, Mr.

Walthrope. How do you do it? I'm sure I don't know. You work your miracles though. Are you an angel? A magician perhaps? You must be."

"A magician! I like that idea! Yes, that's it, Mrs. Henderson—a magician sworn to secrecy. You can never know the secrets of my illusions."

"Illusions? Is that what they are? Are they not real miracles? Whatever they are, I'm grateful you're doing so much. But let's not talk about wool and corn and wheat with Mrs. Robertson here," she said turning to face the guest. Mrs. Robertson was a middle-aged woman of significant proportions and full face. "Was your son at Fredericksburg? Was Stuart in the battle?"

Mrs. Robertson was staying at the cousin's home for the week. She had just arrived from Richmond where she had sought out the latest social, political, and war news. Her son, because of his membership in JEB Stuart's Virginia cavalry, was a celebrity in absentia at Emily's table.

"That's what I've heard," she responded. "Yes, he's safe. I've heard from my brother, Jacob . . . also with Stuart. They were in part of the fight, but had few casualties. That's what I've heard about the entire army. We lost very few! What a blessing from God! But oh! My! The work of death among the Union men. Jacob told me the Yankees charged that hill, and cannon and musket killed them as fast as they came. They didn't have a chance, no chance at all. Jacob said it was Longstreet's men where the greatest slaughter occurred, but mind you, I agree with Emily, Jackson's men held against a terrible charge. Only our General Jackson's leadership saved the day. And I, like you," she said nodding admiringly toward Emily, "take pride that he is a Virginian. But even Longstreet has proven a worthy tool in the Lord's hands. Emily, my love, we have to recognize him as one of our great generals."

Mrs. Robertson continued, "But the battle was both wonderful and terrible. Jacob said it was so bad for the Yankees, that our soldiers . . . the soldiers of the dear Cross of Christ . . . actually felt sorry for the Union boys."

"Sorry for Yankees? Preposterous!" Emily said.

"Preposterous perhaps, but there seems to be some camaraderie among the soldiers on opposing sides," Mrs. Robertson said. "Why I heard from Jacob that my son was among several who went out and visited with the Yankees after the battle. They had an agreement not to shoot at each other, not to fight unless their officers ordered it—even then they'd fight only after giving each other time to get to safety. Jacob told my son not to get involved in that kind of thing again, but Emily, it's going on all the time now."

"I'm quite sure my husband would never do such a thing. He's completely dedicated to the Confederacy," Emily said arrogantly.

Walthrope, perceiving that Betsy was not paying close attention to the conversation, jumped in to soothe the anger that flared in Mrs. Robertson's eyes. Speaking to Emily, he said, "I'm sure Mrs. Robertson's son is completely dedicated to the Confederacy. But keep in mind, these are young boys . . . on both sides. Under different circumstances they might be friends, even close friends. If the war hadn't come along, they might at this very hour be playing one of those baseball games, not battling for life. Or more likely this month, they'd be wearing themselves out in a snowball fight."

Mrs. Robertson responded quickly, "You are correct, Mr. Walthrope. My son is as loyal as any man."

"I hope you are not suggesting, Mr. Walthrope . . . that this war is like a silly game boys might play," Emily said.

"Certainly not." He saw that pushing the point with Emily served no purpose.

Mrs. Robertson was angry and embarrassed. "I must say, I am uncomfortable staying in a home—even after so many years of friendship—a home where they speak of my son as a traitor."

Betsy, reawakening from her private thoughts, sensed the problem and spoke quickly. "Oh, Mrs. Robertson, we are honored to have you with us. So many in your family are sacrificing for our cause: Your husband with the great service he does for the government in Richmond, your brother, your valiant son. Where else in the army could they do better service than in Stuart's cavalry? And you, our dear friend, you driven from your home. The cruel invaders! We have so much to admire you for . . . for all you have done for Virginia. Having you here with us is a privilege. How better to show how much we appreciate you . . . your family?"

"I am grateful for your sentiments," Mrs. Robertson responded, clearly relieved she could stay on with honor. "For a moment, I thought perhaps we were not appreciated. But when a woman who has given so much for the Confederacy says such words, I know I have nothing of which to worry."

Emily sat quietly, accustomed to Betsy smoothing feathers ruffled by her zealous patriotism. Emily fancied herself unrivaled in her allegiance to the Confederacy, and she was quick to share her nationalist feelings. She knew others sometimes didn't appreciate her declarations, but she meant no harm by them. They were merely expressions of her own commitment. Emily often used her husband as an example of courage as he, in her mind, was an extension of her own bravery. Betsy never shared with Emily gossip from neighbors: Soldiers serving with Emily's husband had passed along stories that suggested he didn't live up to his wife's patriotic ideals.

Betsy changed the subject, "Which way is Fredericksburg?"

"From here?" asked Mrs. Robertson, surprised by the sudden question.

Walthrope commented, "It's just about due East. Why?"

"I was just thinking of all the brave soldiers who were fighting there, trying to picture in my mind where they would be . . . what they did."

Emily saw her opportunity to save face and commented to Walthrope and Mrs. Robertson, "When my cousin says brave soldiers, she thinks of our army."

"I do. Emily . . . the other side, too. Courage exists on both sides. It must," Betsy responded gently.

"All Confederate soldiers are brave! You're right about that," Emily responded, attempting to convince everyone including herself that she and Betsy completely agreed.

Walthrope commented, "If there are brave men on both sides, certainly there are cowards on both sides as well."

"Oh, Mr. Walthrope!" Emily scolded, "You are surely mistaken! How could one of our soldiers be a coward when they are fighting for their freedom, their families and their country . . . for us . . . for our second Revolution?"

"You see the world only in its brightest colors," Walthrope responded. "Not all our soldiers are as pure hearted as you—I assure you of that. Next time you write to your husband, ask him if there are cowards in his regiment."

Betsy winced unconsciously at the possibility that Emily would write to her husband about cowards.

"I will do no such thing," Emily responded with consternation in her voice. "To doubt the bravery of our men is to weaken our cause. Sometimes, I must confess, Mr. Walthrope, I am not sure about your loyalty."

Walthrope knew Emily meant no offense, took none and continued eating.

"Come, come now, Emily" Betsy said. "Mr. Walthrope has done so much for the Confederacy. His work at the factory . . . all he's done for us. We are all indebted to him."

Walthrope smiled. "Perhaps someday I will ask for payment in full."

"In that case," Betsy said, "I hope to have, but sincerely doubt that I will have, the resources to pay the full bill. The debt will be very heavy indeed."

Emily was diverted from her passionate patriotism to what she was convinced was Betsy's budding romance and courtship. She smiled and glanced meaningfully at Walthrope who returned the smile and the intent.

"Oh . . . I believe you will!" Walthrope said, turning to look directly at Betsy, hoping for a significant look from her and being disappointed that she was looking down at her plate.

Chapter 4
December 1862, Staunton, Virginia

*L*ater in the evening, Emily found Betsy in a chair staring out a window in the dining room. The drapes were open, and Emily could feel the winter-night chill emanating from the glass.

"What on earth are you looking at?" the cousin asked. "It's dark out there. You surely can't see anything through that window." Emily peered out and saw only the reflection of the room in the panes.

Betsy gave her cousin a preoccupied glance. "Just thinking about those young men . . . at Fredericksburg. They're right out there." She raised her hand almost feebly pointing directly out the window.

"You really are becoming a saint . . . thinking about our men constantly."

"Not all of them," Betsy said laughing.

"Betsy, you've got to stop worrying about them so much and think more about Mr. Walthrope. Come join us in the parlor! One of our invalid soldiers is actually well enough tonight to sit with us in the parlor. Mrs. Robertson is asking for you, and Mr. Walthrope is still here. Come! Think about him for a while . . . think about Mr. Walthrope!"

"Mr. Walthrope?" Betsy said with surprise in her voice.

"Don't pretend that this is a new thought to you, dear Betsy. I know you have fond feelings for him." Then with emphasis, she added, "I know he has feelings for you."

"Mr. Walthrope?" Betsy, paused to consider what her cousin suggested. "Mr. Walthrope . . . feelings for me? Surely you're mistaken!"

"Oh please! . . . stop this! Such protests! You know he has feelings for you. You can't deceive me. I know you so well . . . so, so well. I can see your affection for him. It shines from your eyes when you're together. At supper, I knew what you meant when you said you were indebted to him. He knew it, too. I know he considers asking for your hand."

Betsy was dumbfounded. This was a new idea to her. She said, "Emily . . . I had no idea. He feels affection for me?"

"Affection? No . . . not merely that! He has a great passion for you! I cannot believe you do not know that. Haven't you noticed how he treats you? He fits so well into our home. It's as if—in some respects—that the two of you are already married." She spoke the last words in a way that indicated she implied no scandal.

"Married?" Betsy laughed. "Is that how everyone sees it?"

"Everyone I know."

"How could I have missed this?" She pondered briefly, then added, "Yes . . . he is very kind to me."

"Why do you think he didn't care to make more money at the factory? Everyone's interested in making more money . . . except those in love."

"In love? It can't be."

"Take my word . . . he is in love with you. Haven't you seen it? It's obvious to everyone else. I can't believe you haven't seen it."

"I assure you . . . I can assure you, Emily . . . I had no idea."

"But you can't deny your tenderness for him."

"Feelings for Mr. Walthrope? He is certainly kind . . . but I can't believe he's interested in me. He's just interested in the woolen factory . . . in the war and winning it."

"He's certainly interested in anything related to you," Emily said, laughing gently. She smiled in a distant, romantic way.

"Mr. Walthrope . . . in love with me?"

"It has a poetic sound . . . don't you think? The two of you . . . you're perfect for each other. He's so handsome . . . strong. He always knows what to do . . . to say. He works so hard on our behalf . . . and for Virginia. He's perfect for you."

"But it hasn't been that long since Thaddeus . . . just four months. I'm still in mourning. I'm still draped daily in these black dresses. We shouldn't even speak of such things. I've only known Mr. Walthrope a short while . . . what, a month or two?"

"True. It wouldn't be right perhaps for you to marry him now . . . but wait till next fall . . . an October wedding. It will have been more than a year then. Then you'd have your husband right here with you . . . away from the fighting. Your life would be so pleasant. Think how wonderful it would be!"

"I barely know Mr. Walthrope. I'm certainly not in love with him," Betsy protested. "All we talk about is the factory."

"Don't try to fool me, dear cousin. If you talk only about the factory . . . you must stop it. Talk about other things, too."

Bewildered, Betsy said, "I don't even know what he likes to talk about . . . other than wool. Do you know what he's interested in? What do you talk to him about?"

"We talk about you."

"Me? And what does he say?"

"I don't know that I should say . . ."

"I presume nice things."

"Only the nicest . . . I believe he feels he has found the ideal lady. Think of the advantages! He's becoming so important in town now . . . so respected. He's already paid for a substitute for the army. He's even exempted by his position at the factory. He'll never have to join . . . never. He can stay right here with you. He knows your enterprises. He can take over all of them . . . the mills . . . farm . . . run them for you. You won't have to worry about them anymore. A woman shouldn't have to worry . . . not about such things. You won't have to worry about anything."

"Yes . . . it would be pleasant not to worry. But the farm and mills . . . dealing with them is all that keeps me busy . . . keeps my mind busy. My husband's only been dead four months! This is wrong to think . . . to speak this way. If I didn't have the farm and mills, what would I think about . . . to keep my thoughts off memories? What would I do to keep busy? This is wrong!"

"What did you do before . . . before you were married?"

Betsy answered, trying to remember what she had done with her life in Winchester. "Before? Was there a before? I visited a lot. I had friends . . . relations . . . music . . . the piano forte . . . books. I read a lot of books. There was school . . . and plays, lectures, church, concerts . . . parties."

"You can do all those things again . . . not right now of course. But when you're further along in your mourning, you can do them again. Even now, you can spend more time at the hospital. They have a great need . . . and you are so wonderful with the men. The last time we were there, I overheard two of the sisters speaking of you and the wonderful work you do . . . such praise. Spend more time in the hospital or care more for the patients here under our own roof. Betsy . . . Lucius Walthrope is perfect for you and you'd be foolish not to appreciate that. I can't believe that you're honest with . . . ." She broke off her thought in mid-sentence and smiled. "You are feigning disinterest! I should have known. You are interested in Mr. Walthrope! I've seen it . . . I have seen it!"

Betsy tried to recall what it was that she had done that would have communicated to Emily an interest in Walthrope. She was more familiar with him than was usual among young men and women because they were together so often to discuss the factory. Wool . . . that's all they ever talked about. He was at the house every day, but for reasons of business. It was never personal. She did enjoy his company: He could be entertaining . . . charming. He could also be direct and focused . . . and she liked that in him. Perhaps she had ignored feelings for him. He certainly had done everything he could to win her over. She could see now as she reconsidered memories in the light of this new information.

She recognized the potential of her relationship with him for the first time. She enjoyed the thought. She would like to have someone else worry about the factory, mills and farm. She would like to attend more parties . . . visit more with friends and acquaintances. Hank came to mind. She smiled sweetly, but the pain she had so recently felt had eased. Perhaps her memory of Hank was just her way of wanting to be in love . . . to not be alone. She hoped that was the case. She liked the thought that if she married Walthrope, she would no longer have to worry about Hank . . . except as an old acquaintance . . . a first love. She had not enjoyed this day . . . had suffered much for the Union private. She did not want other such days, as she felt helpless . . . able only to sit . . . fret, hope and pray. She had never felt the same worry and pain for her husband, and she didn't like this feeling as there was no easy remedy for it.

How would she even know if Hank died? No one would think to contact her . . . let her know. She wasn't family. She wasn't even on his side in the war. No one knew he loved her. No one knew she loved him. There she'd thought it. She did love him . . . he loved her . . . and no one else knows it. Her mind stopped processing, paralyzed by a new question:

What if he didn't love her? He might never be able to forgive her for what she'd done in Winchester. He didn't know he was writing to her. He thought it was a widow he'd never met. Her mind began to process again only when she concluded that it would make things easier if she loved Walthrope . . . not Hank. It would be much easier. From that moment and that realization, she began to cultivate a romantic affection for Lucius Walthrope.

Chapter 5
December 1862, Falmouth, Virginia

*T*hree days after the battle at Fredericksburg, Hank wrote to Mrs. Henderson,
My friend,

I hope you are well and that your trust is in God's care. I write to you discouraged as you have done it to us again, that is to say the Confederate Army has done it to us again. I despair for I fear this war will never end, and if it does, I am beginning to believe that your side will prevail. I don't think it's that we're not as brave as your boys. I think it's the generals. You have some great ones. Ours seem to have all the advantages and to make every possible blunder. We fight both the South and our generals, and, unless we can get rid of one of these foes, we haven't a prayer.

We have a new regiment from Michigan that joined our brigade. The 24th. We didn't have much use for them before the battle and treated them pretty bad. I think we thought they wouldn't measure up to the high standard that everyone expects of the Iron Brigade. They call us the Iron Brigade now because we fight as if we're made of iron. We've held in every battle. We don't break, and we don't run. We haven't since we were formed. The boys from Michigan hadn't proved they could measure up. They were what we call bounty boys. We heard they got bounties when they signed up. It makes one question their loyalty, made us wonder if they came just for the money. We had little hope for them.

We didn't have much to do with the main battle over at Fredericksburg. We were on the left end of our lines and the boys from Michigan got in a tangle with some of Stuart's men. It got hot for them, and we were proud of the way they stood up to Stuart. It looks as if they will fit into our brigade after all, and now I'm hearing they never did get bounties to join.

The real test for our regiment came just before we retreated. We were on picket duty, the whole regiment, in front of the lines and a stone's throw from the enemy. I was at a post with two other men. It was a miserable night, very dark. A heavy rain blew in our faces. We had strict orders to be quiet and not to shoot at the enemy, unless they fired at us. There was nothing for us to do but stand there and watch as best we could through that rain for any advance of the enemy. While we were uncomfortable, we weren't too worried about the Rebs as we had a truce with the boys on the other side. Of course, I don't suppose the general knew anything about it, but it made it a bit easier for us out in front like that.

It was nearing early morning when word came for us to pull out very quietly. We thought it a strange order. When the word came to us that our safety and even our very lives depended on our silence, we began to wonder what circumstance had come upon the army.

We were stationed far out front of the army and were told to make our way to the pontoon bridges about three miles from where we were posted. We didn't form or move as a regiment, but moved on our own. We moved as silently as we could, and we were glad we did. As we made our way back toward Fredericksburg, we discovered our army gone. We passed areas that earlier had been teeming with soldiers. They were now silent and empty. It was a very lonely feeling, for we began to think that perhaps we were the only Union boys on the Southern side of the Rappahannock. We imagined the men of our old enemy Stonewall Jackson just whetting their appetites for a little 19th Indiana stew. Picture what we felt when we arrived at the river's edge, where earlier we had crossed on a pontoon bridge, only to find it was no longer there, the engineers were cutting it loose; and we watched it float from the shore. We expected the Confederate cavalry at any minute, and I was sure that any future letters I wrote to you would come from Belle Island or some other Southern prison. The engineers, however, had kept back some boats so they could make their escape. We piled in with them and paddled across the river. Only then did we learn exactly what happened.

Our entire army had retreated. It took place during the night. We were abandoned out there on the field by ourselves. We had no idea what was happening, and I guess we weren't supposed to know. The generals, Burnside and Reynolds, were going to sacrifice us so the rest of the army could get away. The generals in all their wisdom figured that if the rebels heard or saw

something that made them think the Union was retreating, they would push forward and find us still in
their front. They would think the army wasn't retreating after all. Not letting the enemy know you're retreating is important, because if they attack then,
you're vulnerable. So we were to protect the army by
sacrificing ourselves. If morning had come and the
Confederates had discovered the retreat, they would
have killed everyone in the 19th, as I don't believe
there's a man among us who would have surrendered.

Huzzah for our colonel. When the rest of the army
was safely across the river, he pulled us in and we, as
quiet as a thought, made our way to those boats. I was
one of the last ones across, and I'm glad to say that we
didn't lose one man in the retreat.

I am becoming quite regular at prayer now. I said
several fervent prayers as we retreated and crossed
the river. Our Heavenly Father watches over me; I'm
convinced of that and grateful.

Let me describe the battle at the other end of the
line. It's being called a slaughter. I've talked to some of
the boys down the line and they say General Burnside
had them charge over a long, slow rise toward a hill
where all the Confederate guns were firing away.
Some of the boys were making real progress in the
charge when a whole line of your soldiers stood up and
fired. The Confederates were hiding behind a wall in a
sunken road. Our boys couldn't see the road, the wall
or the men until it was too late. They had no idea the
Rebels were there and when they fired into our boys, it
stopped our charge. Our general in all his wisdom kept
ordering more troops across that open field of slaugh-

ter. *Thousands died there at what they call Marye's Heights.*

I don't understand why we don't get good generals. If we had a Lee or a Jackson or a Hill, we'd already be home. It seems God is on your side and is going to bring victory to the South. I hope you're not offended if I pray I'm wrong, or that God changes allegiance. I don't see how he can want the country torn in two or that he wants men to serve as slaves. They say God moves in mysterious ways. Perhaps he's just prolonging the war in disgust for us all, or to humble us, or because of our sins. Maybe he's sending a flood of blood to cover the earth as he once sent rain. I do believe it's because of our sins. I've found sin to be an interesting topic to discuss and would someday like to discuss it with you.

That's enough about the war. I have been healthy. I don't ever seem to get sick out here. Many men are sick. My friend, a fellow by the name of George, from Indiana, has been sick and couldn't fight in the battle. I teased him about not fighting. George is always joking with people, and it was good to make fun of him. He took it hard as he really wanted to fight, but he's been real sick and couldn't have lasted the day. I hope he gets well soon. He's in the hospital, and we miss his company.

I hope you are well and that you remember how much respect I have for you. I continue to look forward to presenting to you the letter I carry from your husband. I hope you don't miss him much, but are happy.

Ever your friend

Chapter 6
December 1862, Falmouth, Virginia

*H*ank's hands were nearly frozen. He put away his pen and sealed the letter. The ground too was frozen, and he made his way across its hard surface to a fire that Nat was feeding. Hank sat down without speaking.

Nat looked up at him, but likewise said nothing. It was more than a minute before Nat broke the silence. "I went to see George at the hospital."

Hank loved to listen to Nat speak. When he spoke it was as if he was singing, and it nearly always brightened Hank's mood just to hear him. Hank responded, "I want to go see him, too. How's he doing?"

"He's real sick, but I think he's gonna make it. Says his coughin' ain't as bad as 'twas . . . course it sounded bad to me. I told him you was still pretty upset he didn't do no fightin' . . . that you talked to the lieutenant and told him you thought he was skulkin'. Hank, you should'a seen him! He got mighty upset. That's when he started coughin' so bad. I suppose I shouldn't have said it . . . but I didn't let him think it for long. I told him the truth. He laughed, then started coughin' all over agin. He said the doctor told him he'd be ready to fight real soon. I hope he is. 'Tis tough to see him there when he wants to be with us."

They both sat close to the fire, huddling with their backs against the cold wind, but it swirled and twisted around, periodically blowing smoke and ashes into their faces. Both men looked forward to making winter camp where they could build a rough cabin for at least some defense against such wind. Last winter, they had made what they considered a good one, and they hoped word would soon come that they were going into winter camp.

"Hank, d'you know I have eight brothers and sisters. I'm the oldest."

Hank looked at him without responding.

"I'm the biggest, too." He smiled. "The rest of my brothers . . . there were three brothers, are 'bout your size. My father always counted on me to do a lot 'round the farm. Never had no chance to go to school . . . always needed on the farm. Pa and me worked hard in them fields. He was from Sweden. I don't think I told you that, did I?" He looked at Hank, but expected no response. "He didn't speak good English, and wanted me to go to school so I'd learn. I was born in Sweden, too . . . come over as just a little boy. Pa changed my name to Nathaniel when we come over . . . said it sounded American. I grew up big and strong. Pa needed me more to help 'round the farm than to go to school. Summer or winter—didn't matter—there was always work for us. That's how come I can't write or read no letters."

Hank listened respectfully. Hank had never heard Nat talk about himself so much. Nathaniel had dictated letters to Hank who had written them out, so Hank knew much of what he heard. Nat, however, had never spoken so freely and directly about it. Hank said, "Nat, you speak English well . . . and you can sing."

Nat smiled weakly, "The other boys . . . they helped with some o' the work, but they couldn't do the work I could do. So when they wanted to go to school, it didn't matter much . . . and they got to go. Pa always needed me. He was workin' hard on the farm . . . he needed help. He once told me when we was out in the field. I still remember the words he said: 'Nathaniel, you go to shool tis year. Be teached all you can, so you can be a goot American boy.'

"I knew he wanted me to be a real American . . . it was important to 'im. But he needed my help on the farm, so I said, 'Pa, I am a real American. I can stay right here with you.'

"He smiled . . . his teeth all showed. You see, Hank, that's what he wanted me to say. He answered me: 'I guess you are an American. You can stay right here vit me'. And he just kept right on smiling. So I stayed there to work with him. Hank, we made a beautiful farm. We were doing real well. The other boys worked on the farm when they could, but my pa and me, we worked hard, every day, from when the sun come up, till it went down . . . even in the winter. That's why being out here ain't so hard on me. There was always something to do, always some work needin' to be done.

"When the war come along . . . my pa says to me, 'We should do our part; 'tis our country now.'

"I understood right then—he wanted me to join up with the Union. He didn't say that to the younger boys . . . just me. So I said to my pa, 'I'm gonna join the Union army.'

"Pa got a big smile on his face and said, 'We're all Americans now. You yoin the army.' I knew my pa wanted me to join, but I didn't want to be no soldier . . . not at first. I never wanted to be no soldier, but pa wanted it. So I joined."

Hank didn't respond, but looked closely at Nat's face and could see a sorrow he'd never seen before.

"Hank . . . I don't think I'll see my pa agin. Who will help him with the farm?"

Hank spoke quickly, "Of course you'll see him again. By spring you'll be right there with him plowing the field."

Nat shook his head vigorously from side to side. "Hank, you're real smart. You know things. I don't mean no disrespect . . . I have a feelin' that I won't see no more springs on the farm."

"Nat, that's nonsense! You're just tired and cold."

"I am tired and cold, Hank . . . and lonely. I want to be a good soldier, so my pa can feel he done what he could for the country . . . so he could feel like he was American, too. Having a good soldier in his family . . . that makes him proud. In my mind, I hear him tellin' neighbors how his boy is fightin' for the Union." Nat sat quietly for a minute, then continued, "When they write they tell how good things are on the farm, and I feel real sad. They send packages with lots of them goodies, and I like 'em. But my brothers don't join the army . . . just me. I write 'em—you know that—but have you ever heard me say they should join the army? I ain't 'bout to say that. 'I tell 'em, stay home. Don't come here.' Hank, remember how excited we was to be soldiers in them early days? I didn't want to join, but when I did, I got excited to fight. Remember how excitin' it was . . . everyone wishin' us well . . . givin' us food, speeches? We was gonna save the Union . . . and fast. Now I write—or you write—and tell my brothers don't become no soldiers. Stay at home! Go to school! Work the farm! Get married to a pretty little girl, but don't be no soldiers. But for me . . . for you, the more we fight, the more we die . . . and we never seem to get no closer to bein' home. Wherever we go, the Rebs are there first; whatever we do, it ain't enough."

Hank interrupted. "Nat, you listen to what I'm telling you. You just wait till next spring, we'll win the big battle . . . big thing. Then Abe and Congress will send us all home. Then you'll go home a hero with laurels on your head."

"I hope you're right, Hank. But I don't know that I can wait till then."

"What would you do? Are you thinking of leaving?"

"No, can't desert. You know that. Pa would lose his soldier . . . wouldn't want me at home like that. No, I have to keep on soldierin'."

Hank looked at Nat and wondered what the conversation meant.

Chapter 7
February 1863, Belle Plain, Virginia

*T*he next letter Hank received from Staunton said,
Dear friend,

I was relieved to hear that you were well. I thank the Lord for his mercy. We had heard horrid reports of how the Yanks were killed at Fredericksburg. I worried about you for nearly a month before receiving your letter, and then to read of your narrow escape. My heart stopped with each sentence. But, in the end, to hear that you were well relieved me of a great burden. Still, I can't stop thinking how close you were to peril when you were left alone on the field. You did right to pray, but know that I pray for your safety day and night. You cannot know how I worry for you who have been so kind to my husband. I only look forward to the day when I can thank you in person.

All is well here. I continue to live with my husband's cousin and both of us are working to ease the burdens of wounded soldiers here in Staunton. Many soldiers are sent here to recuperate from wounds and sickness because the railroad comes here from Richmond. A few soldiers are usually in the house with us recovering from every kind of sickness or injury. A surgeon checks in on them periodically, and the servants nurse them and take care of them for the most part, although we do help when we can. My cousin's house is very big, so we hardly know they're about, and allowing them to recover here is the least we can do.

I like to spend at least a day a week at one of the hospitals in town rolling bandages and caring for the wounded. When I'm there, I imagine that I am caring for you because you have been so kind, and I would like to repay you. Do not think such thoughts disloyal to my husband. If you do, then you misunderstand my intent. I can't care for my husband as he is beyond all earthly care, but my concern for you honors him because you were the last to serve him in this life.

Life in Staunton is busy. We have much work to do to support the war. The town is full of soldiers, and I work to make sure there are uniforms for our soldiers and food for them. As you probably have noticed, I haven't done a very good job as many of our boys from Virginia are without uniforms and are as skinny as fence posts. I hear often how they are even without shoes, but I can't help with that as I don't know how to make shoes. Some shoes are made here in town, but I don't help with that.

Hank smiled as he read her comment about shoes for Secesh. Her comment reminded him of George who often joked that if he were dying on a battlefield, he would take his shoes off and lay them by his body just to save the poor Rebs the trouble of having to pry them off his swollen feet after he was dead. George always called it his final peace offering. Hank continued reading.

I hear only wonderful stories about how brave our soldiers are. Although I do have a friend who told me of one soldier he met while traveling here in the valley last summer who was so stupid that he thought we should turn him over to the Yankees to disrupt their whole army. I think he jests as I have seen only intelligent and brave soldiers among our men. I do think a great deal about the soldiers, especially about you. I have reserved a special place in my affections for the man who served my husband.

For the first time in their exchange of letters, Hank felt hurt. He was sad she was concerned for the very men who were trying to kill him. As a soldier, he was disheartened by her flippant words about a "stupid" Confederate soldier. He finished reading the letter.

My friend, let me close now with the thought that we shall one day, in a time of peace and happiness, meet face to face.
Your particular friend

George, his cough showing signs of improvement, had regained his strength and returned to camp. Shortly after the battle at Fredericksburg, winter camp had been proclaimed, and George, Nat and Hank built a cabin at Belle Plain, Virginia, of log and mud walls, mud floor and tent roof. They expected to be there throughout the winter so they built it well, including a crude stone fireplace in one of its walls.

Hank lay on his bunk in the cabin reading the letter, glad to have shelter. He rolled over as he finished it. The cabin was home only to Hank and George now. Nat was gone:

In January, General Burnside tried to outmaneuver the Rebels through a long march around their flank. It hadn't worked as planned and the movement left the Union army mired in the wheel-high mud of unexpected bad weather. When Hank, George and Nat got back from what they called Burnside's Mud March, Nat was feverish, covered with spots. While they were away, soldiers from Ohio had occupied and desecrated their cabin, but the defilers graciously and quickly vacated when Nat cordially showed them his spots. Hank and George carefully nursed Nat for three days, but he sickened more each day. On the third day, they took him to the hospital. It turned out to be the measles, and he died several days later.

Hank and George buried Nat, but before covering the body with dirt, George had wanted to offer a prayer. Hank lowered his head as George spoke, "Our Father in Heaven, this here body that lays in your ground is your son Nathaniel Andersson from that state o' Indiana. He's comin' home to you now. He was a good man. Hank and me, we never heared him cuss much . . . not too much. He never gambled, and he didn't never go after no harlots. He was a good friend to Hank and me . . . a real hard worker . . . and he could sing. When he sung, it was like listenin' to them angels that you keep 'round that high throne you got yourself. I s'pose you might be able to use him in that choir o' angels. I think he'd be willin'. If you don't need him fer your choir, put him on your farm. He's a right good farmer, and he'll raise some real nice crops fer you. We're gonna miss him down here mighty grievous, so take good care o' him . . . and make sure he ain't gotta share that mansion you give him with no Secesh. He'd rather die than do that. Now, 'bout them Rebels, Na-

thaniel Andersson, he done his share of fightin' 'gainst
'em. Even though you took Nat to yourself, we're gonna keep on afightin' 'em. We'll keep tryin' to whip
those Rebels back into the Union. But we sure could
use some help with that . . . they are very pesky fellas.
Course we know you already knowed that. Whatever
help you can spare would be 'preciated. Thank you,
Lord. Amen."

George finished the prayer and raised his head to
talk to Hank. Hank kept his head bowed. He smiled to
himself as he thought of George's prayer and said one
softly in his heart, "Father in Heaven, Nathaniel Andersson was a good friend . . . a great American. Thank
you for letting me know him, and please take him to
yourself, I pray in your son's name. Amen."

George's piercing stare greeted Hank as he raised
his head. "Hank, d'you think I should become one o'
them preachers after this here war's all over?"

"George Dyer, I think you'd make a fine preacher . .
. better than any they have in this army." He smiled
warmly at George whose stare had softened into a look
of sadness. Hank had the feeling he was going to cry,
but George's sadness lasted only seconds and disappeared behind a jolly look.

"That's what I'll be then . . . when we're all done.
Hank, I'll be 'xpectin' you in my flock, and I want big
freewill offerin's from you, too."

"I'll be the first one to give, George. Don't worry
about that."

Hank and George walked without saying another
word back to their hovel. They both lay on their beds.
Hank lay on his back looking at the roof made of sev-

eral tents buttoned together. He thought of Nathaniel .
. . his farm . . . his brothers . . . his father. Hank pictured Nathaniel's father working the fields alone. He
imagined him getting the news, saying nothing, just
continuing work . . . alone in those fields with silent
tears on his cheeks.

Chapter 8
March 1863, Staunton, Virginia

*R*uth, Emily's house slave, brought the letter to Betsy who had been reading the latest edition of the *Staunton Spectator*. She accepted the letter calmly, set it aside and continued to read the newspaper. The letter was from Hank. She knew it without looking and resisted an urge to read the envelope. Until that moment, reading the war news had thoroughly engrossed her, but once she touched the envelope, she lost all interest in the conflict. She stared at the paper without comprehension as the letters blurred before her gaze. She was torn. She wanted to push the newspaper away, tear the letter from the envelope and devour the words, hoping for some inkling that Hank loved her, Betsy Richman Henderson, not just the widow Henderson as he imagined her. At the same instant, she abhorred the letter as it could only bring her more worry.

In many conversations during the last three months, Emily had suggested an easier solution: a strong, loving man nearby and immediately available. All Betsy had to do was reach out to Walthrope. If she embraced her factory superintendent, then uncertainty could end—the worry and desperate hope she felt for Hank could stop. Her cousin's persistent suggestions had worn down her resistance. At times she continued to

feel the love she had felt for Hank in Winchester, feelings only sharpened by her sense of lost time and opportunity. There were times when she was sure she
would love him forever, but there were other times,
increasing as the weeks passed, when she gave up
hope in his love.

Guided by Emily, Betsy thought more and more
about Walthrope. She thought about how easy it could
be if she abandoned all for him. At those moments, she
would commit to herself to forget Hank.

Her resolve to forget Hank was peaking when she
received Hank's latest letter. At first, she pledged unconsciously not to open the letter. She would rise from
her seat, cast it into the afternoon fire that warmed
the room. It would be done . . . over. But the letter was
tantalizingly close, and she remembered Hank, the
walks they had taken, how he listened to her. It didn't
make a difference what she said, he listened and
sometimes made gentle fun of her. He didn't always
agree with her. He often expressed concern over what
she said or did, but she never felt judged. He was
sometimes impulsive, and she found that exciting. A
gentle snow-ball fight, an unexpected horse race, a
surprise gift. His spontaneity came from a deep love of
life and an inability to see too far into its future.

Walthrope was kind to her, too. But it was different.
He was kind to her as a shopkeeper would be—
seemingly always trying to please the customer to ensure future business. It seemed Walthrope wanted her
to have her whims filled before she spoke them or even
thought them. Hank had always spoken of inner
strength, devotion, a love for others, a purpose. But

she was tired; the war had already gone on too long. She had lost her husband. She was lonely.

Emily's romantic suggestions were pleasing and comfortable. Increasingly over the months, Betsy had begun to feel she didn't want to strive for anything beyond beautiful flowers on a table, happy company, the taste of a fine dinner, the rustling of a new dress. She didn't want to wait any longer. Life had worn her. She wanted physical comforts, not more sorrow . . . not more pain. When Emily had suggested that Betsy loved Walthrope, she accepted the possibility because it was so easy and she was tired. A man's voice, his touch, a gift of flowers, pleasant conversation, a dance, a party, admiring eyes nurturing her . . . they were all now within her reach. They would feel so good. All she had to do was love this man who seemed to love her, and abandon someone so far away . . . imagined . . . wonderful, but unattainable. Emily continued to suggest the possibilities. Walthrope continued to be there, always pleasant, always giving, subtly confirming those same possibilities. The race between suitors was run anew daily, and in each race Hank fell farther behind, not because she loved him less, but because he was so inaccessible, and she craved companionship.

After 15 minutes of inner-struggle, Betsy's resolve to toss the letter into the flame evaporated. Yes, she would probably commit herself to Walthrope—of course she would—a marital union could not be far off. But where was the harm in opening the letter? Young Hank had been a dear friend. She seized it and opened it with shaking hands.

Dear Friend,

I write to you in sorrow today, as I've just buried a friend. He died of the measles. He's not the only one I've seen die from it in the war, but he's the closest one. And I feel it more than all the other deaths combined. He was born in Sweden. Funny to think that he should be born in Sweden and still fight in this war. Perhaps it's not just a war between states, but a war for the world. It seems right that it should be so as we are one of very few countries, if there are any others, where citizens are free and govern themselves, with no monarchy and no despot. If you look around this army, you see people from everywhere. I've met Russians, Frenchmen, Canadians, Irishmen, Scots, lots of Germans, and more. You wonder why they fight for us, but it may be they only fight for themselves. My friend's father was proud to have a son fighting for the Union. It's funny that a man who was born an ocean away would take such pride in having a son at war for the Union, unless he believed that he really fought for liberty. Perhaps that's how it should be.

Hank's words were anathema to the Southern Cause, but Betsy didn't see them in that light on this day. She remembered fondly her father and how he taught her about the great struggle between those who would grant liberty and those, driven by the devil, who, above all else, would seek to exert their wills over others . . . to control others, to mold others as they wanted . . . all for their own glory. She remembered her father recounting the stories of his grandfathers who had fought in the Revolution of '76. As she read Hank's words, she didn't focus on whether her allegiance was Confederate or Union, she focused on her allegiance to freedom and self determination. She felt deeply that they were available to her only because God had willed it through intervention in a revolution and in the creation of a constitutional government based on republican principles, a possibility not even imagined 100 years earlier. Her father had contended that it was a miracle, and she heard his words as she read Hank's letter. She remembered him standing next to Hank.

She continued to read.

I will miss my friend, but I feel especially for his family who will suffer agony for their loss. It's hard to lose a son or brother in this war. It must be harder yet to lose a husband.

I must confess that I have a greater desire now to meet you. To exchange letters is wonderful, but it would give such pleasure to hear your voice for just a few moments.

She wanted to hear Hank's voice, too. She tried to remember what it sounded like, but couldn't. Mildly disappointed, she continued reading.

Friendship has become very important to me. The boys are like family. I would give anything to see my family again, as I miss them more with each passing week. Years ago, I had a friend. It would mean so much to me to be able to once again be her friend, but I can't go back as there are so many bad feelings. So I hope that you will let me be the friend to you that I should have been to her.

The letter brought her up short. Was he writing of her—Betsy Richman? She held no bad feelings! Yet he wrote of bad feelings. It was him . . . he held bad feelings for her. It could never work out then, not for the two of them. She stared at the letter and cried silently. Her decision would be easier to make.

Chapter 9
May 1863, Staunton, Virginia

Walthrope and Betsy sat close together on a couch in Emily's parlor. It was early afternoon and Emily who had been with them had excused herself momentarily, leaving the pair alone.

"Betsy, why won't you call me by my given name? You insist that I call you by yours, but refuse to use mine."

"Mr. Walthrope, it's because of my great respect for you."

"I don't want respect! Don't you know you torture me with your distance? I profess at this very moment my undying love for you. I ask plainly: Do you return my regard?" He paused to give Betsy an opportunity to respond. When he saw she wasn't going to answer, he continued, "Why can't you understand that I labor here only for you? The Confederacy, the war, soldiers . . . none of it matters to me when compared to you. Will you not accept that . . . and my love? Will you not return that love? Don't taunt me; don't ignore my feelings another minute. It's time for you to depend on me more than ever before. I can make your life very comfortable."

"Mr. Walthrope, you know I'm already very comfortable. There are many here in Staunton—soldiers, families, refugees—hard pressed for food, clothing, shelter. Here I am, short on salt, but with an abundance of everything else. I can still buy ready-made clothing. And wool, as long as I want it in gray, I can have as much as I could use in a lifetime. Many are wearing rags—nice, decent clothes fallen apart—that no longer cover their nakedness. It's an abomination. It condemns me . . . us. Some of the poor wretches have nothing but a thin skin stretched over their bones. Doesn't that suggest I'm already more comfortable than I ought to be."

The force and content of her response surprised Walthrope, but he didn't waver. "It suggests you think too much about others, and not enough about yourself. You're generous with them. Betsy, you have a right to what you have! You've earned it. They can't be compared to you."

She turned her face to look directly at him, anger in her eyes, "I, Mr. Walthrope, am a widow . . . not even a year. All that I have 'earned,' as you say, was a gift that came from a family wiped from the earth—the last one by this cursed war. I, unworthy mind you—most unworthy, live off its fortune by the mere chance of a short marriage . . . a fortune earned by sweat over generations and by the blessing of God. What I have earned, you say! Earned? Do any of us earn what we have?"

"Perhaps I didn't speak what I felt. Allow me to attempt it again. You, kind lady, have extended all you have to those around you. Now I ask: Don't you owe it to yourself to find happiness, comfort and ease."

She looked at him. She was angry, but the warmth in his blue eyes softened her feelings. He was just attempting to praise her. She should be flattered. He was surely as compassionate as she was. He was just trying to impress her, to court her. He was just trying to make her happy. She did want to be happy. Her anger passed, and her face took on a flirtatious smile, "The liberties you take with such talk might be hurtful to many a widow or . . . worse yet . . . weaken their resolve."

"Many a widow would be offended, and many, I dare say, would lose their resolve in these days. But not you! You are a rock for many who flounder in the sea of lost hope . . . of heartache and hardship that rides this tide of bloodshed and coercion. It is you to whom many grab hold for safety. But can't that rock that is you be moored for its own safety, for your own safety? You know I'm most sincere in proclaiming my intentions, my devoted love for you. Don't ignore them for another hour! Why will you not accept my love . . . and all it has to offer?"

"And what might it offer?" she said continuing her teasing tone.

"You'll be able to forget your business concerns. You'll have a devoted servant, a companion, who worships you for the remainder of your life."

"Is this a proposal, Mr. Walthrope?"

Walthrope took on a crestfallen look. "I don't think you would accept a proposal, so I don't waste my words."

"Oh, you might be surprised."

"I think not. But I would give you everything you could ever want."

"And what is it I want?"

"Only you can tell me that. What do you want? Tell me, tell me! It will be yours!"

"A large family."

"Sixteen children! I promise it! Shall I swear it on the Bible?"

"I didn't mean that large."

"It's too late. It's already promised. Tell me more! What is it you really want?"

The smile disappeared from her face as the question permeated her being, sneaking safely past her defenses and the game she was playing. She wanted to see Hank . . . to marry Hank. Could he arrange that? A sadness touched her lips as she said, "But there's nothing I want."

"Why do you do that?"

"What?"

"Whenever we have a serious discussion about our future together, you tease, you ignore, till finally we get close to understanding one another. Then it's as if a shade is pulled down over your eyes and all light— light that brings me joy—is hidden. What is it that keeps you from telling me what you really want? Confide in me!"

Void of emotion, she looked up into his face. "Perhaps I just don't think you can bring me what will make me happy."

"Whatever it is, I'll get it for you. If you don't tell me . . . if you don't tell me now, I'll find the answer somehow, and I will get it for you. I will! Is it peace? The war to end? I'll arrange it. Do you want all Yankees skewered and roasting slowly on a spit? I'll arrange that! Whatever it is—just tell me!" He could see she was not going to respond. With determination he said, "I'll discover your secret. I will know what will make you happy."

She shuddered at the thought that he would ever know about Hank. It alarmed her further to think that she wanted to give in, forget Hank, give herself to Walthrope, allow him to take care of her, to think for her, to work for her, to love her. Walthrope had been right: Somewhere deep within she hesitated in giving herself to him, and he saw it. It was not the first time it had happened. At the moment when she would be ready to yield to his will, a memory would surface and rekindle her feelings for Hank. Then it was, as Walthrope said, as if blinds closed over her eyes leaving her alone with her thoughts. She would recognize again in that moment that her love for Hank, as imaginary as it was, overshadowed any feeling she could ever have for Walthrope.

Walthrope was still talking, "I will know, Betsy! I will know what troubles you. I will make you happy."

Betsy laughed, "I would save you, Mr. Walthrope, from a fruitless search."

"It is not fruit I hunt, Mrs. Henderson," he said firmly, staring hard into her eyes.

True to his word, his search began that afternoon. He took Emily aside in the parlor, where they sat side by side on the same couch where earlier he sat with Betsy.

"Why doesn't Betsy love me?"

"My dear Mr. Walthrope, she is madly in love with you. I'm convinced she wants to be yours more than anything else in this world."

"Then why does she hold back her most intimate thoughts and feelings from me?"

"It's simple. Can't you see it? She's torn by her love for my cousin, her responsibilities and duties as a widow, her love for you. I am as convinced that she loves you as I am that the sun will rise tomorrow. I assure you that at this very moment she is tortured by the very thought that she will not be yours."

The cousin rose and walked away happily, leaving Walthrope thinking, worry on his face. He was not convinced it was devotion to her late husband that held Betsy back, and he swore to himself that he would find out what it was.

Chapter 10
May 1863, Somewhere near the Rapidan River, Virginia

*T*he rain was pouring on the Iron Brigade as they marched back from the battle of Chancellorsville. Hank, lost in his thoughts as he often was on long marches, remembered his final visit to Betsy. That day was a sweet memory to him for the first time. Lost was his feeling of humiliation and sorrow. He smiled as the rain dripped from his tall felt hat. He remembered each person in the Richman parlor, the conversation, the description of some obscure instructor at the VMI and how he stood in the rain . . . abandoned even by his cadets. The same instructor, now a general, had just whipped the Yankees again. On this day, they were all in his element.

Hank was disappointed the Union had lost again, but he thought little of the battle as the brigade had never fully engaged and had been far from crucial action in the Union debacle. This experience—marching—would be his memory from Chancellorsville. He leaned his head back slightly and stuck out his tongue. He caught a rain drop in his mouth and felt a childlike excitement. The tiny raindrop refreshed him. In spite of the evil into which the drop fell, it was cold . . . pure . . . innocent. He craved an innocent world. He hoped he would live through the war, hoped the widow would love him, hoped he would love her.

The sounds that swirled around him caught his attention. He began listening—swearing, yelling, rushing here and there just off the road, rumors about how many died and who was left, rumors about Jackson, opinions about how badly they fared and how badly they were led once again. All of these sounds lay over the top of the steady, muffled beat of the infantry's feet upon the deepening mud of the way. He listened, taking hope from the sound. It didn't matter that Stonewall Jackson had just beaten them again. He had done it before, and this army had always come back. The Iron Brigade . . . the First Corps . . . the Army of the Potomac . . . they would be back. As long as feet kept this rhythm, all would be well in the end, as long as they kept marching . . . marching . . . marching. The rhythm captured his subconscious, speaking words in his mind. It proclaimed that the Union would not die, not this army with its failing generals, not this nation rent in two, not this cause Hank now cherished so deeply, not those people who had determined to fight on until peace came to an undivided United States. Hank savored the impression, as he trudged in the rain and softening mud, that all would be well.

Chapter 11
May 1863, Staunton, Virginia

"*B*etsy . . . Oh, Betsy! He's wounded, he's wounded," her cousin said as she came running into Betsy's large, second-floor bedroom. "We've just heard. No one can talk of anything else."

Betsy, who sat in front of a large mirror and table, felt a part of her die. Hank wounded? How could it be? How did Emily know to tell her? How had she heard?

"They say he was shot by his own men," Emily said, and without breaking for a breath added, "Our good General Jackson, oh, our good General Jackson. They say his wife and baby are on their way to him. He lost an arm."

"Jackson, injured?" Betsy responded, oblivious to what she had said. Then it was not Hank after all. Life poured again into her being.

"Yes, his own men shot him . . . North Carolinians. They say he will recover, but what a loss until then. I thought God would protect him, not let anything happen to him. I didn't think anything could happen to him. I don't understand it. What does God intend? Has he fulfilled his mission?"

Betsy responded simply: "He is a great general."

"None better . . . unless it's General Lee," Emily said. "But the battle was a great success. If Jackson hadn't been shot . . . did I tell you that General Hill was wounded, too? If Jackson hadn't been shot, they say we would have crushed the whole Union army. We would have sent them back to New York or Vermont . . . or Hell . . . or wherever those fiends come from."

Under normal circumstances, Emily's last sentiment would have shocked Betsy, but the widow didn't notice it.

"Then the battle wasn't lost?"

"Oh, no! How could it be?" Emily's mode changed to joy. "Is there anything but Confederate victories? It was a great victory. The Yankees scurried northward. With Jackson though, we could have destroyed their entire army. There would have been nothing left! We could have ended their cursed occupation forever. This . . . this . . . this war would have been over. We were so close! Why has God done this to us when we needed his help the most. We were so close to the final victory." She looked meaningfully at Betsy, "You could have accepted Mr. Walthrope's proposal."

"His proposal? What proposal? And what's that got to do with the war?"

"Oh, my dear cousin," Emily said as she moved behind Betsy and began to arrange her cousin's hair, watching in the mirror. "It is so clear to me . . . the only thing that keeps you from his arms is this evil war levied on us by the beast of the North."

"What nonsense! Why would the war encourage or discourage me from Mr. Walthrope?"

"What else could it be? Unless you have some secret you withhold from even your dearest cousin, I can only conclude that it must be the war. You would never conceal your thoughts and feelings from me."

"You misread me," Betsy said wanting to tell her . . . to tell someone at that moment . . . to tell anyone . . . what restrained her feelings for Walthrope. "I am in love. That's what holds me back," she said.

"In love? Of course you are. I know that. Then why hold back? Nothing keeps you from his promise of matrimonial bliss. He is ready. I assure you."

"I'm not in love with him."

The cousin instantly looked thoughtful, then distressed. "I am sorry," she said meekly. "I have forgotten your great love for Thaddeus." Her voice rose as she continued to speak. "I have been so busy encouraging you to embrace a growing love that extends its arms to you that I have forgotten one that stands behind ever pulling you to the past." She spoke softly again, "Betsy, my love, you can't mourn forever. Thaddeus wouldn't want that. You've been faithful to him . . . to his name. I have seen that a thousand times during these past months. Now you must go on without him. There can't be another love like your first love. You can always cherish that love in your heart. But he's gone, dear Betsy . . . sweet Betsy. You can . . . for your happiness you must . . . give yourself again, without any discredit to Thaddeus. Certainly Thaddeus would approve of his dear friend Lucius."

"You're right. It is hard," Betsy said, "to forget your first love." Emily remembered Thaddeus and smiled thinking of Betsy loving him so much. Betsy smiled remembering Hank. Betsy silently said a prayer that he would be safe from harm. Without warning, momentarily oblivious to her cousin's continued presence, she pulled paper and pen from a drawer in the dressing table and began a letter. The cousin watched curiously, confused by this sudden urge to write.

"Betsy, who are you writing to?"

Reminded that Emily still hovered over her, Betsy again craved sharing her secret. She knew Emily wouldn't understand nor approve, but to share the secret with anyone would make it less painful. "I do have a secret I have kept from you," Betsy said impulsively, turning abruptly to face Emily.

"A secret from me? I can't believe it. Why have you done this?"

"It's a very painful secret. Painful to you as well I fear."

The cousin looked concerned, "What can it be?"

"You will be angry with me."

"Then I promise beforehand that I shall not be."

Betsy looked at her cousin, breathed deeply and said, "Do you remember the letter I received from the Union soldier?"

The cousin looked stricken. "How could I forget that day . . . the horrible fight we had. Oh, please don't bring that up."

"I'm in love with that soldier."

"You can't be," Emily said softly with chagrin on her features. "You don't know him." She showed no sign of the expected anger, and that encouraged Betsy to continue. She told her cousin about Hank, his friendship, their love, his proposal, her rejection, his letters, her letters, her pain, her confusion, her befuddling interest in Walthrope, and of something deep inside that gnawed at her and didn't allow her to give herself completely to Walthrope . . . or to let go of Hank.

Emily listened empathetically, compassionately, tears welling up in her eyes several times. She felt none of her usual patriotic zeal as she shared Betsy's sorrow, discomfort and hope, but one question bothered her. When Betsy finished telling her story, Emily asked it immediately. "Betsy, did you feel this way when you married my cousin?"

Betsy looked horror stricken, "Oh no, you mustn't think that. I loved Thaddeus, and was true to him in thought and deed the entire time we were married. To me Hank was dead. It was only when Thaddeus was gone . . . when I learned Hank was still alive, then . . . then all the feelings returned."

Emily sighed inadvertently, then smiled. "Then there's nothing to be worried about. Your feelings will sort themselves out in time. You must be patient, as apparently, so must Lucius. I still believe he is perfect for you . . . and time will tell. In the meantime, you must be true to yourself and your feelings, and commit to no one."

Betsy stared, disbelieving, at her cousin. Where was the Emily ever ready to defend the Confederacy and its citizens against kind words spoken of Yankees? Where was the Emily who inflicted pain on many rather than allow herself to be hurt. Betsy rose from the table and put her arms around her cousin and said, "Oh, Emily, thank you."

Emily allowed Betsy to hug her for a moment, then demonstrating discomfort pulled away from her. "I too have a secret kept from you, though I suspect you know it as well as I."

"It'll be sacred to me if you wish to share it."

"It's about my husband."

Betsy felt her back stiffen. "Please . . . you don't need to tell me."

"I see you do know," the cousin said smiling sadly. "I've known for a time myself. You were right that day that letter came. He has not proven brave in the army. I've heard people talking . . . sometimes when they thought I wasn't listening, sometimes when they knew I was. But Betsy, I love him . . . courageous or not."

Chapter 12
5 July 1863, Gettysburg, Pennsylvania

Dear friend,

I am forever in your debt for allowing me to write to you the feelings of my heart. They are poignant this day. For the past several days, we have been involved in a tremendous battle, and I am wearied by war. I lost a friend who has been with me from the time I enlisted. His name was George. I have lost many friends, and I don't know that the war is any closer to ending, but to lose George is to lose another brother.

We think we are driving General Lee and the honorable soldiers of the South back into Virginia, but I fear they will escape again. Our generals allow the Army of Northern Virginia every opportunity to escape. I worry that perhaps this battle victory will have no clear outcome or purpose. I am not sure that I'm able to continue this fight. I have lost enough friends and seen many die. There are just a handful left in the regiment and even fewer if you consider only those who mustered in with us. If I had family in the North, and they told me to come home, I would leave today and try to never think again about what I've seen and what I've done.

Let me tell you about the battle. Our brigade was among the first to arrive. Our regiment was on picket duty the night before and joined the rest of the brigade as it marched toward this place here in Pennsylvania, a town called Gettysburg. When we got here we were just in time, and we could hear the sounds of musketry, cannon and cavalry carbines just beyond the town. They called us forward and sent us down a hill toward charging Southerners.

Our muskets were loaded from picket duty, so we fired right away and our volley seemed to have a good effect. We chased them back across a creek and up a hill capturing many of them. We won the morning fight, but lost a general, General Reynolds, the same general who planned to abandon us at Fredericksburg.

In the afternoon, the Confederates came back. The fighting was terrible, and many died on both sides. There were many more of them in the afternoon, and they fired at us, and we at them. I could see them fall, but many of our line fell, too. The general told us to hold the position under all circumstances, and as I saw so many Rebel soldiers firing at us, I accepted my fate. I was sure I would not, indeed could not, live under such circumstances.

I was not with George when he died. We chatted during the lull before the afternoon battle, but lost track of each other as the fighting renewed. Today, I went back to that place and found him. He was lying on his back, eyes staring heavenward, legs crumpled beside him. One arm lay twisted under him, the other straight at his side. His musket was gone and his hat lay partially crushed underneath his head. His pockets were cut open. That's what they do to rob you of valuables once you're dead. His boots were gone, and he never got the chance to take them off as he always said he would.

I didn't even know him at first. His body and face were black and swollen. I only identified him because he had pinned his name on his uniform after the morning fight. I wonder now if he knew he was going to die. We buried George. George always took care of me. I wish I could have taken better care of him. We brought back a few of our wounded who had lain there since the battle.

During that second attack, the one when George was killed, many of our men died, and some were captured. It's disheartening to look around and see so few of us left. Black hats were strewn everywhere over that hill and in nearby woods. They were destroying us, but our general kept us there. In the end, the colonel gave the command to retreat, and we did it slowly back up a hill, where we held out a little longer. We fell back again, this time to a barricade of sorts, near what looked like some church buildings. I found out later it was a seminary. Thinking about it now, it seems a strange place to do so much killing. We could have held out there a long time, but those persistent Rebs broke through north of us and began to swarm in our direction. They were charging, shouting at us to surrender. We retreated farther into the town. I wanted to run and save myself. There was a great confusion there. Union men were everywhere running in a thousand directions, Confederates immediately on our heels, and nearly in our midst. It was no use to resist longer. Anyone who stayed to fight would have been captured or killed for sure. A few of us stuck together and moved through the town as quickly as we could in the great tumult and confusion. We retreated until we gathered with others among the tombstones in a cemetery south of Gettysburg.

I made it to safety. Many didn't. It seems a dream that I am still alive to write this letter. George didn't make it. Much of the Iron Brigade didn't make it. I will miss George. We messed together. It was just the two of us. I don't want to eat with anyone else. I hope George's death was worth it. It seems a great victory. Perhaps we did accomplish something worthwhile in this battle.

For the past several days, we've been dug in on this hill. We have, upon occasion, had to hug the earth tightly to avoid destruction from Southern shells. After the first day's battle, it's been frightening. I'll always remember this as a place of death. So many died in this battle. I heard our regiment lost nearly 20 officers and 200 soldiers. We only have 60 men left. This is worse than anything else I've seen. I feel blessed, yet sad to be alive. I'm not even wounded. How can that

be? I've asked myself that question a thousand different times. Why George? Why not me? I don't know the
answers, but the question led me to pray much since
the battle ended.

I've been spared from fighting since the first day
here, but there's been fighting all around us. Some of
the brigade was involved, but not our little regiment. If
I never see another battle, I will be a very happy man.

Other areas of the battle were just as bad as where
we fought. A couple of days ago, there was a tremendous Confederate charge at the center of our line.
Some are saying there were more than 10,000 soldiers
in the attack, many of them Virginians. I heard it was a
beautiful sight to see all the Rebel colors and the men
spread out across the fields moving in order toward
the center of our line. But they were cut down; bodies
were everywhere.

I've had enough war for my taste. I wish I'd never
enlisted. But I did and must see it through or die trying. I think the Union is worth dying for. I hope you
don't take offense at what I'm saying. But I need to
write how I feel to someone, and I know you to be a
true friend. Please forgive me for being so forward,
and remember that I'm a poor soldier who has lost
nearly all of his friends.

I hope this war doesn't last much longer and that I
may deliver to you this letter I hold. Please write as it
makes it much easier for me to endure my lot.

Ever your faithful servant and friend

Chapter 13
July 1863, Staunton, Virginia

*W*althrope sat at the parlor desk when she came in. He was reviewing what to Betsy looked like factory information on production rates. Earlier in the week, he explained that the government was badgering him for higher production, even with the shortage of wool.

"Good morning, Mr. Walthrope. It's an absolutely lovely day."

"Not such a good day for some of us."

"Things don't go well at the factory?"

"Things are going well enough . . . considering we can't get wool. Without wool there is no cloth, without cloth no uniforms. But no one listens. They just want more cloth."

"I know the factory works day and night. You must be finding the wool somewhere."

Emily came into the room quickly, bubbling with excitement, "Have you heard the news?"

Walthrope and Betsy looked at her expectantly. It had been days since either had seen her so animated. Betsy spoke for both of them. "What news? I've heard nothing?"

Walthrope put down the ledger and waited for the cousin to speak.

Emily spoke again, no less animated than before. "I received a letter about my husband. He's alive . . . wounded at Gettysburg, but he's alive. He's in Winchester . . . in a hospital. I've got to go to him."

"He's alive." Betsy repeated. There had been no word from Emily's husband since Gettysburg, and the household was growing concerned that he lay silent north of the Mason-Dixon line he had never wanted to cross. "We should celebrate! Will he come home soon?" Betsy was catching Emily's excitement. "This is good news."

"Do you think I can get to Winchester? Do you think they'll let me?"

"I'm sure you can. Winchester's still in our control . . . isn't it, Mr. Walthrope?" Betsy said, looking for confirmation. "I'm sure we can get you there. We'll work on it right away. Mr. Walthrope can help us." She turned to him. "We've got to get her to Winchester." Then turning to Emily, she said, "You can stay with my mother. She'll be glad to have the company and to hear the news from the upper valley. I'll write her a letter and let her know you're coming, and maybe it will get there before you do."

Walthrope, sensing how important it was to Betsy that Emily go, offered quickly, "I can make the arrangements. Will you take your own carriage? When would you leave?"

Emily spoke as soon as the words left Walthrope's mouth. "Today! Right now! No . . . no. I can't go right now. I have to pack . . . have to pack. When can I go? I've got to go now . . . today! I can't wait till tomorrow."

Walthrope was confident, "Then today it will be." He rose quickly from the desk, leaving the room without further words or acknowledgment.

"Oh, thank you . . . thank you. I've got to pack. What shall I take? There's so much to do."

Betsy put her arm around her cousin's waist to calm her and walked with her from the parlor toward the stairs. "I'll help you. We'll get you ready. You're going to see your husband! This is wonderful! He's alive! And I'm sure it's just a little wound. I'll take care of everything while you're gone: Don't worry about a thing. Mr. Walthrope will make the travel arrangements. I'll take care of the house . . . everything here."

Emily stopped in the front hall, and turned to Betsy and said in a soft, appreciative voice, "I know you'll take care of everything. You always do. I could not have endured these months without you." Then she looked flustered and embarrassed, "Here I am with a bit of good news—I get to see my husband . . . running off leaving you here alone."

"Don't worry about me, I'll be fine. We'll be fine."

"Yes, you've got Lucius. He has been such a good friend to us both."

"He has."

"I think he's helping you forget Mr. Gragg, but don't you ever miss . . . . Oh, forgive me, I shouldn't bring it up."

"Don't be sorry. It's fine to ask . . . especially between the two of us." Her voice changed from kindness to reflection, "I had a dream about him last night."

"You dreamed of Thaddeus?"

"It was a most peculiar dream. I haven't mentioned it to anyone, but it hasn't left me since. Some dreams awaken you in the night and you think you'll remember them come morning. You go back to sleep and by morning you can't remember what it was about no matter how hard you try. This dream was different. It was so real. I woke up as if I'd been there—as if I were still there. I was convinced I had simply to turn my head back and the whole dream would again appear before me. I remember that because I did turn my head as I sat in bed. I fully expected the dream to be there. Only when I saw nothing but early morning darkness and shadows did I realize it never happened. It was only a dream." She finished her last comments with her eyes looking beyond the cousin, her mind focused firmly within self.

"What was the dream? Will you tell me?"

"But we have to get you ready to go," Betsy said with concern.

"I will still have time to get ready." Betsy's strange mood made Emily thoughtful and helped her regain her composure. "I've already sent Ruth to pack," she admitted.

"I can still remember it as well—right here with you—as I could early this morning." The two women stood facing each other in the hall as Betsy described her dream. "I was in a great room with many people milling around. I was trying to get across the room. It was difficult. People seemed to be pushing in every direction. They were all so busy. I admit I pushed my way across the floor . . . pushed both men and women out of the way in the most indelicate manner. When I got to the far side of the hall there was an open space around a table or desk. Thaddeus was sitting there doing some paperwork. I looked at him . . . called to him. He looked up with no surprise in his expression and said matter-of-factly, 'Ah, you've come, then.' He rose and came toward me and I moved quickly to him. By the time I reached him his uniform had become wrinkled . . . dirty. I bent over to brush off the dirt . . . pulled and pushed the uniform trying to make it straight and neat. He watched me the whole time, just stood there watching, smiling. When I finished, I stepped back to look at him . . . to admire him. He was so handsome. He had a kind, benevolent look. I smiled. Then I noticed a button was missing from his uniform. I became frantic. No one was in the great room now, and I was distant from him. I cried out, running to him. I fell at his feet and searched the floor. He just smiled, looking down without saying a word. I began to cry and sob out loud, and he said, 'Don't worry.'

"I responded, still crying, 'But it's missing.'

"'What's missing?'

"'Your button . . . the button from your uniform.'

"He asked, 'Did you find it?'

"'It's gone. I've looked everywhere,' I said.

"He said, 'It can't be gone. It was there. Look again.'

"'I've looked everywhere,' I pleaded.

"'What did you do with it?' He asked in a suddenly accusing manner.

"'I don't have it,' I said, crying . . . feeling betrayed.

"Then Thaddeus' whole attitude changed. His body visibly relaxed. I could see it just as easily as I can see you standing here. He spoke softly to me as if I were a young child, 'Here it is. I have it. Here, you take it. I don't need it now. It's yours.'

"I looked down and saw his open palm extended to me. His hand was bloody . . . in that hand, he held the button. I reached for it, and it was gone."

"The button?" Emily queried.

"The button . . . Thaddeus . . . the dream . . . it was all gone."

Emily didn't know what to say and neither did Betsy. Both were silent. The cousin had hoped she could use the dream and words about its meaning to comfort Betsy, but she could make nothing positive of it. After a moment of awkward quiet, Betsy said with a smile on her face, "If only we had Joseph here to interpret my dream."

They both laughed nervously and moved in unconscious synchronization toward the stairs. As they walked, Emily said, "Why don't you come with me to Winchester?"

"To Winchester?"

"Yes. You could see your mother. You do always worry about her. It's been so hard in Winchester . . . with the war. Come with me. Visit her."

"Winchester," Betsy repeated as she seriously considered the invitation. By the time they had reached the top of the stairs, Betsy had agreed to go and was anticipating the trip with nearly as much excitement as Emily. She would go to Winchester to get her mother. For many months, she had wanted to get her mother out of Winchester, but Rebeka refused to leave. This was the perfect opportunity to go to her mother and convince her to come to Staunton.

By two o'clock the two women were riding privately in a carriage for Winchester. The trip was slow and difficult as at times refugees from the lower valley flooded the road, carrying as many of their possessions as possible. They were fleeing Winchester because of rumors of a coming Union occupation, and the refugees walked or rode among soldiers, many wounded at Gettysburg, who likewise flowed southward. The cousins sat grimly side by side. They had expected a festive, hopeful trip north and were unprepared for the dreadful circumstances among those they passed. They took particular notice of the soldiers, and the sight of each bandaged man made Emily twitch as she imagined for the first time the possible wounds her husband could have. Betsy looked out at the soldiers and ambulances and wondered if Hank was wounded. She took comfort in the thought that if he had been, he was at least still among friends in the North. He would not have to shuffle or be carted to safety as were these struggling soldiers.

Late on the third night, they stopped at a Woodstock tavern overcrowded with refugees from Winchester. Throughout the trip, Betsy had wanted to stop in Woodstock and meet members of Hank's family. Her father had visited the Graggs many times, but she had never met them. To her, Hank had never been connected to anyone in the world other than his uncle's family with whom he had lived in Winchester . . . and to her own. She now felt embarrassed as she realized she had never shown interest in meeting his family. As they traveled she could not deter her mind from thinking about the Graggs. When the party was informed that the town's inns and taverns overflowed with travelers, Betsy made up her mind. "Isaac," she said to their driver, one of Emily's servants. "Ask in the tavern where the Gragg family lives. I believe they might welcome us into their home." Emily looked at her curiously, but said nothing.

The driver disappeared only to return in minutes. "Ma'am," he reported, "they live 'bout a mile and a half south o' the town . . . just off the Turnpike."

"Let's go visit them."

When they were back on the road, Betsy turned to Emily and said in a soft voice, "I'm not going to tell them who I am."

Emily didn't respond immediately. She looked out over a field they were passing, watching the haphazard flashes of fireflies. Finally she spoke. "Do you think that's wise?"

"I just want to see them . . . see what they're like. I don't want them to know that I'm . . . I'm Betsy Richman, the one who rejected Hank. Can that be wrong?"

"Wrong? I don't know. Maybe not. But it is risky. They may find out."

"We'll be careful. We won't be there long. I can hide my identity that long. After all, my name's not the same as it was."

"They may know who you married. They may know your married name."

"I think not. If Hank didn't tell them—and Hank doesn't know—how would they know? Why would they know or care? They don't know anyone in my family . . . other than my father. He's gone, so he didn't tell them."

Within a half hour they were at the front entrance to the Gragg home. Dogs ran around the carriage and the driver and both women waited to see if someone would come out.

Chapter 14
July 1863, Woodstock, Virginia

Almost at once John approached the front of the carriage. He had been at the side of the house when they drove up, and he quickly greeted Isaac.

"Good evening," John said, clad in a Confederate cavalry uniform.

"Evenin', sir."

"Looking for someone?"

"Yes, sir. We're lookin' for the Graggs. There were no rooms in town. My mistress and Mrs. Henderson wants to stay with y'all the night."

Hank's father appeared at the door, and John left Isaac's side to speak softly to his father. Robert Gragg responded in similar low tones and went back in the house. All of this was done in shadows, so Betsy was unable to see the face of either man. She was feeling anxious. Seconds later, the front door swung open and a woman came boldly through it. "Oh . . . do come in," Margaret Gragg called warmly as she approached the carriage. Looking in at the faintly lighted faces of the two women, she repeated the invitation. "Do come in! You must have had a very difficult time of it. We've heard the Pike has been full of refugees all day . . . for days. It must be terribly frightening. The inns are busy . . . everyone's running from Winchester. They're all afraid the next Union occupation is going to be as bad as the last one. Do come in!"

Emily looked at Betsy questioningly and Betsy responded to Margaret. "Thank you. We're tired and could very much use a good night's rest before continuing on."

"We're delighted to see to your needs," Margaret added.

Isaac opened the carriage door for the two women, and they descended.

Margaret nodded her head in an indication of friendship, and they responded likewise.

"This is very gracious of you, Mrs. Gragg."

"It's a privilege. We don't get many visitors here . . . even with so many on the road now."

"Mrs. Gragg . . . we're not leaving Winchester."

"You're not? Then where do you come from?"

"Staunton. We may be the only two people in the valley who are traveling to Winchester."

"Is that wise . . . with the Union soldiers coming?"

"My cousin," she responded nodding to Emily, "is going to nurse her husband back to health. He's in Winchester recovering from a wound . . . wounded in Pennsylvania. I'm going to visit my mother in Winchester . . . take her back if I can to Staunton, if she'll come."

John entered the conversation, "Ma, I don't think Winchester's as dangerous as you believe. All this fear of Yankees coming to Winchester, that the human monster General Milroy is coming back is just that . . . fear." He looked at the two guests. "You'll be fine in Winchester."

His mother dismissed his comment, saying "I'm glad to hear that, John." She turned to Betsy and Emily, "John may be right, but what I know is that you are both brave women to go down the road toward Winchester . . . toward trouble, when all the world goes in panic the other way. Courage . . . courage . . . that is courage. And either way—coming or going—you're welcome in our home. We have the space to make you comfortable and would cherish the company. You can tell us all the news from Staunton . . . and you," she said looking kindly in Emily's direction, "can get a good night's sleep. You'll need your strength to care for your husband. I trust God will heal him and protect you all." She changed the subject to arrangements, "John have the bags taken in. They'll be staying in Hank's room." Betsy's heart accelerated at hearing his name from his mother lips. Margaret continued giving instructions, "Put the servant up out back. We'll send him supper shortly. Make sure he gets whatever else he needs." Hank's mother turned to the women again as she ushered them into the house, "I'm sure you must be hungry as well—all day on the road. Lucy," she called, "have supper prepared for our guests. They must be famished."

Margaret and Robert ushered the women into the parlor and invited them to sit. Betsy in a flash took in every detail of the comfortable room, noting with particular interest an overstuffed bookshelf that sat in one corner of the room. She had the impression that Hank was in the room and smiled when she caught a glimpse of Lucy peeking in at the visitors through the doorway.

Margaret continued to talk. "We'll have food ready for you briefly. Rest a bit here while you wait."

"You're entirely too kind, Mrs. Gragg. We ask only a place to rest for the night."

"And you'll have that, but we hope you'll be comfortable as well. Now who was it that suggested that you come to our home. I must thank them. It's such an honor . . . such an honor . . . to have you here."

Emily looked at Betsy, waiting to hear the answer.

"Oh, dear," Robert said, "We're so glad to have you with us that we have not been properly introduced. He began introducing himself and his wife; then introduced in absentia John who was still making arrangements for the guests and Lucy who was in the kitchen with several servants who were preparing the food. "We are honored to have you with us."

"Again, I cannot express how grateful we are for your hospitality," Betsy said. "I'm Mrs. Thaddeus Henderson. This is my cousin. We're both from Staunton." She introduced Emily and explained how eager they were to find Emily's wounded husband.

John came into the room as Betsy introduced herself and Emily. Taken by her beauty, he responded simply, "Mrs. Henderson."

"I must confess," Betsy said. "I was acquainted with one of your sons. Knowing him as I did, I knew we would be welcomed—and comfortable—in your home."

"One of our sons?" Margaret responded. She thought sadly of Daniel.

"Yes. Before I was married, I knew your son, Hank."

"Henry! You know Henry?" Margaret said in a clearly surprised tone.

John, irritated that Hank knew such a beautiful woman, spoke. "I don't remember Hank spending time in Staunton. Did you meet him there?"

"My mother's in Winchester. I was raised there. That's where I knew Hank."

John laughed. "Hank went to school in Winchester, and even when he wasn't in school, he was always looking for reasons to go down there. He spent a lot of time in Winchester . . . more time there than working on the farm."

"That's unfair, John," Robert said patiently. "You know Hank was a hard worker."

"That he was. I'm just saying he loved Winchester . . . was distracted by Winchester," John responded with a smile still on his face. "He had a special friend there. Mrs. Henderson, do you know of any special friends Hank may have had there . . . perhaps a Miss Richman?"

Emily glanced nervously at Betsy, and Betsy looked John directly in the eye. He looked a little like Hank, but his voice was deeper and he was bigger. "I'm sure a fine young man like Hank always has special friends. I certainly felt he was a special friend of mine."

"Have you seen Henry?" Margaret asked. "We lost track of him for several years. Perhaps you had heard he was dead?"

"I had heard that. I, too, was concerned for him. Then you've found him?"

"We found out just last year, he's still alive . . . doing well. He's with the army."

The cousin waded hesitantly into the conversation, "Was he at Gettysburg? That's where my husband was wounded."

"I'm sorry. We don't know. We don't correspond with him. We're just glad to know he's alive and hope to see him again after the war."

"After the war? Can't you write . . . doesn't he ever come home?" Emily asked, not understanding how Betsy could get letters from him in Staunton when his family couldn't get them farther north.

Betsy, intuitively recognizing the dangers of a valley family corresponding with a son serving the Union, came to the family's aid. "I'm sure he's busy fighting for his country—so busy it's hard to write . . . or visit." She felt honored and a stab of guilt that he would go to such lengths to write to her instead of his parents.

John laughed again. "That's probably right."

For Betsy's benefit, Emily defended Hank by unleashing her patriotic zeal on John. "It looks like you find time to visit home. Shouldn't you be with the army somewhere . . . instead of visiting here?"

John took no offense and laughed. "Pretty plain to see, isn't it. I'm cavalry . . . lost my horse in a skirmish. I'm home to get another horse. Sure don't want to end up in the infantry. I'll be back with the army in a few days."

Emily looked at Margaret and said, "Do you have other sons in the army?"

Margaret's expression saddened, but she felt relief that the conversation had changed before she had to reveal that Hank was a Union soldier. "I had a third son . . . killed at Second Manassas, the first night of the battle. He was in the Stonewall Brigade."

Emily looked at Betsy with surprise.

Margaret mistook this response as an indication that they knew Daniel. "Did you know Daniel, too?"

"No, Mrs. Gragg," Betsy said sadly. "We would like to have known him . . . very much. We never were so fortunate. I am deeply touched by your loss." She bowed her head reverently.

Emily said, "Tell them about Thaddeus."

Betsy raised her head and smiled graciously. "My husband was also killed at Manassas, so I understand how you must feel."

"My cousin was a hero," Emily said. "He was in the Stonewall Brigade, too . . . showed great bravery in all their battles. His men loved him. He was very important, no, he was vital to Jackson's victories here in the valley."

John, who had become visibly more energetic since learning that Betsy was a widow, asked, "Which regiment was your husband with?"

"Thaddeus was in the Fifth Virginia."

"Daniel was in the 33rd Virginia, Company C, the Tenth Legion Minute Men."

Betsy smiled again, "They may have known each other. They no doubt are together now." Betsy noticed Robert's and Margaret's eyes moisten as they thought of Daniel. She wished her eyes still moistened for her husband.

Lucy called Margaret from the other room and the matriarch excused herself. When she left, the conversation turned to the weather. No more was said of soldiers and war that evening or the next morning.

Throughout the visit, Margaret had the distinct impression that Mrs. Henderson wanted Margaret to like her and that impression flattered Hank's mother. She later asked Robert about her perception. He indicated that Mrs. Henderson was a kind, refined young lady who seemed concerned about everyone. In spite of his words, Margaret retained her notion. If Hank had wanted to marry this lady . . . instead of that Richman girl, everything would have been different . . . much happier. Margaret had liked Samuel Richman and appreciated all he had done for Hank. Samuel visited the Graggs whenever he passed through Woodstock, and the family had always warmly welcomed him. But Margaret's affectionate feelings no longer extended to his daughter. Margaret blamed Betsy for what she thought at the time was Hank's death. At one point during Betsy's visit, Margaret had weighed mentioning the Richman girl. She hoped Mrs. Henderson might utter ugly words about her, but Margaret resisted the temptation. By the time the carriage pulled away at eight o'clock the next morning, Hank's mother had concluded that this wonderful lady could not even know the uncharitable Miss Richman. They could not have been friends . . . they had no traits in common.

By evening the carriage was approaching Winchester. Refugees and wounded soldiers continued to impede their progress, and Emily became increasingly agitated as she neared her husband. Her early-felt excitement that her husband was alive and that she would soon see him had deteriorated completely, leaving only trepidation that she would find him crippled, dead or on death's verge.

For Betsy the day passed quickly. She had fallen in love with Hank's family, and her only vexation was remembering she hadn't said yes to him. She wondered if Hank would be dead on the battlefield in Thaddeus' stead if she had accepted his proposal. He would never have left Virginia and might have sided with the Southern Cause . . . or perhaps they both would have moved north before the war. Today, instead of riding in this carriage, she would be in his house fixing supper for him, her husband . . . waiting for his arrival after a long day of work. For them there would have been no war. She tried to remember how far Indiana was from Virginia. In a less rational moment, she felt bitterness remembering Thaddeus: He married her. He robbed her of happiness with Hank, happiness in Indiana. Thoughts of Walthrope interrupted these notions. He had kindly made the arrangements for their trip. He was always there for her. Thoughts of Walthrope brought her back to reality, and she reminded herself of what Emily had so often said . . . that she was only imagining a romance with Hank—one that didn't exist.

Chapter 15
July 1863, Winchester, Virginia

*T*he Confederates were still in control of Winchester as the carriage drove into the town, but it was clear by the clatter and activity that the army was preparing to move south. Betsy wondered what would become of the town after the soldiers left. Winchester already wore dramatic marks of destruction. Beautiful lawns were gone, replaced by patches of dirt more akin to common roads than to their verdant green pasts.

The town was dirty, the remaining houses looked worn and many outbuildings Betsy distinctly remembered no longer existed. Fences that once set neighborly boundaries around the town were gone, taken by soldiers of one side or the other for their camp fires. Evidence of destructive fire was everywhere. Windows were broken in buildings that still stood, and a few structures and homes were totally demolished. Some houses looked much the same as when she had left, but her eye seemed drawn to those that were not.

When the hated Union General Milroy governed the town, rumors claimed he would eventually burn it. When he hadn't burned it, rumors confirmed it escaped destruction only because the Confederates drove out Milroy before he could torch it. Nonetheless, Winchester had tasted its share of spoliation, and

Betsy wondered if what she saw was just the appetizing course for a coming Union feast of devastation.

As she took in the wrecked town, she appreciated the Confederate presence. Soldiers seemed to be guarding every corner. But she shuddered to think of what her mother must have suffered. Since her marriage and move to Staunton, Betsy had corresponded regularly with her mother. Even when the Yankees controlled the city, they wrote to one another, resorting like others to smuggling letters in and out of the city. Her mother was adamant about staying in Winchester, and she never wrote or hinted at difficulties in the town. She visited Betsy in Staunton shortly after the war started, but she refused to leave Winchester permanently and now refused to leave even for short visits to her daughter's home. In every letter Betsy had written, she pleaded with her mother to come to Staunton; but her entreaties were to no avail.

The cousins didn't know where to search for Emily's husband so they directed Isaac to Rebeka Richman's house. Betsy gave street-by-street instructions to the slave who had never before been to Winchester. She was relieved when the house came into view, looking as if it had weathered well the Union storm. Fences and spring house were gone, the lawn no longer existed, but the main house survived.

They pulled up to the front porch of the home and both women quickly descended from the carriage. Betsy pushed the front door open and ran up the stairs to her mother's room. She opened the door and burst in. No one was there, and she returned to the stairs. At the bottom of the steps, she saw her mother standing, looking perplexed, face to face with Emily.

"Who are you? And what are you doing in my house?" her mother demanded, having not yet seen Betsy at the top of the stairs.

"Ma!" Betsy called out as she flew down the stairs.

Rebeka turned to face Betsy as she reached the foyer. "Betsy?" her mother said guardedly in a gentle voice. Both women fell into one another's arms. Rebeka stroked Betsy's hair, but was silent. She eventually asked, "Betsy, why are you here? I hope everything's all right. Nothing's happened has it?"

Betsy laughed softly at the irony of the question, "Mother . . . Mother . . . I've come to take you to Staunton. You must come live with me. I don't want you here. The town's nearly destroyed. I can't think what will happen if Milroy comes again. I've heard so many stories from refugees I've seen in Staunton about how bad it was here when he was in charge. I won't let you go through that again! You must come with me!"

"This is my home," protested Rebeka quietly. "I survived General Milroy once. I can survive him again . . . or any other Yankee general they send." Her voice took on a nostalgic tone as she looked around the hallway, "If I leave this house, it will be destroyed. That's what happens to abandoned houses."

"You must come with me. Come back when all this is over. We'll rebuild the house . . . if we need to."

"If I stay, we won't need to rebuild."

"The house doesn't matter. Come . . . live with me. There aren't any Yankees in Staunton. I won't leave unless you come."

"Oh, Betsy, you can't stay here. This is not a good place to be."

"If it's not safe for me, it's certainly not safe for you. Have Rose pack your things! I won't leave unless you go with me."

Betsy noticed how tired and worn her mother seemed. There was gray in her hair.

"I can't leave my home. Many of the better people have left town, you know. Some of them, the Yankees kicked out just so they could have their houses for an officer . . . or hospital. Milroy did that. It's not the same as it was when you were here, Betsy . . . you look so beautiful. It's hard to find beautiful things here any more. But I can't leave. Your father will expect to find me here when he comes."

The mention of her father saddened, but did not surprise Betsy. He had died while traveling on business before the war. Everyone, except her mother, accepted his death. Samuel had been visiting Rebeka's brother in Martinsburg when he became mildly ill. His condition worsened quickly, and he passed away before his family could be notified. When word came that he was dead, Betsy had opened the message, but had been unable to approach her mother. Instead she sent a note to Hank. Hank had rushed to the house and at Betsy's importuning had gently told her mother. Her mother reacted desperately to the news. She shrieked . . . wept . . . hugged Betsy . . . then Hank. She lamented his death for more than two hours, all the while the two young people tried to comfort her as best they could in her increasing frenzy.

They never brought his body back to Winchester; Rebeka hadn't wanted it brought back. Instead they interred him in her family's small cemetery in Martinsburg. Betsy knew he was dead; there was no question about that. Hank and Betsy had gone to Martinsburg for the funeral. They had seen the body and grieved at the grave. Her mother had refused to go, and with each day, increasingly behaved as if he were not dead, but merely away from home. She refused to grieve or even to allow Betsy to lament her father's death. Her mother's refusal to wear appropriate attire and her insistence that she continue her social life as before created a social stir in the town. As Betsy thought about her mother's delusion, she remembered morosely the day she had returned from Martinsburg. Hank had come to the house and Rebeka had greeted him happily . . . as if nothing had happened. Betsy asked Hank to speak with her, to make her mother understand her husband was dead and never coming back. Betsy hadn't wanted to be there when he told her. It would be too painful . . . it had been too painful when they initially told her of his death. Betsy went quietly to her bedroom to wait, leaving Hank alone with her mother and his doleful mission. Hank left quickly late that night without saying good-bye to Betsy, and Rebeka had never again welcomed Hank into the Richman home. Neither Hank nor Rebeka ever mentioned what happened, and Betsy had been too frightened to ask.

Emily's soft cough distracted the two women from their conversation and thoughts. "Oh, Mother," Betsy exclaimed. "I've totally forgotten. We've got to find a soldier." She introduced Emily, explaining her husband was somewhere in Winchester.

"I know a colonel who can help us," her mother responded. "Everything's chaos, but I think the colonel can find him for us. If he can't help, General Ewell's still here. Perhaps we could go to him." She nodded politely to the cousin.

"Thank you, Mrs. Richman."

The colonel, who was busy preparing to leave town, quickly located Emily's husband at a home converted to a hospital, not far from the Richman's house. The women asked about his condition, but the colonel could give them no additional information.

Rebeka had known the owner of the house before the war. She heard they were Union sympathizers and abandoned their home to move north into Western Maryland shortly after Milroy's escape from Winchester. As the carriage pulled to the front of the house, the trio noticed an effort to move men from the hospital into waiting wagons and ambulances.

The women descended from the carriage. Emily immediately went to the wagons and ambulances searching the faces of the men already crowded into each. The task was difficult as in some wagons men lay squeezed on their sides, allowing more patients to be placed in each wagon. Emily then followed the stretchers being carried from the house, again looking each man carefully in the face. She was nearly frantic;

Betsy and Rebeka watched with sympathy as she searched for her husband.

Emily worked against the tide of men and stretchers that passed out of the home. Betsy and her mother followed her into the make-shift hospital. Emily darted frantically from one man to the next as they searched each room. Her visible agitation increased, and she seemed to feel she was too late—that they had carried his lifeless body out just minutes before she arrived. They looked for her husband on the main floor of the house, then made their way to the stairs. There was less commotion on the second floor as the army removed men able to travel from the main level first.

Emily ran up the stairs, periodically leaping over a step. By the time the others alighted on the second floor, Emily was already coming out of the first room, having searched it.

"He's not here! He's not here! Where have they taken him?"

Betsy tried to calm her. "He's here. We'll find him. There are other rooms." Emily didn't hear her as she had already entered the next room. Before the two other women could reach its door, Emily emerged from that room and pushed by them to the third room on the floor. She was nearly running and Betsy and her mother recognized that to try to keep up with her was hopeless.

Being near so many wounded men touched Betsy and Rebeka, and they slipped into the room Emily had just inspected. They walked among the men who lay on thin mattresses or straw on the floor and bent over each, touching their hands and speaking softly to them. They could hear in the distance Emily's small shoes clattering across another room. They forgot about her and her husband as they touched and visited each of the soldiers. The mother and daughter worked together engrossed in being with the men. They heard Emily's footsteps descend the stairs and her voice raised below. She must have found him, but neither woman left her efforts. As they worked down the row, they came to one who looked vaguely familiar to Betsy. "Do we know him?" she asked her mother. Whispering back, her mother said, "I don't believe I do."

"He looks familiar," Betsy said as they approached him.

He was pale, little meat left on his face, and lay silently on a mattress, desperation in his eyes.

"Can we help you?" Rebeka asked.

In response, panic animated his expression. His eyes darted wildly. "Don't let . . . let her leave," he said in a barely audible, broken voice.

Upon hearing these words Rebeka moved aside and motioned for Betsy to move closer to him. She whispered, "He seems to know you. Don't leave him."

Betsy had a strange thought: Was it Hank? She moved to his side, hoping that somehow it was him, that he had asked for her. She got close. It wasn't Hank. Yet . . . she did know him. Who was he? She searched her memory.

"Betsy . . ." he began in his weak, strained voice.

Betsy looked at him. He knows me, she thought.

"Don't let her leave."

The revelation raced through Betsy's mind. She had met him a few times before the war, but he was vastly altered. "Mother," she said softly. "We've found him." She knelt close to the man and spoke reassuringly, "She won't leave. We'll bring her back." She could hear her mother move swiftly to the door. Betsy held his hand with hers and gently placed her other hand on his forehead. "We'll bring her back. We'll take you home and nurse you back to health." His head was hot. She could feel him respond to her touch so she left her hand still. She turned and called to no one in particular, "Bring a litter! We need a litter!"

Betsy heard him say softly, "She was here."

"She still is here. My mother's gone to get her. You're going to be all right. Rest now. She'll be here soon. She won't leave you. We've come to take you home."

Betsy could hear Emily approaching from behind, and she removed her hands from the soldier's head and hand, trying to step out of the way before Emily arrived. But it was too late. She was trapped between Emily . . . her husband . . . the wall . . . and the soldier who lay next to him on the floor. She was uncomfortable, feeling as if she were intruding in the couple's reunion. She turned to the other soldier, a lieutenant, and knelt at his side. She looked at his face. Her mind instantly fixed on memories of her friend from Winchester, Marie Ann Allen. The lieutenant lying with eyes closed was the young, innocent, arrogant, enthusiastic cadet from the VMI who had completely won Marie Ann's affection. She didn't hear the conversation and clatter behind as her mother and Emily and a male voice discussed how to move the wounded husband to the Richman house. Betsy looked at the former cadet. His clothes were no longer neat and orderly as they had been in the parlor so long ago . . . he no longer looked fresh and bright. She wondered if Marie Ann knew where he was and wondered where Marie Ann was. Betsy had lost track. During the war, she had lost track of so many people. She smiled sadly as she looked at the boy as he slept.

"Betsy," her mother whispered from behind her. "It's time to go."

"Oh . . . Ma," she whispered in response, rising to her feet and turning to face her mother in one graceful movement. "Go without me, take Emily's husband to your house. Send the carriage back for me. I want to stay here for a little while."

"Why would you stay here? We've done what we came to do. I know these men need help, but right now, we need to think first of Emily and her husband. Come. Come now!"

"Do you remember a cadet from the VMI . . . the cadet that Marie Ann married?"

"Yes . . . vaguely. Did they get married? I don't remember that."

"He's here." Betsy said indicating with a nod of her head the unconscious lieutenant at her feet. "Surely they married! Marie Ann was set upon marrying him."

The mother stepped to Betsy's side, "Oh, my!" And without pause added, "We'll take him as well." After considering the situation, she hesitated, "But they won't both fit in the carriage with us.

"Isn't there another wagon . . . or ambulance?" Betsy asked looking back at the officer who had accompanied her mother into the room.

"I'm sorry," he shook his head negatively. "We're using all the wagons we can find to move the more promising patients south. I'm sorry." He looked sadly at the VMI alumnus and said, "He doesn't have much time."

"We have a wagon at home still," Rebeka volunteered softly. "No one's taken it yet. We'll get it."

"No, no, Mother," Betsy said calmly. "We can use the carriage for both. Go home. Take Emily and her husband. Send the carriage back. I will bring . . . what was his name? Do you remember?"

"It's been so long."

"I should remember. He brought me that first message from Thaddeus. I only met him that once. Thaddeus sent him asking if he could call on me. I can't leave him here to die . . . or fall into Union hands, not after that."

"Let me take Emily, then. I'll send the carriage back."

"Is Marie Ann still in Winchester?"

"No . . . no, she's not in Winchester. If I remember correctly, she and her family left early on, but I don't know where they went. I never knew they married. But don't worry about that right now. We'll find her later. I'll send the carriage back."

Betsy watched her mother leave and knelt again by the lieutenant. She touched him this time, touching his head as she had touched Emily's husband. His head was on fire, and she involuntarily grimaced as she felt the heat.

She rose quickly and went down the stairs. She found a doctor and asked for water to cool the soldier's forehead. Without feeling, the doctor responded that there was a well out back that had good water and that many of the men had fevers. He continued to talk to her, perhaps frustrated that so few soldiers left under his care could respond. He said he was staying behind with those not well enough to travel, even if it meant capture. He hoped that some could eventually travel . . . that he could save a few. Emotion rose in his voice as he explained that some men should not be moved. Two ladies had just taken a man who would die within a day because they moved him. It was the injured soldier's wife, so if she wanted to move him she could. The man wouldn't do any more for the army anyway. He tried to persuade the woman to leave her husband here for a few more days . . . that it would be better. But she and the other one, they insisted upon taking him at once.

Tears welled up in Betsy's eyes as she moved slowly from the doctor. Her departure didn't slow his conversation, and she heard him continue talking as she made her way to the backyard where she found the well and fresh water. She took water up the stairs and knelt again by the soldier. She tore off a piece of her petticoat, folded it in several layers, dipped it in the cold water, and placed the wet cloth on his forehead. Cadet Moore . . . that was his name. His head moved and, for the first time since she discovered him, he opened his eyes. She could see his body tense. He said in an unsteady voice, "Miss Richman."

"Where is Marie Ann?"

He had a look of confusion and said, "Where am I?"

"In Winchester."

"Winchester?"

"Yes . . . Winchester. Do you know where she went? I'll get word . . . ." She changed her tactic in midstream and lied: "She's coming for you. Where is she coming from? Do you remember? I want to tell her exactly where you are. I'll write and tell her."

Before he could answer, the lieutenant's body again went limp, his head rolling to the side. The little bit of life she had seen in his face faded and his complexion became a grayish white. His eyes stared vacantly to the side. A soft "no" slipped through her closed lips. "No," she repeated almost inaudibly. She ran down the stairs to where the doctor was working. "Doctor, come quickly! One of the soldiers is dying!"

The surgeon looked up from his current patient. His eyes seemed to consider the entire room of men as if to say as they are all dying, why should I leave this one for that one. But he said nothing. He wiped his bloody hands on an apron he wore and followed Betsy up the stairs. She led him to Mr. Moore, then stood staring at the doctor as if she expected him to say—to do—something at that instant to heal the soldier. He looked at the patient, then at Betsy. He remained standing, speaking compassionately, "He's beyond hope."

"Beyond hope?" she said looking down at Mr. Moore. "That can't be."

"I'm sorry, it's just a matter of time. He will not live out the night."

"Then, he's not yet dead? Can I move him?" she asked defiantly.

"You can do whatever you like. He will not last the night. Listen to his breathing."

Betsy turned her head to look at the former cadet and listened for his breathing. She could barely hear the shallow, rapid breath—but at least it was breath. Her emotions were in conflict. She wanted to give in to the doctor's words and will and accept his death, but feelings deep within propelled her not to give up. Perhaps it was this former cadet's connection to her husband . . . or Marie Ann's friendship. Whatever the motive, it was deeper than her despair, and it won out.

"Doctor, he won't die! I'll see to that. I'll take him home."

The doctor looked kindly at her, "Is he your husband?"

"No . . . a friend."

"I am sincerely sorry. I wish the best for him . . . and for you. We can do no more for him. You may take him. Perhaps your love and care . . . and God's mercy . . . if there is any left . . . will heal him." The doctor turned and walked out of the room, returning to the patient he had left unconscious on the operating table.

Within a half hour, Isaac and the carriage had returned. The surgeon sent soldiers with a litter to carry Mr. Moore down to the carriage. Betsy walked alongside the stretcher. She kept a moist cloth on his head as they bore him. She saw some color in his cheeks now. The soldier, however, lay motionless as they carried him, making no protest. At the carriage they laid the stretcher slightly at a diagonal across the seats from front to back, so only its middle was unsupported by the seats. Betsy sat in the carriage near the young man's head and with her back to the driver.

Chapter 16
July 1863, Winchester, Virginia

Rebeka was waiting for Betsy at the door when she arrived. With Isaac's help, they carried the litter into the house, struggling up the stairs and getting him into a bed. In the process, they uncovered his wound: The doctors had amputated his right foot. The un-healed wound looked red, swollen and oozed bloody water and pus.

As they labored to get him into bed, Betsy noticed for the first time that no house slave assisted. "Where are the servants?" she asked matter-of-factly as they struggled with the awkward body. "Call them to help us."

"They're gone."

The soldier lay on the bed. Betsy's mother slumped into a nearby chair and dismissed Isaac.

Betsy looked at her mother, perplexed, but waited until Isaac was out of the room before speaking again. "Gone? Gone where?"

"Ran away."

"Away?"

"Milroy, the demon, and his men encouraged them to leave. That wicked proclamation from Lincoln talk-ing of freedom, it made them all crazy . . . crazy for freedom, crazy to get away . . . away from me. Don't know what happened to them or where they went. William, Rose . . . they're all just gone! Left one by one, or in little groups . . . all gone. Not here. Gone . . . good riddance! They never did much work. Life's easier without them." Betsy noted her mother's bitterness, but her mother's tone changed to sorrow. "They were like family. Didn't we treat them like family? Rose: she was in the family from the time she was born. My father gave her to me when I got married. She was with us longer than you were."

"Maybe you should have freed them, Ma."

"Manumition? Never! Why should we? They were ours. Besides, I couldn't make a decision like that, not alone . . . not until your father gets back. He owns most of them. Rose . . . she had all she could want. I took care of her. How can she survive without us, without me? She was like a child; they all were. They couldn't think for themselves. Whenever they needed something . . . to make a decision, or they had a squabble or a fight, they came to me. I bore a heavy responsibility. I told them what to think, what to do. I gave them food, their clothes. Rose ate our food. I worry about her. I'd like to help her . . . wished she'd stayed. The others, they're gone and forgotten. Not Rose. I'd have taken care of her."

Her mother's feelings for Rose affected Betsy. It had always seemed to her that Rose and her mother had been together for so long that they looked alike—almost like sisters. But Betsy had never suspected her mother's love for the slave woman. She wondered why her mother had never treated Rose with special respect or affection . . . or any affection at all. She wondered what her mother's feelings and expressions indicated. Was it Rose she loved and missed, or was Rose symbolic of her lifestyle withering?

Betsy thought about the slaves she had inherited from her husband and from her father. She wondered what she should do about them. She'd have to consider this carefully, soon. Then it came unexpectedly, the realization: They would be free. With melancholy, she reflected that Winchester, or what was left of it, made that clear to her. The South was losing its strength. It was ebbing away. There would be no slaves someday, someday soon.

With no further words between the women, Betsy straightened Mr. Moore's body on the bed. She washed his wound, reapplied a cool, moist cloth to his forehead, all the while speaking softly to him. She told him how lucky he was to have Marie Ann. She told him how much she appreciated his introduction to Thaddeus. He lay motionless other than his shallow, rapid breath. She sat by him, falling asleep in a chair she had pulled close to the bed. A similar scene had taken place in the next room where Emily nursed her husband with wifely tenderness, soft words and gentle and superficial cleansing. Betsy, as she lapsed into sleep, had forgotten Emily and her mother. She fell asleep and dreamed: The cadet was at her house, it was his first visit. Hank was there and proposed. In her sleep she said, "Yes." She slept soundly.

The next day became the pattern for the following two weeks. A woman sitting beside each wounded man, sleeping in bedside chairs, leaving their patients' sides only to take care of personal needs, becoming increasingly drawn, increasingly worn. Neither man died and each made incremental improvements that were virtually invisible to the two women as they performed their perspective vigils of devotion. Rebeka, likewise, had no rest. She made meals, cleaned the house, did the laundry and sat with the patients as the nurses briefly took care of their own needs.

During this time, the Confederate army retreated south of Winchester leaving the city open to enemy raids. A few raids followed, but Rebeka had shrewdly hidden the horses, carriage, and wagon so that they went unnoticed by the Union cavalry. With each raid, however, Isaac became increasingly agitated. By the end of a fortnight in town, he had become contraband, hitching his future dreams to serving a Union cavalry officer.

Rebeka was unconcerned for Emily. Emily nursed her husband, correct behavior for a wife. Betsy's commitment to Mr. Moore was another matter, however. To Rebeka it was as if this soldier, in Betsy's mind, was Captain Henderson. She could understand how difficult it had been for Betsy to lose her husband, to let go. It would be hard for her to lose Samuel. Eventually Rebeka decided it was unhealthy—this attachment to Caleb Moore—and began to encourage Betsy to take a day for herself: go for a ride, visit an old friend if there were any left in town, do anything that might divert her for a while. Subconsciously, Rebeka believed the still-weak soldier would die without her daughter at his side. She anticipated his death in spite of his progress and believed her daughter could only postpone the outcome for a short time.

Her mother's suggestion of a day out distracted Betsy. For several days she began to think of her life in Staunton, wondered how her enterprises fared, what Lucius Walthrope was doing to deal with wool shortages, worried about the mills. She brightened at the thought of Walthrope; thinking of him reminded her there was happiness and laughter at that same hour . . . somewhere . . . outside what had become a dark prison room for her. She slowly withdrew emotionally from the former cadet and soon was ready to take her mother's suggestion for a day's outing. Her mind quickly latched onto thoughts of Naomi.

Betsy had been curious about Naomi since receiving Hank's second letter. This was her opportunity to find out who she was, what she was like—this woman, her only concrete connection to illusory Hank Gragg. One evening as she sat at her post by Mr. Moore, she announced she was going to take a short trip into the country the next day. Her mother's concerns instantly changed from Betsy's seeming obsession with Mr. Moore to her daughter's safety. She fretted that Betsy might run into Union cavalry . . . or worse . . . in the country. Betsy assured her mother she would be safe: The North was not so degenerate as to insult women. Her mother was not convinced having been an eye witness to General Milroy's occupation of the town and having heard of General Butler's humiliating "Woman's Order" in New Orleans. But there was no way she could now deter Betsy from a country outing.

Chapter 17
August 1863, Shenandoah Valley, Virginia

*T*he next morning Betsy rode one of the horses beyond Winchester looking for Naomi's farmhouse. She knew generally where Naomi lived because she had sent letters for Hank to her, and several local farmers gave Betsy specific directions as she neared the farm. Before the morning was over, she had made it to the house unmolested by anyone from either side.

At the farmhouse, Betsy could see someone watching her from inside, but no one appeared at the door. She climbed down from the horse, tied it to the porch rail, climbed the stairs and knocked boldly on the door.

From inside a harsh, shrill voice said, "Who's there, and what d'yuh want?"

"I'm looking for Naomi Callister. I thought someone here could tell me how to find her."

"What yuh want with her?"

"She's done me a personal favor. I'm here to thank her."

"What service she done yuh?"

Betsy heard the voice soften just a bit, and she determined it was Naomi. "Naomi, my name is Elizabeth Henderson, widow of Captain Thaddeus Henderson."

Naomi didn't answer, but Betsy could hear her working to open the door. When it finally opened, Betsy saw Naomi—a small, skinny woman with a weathered face. A broad smile enchanted Betsy. "So yuh're the widow Henderson."

Betsy smiled in return, "I'm widow Henderson."

"You don't seem too worn for an ole widow."

"Thank you for that compliment."

"It ain't worth thankin' me none." She held out her hand awkwardly to Betsy. "It's a pleasure to meet yuh, Mrs. Henderson."

"The pleasure's mine," Betsy said gracefully as she took Naomi's hand.

"We both got the same friend," Naomi said bluntly.

"I believe we do. That's why I've come."

"I figured that. Can't imagine yuh'd come out just to see me—though yuh'd be welcome—for a social call."

"I would if we knew each other."

"Mrs. Henderson, don't yuh go playin' no games with me. I know I don't know much, but I know enough to when someone's sayin' something' sincere and when they ain't." She paused, then spoke again. "Hank Gragg, I know he always talks true. I was hopin' yuh was like that, too. Don't yuh go flatterin' me none. I know what I am. No words can change that, or make me see myself different. Save yor flatterin' tones for folks what want to be fooled."

Betsy felt justly chastised and responded, "You're right. I apologize. I only want you to know how much I appreciate your sending our letters."

"I ain't sent many, but come in. I'll put us on some coffee. I've got me real coffee."

"I'd like that." She didn't pause for Naomi to fix the coffee but continued to speak. "The few letters you've already sent have given me a great deal of happiness." Betsy almost said "hope" instead of "happiness," but she couldn't bring herself to say it.

"I knowed I should'a read that first letter."

"You read our letters?" Betsy said, embarrassed at the thought.

"That was the deal—the deal what I made with young Gragg. It's fair! I do like romance."

Betsy overcame her discomfort and smiled. "If you don't mind, I'll remember while I'm writing that you read them."

"Hope yuh will. Make 'em real romantic for me to read."

"I'll try," Betsy said laughing, caught off guard by Naomi's simple forthrightness.

There was an awkward silence, broken by Naomi as she put the pot on the stove, "It don't make no sense."

"What don't . . . doesn't make sense?"

Naomi ignored the inadvertent correction of her grammar and said, "Why yuh're so interested in a boy what yuh don't know . . . what's a Union soldier. The Union soldiers are them that kilt yor husband. It don't add up in my figurin'."

"You're right, Naomi."

"Then why yuh doin' it? Why yuh really here?"

"For the reason I told you. But what I haven't told you—and what Hank doesn't know . . ." Betsy paused and looked directly at the woman. "Naomi, I knew Hank before the war, before I was married, before he wrote to me." She waited for the news to sink in. "But he doesn't know he's writing to me. He's writing only to my married name."

Naomi was astounded. She let out a long, loud whistle that startled Betsy. "He done knowed yuh already? Huh! Then why don't yuh tell him?"

Betsy swore Naomi to secrecy, then told her the entire story.

"Sounds like the two o' yuh s'posed to be together. If yuh wasn't, none of what's happened would o' ever happened."

"Perhaps." Betsy said. "Perhaps for me it's a second chance . . . a second chance that may end at any moment with a bullet from a Confederate gun—a musket from our own nation. Naomi, maybe I'm just making up this romance in my head."

"Hank, he's been mighty lucky up till now. I seen him near kilt by some men out on that field, but he's still alive. He's gunna live. Don't yuh go worrin' none 'bout him." Then she became excited, "I feel like I'm that fella with the arrows what's always shootin' folks' hearts . . . what makes 'em fall in love. Yuh'll make your letters real romantic, won't yuh?"

"Naomi, I will fill them with romance just for you."

"Yuh're very kind to me. I thank yuh."

"No. No, I'm the one who should be . . . who is grateful. Is there anything I can do for you, Naomi? Can I pay . . . ."

"Pay?" Naomi shrank at the suggestion, anger in her eyes, and spoke emphatically, "I ain't doin' this for no money. Don't yuh ever think that, not for the shortest moment. Ain't 'nough gold in the world what would make me do this . . . or the other things I done. I think love is nice. Course my husband—he don't—left me here to go fight. Hope he ain't dead, but I'm thinkin' he is. He don't never write none."

Betsy smiled compassionately, "I will pray that he will be all right."

"That would be nice. I know the Lord . . . he listens to a fine lady such as yuh'self."

"I'm sure the Lord listens to a fine lady like you, too."

Betsy could see Naomi take offense, "I warned yuh 'bout flattery. I'm tellin' yuh, it's the devil's own tool."

"I say that sincerely."

Naomi's expression softened.

Betsy spoke again, "Remember now, neither of us can tell Hank who I am, not till I see him face to face. If he learns it's me before that, he may never give me the chance to see him. He'll never come to me . . . not after what I've done to him." Her words didn't reveal her increasing belief that the love Hank and she had once felt for one another was destined to die, that it could not endure, that they would never again see each other.

"That's gunna be hard," Naomi said. She already felt a desperate urge to write to Hank of the good news— that the widow was his long, lost and beautiful love. But she restrained herself and made the commitment. "I'll 'bide by it."

"Thank you."

As she stood to leave, Betsy embraced Naomi. Naomi tentatively returned the hug, but as she felt the warmth of Betsy's body and touch, she relaxed and hugged the young woman tightly.

Chapter 18
August 1863, Shenandoah Valley, Virginia

As Betsy returned to Winchester, she thought about Naomi. She silently prayed for Naomi's husband . . . that he would come back to her . . . that they would live a long and happy life. She then thought about Hank. She had an inexplicable and overwhelming desire to write to him, confess her identity, beg him to love her. Then Betsy's thoughts shifted to Walthrope. She had attended a party with him just before she came to Winchester, her first social event since Thaddeus' death. Walthrope had been particularly solicitous that night, and they had ridden home together in the carriage. She was uncomfortable with the memory, yet attracted to it, as she had been to him that night:

"And what did you think of Mrs. Briggs? Had you met her before?" Walthrope asked.

"She was lovely."

"Lovely?" He laughed. "You are too kind, or were there two Mrs. Briggs there."

"You're being uncharitable."

"And you, Betsy, are being too charitable."

"Mrs. Briggs means to do good."

"Perhaps, but I think her own comments best sum her up. I think she really does believe Gettysburg was not a fatal loss. She believes God will still repulse the 'horrible invading infidel' if we will only," he paused to laugh, "repent of our sins. But we have to repent—all of us, Betsy. If only Jeff Davis would set another day of fasting for the nation, if only everyone would pray that Jackson come back in spirit to fight once again for the country. I really think she believes all that!"

"Mr. Walthrope, you are a terrible man! Mrs. Briggs is a fine Christian. I share her conviction. We must repent if we are yet to win this conflict."

"You, in that beautiful head of yours, cannot share a similar thought with Mrs. Briggs! She is so ignorant, and you are not. You are perfection! Mrs. Briggs clearly is not!" He laughed again, then sobered and leaned across the carriage. He took Betsy's hands in his and looked into her face. She could see his handsome features in the night light. "You're different . . . so strong! But Betsy, words don't convey my true feelings for you. When I am in your presence, my heart thrills. Each heart beat is stronger than the last. I've never felt this way before, about anyone. Only you can make my life complete. Being near you these months has shown me I can only find happiness with you. Your beauty overwhelms my senses. Your kindness touches me." He lowered his head and pressed his lips gently against her hand.

She closed her eyes as she remembered the moment . . . and her impulse to pull him close. She craved his embrace that night in the carriage. As she relived it, she craved it again. Why had she held back? He was so strong, so real. And Hank, merely the sweet memories of a young love, as unreal as a Winchester untouched by war. Naomi's fascination with romance helped

Betsy understand all of this. For Betsy, Hank was not real, except as a distant memory, a wish for romance that could not be. He in some way now belonged to Naomi. For Naomi he had become a delusion that fueled her fantasies of a gentler world and gentler men. Betsy entertained the idea of not writing him anymore, but came to no decision.

The women's resources in Winchester were dwindling. At the end of the third week, they had little left in the house to eat . . . or to sell for food. Thanks to Rebeka's ingenuity, they still had the horses, carriage and wagon. She was thinking for all five occupants of the house now and knew their luck was running out . . . that before long one of the armies would conscript the horses. From the day Isaac disappeared, she suspected it would only be a matter of time before he would return, leading his new, and first, employer to their hidden horses. They had to move quickly if they ever were to leave. Rebeka desperately wanted to stay in Winchester and would have stayed were it not for the others. She had to get them to safety. Staying in Winchester would guarantee the death of the two patients, and the women would become refugees . . . or worse. When Samuel returned, he would understand: She was leaving for Betsy.

Rebeka acted without telling anyone: She prepared as much food as she could for the trip south and packed for the two nurses. At sunrise she woke both women as they slumbered by the beds of their patients and told them of her plans to leave immediately. The three women laid a mattress from Rebeka's bed in the wagon, and placed the lieutenant on it. They brought Emily's husband out of the house on the litter and placed it across the seats of the carriage.

Emily drove the carriage. Her husband's strength had increased, and he was able at times to sit up in bed and visit with his wife. During those visits, the two of them never spoke of the war or his experiences in the army, and they seemed increasingly distant from Betsy and her mother. Now the reunited couple would make the journey by carriage to their Staunton home.

Mr. Moore showed few concrete and enduring signs of improvement. He rallied several times, but his energy soon waned. Rebeka drove the wagon and Betsy sat at his side in the back of the wagon, nursing him as she had for the weeks he had been at her mother's house.

Once they were on the road, Betsy's mind opened up again, and she considered life beyond caring for this young soldier. She pictured herself with Walthrope in the church at Staunton. She could see him dressed in a dark suit and imagined that she wore an exquisite wedding gown. She heard her own lips speak the words, "I do," and imagined him pulling her close . . . his embrace . . . the warmth of his kiss. She envisioned the scene over and over again as they traveled south the first day, covering the discomfort of the ride with the sweetness of her daydreams.

Chapter 19
August 1863, Staunton, Virginia

As the wagon traveled the Valley Turnpike, a long-time acquaintance visited Walthrope in his Staunton home.

The friend spoke. "You've worked it quite well . . . well indeed. I couldn't imagine you doing it better."

"It has gone even better than I planned. For a brief while she was only interested in business, but I do believe she has warmed to my many charms. There is a slight complication, but things will work out."

"A complication?"

"Just a little difficulty. It really doesn't matter. The way I have arranged everything, I'll be fine whether she marries me or not. Making money in this factory of hers is the easiest speculation and safest smuggling I've ever seen."

"Must you always call it that? Speculation . . . smuggling . . . such ugly words."

"Call it what you will. I'm making all the money I could want. Once I get her, I will be wonderfully wealthy. Thanks to her family name, Matthew, I'm already a respected member of the community. Imagine that. Everyone in town wants to hear my opinion. If I told them to lay down their arms today . . . tonight . . . and free their slaves, they would do it in a moment. I could easily do what Lincoln has been trying to do, and I could do it without another dead soldier."

"Yes, my dear Lucius," Matthew responded. "But think of the money lost because of your generous concern for humanity. I say let the thing continue . . . as it is, at least till we have more . . . much, much more."

"I'm not planning to end the war." Walthrope laughed. "It's just hard to imagine a better decision than mine to woo this fine lady."

"How could you so easily win her heart? She suspects nothing?"

"It hasn't been easy . . . but she suspects nothing." Walthrope said laughing.

"How can that be?"

"I don't know why she loves me so, only that she does," Walthrope said in a mocking tone. "For me, knowing that is enough. After all, as long as she loves me, she won't notice the skimming and speculating I do . . . with Stokes' help."

"Who's Stokes?"

"Stokes is a somewhat weak but clever man over at the factory . . . my right arm to all who are watching. He's delighted to work with me. He doesn't share my fondness for the honorable Mrs. Henderson. He hated her husband before the war. He was just delighted to see Captain Henderson go off and get himself killed."

"Do you not take offense at his lack of admiration for your future wife?"

"Offense? Why should I?"

Matthew laughed. "You're heartless, Lucius."

"Perhaps."

"I know you've done all this before, but don't you feel guilty stealing from a widow?"

"Stealing? Remember when she is Mrs. Lucius Walthrope that factory will be mine . . . at least that's the plan. What difference does it make then that I've already taken profits? Can a man skim off his own profits?"

"Just taking your share a bit early?"

"It will all be mine . . . eventually. I'm just making sure I get what should be mine, even if something should distract the widow from her duty to marry me. If she doesn't marry me, that's fine. I'll continue to skim off the cream. I'm doing her a great service. She'd be losing money in the woolen business if it weren't for me. I've expanded her business, made sure she's reaping profits from prudently holding, selling, shipping: salt, sugar, coffee, tobacco, cotton. The list goes on. Businesses she doesn't even know she's in. My, or rather her, only profits . . . not that she sees many of them, come from those ventures, and she doesn't know anything about them. Doesn't even know they exist. She has nothing to do with them. It's been so easy with my friends . . . and her good name."

"Isn't the factory under government control? How do you get away with it?"

"Matthew, I take good care of certain Confederate authorities. They're so pleased with my production methods: They encourage all my endeavors. Valuable rewards find their way to them. As long as I appear to keep woolen cloth rolling from the factory periodically . . . and money flowing into their pockets continually, no one will question me. It's done so easily, and the

longer I do it, the better I'm getting at it. But Matthew,
what I can't afford is to have her marry someone else.
That would end the whole scheme . . . do me in. And
I've discovered a possible suitor—a strange suitor. So
my only recourse is to marry her myself and marry her
as soon as possible. I'm working toward that . . . working hard. Once we've married, I'll have nothing to
fear."

"You are a very creative thief, Lucius. It's no wonder
that Ben has always been so fond of you."

Walthrope smiled, "Matthew, the words you use!
They wound me! I thought I was among friends."

"Another suitor? Do you know him?"

"I don't . . . oddly, neither does she." Matthew
looked confused, and Walthrope continued the explanation. "It's very peculiar. Before she left for Winchester, I felt I was making real progress toward conquest.
At one point I thought she was ready to accept my
proposal. But whenever I got close enough . . . so close
I could taste it . . . something would happen, something would stop her and she'd back off. I could feel
her moving away. I asked her what it was; she denied
there was anything."

"Then how do you know you have a rival?"

"Her denying it confirms it to me. But there's more:
After she left for Winchester, I went to her cousin's
house—she's living at her cousin's house—and asked a
servant to see her business papers for the factory. I
told the house servant that Betsy had asked me to re-
view them. She gave me all the papers I'd given to
Betsy. I'd seen them all . . . nothing new. Of course, all
of them, I'll have you know, were fabulously inaccurate

but creative records composed just for the enjoyment of our Mrs. Henderson. Then it came to me: Ask for any letters she had received . . . pretend there were some business letters among them. The slave brought me letters from Betsy's mother, uncle, friends. Still no suitor . . . nothing more than a bit of good gossip here and there. . ."

"Anything worthy of blackmail?"

Walthrope laughed. "Nothing so valuable . . . just interesting. Then I asked her for letters she'd forgotten or overlooked. They would be special letters just on the factory. Betsy would take uncommon care of them . . . perhaps keep them separate from all her other letters. There was a flash of recognition on her ignorant slave face. Betsy kept a few letters in her bedroom. Yes, those would be the letters, and she fetched them."

"How could she give you the lady's letters without permission?"

"They know me so well in the house. I have access to everything. I'm trusted. Why should a servant question my inquiry now? Betsy and Emily honored all my requests while they were at home. Why not when they're away. The daft girl brought me the letters, and I pored over them. There weren't many, just enough. It seems some Yankee—Can you imagine?—a Yankee. Our great patriot's getting letters from a Yankee. There is no purity in the world, Matthew . . . no purity at all. It turned out he'd been with her husband when he died. The lecherous boy just wanted to keep up correspondence with the captain's virtuous widow. Very touching letter, Matthew . . . very touching. Almost brought me to tears." Walthrope smiled sarcastically.

"Unfortunately, I don't know what she wrote back. But she must have encouraged him. Some woman in the lower valley apparently smuggled letters between the two . . . Naomi something or other."

"Wouldn't that information be worth something?"

"It won't do, Matthew. The woman can't have much. She can barely write her own name, judging from the address on the envelopes. I'm sure she's poor. So that's my competition: some plotting private in the Union army. It doesn't sound like much . . . but I think he's what holds her back."

"Maybe it's the memory of her husband."

"No. No. I don't think so. You wouldn't either if you read the letters. There's something brewing there. I can't believe he would keep writing unless she encouraged him. She certainly takes good care of the letters. She feels something . . . that's clear."

"Lucius," Matthew spoke in an exuberant tone, "you have nothing . . . nothing . . . to worry about from a private in the Union army. He'll be dead before the war ends. He may already be dead. Don't let him disturb your tranquility. Tell me when you will propose."

"I've thought a lot about that. She will be ripe for picking when I can convince . . . when I can subtly persuade her to let me manage her mills and farms, then I'll know she's totally in my hands. They're her last grasp on independence, don't you see? Did you know she has over 1,000 acres? It's an immense place! Once I have control of those, I'll be convinced she'll accept my proposal. She'll be mine. Then I'll insist she join me in holy matrimony . . . or at least legal matrimony. That's the key element—legal matrimony. Until then . .

. until she shows that confidence in me I don't think I'll have succeeded in overcoming the barriers. It will be too risky to insist before then. I can ask her, suggest it to her, guide her, but I can't insist, not until she's totally dependent on me. I can't insist until she's ready. She might turn me down definitively. And I don't want that. That's one thing I can't have. She can't close the door on me. The door's got to stay open."

"Will you be happily married?"

"I will. She is good-looking, even in black . . . perhaps especially in black." Walthrope said thoughtfully, smiling to himself. "She's charming, smart, a bit naive." His eye took on a distant look and his voice became more sober. "To be honest with you, Matthew, I'm even beginning to think I might like her. There are moments . . . at times, I actually consider her wishes. It's never happened to me before. And it's only because she is so unusual." As he finished the statement, his eye focused again on Matthew. "All her traits, Matthew . . . all of them . . . will be useful for a man who aspires to much. With her wealth, I will become very influential. The possibilities will be unlimited in the Confederacy."

"The Confederacy? When did you become an advocate of the southern nation?"

"Confederacy . . . Union . . . what does it matter? I'll prosper in either with what she brings."

"I am relieved to hear you haven't lowered yourself to patriotism."

"Oh, but I have . . . I have, my friend. The confusion this war and patriotism set loose, has given me . . . and you . . . and others . . . such opportunities. Praise be the god of patriotism and the god of war. Bow down to them, Matthew, if you know what's good for you. Worship them! Men like us always survive and prosper, don't we—the lifeless bureaucrats and us. We always survive! It doesn't matter if it's war or peace. We're the ones who rise to the top. We are the cream. We know what to offer the people and governments, and they're always willing to pay our price. They look down on us, speak ill of us. Smugglers, speculators, scoundrels, crooks . . . a thousand other names they call us, and we do serve in so many roles. But they need us, they crave us. And, in return, we give them what they really want. Right now, they need our services to keep this war going. They know it. They just wouldn't dare say it out loud. We accept their scorn as long as they're always willing to pay our price: power and pleasure in its many splendid forms. It doesn't matter which side we're on, we flatter them, bribe them; then, in the end, we frighten them . . . control them . . . bathe ourselves in wealth and prestige that comes from it. It is the drive to serve ourselves at all costs that makes us so powerful . . . more powerful than the president of either country. May neither president ever be victorious. Law, custom, protocol—even personal conscience—restrains presidents . . . makes them weak. The good people of the world need no laws. We keep them under control with imaginary principles: 'Thou shalt not' is already affixed in their minds. We . . . and kindred spirits . . . have no constraints. Our own passions and desires, they are our only limits. And you know only too well that those passions grow with each minor gratification. Passion expands to infinity. Each day . . . each experience . . . teaches us to better satisfy our cravings of tomorrow. They increase our ability to want more. Oh . . . so much more. The potential goes on and on. I get a chill just thinking about it. You know what the real tragedy is, Matthew? When the good, hardworking people of the world wake up after death, they'll find even in those lofty worlds they so often preach and dream of, that we, who have learned the real lessons of life, we will be on top. They will serve us . . . or be punished. That is heaven! Anyone that teaches otherwise does not understand. I ask you would God really want the meek surrounding him? It's impossible to conceive it. Why . . . how . . . would he reward the weak when the strong have already taken all the rewards? Gratify yourself! That is glory . . . and that may be immortality. Who is there that can say, or know, otherwise?"

Matthew laughed. "You should have been a preacher."

"Matthew, my friend, don't you remember? I have been a preacher upon several different occasions . . . when it suited my purposes. Before it's all over, I may well serve in such a high and diabolically divine role again."

Chapter 20
August 1863, Somewhere on the Valley Turnpike, South of Winchester, Virginia

*T*he heat and humidity sapped the women's strength as they made their way south. Sweat that wouldn't evaporate drenched them, and their patients suffered from the heat, dust and constant jerking and bumping of the wagon and carriage on the road. Emily's husband weakened in the sun in the uncovered carriage and was litter ridden by early afternoon. Caleb Moore, sheltered from the sun by a tarp clumsily arranged over the wagon, moaned at periodic moments and mumbled about the pain in the foot that wasn't there. The two vehicles traveled slowly, taking twice as long as Betsy and Emily had taken traveling north. They spent the first night at a farmer's home south of the Confederate line. The farmer and his wife welcomed them into their home, fed them and sat with the soldiers throughout the night. The three women collapsed from fatigue and slept until well after first light. The farmer and his wife continued their hospitality, serving them breakfast, hitching up the horses and sending them on their way. Betsy and her mother joked that they were sure the couple was delighted to see them leave and must have gone immediately to bed for the day.

The second day was hotter and more humid. Emily and her rested husband were able to make better time and seemed resentful of the wagon's slow pace. They suggested, and everyone agreed it would be better if the carriage went ahead. Betsy had decided to move back into her own home; by going ahead, Emily could make those housing arrangements.

The mother, daughter, and patient made slow progress during the late afternoon of the second day. Betsy tried to keep the patient covered and protected from the sun, but as the miles passed, he moaned less. Late in the day his face became pallid again. As they had weeks ago, his eyes gazed vacantly and his head slumped to the side. "Mother," screamed Betsy. "We're losing him! We've got to stop!" Betsy worked on her patient with all the nurturing skill she had developed, and Rebeka pulled the wagon off the turnpike, across a field and, after wandering back roads, found a nearby farmhouse. She called for help. A farmer, wife and servant rushed to the wagon. Without looking up, Betsy worked furiously to revive the man. Rebeka called out to them as they approached, "We've got a wounded soldier in the wagon. We're transporting him south, but he may be . . ."

She was cut short by the farmer's wife. She had looked into the wagon and said in a startled voice, "Mrs. Henderson!"

Betsy looked up. Horror seized her. Margaret Gragg stood beside the wagon looking at her with concerned affection. They would discover she was really Betsy Richman. Betsy could feel the blood rush from her face, and she felt dizzy. Margaret reached into the wagon and grabbed her as she slumped backwards . . . unconscious.

Rebeka explained, "The poor girl has worn herself out trying to save this soldier."

"We've met Mrs. Henderson," Margaret remarked as she climbed carefully into the wagon and laid the young woman down into its bed. She called for water and fanned Betsy with her hand.

Robert Gragg and the servant, a slave hired to work in the Gragg's fields, lifted the soldier from the wagon and moved him to the parlor where Lucy took over as nurse.

Robert returned and lifted Betsy carefully from the wagon. "Take her to Hank's room," Margaret directed. She hurried ahead of him, and pulled back the bed coverings. Robert laid Betsy clothed, her face and collar drenched from sweat, on the bed. Rebeka Richman followed the entourage.

Robert quickly excused himself and the two women worked to remove Betsy's shoes, dress, and some underclothing. Rebeka spoke as they worked, "Thank you so much. Your hospitality is totally unexpected, but greatly needed. Betsy is my daughter and has worn herself out trying to save the life of that young man."

Margaret responded, "I'm honored to have you in our home. You're most welcome to stay as long as needed. We will do what we can to make you comfortable. We're very fond of your daughter—she was a friend to one of our sons years ago."

"She was! How remarkable then, that we should end up at your door in our very hour of need."

"Mrs. Henderson didn't suggest you stop, then?"

"Betsy was busy trying to save Mr. Moore. I don't think she knew until you called her. You were there just at our moment of most need. Thank you."

Margaret nodded graciously to Rebeka. Betsy's color and breathing had returned to normal, and she slept.

"I do believe she is just totally exhausted," Rebeka said. "She has had a very difficult three weeks."

"I only wish we'd known. We could have done something. She stopped here on her way to Winchester. All the inns were full," she explained. "In the brief time she was here, we became very fond of her. Perhaps . . . if we'd known . . . ."

"You have done more than enough already. Thank you."

"Would you like to sleep in here with your daughter? We could bring in a small bed . . . or could put you in another room . . . whichever would make you most comfortable."

"I'd like to stay with Betsy . . . at least until she's feeling better."

Betsy tossed in the bed and spoke unintelligibly.

"I will have your bags and a bed brought up for you."

There was a soft knock at the door.

"Come in," Margaret called.

Robert came through the door, asking, "How's our upstairs patient?"

"Resting," Margaret responded as Betsy tossed on the bed. Margaret smiled. "I hope the sight of me doesn't cause too many people to faint like that."

Rebeka spoke quickly. "Oh, no, it wasn't that! She fainted from relief . . . knowing she was safe at a friend's home."

Robert nodded politely to Rebeka and said, "Your soldier's wound doesn't seem to have healed. It doesn't look good. I've called for a doctor. I hope that meets your approval."

"That's wonderful. Poor Betsy has been nurse and doctor to him. To be honest, I don't—didn't—think it worthwhile to call a doctor; I didn't expect him to live."

"Well, one's been called. He can tell us if there's hope. Who is the boy?" Robert asked.

"He's married to one of Betsy's friends."

"Betsy?" he asked.

His wife quickly interjected, "Mrs. Henderson. That's her name, Betsy."

"Ah," he responded.

Robert nodded again to Rebeka, "I'm sorry . . . I haven't had the pleasure of meeting you officially. Surely by now you have formally met my wife, Margaret . . . and I'm Robert Gragg."

The color drained from Rebeka's face. She knew instantly who their son was, and why Betsy had stopped here on her way to Winchester. She surmised that Betsy fainted when she saw that Margaret and Rebeka would meet face to face. But they didn't know her first name! They didn't know who Betsy was! Dread came over her. Hank appeared in her mind. She inwardly recoiled at the image. She hated him. He had brought the lies. She remembered it all so vividly. He was there . . . in her house . . . saying her husband was dead. Dead! Buried! It was as if Hank had killed him and hidden the body. In her agony that night, she remembered . . . it was impossible now to conceive it, but she began to think Hank was Samuel—they looked so alike. She knelt at Hank's feet, begged him not to leave her, kissed his hand over and over again . . . as if he had really been Samuel. When she came to her senses, it wasn't Samuel before her. When she realized what she had done, she was horrified, humiliated . . . humiliated before the boy. She wanted to believe it had never happened, that he had never seen her humbled like that. Then it dawned on her: Samuel wasn't dead. The boy lied to humiliate her! She would never countenance him again. He had disgraced her. Samuel was not dead. He would come home. He would throw out the liar . . . the boy who had humiliated his wife. She had spent these years waiting for Samuel's return. He would return. Hank would see! Hank would know that she knew he lied. Her dread heightened. She needed this family right now, and she remembered her treatment of Hank. Hank surely reported her meanness to his parents. She had heard of his disappearance without regret, as proof he had lied; yet Samuel had been so fond of him. He had saved Samuel. Why then did he have to lie about Samuel's death? She felt guilt . . . remorse. The Graggs would surely ask her to leave, even with Betsy desperately needing rest and Cadet Moore dying. Knowing the dishonor of the son, she expected it of the parents. They would force them to leave. The parents would throw the three of them out now just when they needed their help. Why had she been so cruel to Hank? He had been like family . . . a son; then to lie . . . to tell her Samuel was dead. Why had he done it? All of this she remembered . . . wrestled with. But Rebeka, toughened by face to face interaction with Milroy and his Union men, recovered quickly. "Then you must be the parents of Hank Gragg," she said pleasantly.

Robert and Margaret looked at each other discreetly. Margaret spoke for both of them. "We are."

"He was a fine young man. As I recall he disappeared before the war. I am sorry." As these last words left her mouth, a broad smile crossed Margaret's face.

Margaret spoke with animation, "Don't worry about that. Henry is quite well. He's in the army."

Surprise registered on Rebeka's face. She forced out the words, "I'm so pleased to hear that. I know Betsy worried greatly when he disappeared." Their graciousness made her angry. She hated Hank. Why were they so kind? It was obvious they didn't know who she was. When they found out, they wouldn't be so kind. No, not nearly as kind. Yes, there was no doubt; they were just like their son.

Betsy lay calm in the bed.

Margaret spoke again, "Robert, bring up their luggage. Mrs. . . . " She redirected her comments to Rebeka, "I'm sorry . . . I only know Mrs. Henderson, Betsy, by her married name."

Rebeka was horrified, embarrassed and frightened. They weren't kind. They were like Hank. They would throw them out. Now was the moment, Rebeka thought. She considered lying. "I'm Mrs. Hancock," she could say. But they'd find out. Maybe by then Betsy would be rested. She wanted to lie and determined she would. But when she opened her mouth, she meekly said instead, "I thought you knew. I should have told you before we came in."

"Nonsense," Margaret responded. "You had much on your mind."

"I'm Rebeka Richman."

Neither of the Graggs responded. They knew the last name. Rebeka watched as the shock she had felt moved to the Graggs. In that moment, it became clear to both of them that Betsy was the girl who had rejected Hank. Margaret glanced inadvertently at the young woman, her pleasant smile momentarily replaced by a look of sorrow. This girl was the cause of her pain, Daniel's death, Hank's disappearance.

There was an uncomfortable silence. Rebeka wanted to apologize for her treatment of Hank—perhaps then they wouldn't drive out Betsy and the soldier—but she remained quiet. She considered, strangely, that she would understand if they expelled them. Some part of her wanted them to do just that; it would prove her right about Hank . . . about them.

Margaret recovered enough to complete her statement. "Robert," she began again, "Won't you please bring up their luggage and a bed for Mrs. Richman," she smiled at Rebeka, "for Rebeka. I think they'll be here a while." Robert left the room immediately without saying a word.

Betsy squirmed in the bed and cried out. Rebeka slipped to her side and stroked her beloved daughter's hair, turning her own face from Margaret. Rebeka's eyes filled with tears.

"I'll go down and check on the patient. Please excuse me," Margaret said.

"Yes, thank you. Thank you. You've been kind." Rebeka did not raise her head to look at Margaret, but Margaret never noticed as her own thoughts preoccupied her mind.

Chapter 21
August 1863, Woodstock, Virginia

Margaret walked from the bedroom, down the hall and stairs. She stared straight ahead. Her mind was an ocean of conflicting thoughts and emotions. She couldn't help feeling compassion for Betsy as she lay collapsed in the bed upstairs. She cherished the feelings she had when, on her last visit, Betsy had shown her so much deference and affection. Simultaneously, a bitter anger at the same beautiful young woman gushed from her heart, tightening her jaw till her teeth ground together. This woman had destroyed Margaret's family. She didn't even think of Betsy's mother. The conflict in Margaret's mind encompassed only the daughter, a girl whom she had wished upon Hank . . . the despicable girl who had destroyed Hank's life, a girl with whom she had so rapidly fallen in love . . . a girl who had so completely deceived her.

When she reached the bottom of the stairs, Margaret walked directly into the parlor. Lucy sat next to the motionless soldier. Margaret looked down on him and suffered for the young lieutenant. His life had been destroyed, but he still grasped its vestiges. The doctor would come soon.

She wondered what Betsy's real relationship was with the soldier. Why would she be so frantically attached to him if there wasn't something more to their relationship? She grimaced at the thought. She did not—could not—believe it. She didn't want to think badly of Betsy . . . of Mrs. Henderson. She tried to rid her mind of such thoughts, but they kept coming back. Margaret excused herself, exchanging hushed words with Lucy about the soldier's condition, tenderly touching her daughter's face before going to bed. The sun had not yet set.

As Margaret lay in bed, thoughts swirled. She couldn't silence them or find solace in sleep. Some of the meanest and worst thoughts made her feel the best and most powerful. Yes, it must be that this young soldier was Betsy's illicit lover . . . always had been . . . even while she was married. Betsy had betrayed her own husband! She was an adulterer! He had joined the army just to get away from her infidelities. As Margaret lay in bed, the satisfaction of knowing it was all true consumed her. Betsy destroyed all she touched. Margaret drifted into a shallow and unsettled sleep and dreamed:

Betsy stood before her, taller, broader than in real life. She looked down at Margaret and laughed. Margaret implored her to stop, but Betsy continued. "Please have mercy. Please stop!" begged Margaret.

Daniel appeared behind Betsy, and Betsy laughed louder.

"Mercy . . . please." Margaret implored.

"Mercy from her?" Daniel said facetiously. "I'm dead because of her—she killed me." Then Daniel became Hank.

"Can you have no mercy?" Margaret asked rhetorically.

Betsy and Hank disappeared and the image of a battlefield appeared where lay dead soldiers without visible wounds. She walked among them and spoke quoting a verse from the Bible, "Behold, the day cometh that shall burn as an oven; and all the proud, yea, and all that do wickedly, shall be stubble . . . ."

She looked closely at the men who lay upon the field. Betsy was there, too, young and beautiful, smiling, walking happily among the dead.

In her anger, Margaret yelled, "What have you done? You've lied . . . killed! Betrayed me! Betrayed my son! Your husband! Have you no mercy, no compassion, no shame?"

Betsy stood, motionless. Her face took on lines of sorrow, and she lay down on the field as if she too were dead.

Words came to Margaret's mind: "Will you add another body to this bloodless field of hatred and death?"

Betsy lay as if for burial, her eyes closed, arms folded across her body. Margaret stood above her, looking down. Betsy opened her eyes and spoke, "Mercy, please!"

"Mercy on you?" Margaret laughed, then spoke sternly, "You deceived me!"

The words came to her mind again, "Will you add another body to this field?" Margaret bent low. Betsy's eyes were closed again, and Margaret impulsively, but gently, touched the girl's pale cheek and rested her hand there. There were the words again: "Will you add to this field?"

Margaret awoke and lay in the dark looking toward the ceiling. Tears ran freely down her cheeks. She reached out her hand and felt for her husband to pull close to him for comfort, but he wasn't in bed. She thought of Daniel . . . of Hank . . . of Betsy. She rose impulsively, covering her summer nightgown with a light shawl, and stepped into slippers. She made her way to the top of the stairs. She could see a light still glowing in the parlor and could hear hushed male voices. She wondered what time it was. She made her way back down the hall to Hank's room and carefully turned the knob, pushing the door open slowly. She quietly stepped in and closed the door behind her.

As her eyes became accustomed to the darkness, she could see Rebeka asleep on her small bed and Betsy on Hank's bed. She moved silently to the side of the larger bed and looked down on Betsy's form. She thought of her dream and of mercy and prayed silently. She prayed for a long time with her eyes unconsciously squeezed tightly closed. When she opened them and looked at the girl again, she directed her thoughts to her: "Mercy is not from me. It's beyond me. I'm not that strong. It's a gift for you . . . for me." She bent over the sleeping woman and softly kissed her cheek. She felt tears fall from her eyes onto Betsy's face, and the young woman shifted in her sleep. Margaret collapsed into a chair by the bed and remembered words she had read that morning, ". . . unto you that fear my name shall the Sun of Righteousness arise with healing in his wings." She mouthed the words, "Thank you, Lord. Thank you, Lord." At that moment, a powerful feeling of warmth overwhelmed her. She smiled in the dark and again repeated, this time almost audibly, "Thank you, Lord."

At daybreak, Rebeka Richman opened her eyes to find Betsy still sleeping soundly on Hank's bed and Margaret Gragg, slumped forward, asleep in a nearby chair. She raised herself on her cot and sat on its side. She couldn't take her eyes off Margaret. She wondered how long she'd been there. She wondered about the struggle through which she must have gone . . . and thought of her own struggle. She wondered at the strength of the woman and felt ashamed of herself. She missed her husband. If only he would come. With her eyes on Margaret, and thinking of the woman's grief and sorrow, she responded to her own thoughts, consciously acknowledging to herself for the first time since her husband's burial, that he was not coming . . . that he never would. Samuel Richman was dead. She had known it all along, but it had hurt so deeply . . . too deeply; only when she feigned he still lived was the pain bearable. Margaret's compassion in suffering had opened Rebeka's heart and mind. She faced Samuel's death, crying silently for her dead husband.

Chapter 22
August 1863, Woodstock, Virginia

*T*he evening on the lower level of the house had proved just as eventful as the conflict upstairs. They had summoned the doctor who found the leg was not healing and that there was little chance Mr. Moore could survive. The only hope was to amputate more of the leg. The men in the house had quietly transformed the parlor into an operating room where they chloroformed the patient, took off the leg well above the knee, and cleaned up. The doctor had gone home after the surgery.

Robert Gragg had fallen asleep on a couch in the room because he didn't want to awaken his wife. He knew she would have a difficult time sleeping after learning Betsy's identity. He didn't share his wife's concern as he had never blamed Betsy for Hank running away. He blamed only Hank.

He remembered the many times Margaret told him of her "unholy hatred" for the Richman girl and how she hoped they would never meet face to face. Under such a circumstance, she professed she would never be able to control her feelings or her words as someone who belonged to Jesus should. She feared that meeting Betsy Richman would be a test beyond her capacity for charity. Margaret had lived for four years in constant dismay because she firmly believed she fell short of Christian ideals because of her feelings for the Richman girl. Robert assured her many times that she had nothing to dread; their paths would never cross and those feelings would subside in time. After Hank reappeared, Robert affirmed to his wife that it was all over. Betsy, and whatever she had done, didn't matter anymore, and surely now she would never have to face the young woman. He could never have imagined the previous night. He had fretted much of the evening about his wife . . . only enduring the trial by keeping busy and distracted with his assistant surgical duties.

Robert had left the windows to the parlor wide open overnight to dispose of the smell of the operation and of the patient's injuries, and a light, but moist, breeze ruffled the drapes of the room shortly after dawn, awakening him. He rose quickly from the couch. He could hear someone already working in the back of the house. He stepped to the patient's side and examined his face carefully. He could tell nothing from the face, and looked around the room to ensure he had cleaned up all evidence of the operation and that the room looked as it had when Margaret had gone upstairs.

Robert quietly climbed the stairs to his bedroom to check on his wife and was distressed not to find her in bed. He moved down the hall wondering about Betsy. As he approached her room, the door opened and Margaret and Rebeka quietly slipped through the doorway. They were clearly in the midst of an ongoing conversation. Rebeka seemed subdued, but Margaret was as animated as she had been when Betsy arrived the evening before. The two women passed Robert without acknowledging him and descended the stairs.

It was later in the morning when Betsy finally stirred. As she roused herself, she awoke to two women at her bedside. Her mother sat on the bed itself to be close to Betsy. Margaret sat in the chair in which she'd spent the night. Betsy slowly opened her eyes. She recalled what had happened and was horrified. Quickly she closed them again, hoping the two women hadn't noticed she was awake, hoping they would give up their vigil and leave her alone.

The women were talking softly, and she listened. They were speaking of Hank. Margaret told Rebeka how he had visited them for several days, and how wonderful the days had been. She spoke openly of his being a Union soldier and said they didn't expect to see him again until after the war. Rebeka told Margaret of how much Hank meant to their family, how much her husband had loved Hank, how much she had loved Hank. She cried when she told Margaret of Samuel's death and how she refused to accept it . . . blaming Hank. Yet Hank had saved Samuel's life once. She told Margaret how she had been unkind to Hank, how she suddenly hated Hank. Margaret said only that she understood; and she did. For the first time it was clear: It had been Rebeka who had rejected Hank in her pain and sent him away . . . not Betsy. Rebeka asked Margaret for forgiveness for her mistreatment of Hank.

Margaret responded, still feeling the warmth, compassion and generosity of her midnight gift, "That was all a long time ago. Much has changed since then. These are difficult times. The world's a different place, and we are all different people." Her voice trailed off.

Betsy again relived the moment when she had rejected Hank's offer. She wanted to have that moment again. This time she would accept. Kneeling to him . . . kneeling at his feet, she would beg him to take her. She would be Rebeka's daughter, Margaret's daughter—the thought appealed to her. Precisely then, Margaret's phrase passed through her mind. "We're all different people," and she thought, we can't go back. What was possible then, it's now impossible. It's too late for Hank . . . for me . . . for us. She opened her eyes and said sadly, "Mrs. Gragg."

Both women looked down at her, surprised she was so quickly and apparently fully awake.

"Forgive me."

Margaret looked at Betsy; her eyes became thick, anticipating tears. "I have."

Betsy continued her confession, "I didn't mean to harm Hank or to lie to you." A great weight fell from her shoulders as she spoke his name out loud again to his mother. "I couldn't tell you the truth. I wanted you to like me."

Chapter 23
August 1863, Woodstock, Virginia

*W*ithin a week, the soldier was well enough to sit up and take nourishment. It was then that Betsy decided he was also ready to answer questions about Marie Ann's whereabouts. As she sat by him holding a tray from which he took his food, they began their first serious discussion. Always before when Caleb Moore had begun to thank Betsy or anyone else in the house for their care, they would push it aside with, "Save your strength. There will be plenty of time for that later." This morning was different. Betsy commenced the conversation, "Mr. Moore?"

"Miss Richman . . . please call me Caleb."

"Caleb, I married since we last met. You seem to always forget that. I married Captain Henderson . . . Thaddeus. I'm Mrs. Henderson. Don't you remember?"

"You married him?" He looked momentarily confused, then said, "I know that. Why would I not know that? I remember hearing of it. I was pleased. I liked Thaddeus so much." His face darkened. "But he died."

"He did."

"I'm sorry."

"Thank you, but you must tell me where your wife is. I'm sure she's . . . ."

"My wife," Caleb blurted out. "I have no wife." He then added playfully, "I'm available."

Betsy swallowed hard to avoid the smile that instinctively arose when he announced his eligibility. She focused on his first response. "Not married! I thought you . . . didn't you marry Marie Ann?"

"Marie Ann?"

"Yes, Marie Ann. The young woman with whom you had a most particular friendship . . . your betrothed. She was there at my home when you visited. Why can't you remember any of this? Perhaps you are not well enough yet to talk about it. The wound has made you forget everything. You are not yet yourself."

"I may not be myself, but I'm well enough to remember I'm a bachelor and not betrothed to anyone . . . and to remember Marie Ann. What gave you the idea that I would marry Marie Ann?"

"Didn't you correspond with her? Weren't you betrothed to her?"

He laughed softly and briefly, "Mrs. Henderson . . . I corresponded with many beautiful girls. I assure you I did not have and never indicated that I had any particular interest in Marie Ann . . . beyond mere friendship. Perhaps she read something into my letters which I never intended."

Betsy looked at him with disgust and spoke with emphasis, "Well, Caleb Moore . . . you should be very grateful to Marie Ann."

"To Marie Ann? I am grateful beyond words to you . . . your mother . . . this kind family. To Marie Ann?" He leaned his head back. "I barely know her."

Betsy looked at him severely. "Marie Ann was a close friend of mine."

"Then I will speak nothing more of her without respect because of my unending admiration for you."

Betsy ignored his compliment and stated emphatically, "That's the only way you should speak of Marie Ann for she saved your life."

"I've heard you were modest, but even your modesty cannot hide the truth. I know to whom I owe a heavy debt for preserving my life. It's to you, Betsy. You are my guardian angel. I am your humble servant, forever."

"You are wrong!" she said heatedly. "I'm not anybody's angel . . . most certainly not yours. I saved someone I thought was the husband of Miss Allen . . . because of my concern for her. You just happened to get the undeserved credit of having the decency to marry a girl as lovely as Marie Ann. You are alive today only . . . only because I mistook you for someone wise and kind." She rose indignantly with the food tray. "You've had enough to eat. You're sick!" She walked out of the room saying, "You were saved by accident, and there won't be any more accidents around here . . . not if I have anything to say about it."

Caleb followed Betsy with his eyes. He felt weak and was trying to comprehend what had just happened. As it became clear, he laughed loudly for the first time since his injury. It felt good, but it wore him out, and he quickly slid back down on his make-shift bed.

Betsy marched quickly into the kitchen, and by the time she reached its door, she too was laughing.

There, seated at a kitchen table, were her mother, Margaret and Lucy. Both mothers looked up and smiled to see her so happy.

"What's happened to make you so cheerful?" her mother asked.

Betsy tried to control her laughter, but the more she tried to control it, the more she laughed. "He's . . ." she laughed. "He's . . ."

"He's what?" her mother asked.

"Cadet Moore's . . ." she laughed.

"Is he all right?" Margaret asked.

She nodded as she continued to laugh. "He's not married . . . not interested in marrying Marie Ann."

The two older women looked at each other, perplexed.

"Not married? Not married to Marie Ann?" her mother asked.

With her laughter momentarily under control, Betsy said, "I saved the wrong man." She broke into laughter again.

This time her mother stood up and moved to be by her and held her in her arms as Betsy's laughter became tears of exhaustion, frustration and mourning. As she listened to her daughter's sobs, Rebeka said softly, "Just because he hasn't married her yet, doesn't mean he won't in the future. You've just got to get them together."

Betsy instantly stopped crying. She wiped her eyes and nose with a handkerchief and thought briefly. "You're right," she said. Then, she smiled broadly and added, "It will be harder for him to run away from Marie Ann now . . . with just one leg."

Lucy, unprepared for the comment, laughed out loud momentarily, blushed, and muffled her laughter.

Within days, they had contacted Caleb's family in Southeastern Virginia and told them where he was and of his situation. Betsy wrote to them that Caleb would be her welcomed guest at the Henderson home in Staunton until he fully recovered. Betsy also sent a short note to Marie Ann Allen to begin dialogue with her. She had learned through inquiries during Caleb's recovery that the Allens had relocated with other refugees to Lynchburg. Betsy would invite Marie Ann to visit Staunton once they settled.

Three weeks after the women arrived unannounced at the Gragg farm, Betsy, her mother and the rapidly recovering patient—now able to move about on crutches—were riding in a carriage the Graggs provided for the long trip to Staunton. The trip was much more enjoyable than the trip from Winchester. The weather was cooler, the patient healthier, and the carriage more comfortable than the wagon they left behind.

Chapter 24
September 1863, Near Staunton, Virginia

After several days they reached Betsy's house near Staunton. It was afternoon, and the travelers were tired and sore from the journey. John, the old house slave, greeted them from the porch. "Welcome home, ma'am."

"Thank you, John."

Out of the front door came Walthrope. "The refugees have arrived," he said smiling. "Welcome home, Betsy. You look more lovely than ever."

Betsy ignored his compliment and said brightly, "Mother, may I present Mr. Lucius Walthrope? Mr. Walthrope, Mrs. Rebeka Richman."

Walthrope moved quickly to the side of the carriage where Rebeka sat and extended his hand to assist her descending from the carriage. "It is a pleasure, Mrs. Richman. I am at your service. If there is anything I can do for you . . . at any time . . . you have but to ask. It will be done."

"Thank you, Mr. Walthrope."

"Lucius . . . please call me Lucius."

"My daughter has told me only the most wonderful things about you."

Walthrope laughed, "Your daughter is kind."

Betsy addressed him again, "Mr. Walthrope, let me also introduce you to Lieutenant Caleb Moore of the famous Stonewall Brigade. He's an old friend of mine. As I wrote, he'll be staying with us for a while."

"Mr. Moore, it is an honor."

"I likewise am honored, Mr. Walthrope."

"Lucius. Please . . . you must all call me Lucius."

"And you, sir, must call me Caleb."

"I will do that, Caleb. Do you need help to get inside?"

"No . . . no. I can manage it."

Walthrope walked Rebeka to the door, while Caleb pulled himself down and with crutches made his way slowly into the house.

Betsy didn't follow the others inside, but turned and looked out over the land. She walked to the door and called to John. "Make sure they're comfortable, I'll be back in a while." She arranged care for the Graggs' carriage and the horse, then rode a different horse down to one of her mills. She was enjoying being home . . . the freedom . . . being far from the war's front. She fervently hoped the war would never come this far south in the valley. It was comforting to see Walthrope. She could always rely on him. Without him, she couldn't have left all to go to her mother in Winchester.

On returning from the mill, her feelings and thoughts had changed dramatically. Her overseer at the mill had asked her if she had been to the woolen factory.

"No . . . not yet. I just got back and came to see you first—you being my favorite." The overseer had not acknowledged her answer, and it made her uncomfortable.

"Why do you ask?"

"No reason," he said, "Just heard things . . . been hearing them for a long while now. Hearing a lot more these days. Just people talking, mind you. Nothing . . . really."

"What have they been talking about?"

"Oh, Mrs. Henderson . . . it ain't my place."

"No . . . please . . . tell me what you've heard."

"Mrs. Henderson, you know I wouldn't 'less you force me. I don't like passing on this kind of talk."

"I'm sure you never would, but I insist."

"If you're insisting then . . . some people are saying the factory ain't doing good things."

"I know we've had shortages of wool. With the war, you've got to expect that."

"No, that ain't it. People say they don't like that Mr. Stokes you have up there."

"He can try the patience of Job, but he knows . . ."

"It ain't like that, ma'am."

"Oh?"

"That Stokes fellow is getting mighty proud . . . meaner than he used to be."

"So that's it. I'll visit the factory tomorrow. I'll have Mr. Walthrope take me, and we'll visit Mr. Stokes."

"You're taking that Walthrope fellow with you, then?"

"Why wouldn't I take him? He's the factory superintendent."

"Yes, ma'am."

She was losing her patience with this long way to the overseer's point, but she suspected if she rushed him, he would clam up. "You don't think I should take Mr. Walthrope?"

"No, ma'am. Wouldn't it be good to see the factory without that Walthrope fellow?"

"Then I assume I should go without an appointment."

"Ain't it your factory? Why'd you need an appointment to visit your own factory?"

"Unless something changed while I was gone, I'm the proprietor."

"Yes, ma'am . . . 'less something changed."

She lost her patience. "Out with it! What are you telling me?"

"Nothing, ma'am. Just that people are noticing things changing."

As she rode from the mill, she tried to understand what the man suggested. Instead of going home she rode directly to the factory. It was quiet. Since the war began, she had never seen the factory idle in the late afternoon. The government demanded that production be maintained. How could it be closed? She walked around the building, found all the doors fastened and bolted and inexplicably felt danger. She knocked loudly to raise someone, but there was no response. She decided she would come again the next day. As she rode home, she kept thinking about the words of the overseer. She wondered if she would get a similar story from a second nearby mill and rode to find out.

The second mill was a large steam-driven operation near the railroad depot, and when she reached it, the overseer greeted her warmly and treated her with the deference he had always shown her. She probed. How was everything in town? Well. How was his family? Well. He was a grandfather now. How was business in town? Good. With the railroad from Richmond and war demands, it kept the mill busy. Flour was always needed.

"I've heard my woolen factory is busy."

"Yes, ma'am."

"But something doesn't seem right to me."

"It don't. Hope you find my service valuable. We've been very busy."

"I know you have, but the factory seems slow."

"It does?"

"I went by there this afternoon. It was closed up, can't figure out why it's not open."

"Don't know why that'd be. You got that Walthrope gentleman. Ask him."

"Yes . . . I could ask him . . . and I will." She spoke tentatively, hoping to draw out from the overseer any rumor he had heard. "But it seems strange . . . something doesn't seem right."

"Does seem strange don't it. It ain't like the factory 'fore Walthrope got here. Got those other businesses there now."

"Businesses. What other business?"

"Oh, ma'am, you know 'bout them: The merchandise . . . sellin' . . . buyin' . . . that kind o' thing. They say you's gettin' mighty rich from it."

"Oh, yes . . . that . . . of course."

"Buyin' and sellin', it ain't as hard as mill work, but the mill's all I know . . . I 'preciate the work."

"You do a fine job. Do people think what's going on at the factory is bad?"

"Don't know what folks think. Course . . . excuse me for sayin' . . . I don't see how it's helpin' the war none. But you's doin' it, so it has to be helpin'."

It was dark by the time she arrived home, and the house was frantic. Walthrope had been down to the first mill she had visited and found she had left hours earlier. He had just returned and was preparing to search for her again. She promised them she wouldn't go on any more solitary evening rides and calmed everyone's nerves but her own.

After supper, Rebeka, Walthrope, Caleb and Betsy retired to the parlor to visit.

"Where did you go this afternoon?" Walthrope asked.

"To the mills."

"Mills? Of course, I didn't think of looking at the other mill. Always conscientious: first day back and visits two mills. You have a very unusual daughter, Mrs. Richman."

Rebeka and Betsy ignored his comment, and Betsy casually added, "I went to the factory as well."

Out of the corner of her eye she saw Walthrope's head rise quickly. She didn't look at him.

"You did travel today, didn't you?" Walthrope said. "And did you find everything in order at the factory?"

"I would expect so with you in charge, but I got there after it closed."

"After it closed?" There was a touch of surprise in the question. "Well . . . just let me know when you want to go. I'll take you when it's open. You know how old Stokes feels about women proprietors in the factory."

"I will visit it some time soon."

"What about tomorrow? I'll swing by about 10 o'clock and take you for a visit."

Betsy laughed. "Ten? I don't think I'll visit at 10."

"I understand. You'll need to rest after such a long trip. You just let me know when you want to go. I'll make the arrangements."

"I knew you would."

"Now if you'll excuse me, I must be leaving. You've had a long day. You should rest. Mrs. Richman, it was a great honor to meet you. I look forward to seeing you again."

"Mr. Walthrope . . . Lucius . . . thank you for taking such good care of us today." She added, reaching out to take Betsy's hand who sat nearby, "And for taking such good care of my daughter."

"I assure you I have gotten far more pleasure from it than any of you. Service . . . especially to Betsy . . . is a joy." He nodded to Caleb. "Lieutenant Moore, good evening."

Caleb nodded without rising from his chair. "Good evening, sir."

Betsy rose.

"You needn't show me out. I know the way."

"I want to," Betsy said.

They walked without speaking to the front door which Betsy opened. They stepped out onto the front porch. The evening was cool and Betsy shivered.

"You'd better go back inside. It's cold," Walthrope said. "And you've had a very long day."

"It's nice to be home. It's been nearly two months since we left. It feels wonderful to be here."

"I missed you. I'm so glad you've come home. It was a long time."

"It was. I thought a lot about you while we were gone. I've thought a lot about you this afternoon as I took my ride."

"I've thought a lot about you, too, Betsy. You have become very important to me. I just hope I have proven trustworthy of more confidence . . . that you will expect even more of me."

"You have become entwined in every part of my life."

"I'd best take my departure, Mrs. Henderson," he said, suddenly formal. "Till tomorrow."

"Till tomorrow," she responded. "Why don't you come down around in the afternoon . . . say about two, and tell me all that's been happening at the factory."

"Two o'clock. I will be here. I'll bring the reports. You know you're lovely, don't you?"

She smiled warmly at him. "Good night, Mr. Walthrope."

"Goodnight."

Chapter 25
September 1863, Staunton, Virginia

Walthrope rode directly to Stokes' home. He pounded long and hard on the man's front door. Stokes, who lived alone, reluctantly opened the door, and Walthrope pushed his way into the front hall.

"Mr. Walthrope, what are you doing here at this hour?"

"The question, Stokes, is not about the time." Stokes could see Walthrope's rage. "The question is what you are doing closing the factory. We must keep up appearances. The government . . . remember the government."

"We are making so much from our other enterprises that . . ."

"'We are making?' 'Our enterprises?' Let me remind you," Walthrope stepped closer to intimidate the balding, ashen-faced, short, stout man. "There is no 'our business.' Never . . . never presume to be my equal! Do you hear me? You're lucky I don't shoot you right here . . . right now!"

Stokes unconsciously stepped away from Walthrope, but the visitor matched his retreat.

"Why are you so angry? I'll keep the factory open if you think it's that important."

"If I think it's important!" Walthrope yelled. "You don't understand! Let me help you see how things are. Listen carefully, Stokes, so you do understand. Men like you have disappeared in the past. If you don't get it right, you'll join them. Listen, my good Mr. Stokes . . . or hear nothing more . . . ever. Am I clear? Do you understand?"

Stokes had never seen Walthrope angry. Walthrope had always behaved as a gentleman, always smooth, albeit with strong tendencies toward greed and disrespect. For the first time in his relationship with Walthrope, he understood the man and his drive; and that understanding scared him.

"You will keep the factory open . . . operating as it always has," Walthrope continued. "You will take no more afternoons off. I don't care how little we make on wool . . . or how little wool we have. With a war going, the government . . . the people expect the factory to be working . . . constantly working. Everyone's already suspicious about what goes on there. We are shielded only by the reputation of our benefactress; no one looks too closely because it's her factory, so it must be honorable. They expect only good from her. If our dear Mrs. Henderson—or the Rebels—lose confidence in us, the venture won't last long . . . even with our friends. If you can't get that right . . . if you can't keep them happy, I'll find someone who will work the factory right. You fool! Saint Betsy returned today. She went to the factory."

"You accuse me?" Stokes saw the cause of Walthrope's wrath and was becoming angry himself at being unfairly chastised. "She is your job." His voice rose accusingly, "You were to keep her away, the government off . . ." Stokes' words stopped short as a fist struck him hard in his face. He stumbled back in shock, but animal instincts took over, and he dove forward driving his shoulder hard against Walthrope's midsection. Stokes' blow pushed Walthrope backward. He doubled over and the two men fell hard against the door and floor. Walthrope raised his fist quickly, instinctively and brought it down hard on the back of Stoke's neck. Walthrope raised his knees hard pushing Stokes off him, and Stokes tumbled backward. Walthrope was on his feet in an instant, picking up a brass spittoon that rested in the corner of the hall, holding it in both hands and bringing it down hard on Stokes' head three times. Stokes, who rose to his knees after the first blow, fell on the floor after the second and remained motionless . . . his head visibly crushed and bleeding.

It was over too quickly for Walthrope; his animal fury not yet spent. Angry that Stokes lay lifeless on the floor, he kicked the corpse and walked noisily around the hall, until he finally settled on a chair to think. Stoke's death would be a burglary interrupted. There were many soldiers in town. Assaults had become frequent in Staunton, and this incident would be just one more. He would plant a Confederate forage cap and mess up the house a bit. That would be enough. They would never suspect him . . . he had been on such seemingly cordial terms with the dead man. He walked through the house in the dark taking small trinkets from each room, pulling open drawers and cabinets. He quietly stepped outside and carefully, softly broke

the window in the kitchen, leaving the kitchen's outside door ajar. But he never saw the smallish woman
who huddled in fear in a corner of an upstairs bedroom
and who scurried from the back door after he left the
house to find a forage cap.

The next morning, Walthrope was at the factory early when word came by way of a visit from the sheriff
that a wayward soldier had broken into Stokes' house.
In cahoots with a woman who had apparently seduced
Stokes, the soldier had burglarized the house and
killed the foreman. On hearing the news, Walthrope
appeared shocked, and he was. A woman? Was there a
woman in the house? Was there a witness? He could
feel the sweat on his brow. He was rarely without
words, but he sat stunned by the revelation. The sheriff took his behavior as surprise and profound sorrow
and apologized for bringing such sad news. Walthrope
recovered enough to show the visitor out.

By 10 o'clock the news had reached Betsy, and
when Walthrope came for their interview at two, they
discussed the sad event. Walthrope had regained his
equilibrium and wove a fantastic web for Betsy. Last
night he had been disturbed to learn the factory had
been closed when the soldiers needed so much. He
had not fulfilled Betsy's high expectations and had
gone to the factory early that morning. There he found
evidence that Stokes may have been using the facility
to hoard goods, speculating on them. He was angry
and awaited a confrontation with Stokes. Regrettably
that encounter never happened. Stokes' death devastated him, but he was more heartsick that the crafty
fellow had swindled him when Betsy and the country

had placed such responsibility upon his shoulders. He would do more . . . far more . . . in the future. She would see—he would prove worthy of her respect.

As he explained it, she believed him. In her turn, she confessed to him everything she had heard the day before. She had always been uncomfortable with Stokes. Yes, she pointed out that Walthrope had gotten sloppy, but she excused it because she had kept him so busy seeing to all her needs. He had kept everything together while she was gone, had gotten the house ready for her return. She understood: She had asked too much of him. It had been Stokes who had misused the factory. She was relieved to know it had not been Walthrope.

He assured her that she had not asked too much of him, but that he had failed because of his lack of diligence. He would show her. He would work harder . . . try to make amends. It was hard to keep the factory operating at any profit, but he wasn't interested in money, only in fulfilling her wishes. He conjured up her religious feeling by referring to proving himself a worthwhile steward . . . a phrase he had heard preachers use. He would dedicate himself completely to the factory, to the cause, to her.

In his mind, the interview went better than expected. She responded that under the dire circumstances, he should devote himself solely to the Confederacy. She held him in awe because of this sacrifice and looked forward to the end of the struggle and for more peaceful times when they could be together.

By the time he left, she had forgotten the need she had so desperately felt the night before to inspect the factory. All was clearly well; she felt justified in her long-held distrust of Stokes. Walthrope was now fully engaged in the work. She could focus on the mills, the farm, her mother, Caleb's recovery and the plan to marry Caleb off to Marie Ann Allen.

In the coming months, Walthrope did work longer hours in the factory and reported wonderful results to Betsy. He indicated everything was running more smoothly without Stokes. He assured Betsy that receipts of raw materials into and shipments from the factory had never been so frequent. Independent witnesses inadvertently supported his reports saying activity, including deliveries and shipments at the factory, had never been greater.

Caleb Moore, in the meantime, continued recovering rapidly and had become a welcome addition to the household. Even in his weakened condition, he took on management of the farm and mills. Rebeka Richman settled into her new life on the farm and kept up, in Betsy's mind, an unlikely correspondence with Margaret Gragg.

Betsy enjoyed Walthrope's company. She left operation of the factory totally in his hands, and she was like a school girl as she received the unending train of gifts he now sent. Her mother never spoke of Walthrope, but each time Betsy received a gift from him, Rebeka with a wry smile would quote the Bible: "Thou shalt take no gift: for the gift blindeth the wise . . . ." Walthrope and Betsy had begun to discuss marriage, and she was growing excited and anxious at the prospect. No specific decisions or arrangements had been made, but as the year ended, Walthrope suggested they marry right away.

Betsy had not written once to Hank since she had come home, and she barely scanned the two letters he had sent her. She tried not to think about him or his family. She also strove not to think of Emily, but for a different reason. Emily had avoided Betsy when she arrived in Staunton, and Betsy assumed it was because she knew of the cowardice of Emily's husband. Betsy tried repeatedly to visit her, but to no avail. Emily made it clear she would have no further contact with Betsy.

Chapter 26
January 1864, Near Staunton, Virginia

*F*ive months after Betsy arrived home, a cold, blustery January afternoon brought a small, unimpressive woman to the door of the mansion-like farmhouse. John announced and ushered her into the parlor where Betsy sat quietly reading.

"Sorry to oppose on yuh, ma'am."

Without rising or lowering her book, Betsy responded, "You're not imposing. Won't you please sit down?" She motioned to a chair near her own.

The woman timidly sat on the edge of the chair as if she feared soiling it. She was silent, her timid eyes looking at Betsy.

"Yes," Betsy said when she understood that she was to begin the conversation. "How can I help you?"

"Oh . . . then yuh will help me?" the woman said with despair in her voice. "I couldn't go to no one else. I knew yuh being a woman, yuh would understand. Yuh'd help me."

Betsy felt anxious. She frowned, her forehead creased, she leaned toward the woman, putting down the book without marking where she read. "What brings you here?"

"I saw who killed 'im."

Betsy's mind flashed to the battlefield at Manassas. Does this woman bring another witness of his death? The first witness still haunts me. But it was only a thought, quickly dismissed as inconceivable.

"Who was killed?"

"Jeremiah."

"Jeremiah?" She thought over her acquaintances and said, "I don't believe I know who you mean."

"Jeremiah . . . he worked for yuh."

"Worked for . . ."

"Jeremiah Stokes . . . at the factory."

Betsy's body moved slowly backward until she rested fully against her chair as she considered what the woman said. Clearly Stokes had been someone important to this woman, and she had come to Betsy believing his employer held him in esteem as well. She needed to be gentle. She wanted to ask why she hadn't gone to the sheriff, why had she come to her. She restrained the impulse. "You were there?"

"Heard it all. I was there in his house that night."

"I am sorry. It must have been frightening for you."

"I'm still scared, ma'am . . . scared o' 'im."

"Of him?"

"He killed Jeremiah. He'll kill me, if he knows I seen 'im."

"Why haven't you told the sheriff?"

"The sheriff won't listen to no woman like me . . . don't like no women like me."

"If you tell me . . . and I tell him, you think he'll believe it? Is that it?"

"I know he will."

"But I wasn't there. I didn't see it. I can't tell them something I haven't seen."

"They think a soldier and a woman done it. If I go to 'em, they'll think I done it . . . me and a soldier. They won't believe me. They'll believe yuh. Yuh can speak for me."

"You want me to tell them what you told me, then you'll talk to them?"

"Don't tell him though! I'm scared, but he don't know I seen him. He thought the house was empty."

"Who is he?" Betsy asked haltingly.

"The man that works for yuh. The one at the factory . . . Mr. Wiltroop."

"Walthrope?"

"Yes, ma'am, Mr. Wiltroop."

Betsy's face was expressionless, but inwardly the news stunned her. He couldn't be the murderer. This woman was wrong! How could she believe such a woman? She knew Walthrope. She could trust him. Couldn't she? A doubt leaped into her mind. "You must be mistaken. It can't be him! Are you sure?"

"Yes, ma'am. It was him. I seen him in town. It's the same man . . . sure of it. I asked someone at the factory his name. They told me."

The woman proceeded describing in detail what she had heard and seen, and it disturbed Betsy. She imagined herself at the altar with Walthrope . . . as she had so many times before. Horror filled her being as she now saw his face as the face of a killer. She shuddered, thinking that minutes earlier she would have married him without hesitation . . . a murderer. She felt a deep revulsion. She was numb from shock. It couldn't be true! Impossible! She couldn't believe it! Yet . . . if she were honest with herself, it confirmed something she had long felt subconsciously . . . even amidst talk of marriage. It was somewhere north in Winchester or Woodstock, an impression discomforted her. She was glad she had never told him she loved him. He attracted her, and she wanted the easily attainable stability he promised; however, in quiet moments, she was troubled. She knew, nonetheless did not want to believe, that he was not whom he pretended to be. It was not really Lucius Walthrope she loved. But could he be a murderer? It didn't seem possible. Betsy spoke earnestly, "Tell no one! You must tell no one. Do you understand? No one."

"But yuh said yuh'd help."

"And I will." She thought of how influential Walthrope had become in Staunton and beyond in the past six months and cursed herself for her naiveté. She comprehended for the first time that his influence came from speculation . . . using her factory for speculation and from siphoning her wealth. "But we must be very careful," she said.

A shuffle in the hall and the door swinging open accompanied her last words. Walthrope walked boldly into the room with the words, "Ah, my dear." He stopped immediately, startled to see the woman. "I'm sorry. I didn't know you were entertaining. Please excuse my intrusion." He bowed almost flippantly to the woman.

Betsy could see the abject fear in the woman's eyes. The woman froze, face and body. Betsy panicked as well when she realized she didn't know the woman's name or where she lived. How could she contact her? Betsy stood and moved quickly to the woman's side. She crouched by the chair, put her arm around her waist and raised her as she said, "Thank you for coming. Your news means a lot to me. I will help you . . . I will. I promise."

The woman still stared dumbfounded at Walthrope, who smiled pleasantly in return.

"Come, I'll show you to the door." Betsy said. "Mr. Walthrope, I'll be right back. Make yourself comfortable. I'll only be a moment."

Walthrope, who was in high spirits, spoke to the woman, "You can be sure my dear Mrs. Henderson will do all she can to help you get whatever it is you deserve."

Betsy shook her head involuntarily in response to Walthrope's words. She glanced at him. Was he threatening the woman? She led the terrified woman past Walthrope into the hall and to the front door. Still with her arm around the woman, Betsy pulled her through the door and onto the front porch. She released her hold on the woman and closed the door. Betsy turned to face the distressed visitor. The woman's fear riveted her eyes wide open and fastened her mouth tightly closed. Her eyes darted wildly from Betsy to the street and everywhere in between. Betsy spoke, "I will contact you. What's your name? Where do you live? How can I . . ."

The woman bolted from the porch without looking back, and Betsy, with Walthrope so close, was afraid to call out to her. Betsy watched her hysterical run. Betsy shared her alarm and feared the woman fled supposing Betsy had deceived her . . . that she would give her away to Walthrope. The woman was like a wild animal trying to elude a predator. Betsy pitied the woman . . . and herself, and didn't know how to help either of them.

Chapter 27
January 1864, Northern Virginia

*L*ate in 1863, the U.S. government offered a 30-day furlough and $400 bounty to any three-year volunteer whose term ended in the coming summer if they would reenlist for the war's duration. Hank welcomed the chance and reenlisted quickly. He was not particularly eager to sign up again. He dreaded unending war . . . more battles . . . unimagined anguish . . . continued suffering. But those were in the distant future. He needed a furlough soon for the plans he had hatched.

In January of 1864, the reenlisted men of the 19th turned in their muskets and boarded a train for Indiana and their furloughs. Hank joined the regiment on the train first to Washington, then on to Indiana where he impatiently endured a community-sponsored celebration paying tribute to the volunteers. He cared little for the afternoon's activities and accolades. He was there only for the furlough.

Official furloughs began the next day, most of the men dispersing to their Indiana homes. Hank, wearing new civilian clothes with a new pistol in his belt and pockets full of bounty-won greenbacks, turned eastward toward Virginia. He headed for Staunton and what he now perceived as his destiny. He hadn't written to Mrs. Henderson to tell her he was coming; had given her no clue. But he had to go; he had to see her. He worried for her safety as he hadn't received a letter from her since Gettysburg. He feared some mishap had befallen her. As he made his way toward the Old Dominion, one memory haunted him:

Less than three months earlier, he had gone back to his first battlefield. He, along with other selected Iron Brigade soldiers, had returned to re-inter comrades. Unhappily they found their bones bared and bleaching in the elements on the farmer's field. The soldiers' original graves had been a thin covering of dirt that closely marshaled-Confederate stragglers had grudgingly thrown over the Union bodies where they had fallen. Rain made quick and easy work of disrespectfully exposing the bodies. Re-burying the men was hard work, but Hank appreciated the opportunity to pay last respects to comrades as he tried to identify them and carefully laid their final remains to rest. These men left on the field were no longer identifiable by their hair color, quick wit, or ears that stuck out a little too far. They were discernible only by the still-attached cartridge box, the uniform fragment, the leather belt, anything that might bear identity's clue.

In spite of being surrounded by men who worked as diligently as he did, he felt oddly alone. Once during this time, he slipped away from the other men and walked across the field amid the graves. He tried to remember where he had stood less than 18 months earlier. He felt older and tired. Gettysburg had taken much out of him. He hadn't recovered his energy, his enthusiasm. He took what he imagined had been his

own position in the battle and stood there remembering. He tried to picture where he had found Captain
Henderson, but couldn't quite locate it. He tried to
imagine where Daniel would have been. Did he fall
here? He made his way across the battlefield and
stood on the Confederate side. He turned around and
imagined where George Dyer had stood, where Nathaniel Andersson had fought . . . his friends . . . gone
now. He tried to remember why he originally joined the
army. He walked across the Manassas battlefield to the
unfinished railroad the Johnnies had held and walked
along it a ways. He tired of that and made his way, still
alone, back to the farm, back to where they had
fought.

He stopped on the Confederate side again and
gazed at the woods through which he had raced to
reach his first battle . . . green . . . untested . . . innocent. He couldn't have imagined what was beyond the
wood; he wouldn't have wanted to. He breathed in the
smell of decaying fall leaves and thought about the
war. He imagined it as a forest fire. He saw accumulated on the ground the debris and kindling of slavery
and a new aristocracy. He imagined the sparks of John
Brown's raid, Lincoln's election, Fort Sumter. He pictured winds of hateful and proud words from unthink-
ing politicians and zealots . . . north and south . . .
blowing the sparks into flame upon the dry tinder. He
imagined the growing fire, progressively hotter, con-
suming the hard wood of men's lives. The winds blew
stronger and the woods, the trees, the lives burned
faster and ever hotter. Men became accustomed to the
horrors of the battlefield, desensitized to their own

pain and discomfort and to the pain of others. Tree after tree of men and their lives were touched, fired, burned, consumed, till nothing remained of them but charred, smoking stumps. Even trees spared final consumption were scarred by the heat. He could feel the hot wind of hate and bitterness still blowing on the fire. He imagined thousands of acres burned . . . destroyed.

He looked at the November woods with their rapidly falling leaves and knew his figuratively burned fields would regenerate into beautiful forests, but the trees would not—could not—be the same ones. Comeliness would return, but these trees, these loved trees that had sheltered and shaded him were gone forever: George, Daniel, Captain Henderson, Nathaniel . . . gone forever. They were all part of the same forest, and they were gone. He wondered if it would be worth it. Were pride and hatred ever worth it? When the war was over, would the pride and hatred be gone?

It was getting dark. He looked along the line and imagined that he was beside Daniel.

As Hank made his way from Indiana toward Staunton, these memories were his most frequent companions.

Chapter 28
January 1864, Northeast of Winchester, Virginia

*H*ank traveled rapidly, taking little rest, from Indiana to Naomi's house. In his mind, Naomi had become family, a mother-figure to him. She gave him life when he faced death, nurtured him with letters from Staunton, lighted his way to happiness when he had been surrounded by benumbing darkness. He wanted to see Naomi almost as much as he wanted to see Mrs. Henderson. He approached her farmhouse openly and calmly. He almost felt he was home. It was evening and his soft knock on the door brought her small head to a nearby window. He heard shifting and fumbling with locks and knob. She opened the door. There was no gun at her side this time. She wore a wide smile and said, "Well, if it ain't young Hank come back from the war . . . and lookin' so handsome, too."

"Naomi." He rapidly approached her with extended arms, and she responded with a warm embrace and an invitation to supper.

"I was just sittin' down when yuh come. Join me? Yuh're so skinny, Hank. Yuh're lookin' more Secesh than Union. Don't the government feed its soldiers 'nough these days?"

Hank noticed a dirtied bowl on the table, concluded

that someone else had already eaten, but thought nothing more of it. After exchanging pleasantries, they sat down to a heavy soup.

As they were eating, Naomi said, "I saw her."

"Who'd you see?"

"Yor widow lady." Her comment made just the impact she had hoped to see, and she enjoyed his shock. He stared at her in disbelief.

"How did you . . . you went to Staunton? You haven't been delivering the letters yourself, have you?"

"Calm yuh'self! Calm yuh'self! I don't never travel none. The ole widow . . . she came right here. She was sittin' right where yuh's sittin'. She was talkin' to me just the way yuh's talkin' to me, 'cept she talks prettier."

"Why did she come to see you?"

"Oh . . . Hank. I thought yuh was a smart lad. She come for yuh. She come just to talk to me 'bout yuh."

"Me? She came here to talk about me?"

"Yep. She come. She's real pretty. She looked a mite tired when she come, but she warn't old. Yuh'd be proud to see how pretty she is. I reckon that if yuh'd seen her, she'd be just what yuh'd like."

Hank laughed, "Naomi, how do you know what I'd like?"

"I just do. Don't ask no questions 'bout how I know. I just know."

"When was she here?"

"Back . . . uh . . . late summer. The corn what was planted—which ain't much—was high by then."

"She was here." Hank repeated.

"She visited family in Winchester, so she come out

to see me. She come out here on a horse . . . rode by he'self. Everyone right then was anxious 'bout the Union coming back. Course they ain't come back in yet, and that makes it all tougher 'cause men on both sides is in the country causin' problems for folks. Yankee cavalry come through here just last week. Looked like they was goin' to Winchester, but never heard nothin' more 'bout them. They didn't bother me none."

"What was she like?"

Naomi smiled wide, "I thought yuh'd git 'round to askin' that. What I thought was real pretty was her eyes. They was like one of those green stones . . . emeralds—I think that's what they call 'em. They was big, big eyes; couldn't help but see 'em. She didn't blink none, so I was afeelin' she was seein' right through me. Course she couldn't, that's just how it felt. She had yella' hair done up pretty. Her dress was a rich blue, real soft. I felt it when she done hugged me."

"She hugged you?"

"Yeah, she hugged me. That surprise yuh? Course she hugged me. It was like we was ole friends . . . ain't seen each other for a season or two. Her voice was real soft. I liked her voice. But she says some things she don't mean . . . tried flatterin' me. She must o' thought it real 'portant that I like her. Hank, why d'yuh s'pose she was feelin' like that?" She smiled impishly. "Course I told her that waren't right. She had to say the honest thing or I waren't gunna help her no more. She understood that kind of talk . . . didn't say nothin' more that waren't right."

"She's beautiful then."

"Very beautiful . . . looks a lot like me, only I ain't got them green eyes." Naomi laughed. "But I ain't got no letter for yuh since she was here. Maybe I scared her off."

"Well, if you did, she probably deserved it."

"I ain't thinkin' she's scared off none. I'm thinkin' she wants to meet yuh just as soon as yuh can git there. That's what I'm athinkin' anyways."

"I just hope nothing has happened to her. Is she still in Winchester?" Hank asked hopefully.

"She ain't. Been a long time since she was sittin' where you is. She didn't say nothin' 'bout stayin' in Winchester . . . just see to her family, then goin' back home—think it's a farm what she's got."

"Not in town then?" he mused. "I'm on my way to Staunton now, and I'm not leaving till I see her this time."

"That's good. Course yuh know yuh's still likely to get caught by the whole Secesh army or worse yet by those renegades."

"Renegades? They still causing problems?"

"They always is."

"How about that Cole fellow?"

"He's still 'bout, causin' problems for folks on both sides. Everybody just as soon get rid of him, but he's charmed. Never gets caught, never gets shot. He's pretty much by hisself all the time now. The other men what was with him is all dead . . . or captured . . . or gone home. He still talks 'bout yuh every time he's in these parts. Whenever he comes, I cook him up something to eat and he talks and he talks and he talks, always talkin' big things. He talks 'bout how he's waitin' for yuh to pop up. Says he's gunna get yuh. So mind me, watch out for him. Yuh hear?"

"I will."

"Yuh stayin' the night? Yuh can sleep out in the barn. May be someone else out there with yuh. Don't pay him no mind. I'll talk to him 'fore yuh go out, tell him to stay out o' yor way. Yuh'll be comfortable out there in the barn. Yuh can stay long as yuh want—though I'm thinkin' yuh's gunna want to get to the ole widow lady real soon." She smiled and looked hard at Hank, "Once yuh been shot by that fellow with the arrows, yuh can't hardly hold yuh'self back."

"Naomi . . . thank you." Then he added as an afterthought: "Is she old?"

"Is she old?" Naomi laughed, "Yuh was sittin' there the whole time wonderin' if yuh was in love with someone's grandma." She laughed again. "She's so young I waren't sure if I should rock her in my rockin' chair so the child could sleep or give her back to her ma for sucklin'. She's just right for the likes o' yuh. Now, d'yuh get enough to eat?"

"I've had enough. Thank you. Naomi, have you heard from your husband?"

Naomi sighed and squeezed her thin lips together, "He ain't comin' back."

"I should never have mentioned it. I'm sorry. I was just hoping . . . hoping you had good news."

"Oh, it's fine, yuh bringin' him up. I ain't sad 'bout it . . . not much . . . no more, anyhow. Hank, it waren't no surprise to me. I 'xpected it the whole time . . . since he gone away. He said he was gunna join the infantry, fight for the country. That's what he said. The way yuh done—fight in the war. He never said which army, Secesh or Union." She stopped and looked at Hank for a long time. He detected sadness in her eyes and could feel she wasn't finished. He waited without speaking. "He's dead," she continued. "Got the news just a few days past. Got kilt . . . shot . . . in Californy. Hank, you know 'bout any big battles in Californy. I heard 'bout Vicksburg . . . Shiloh . . . Chattanooga . . . all out west. I keep up on war news, but I ain't heard o' no battle in Californy. Hank, you heard o' any battles out there?"

She waited for his reluctant reply: "I haven't."

"I ain't neither . . . nary a one. He never joined no army. He just run away, makin' a new life for hisself . . . leavin' the ole one—that's me—leavin' his ole life behind. But Hank, the ole one . . . she's ploughin' on . . . on a good spot o' soil, gittin' real happy. She h'ain't never had a whole lot. But what she got, she's usin' for the good. It's good what matters, ain't it, Hank? Can't yuh see that, Hank?"

Hank wanted to hug her, but he responded simply, "I do see it, Naomi. Good is all that matters."

A smile pushed the sadness from her face, "Oh, Hank, I done knowed he waren't never comin' back . . . knowed that when I got no letters. Now I'm sure of it. I was just teasin' folks sayin' he was comin' back. He waren't comin' back. Hank, now I'm a widow, too. Know any soldiers what would like to write romantic-like letters to a widow?" She laughed.

Hank responded tenderly, "I know of one soldier already in love with you."

Naomi looked down at the floor and smiled. There was a pause in the conversation. Naomi broke the silence, "Well now, if yuh've eaten enough, go on out to the barn. It will be a bit cold, but I don't want to hear nothin' more from yuh 'till the morrow."

Naomi hurried Hank out of the house with a lantern in her hand. She entered the barn first, reappearing several minutes later. She took him into the barn and showed him where to sleep, then quickly returned to the house. Hank rolled out his bedroll, buried it deeply in the hay and slipped quickly into it, expecting to shiver all night. But he slept undisturbed until after sunrise.

Chapter 29
January 1864, Northeast of Winchester, Virginia

Voices outside the barn awoke him. He instinctively felt the ground for his gun. It wasn't there. He panicked. He searched frantically for the pistol until he remembered he had left it in Naomi's house when she had hurried him out. Someone was yelling at Naomi . . . a man's voice shouting threats at her. The male voice was getting closer to the barn. Hank watched the barn door as it swung outward. Cole walked in, standing in plain sight.

"Come on out!" he yelled.

He hadn't seen Hank, and Hank moved behind a stall wall and waited. His mind raced. No gun. He hadn't seen a gun in Cole's hand either. He would charge him . . . take his chances in a fight. But the sharp report of a rifle shot changed his mind. He could hear Cole methodically reloading. Hank froze in place, thinking, waiting for an opportunity to escape. Cole fired again. The last shot passed near Hank. Hank could hear him reload—it was a muzzle loader.

Hank saw someone move several stalls away and remembered Naomi's strange warning that someone else would spend the night in the barn. The man moved again and Hank saw his black hand—a runaway slave.

"You may as well come out, or I'm gunna put a ball through every inch of this barn. I'm gunna find you! I know you're in here. If you're one o' those runaway slaves like last time, I'm gunna hang you from that tree we used for the last fellow. Naomi don't want no slaves usin' her barn."

Hank looked across the stalls in the direction of the slave, thinking. If Hank surrendered the slave would have a chance. If he didn't surrender, Cole would probably find and kill them both. He had no choice. "I'm here," Hank called.

"Where? Stand up! I want to see you."

Hank hesitated.

"Where are you? Stand up . . . or I'm gunna shoot agin . . . and you're gunna be dead."

"I'm here. Don't shoot!" Hank slowly stood up and stepped out from the stall.

Cole looked sincerely surprised and called out happily, "If it ain't our friend, Mr. Gragg." He yelled to Naomi, "It ain't no slave—better than that. I got myself a real treasure this time. Mr. Gragg, I know I promised not to shoot if you came out, but I didn't know I was talkin' to you. You merit killin'."

"Don't shoot," Hank said coldly. He had the sense the slave was watching him, but couldn't look to confirm his feeling.

"Sorry, I have to shoot you. I've been waiting for this moment too long. Last time I didn't shoot you, I ended up losin' out on the fun. That's twice now. That's too many times. I've been thinkin' about this moment, about you for quite a while, ain't I, Naomi? It's been pleasurable thinkin' about it. You've died so many times . . . in so many ways. This last and final time you ain't even gunna notice. This time I ain't waitin' for nothin'."

He raised and sighted the rifle. "Maybe you could die with the first ball, not slowly. But then maybe . . ."

"Don't do it!" a small, high-pitched voice commanded from outside the barn. Hank couldn't see Naomi. He could see out of the corner of his eye the slave crouched and still.

"Are you tellin' me what to do?" As Cole spoke, he turned his head to look at Naomi. Hank felt like charging him while his head was turned, but he remained stationary. It might have been his only chance to escape, but his legs wouldn't move.

Naomi responded, still out of Hank's view, "I think I'm just askin' yuh . . . but I'm feeling mighty insistent."

"It's good you wasn't here when we caught that runaway slave hidin' in your barn. You'd probably tried to save him, too. We was just helpin' you by hangin' 'im while you was gone." Cole laughed.

"Cole, yuh's a fool. Yuh could'a taken that slave back . . . got a bounty."

"Some things are more important than money. It was more fun hangin' 'im, watchin' 'im struggle, choke, swing. Like a clock, swingin' back and forth till he all run down." Cole looked toward Naomi. "You don't know how to use that. You're good at carryin' it, makin' threats, but I ain't seen you use it."

"I don't have to prove nothin' to yuh, Cole, but I will if I has to . . . I will. From where I stand, yuh's makin' a mighty fine target. I been shootin' since I was a little girl . . . the size of a churn. My pa . . . he taught me . . . taught me good. Yuh's a mighty big target from here. Why don't yuh put yor gun right on the ground and then kick it way out o' the way so there ain't no accident to clean up. Yuh know I don't mind yuh doin' what yuh do—that ain't none of my affair—but not on my land. Now yuh put that musket down. Yuh can't go akillin' at my house. If yuh keep doin' that, pretty soon won't nobody come to visit me. I do like visitors. Yuh go on, let Mr. Gragg get off my land, then yuh can have yor musket and git him."

Cole lowered the gun and kicked it away from him. "If he gets away this time, somebody's gunna pay. And Naomi—it will have to be you."

"Come, come, how's he to get away? Yuh got a horse. He don't. Yuh got a gun. He don't. If yuh don't catch him, yuh ought to disappear on account o' shame. I'll be tellin' everyone what yuh done if he gits away. Then ain't nobody gunna be scared o' Cole no more. So, yuh better git him, but off my land. Course, yuh can always just let him go. I won't tell nobody if you let him go . . . don't want to see no one shot. Now, Mr. Gragg, yuh come on out o' there. Don't yuh go pullin' no tricks. I can shoot yuh myself if I has to. Mr. Cole ain't that far from his gun. He can git his gun and shoot yuh faster than yuh could do me harm. So come on out. Slow . . . real slow."

Hank walked carefully past Cole, sidling toward Cole's gun. "Don't bother with the gun." Naomi warned him again as he moved toward the rifle. "I'll shoot yuh myself if yuh take Cole's gun. I thought I told yuh. Yuh just go on, get out o' here. I don't need to tell yuh not to come back here no more. I've been real nice to yuh the few times yuh come 'cause I feel bad for yuh. Next time, I'm gunna shoot yuh myself. Always like company, but not yors no more. And don't forgit your hat! Yuh hear me? Take yor hat. I don't want it layin' in the corner of the kitchen no more. Sure as Rebels yell, I don't want yor hat what yuh left in my house. Take yor hat, and yuh skedaddle. Now, git! It's in the corner of the kitchen. I'll give yuh five, maybe 10 minutes, then I'm gunna loose Mr. Cole. So make sure yuh run fast, hide real good . . . poor boy." She laughed callously. "Go on, git out of here. Run!"

Hank who was passing Naomi didn't dare look at her, but broke into a run for the house. There he found his hat and pistol resting neatly on a chair near the table, but he remembered Naomi saying his hat was in the corner and looked in that direction. There, resting against the wall, was an Enfield rifle musket. He smiled, grabbed it, checked to see if it was loaded and primed, and ran out the front of the house. He was careful to keep the house between him and Naomi and Cole.

He ran at an easy pace over several hills and beyond the tree line marking the boundary of Naomi's farm. If Cole came after him, Hank would have to deal directly with him. A shiver went down his spine. He remembered it was Cole all those years ago who had assault- ed Samuel Richman. Hank had heard his voice that night—his odd voice. Remembering, Hank felt momentary gratitude to Cole: Hank had met Samuel, his dear friend, only through Cole's depredations. Samuel had recovered; no long-lasting harm had come to him. Samuel had practically adopted Hank, all thanks to this man . . . this Cole, who had no idea that Hank's life and his own had become so entangled. Did that entanglement have to preclude both of them surviving? Cole would kill Hank. Hank had to shoot him first. Likely death, and his resolve to shoot a man, dismayed Hank. He climbed a nearby hill, lay down—looking back toward Naomi's farm—and waited. He was uneasy, worrying about Naomi and the runaway slave. Minutes after he settled on the hill, he heard a rifle shot from the farm; then all was quiet. What would that mean?

He thought about Naomi and Samuel. He could see Samuel vividly, finding him on the ground, still conscious, brutally beaten. He remembered Samuel's death; trying to tell Rebeka her husband was dead and buried. He remembered her patiently, quietly at first, explaining to him he was mistaken—it was all a mistake. She kept talking, becoming more distraught as the minutes passed. Soon she was yelling at him. Then strangely, she was on her knees at his feet, crying, calling him, Samuel, begging him not to leave her, not to abandon her. But she had stopped her confused supplication suddenly and rose to her feet. He remembered her sudden despondency, refusing to talk to him, refusing to even acknowledge him further. He could still see her calmly going around the room, dousing the candles and walking out as if the room were empty, leaving Hank in the dark. He remembered stumbling as he made his way to the door. He had never told Betsy what had happened, had never mentioned it to anyone. It was too unpleasant to think about. It would have been unbearable for Betsy.

He remembered Betsy, her anguish at her father's death, her despair at his burial, how she begged Hank to tell Rebeka. She couldn't do it. She couldn't stand to see her mother suffer again. He remembered Captain Henderson's widow, Ellie. How grateful he was that she had come into his life, replaced Betsy in his affections, saved him from grief he kept bottled within. He liked the name . . . Ellie. He whispered it, but he was here to kill a man. He had but to kill him, and she— Mrs. Henderson . . . Ellie—would be his. He had to kill this man, this Cole, with his pistol and one bullet loaded into the musket. Nearly an hour passed. Perhaps Cole had decided not to follow him. Perhaps he had other more urgent business, had gone about it, hoping to deal with Hank at some other time. Perhaps Naomi had persuaded him not to kill Hank. He prayed it was so. He didn't like to think it, but perhaps Naomi had been forced to kill Cole: Hank had heard the one shot. Hank shivered from the January cold.

Enough time had elapsed. If Cole was coming, he would have been here. Hank roused himself from his remembrances and thoughts, lowered his guard and stood to leave. As he reached his feet, the sound of distant galloping jarred him. The sound came from beyond a hill in the opposite direction of Naomi's farm. He ran down the hill on which he had hidden and rapidly climbed the next. He looked over its crest and saw a horse and rider ascending the other side. He was closing the distance rapidly. Hank inadvertently held his breath and knelt. He watched as the rider approached. He had seen Cole ride enough times to instantly recognize him. Cole had toyed with him, led him to believe he was safe—just to show up to kill him. Why hadn't Cole just left? Why did he force this on them both? Cole's persistence and hatred wearied Hank.

Hank put the Enfield to his shoulder, took careful aim as Cole came closer. Only one shot. He had to stop Cole with it—the pistol wouldn't do. He had to stop him with the Minié ball or Cole would kill him. Cole didn't suspect, perhaps couldn't yet see Hank's musket. Hank was uncomfortable. This was different from battle where the immorality of killing was dulled by men standing on both sides, men who shared the burden of guilt. He felt like one of the sharpshooters he hated so much. He had little choice and took deliberate aim. Cole rode with a visible rage, and Hank could almost feel his anger as he sighted him. He could see Cole raising his musket as he rode. He had seen Hank's. Hank trained his musket on Cole's head . . . held his breath . . . waited . . . waited . . . waited . . . fired. Missed! Hank heard Cole laugh, and the rider lowered his rifle; he was saving it for a closer, more sure range. Hank pulled his untested revolver from his belt and aimed it at the rider. A first, a second, a third shot were off the mark and Cole kept coming. He was close enough for Hank to accurately bring him down, but he fired and missed again. Then he thought: bring down the horse, and he quickly fired at the horse's head. Hank's shot was perfect.

The horse's head went down instantly, and Cole was thrown over the head of the stumbling horse. He fell hard on the ground, but rose at once. Standing, wobbling from the fall, he retrieved his musket from the ground where it had fallen and took aim. Hank raised his pistol quickly. Both men fired. Cole missed, and Hank's gun misfired, firing seconds after he pulled the trigger, hitting the ground well in front of the now quickly charging Cole. Neither had a bullet left, neither could take the time to load. Hank rushed at the advancing Cole. They converged in a mighty blow that shocked both men and left them hurting, intertwined, and wrestling on the ground. Cole was strong, far stronger than Hank had anticipated. Hank was no match for such strength, and Cole quickly pinned him with powerful legs. He grasped Hank's throat with bear-like ferocity. Cole's teeth were clenched, his eyes ablaze. Hank couldn't breathe or move. The same panic swept over him that he'd felt before his first battle. He was desperate, struggling uselessly, completely overmatched. The panic deepened. He needed air. He had to move. He pushed hard against Cole, but couldn't budge him. He kicked his legs and wriggled, and Cole's grip slipped. He released his grip on Hank's throat to regain control of the smaller man again. As Cole shifted his weight, Hank sucked air deep into his lungs and slid from his grasp. Hank crawled quickly from his attacker, tried to get to his feet, to run. But Cole grabbed him again, this time pushing Hank's face toward ground. He grabbed Hank's neck again, cutting off the air. Then Hank saw it—was it just lack of air, was he hallucinating? It was a pair of bare black feet against the cold ground, seemingly standing beside Cole. Hank heard a loud pop, and felt Cole's grasp slowly lessen . . . his strength dwindle. Cole was yanked off him roughly, and Hank rolled over. There he was—William, Samuel Richman's former slave, standing above him.

"Y'all right, Hank?"

Hank didn't answer. He stared at William.

"Yuh just sit there a while, yuh'll get to feelin' better. I didn't know yuh was the man in that barn last night, else we could'a spent all the night talkin' . . . talkin' just like we used to. Didn't know it was yuh till that man called yor name. I can't believe yuh're 'live—thought yuh were dead. We all thought yuh were, and now here yuh are."

Hank said nothing. He was trying to understand what had happened, what was happening. He looked at Cole. He lay on the ground, his neck at a strange angle, his eyes, bulging, stared vacantly toward Hank.

William saw him looking at the body and said, "Had to do it, Hank. He was killin' yuh. He already killed that lady. He would'a killed yuh, too."

"What lady? Naomi?" Hank asked frantically. He groaned and rolled on the ground in grief, clutching his head.

"After yuh left, she let him get his gun. He bent down, took it from the ground. He was visitin' with her friendly, laughin', sayin' how he's gunna find yuh, kill yuh. He started walkin' away then turned 'round like he forgot to say something to her. I saw it from the barn, and he said, 'Yuh should'a never done that, lettin' him go like that.' Without sayin' another word, he raised his gun and shot her. She never knew what he was gunna do. He just done it. I think she was dead right then. Didn't scream or cry out—nothin'. I saw it all . . . from the barn. The man . . . he just walked away, didn't say nothin' . . . just walked to his horse like nothin' even happened and rode away."

Hank looked up vacuously at William, rose to his feet and said, "I've got to bury her."

"Hank, ain't time." Hank ignored him and walked, unsteady, toward the farm. William ran to block his way. Hank pushed into him to clear his path, but William was immovable. William repeated his words. "Ain't time!"

"I can't leave without burying her," Hank said desperately.

"Hank, don't yuh worry 'bout that. I already done it." William said sheepishly, lying. "I don't need no one thinkin' I done it, thinkin' I killed her . . . a white woman. I buried the body 'fore they found her and said I done it. Hank she's buried. We have to leave. We have to leave. We can't stay here."

Hank's feelings were confused. He couldn't believe Naomi was dead. He couldn't believe he was there with William, but he slowly recovered his senses and looked closely at William's face. "You saved my life," he said, sighing heavily.

William lowered his head, looking timidly at the ground.

Compassion for William touched Hank, and he said, "You've always been a good friend . . . and now this. How did you come to be at Naomi's barn last night? Did you run away from the Richmans?"

William, with eyes still gazing at the ground, smiled. "I done that a long while ago. Thought freedom . . . freedom with them Yankees was gunna be fine. Wasn't so. Them soldiers treated me like one of their animals . . . worse than their animals. Didn't have hardly no food. It was bad, real bad, Hank. Didn't give me money—the money they said. Richmans, they always treated me better, always treated me good. Just didn't have my freedom. If I'd'a had my freedom, bein' with them would'a been good and with Molly. Course it was just Mistress Richman there at the end, and she was good to me. But I had to run away . . . try that freedom; still want it . . . just don't want it with them soldiers. Where do I go to find it? I just want to be a free man. I could take care o' horses. I'd be real good at that. Know all about it. Yuh know that, Hank. So where do I go? Think it'll be better when it's all over? Think there's somewhere they'll let me show them what I can do?"

Hank noticed William no longer addressed him as Master. The lapse bothered Hank, and he was annoyed with himself for letting it bother him. He responded, "Oh, sure there will be a place . . . a free place for you. When the war's over, you can go where you like, do what you like."

"Hopin' yuh're right. Hopin' yuh're right."

"That's what this war is all about, William."

"I heard that, but I ain't seen it. Yuh know what they called me . . . the soldiers. Some ain't nearly as old as yuh. Called me Willie Boy. Willie Boy, cook me up something! Willie Boy, you take my horse! Not as old as yuh, and they were callin' me Willie Boy. Then they don't give me my pay. Ain't right, Hank." A look of concern entered William's eyes, he cocked his head and said, "You ain't gunna take me back are yuh, Hank . . . back to Winchester?"

"I'm not. Of course, not. I'm not Secesh. I'm Union . . . a Union soldier, and I think you should be free . . . today . . . right now. You are free, thanks to President Lincoln."

"Yankee!" William smiled broadly. "Welcome news . . . welcome news. Never thought yuh might be a soldier . . . Rebel or Union. Didn't think of yuh and the war together. Think of yuh only at Marster Richman's. Those were the days, Hank. Remember them talks we had. Yuh were learning so much, and yuh always was helpin' me learn . . . even though I was old. Remember?"

"I remember," Hank responded. "Where's Molly?"

"Molly?" William eyes saddened. "She died last year. She was a good wife and mammy. A slave preacher married us. Did yuh know that? Marster let us do it that way. Molly's marster didn't never care, so we got married at the Richman place. Course we jumped over the broomstick, too . . . that was the real weddin' for most. But Marster, he let us have a preacher. Molly . . . she wanted to jump the broomstick. She didn't give me no reason, just said we had to do it. So we did. Marster Richman held it a little ways off the floor, and Molly jumped it backwards, jumped real high right over the broomstick. And everybody was smiling and laughing, saying how good she jumped. Especially little Miss Betsy—she was just a little girl then. Course Molly wasn't much older—those marsters wanted them girls to have babies real early. She wasn't my first wife you know. Then it was my time to jump. I got real close to the broomstick and jumped . . . jumped high enough. I should'a been over . . . but old Marster, he was sneaky. He raised it when I started to jump, and I jumped right into it. Everyone started to laugh, and Betsy . . . she laughed loudest and said that meant that Molly was gunna be boss of the family, cause she made it over and I didn't. They all tricked me and laughed 'bout it. Spent every Saturday night with Molly till she got sick—got sick and died real sudden. Don't know what happened to the children. Hope that woman wasn't too close to yuh."

At first Hank was startled at the sudden shift in the conversation and thought William meant Betsy, but soon realized he spoke of Naomi. Hank answered softly, "She was close to me. And if I hadn't come back, she'd be alive right now, helping you."

"No . . . that ain't right, Hank. She would'a died protectin' me if yuh weren't here. I think she was just that way."

The two friends visited for a few minutes more, never again mentioning Betsy. William explained to Hank he was traveling north to join the army—had heard about black soldiers and wanted to be one, but not in Virginia . . . not near the soldiers who had treated him so badly. He came to Naomi because she had helped him when he had escaped his mistress. He thought she'd help him again, thought she'd know what to do. He hoped the army would take him. He was old, but still strong. They'd see.

Their reunion ended sadly as they took leave of one another: Hank to continue his search for his widow and William to search for a Union regiment that wanted an older, but still strong, black soldier. They left Cole where he fell.

Hank walked away without turning to look back. He made his way to a north-south road and walked openly toward the south. It occurred to him as he walked that he hadn't eaten breakfast, but he didn't care. Naomi was dead. Would food stop the pain? Within minutes, a farm wagon traveling southward approached. Hank hailed the wagoneer to stop.

"You have room for me?" Hank asked.

"Sure. I'd appreciate the company."

"How far south you going?"

"Strasburg."

"I'll go the whole way . . . if I may."

"You're more than welcome." The man responded as Hank climbed onto the wagon and it began to roll forward. "You with the army?"

"On furlough."

"Were you at Gettysburg?"

"I was. It was a terrible fight. I never want to fight again."

"Were you with them when they made that charge?"

"No."

"I've heard that charge was the most glorious charge ever made by man . . . almost took the day. Don't know why it failed."

Hank didn't comment. At that moment, he didn't care. He was busy thinking about Naomi. He couldn't understand why she did what she did . . . for him . . . for William. He wanted to talk to her again, but he couldn't, and he felt lonely and empty.

He stopped in Strasburg long enough for a meal, to warm up and to catch a ride south. He decided at the last minute not to stop to see his family. He couldn't wait any longer to see Mrs. Henderson. There would be enough time for everything else once he knew: Would she love him as he loved her?

Chapter 30
January 1864, Near Staunton, Virginia

*T*he woman's testimony weighed heavily on Betsy, but she couldn't determine what to do. She had no proof other than the word of a woman of slim reputation, half out of her mind with fear, who told a story inconsistent with newspaper reports. Nonetheless, Betsy was frightened to be near Walthrope now . . . and repelled. She tried not to show it; she tried to act with him as she always had. She wondered if it were fair to conclude he was guilty without asking him directly about it, but she knew she could never do that.

Walthrope still pushed for marriage. He would say, "Why not now? Today! We can be in the church in 15 minutes. Your mother and Caleb can come."

She brushed such comments aside quickly. "Not yet," she would simply say.

She confided in Caleb about many of the things that had happened. She told him of the ambiguous warning she'd received from the miller, that she thought it odd that Stokes had been killed, that she couldn't marry Walthrope . . . not now—she couldn't trust him because it might be true. The intimacy Caleb enjoyed with her flattered him, and for the most part, he just listened to her concerns.

One cold evening, they reminisced about life before the war and eventually visited their memories of Betsy's Winchester parlor. He asked her what happened to the others who had been there. She was excited to have the opportunity to bring up Marie Ann and proceeded to tell him that she had invited her several weeks earlier to visit. Marie Ann would arrive any day. Caleb assured Betsy he was pleased that another beautiful nurse was on her way to care for him.

"You hardly need a nurse, Caleb."

"A man always needs a nurse. Where are the others, now?"

"Other nurses?"

Caleb laughed. "No . . . the others who were at your house that day."

Betsy thought back on the day. "Richard Lewis . . . he's dead," she said somberly. "Died in a Northern camp. He was wounded at Antietam, recovered just in time for Gettysburg. He was wounded there and captured. He got sick at a prison camp and never recovered." She remembered Robert Harris fondly. "Brave and solid Robert Harris. Robert died as well— Smallpox—Jackson, Mississippi, last May just before Vicksburg fell. So the two of them died within a couple months of each other." Betsy looked sad.

"Ended up in the west, huh? And the other fellow?"

"Other fellow?"

"Yes. Came in later, with your mother. Created a scene, disrupted the conversation."

"Ah," she smiled thinking it absurd she had not included Hank in the report. "Henry Gragg . . . he's a Federal soldier somewhere in Virginia."

"Union, huh. I figured that," he said disdainfully. "And he's the only one left alive."

Betsy ignored his disdain and said, "I'd say you're doing a fair job of living."

"Yes, if you call walking on crutches or a peg leg for the rest of your life living."

Betsy scowled at him.

"Ungrateful, I know," he responded. "But there are times when I wish you'd just left me there in Winchester. It's not the pain. The pain is bearable . . . as long as I have my little pills. It's not the pain. Can you imagine anyone wanting to marry me now? Before the war there were so many . . . the pick of all the most beautiful. Any of them would have been delighted to become Mrs. Caleb Moore. Now?" He laughed morosely. "Would you want to be married to a cripple for the rest of your life?" he said in a slightly hopeful tone.

Betsy looked at him thoughtfully, consciously ignoring his tone of voice. "You may wish you were dead," Betsy said directly. "But I'm glad I didn't leave you back in that terrible hospital with that awful surgeon. Of course I'm being selfish. It's just too nice to have you around here—when you're not feeling pathetically sorry for yourself." Betsy smiled at him. "You bring such fun and happiness to the house. We couldn't do without you. I know it's hard: the pain, the feeling of being tired, the loneliness. But you'll be surprised— any of those same girls would still like to be your wife. If circumstances were different, I'd be honored to be Mrs. Caleb Moore myself."

Betsy worried when Caleb began grieving for his lost leg or the war. His mood would turn dark. She knew he suffered, had heard him cry out in the middle of the night, awakened from some morbid nightmare or phantom pain. Months earlier, she had determined she would not let him sink into self pity. When he complained of his leg or spoke of the war, she changed the subject as she did on this occasion. "I have a question for you," she said with a mischievous smile. "As I recall, you were giving us grand renditions that day of the life and follies of a professor at the Military Institute. Oh, what was his name? Please tell me what became of him."

"Professor?" Caleb responded, distracted from his distress and sincerely not remembering.

"Yes. He had a nickname. Oh . . . what was it you called him. 'Old . . . Old. . . Tom . . . Tom Fool?' That was it."

Caleb blushed, remembering in detail his description of a now legendary Confederate.

"As I recall it, Mr. Moore, you guaranteed he wouldn't measure up in war. Now what was his name? I do want to know what funny things he did in the war. Won't you please tell me?" she teased.

"Now you've had your fun," he said smiling.

Betsy laughed loudly.

Caleb became serious, "I only wish we had him now."

Marie Ann arrived the next day and the couple took up the roles they had played in Winchester. Caleb filled the air with stories of valor and funny anecdotes, and Marie Ann begged him to tell more. Betsy watched them with amusement, almost believing that some unexplained modern miracle had taken them back to Winchester as it had been before. Betsy concluded she had been right to save his life.

Such distractions, however, did little to ease Betsy's mind: What should she do about the woman, Stokes and Walthrope. Eventually, she enlisted the aid of Caleb and Marie Ann. Would they go to town and visit the factory? Find Stokes' friends. He must have had some. See if any of them could identify the woman. She charged them strictly not to reveal under any circumstances their mission to Walthrope. Marie Ann was excited to be involved in such espionage, but Betsy confided the details of the woman's visit only to Caleb. Betsy directed Caleb to take special care of Marie Ann. "Do not place her in danger . . . ever!" were her exact words. Once instructions were given, Betsy was left to wait and worry for the investigation's outcome, knowing it decided her future.

The next morning, the young couple took a carriage ride to the factory. Walthrope, who for weeks had pestered Caleb to visit the factory, greeted them most heartily. He had affirmed to Caleb that there were many good positions at the factory for him now that he was recovering and had received his discharge. Walthrope had confidentially mentioned to Caleb that working at the factory would be far more lucrative and valuable than overseeing the mills and farm. He was confident Caleb and he would work well together. Caleb had been uninterested in visiting the factory, and his beautiful hostess aided him in avoiding a visit by insisting that Caleb was needed right where he was.

Walthrope had heard of Marie Ann's arrival but had not met her as he had claimed the factory too busy for him to visit the Henderson home. So he was particularly pleased to be introduced to her and treated her with singular hospitality. He began a carefully orchestrated tour of selected areas of the factory, but midway through the tour, Marie Ann blurted out, "And where did that poor man work?"

Caleb's heart froze. He had planned it all out so carefully. He was going to get the information subtly. Walthrope would never suspect the couple was even mildly interested in Stokes or that Marie Ann even knew about his death. Unfortunately, he hadn't shared his plan with Marie Ann. He'd thought the entire operation rested on him, that she was along only to provide cover. Kept in ignorance she had developed a strategy of her own and put hers in motion first.

Walthrope looked bewildered, "What poor man?"

"The one who was killed."

"Oh, Stokes," Walthrope said flatly.

"We don't need to talk about him," Caleb interjected nervously.

Marie Ann looked and sounded indignant. "I'd like to know why not. It's a pity if we can't remember a man when he's gone. Why I bet his friends right here in the factory would appreciate a kind word about him."

"Friends?" Walthrope said abruptly. "Stokes had no friends . . . not here at any rate." He laughed softly, but coldly, and said, "If you're looking to comfort Stokes' friends, you'll have to look elsewhere. He was hated by everyone here except for me, of course."

"Mr. Walthrope, I'm disappointed. Mrs. Henderson's been saying such nice things about you and here you are speaking ill of the dead."

Walthrope paused, looked at Marie Ann and smiled warmly, "I am convinced that Mrs. Henderson is always correct, so I must be a wonderful person. As a wonderful person, I would never speak so of the dead. You have misunderstood my intent. I apologize to you. Mr. Moore, who," he smiled and winked at Caleb, "I'm sure is not as sensitive to such matters as you and Mrs. Henderson, will understand my human frailties. Even so, if you want to pay your respects to his friends, I suspect you'll have to search elsewhere among those who never had to take orders from the man. I assure you my observation isn't a judgment. I did not mean to offend you."

"But I have taken offense. And in your apology—which I graciously accept—have you not forgotten someone?" Marie Ann asked.

"Of course. I apologize to the departed Mr. Stokes, my highly valued business partner of many months whom I sorely miss."

"There, then! You are just the man Betsy described . . . a gentleman, Mr. Walthrope. I have had a wonderful time meeting you and getting this grand tour of your fine factory."

Marie Ann started walking toward the door and Caleb smiled, shrugging his shoulders in response to a questioning glance from Walthrope.

"May I assume she's not interested in the rest of the tour?" he asked Caleb.

Caleb smiled again and scurried on his crutches after her, calling over his shoulder, "I think you may. Thank you, Lucius. I'll be back another time for the rest of the tour."

Walthrope watched them go and said to no one in particular, "Perhaps when you're alone and can stay a while. You're just the man to take Stokes' place."

Chapter 31
January 1864, Near Staunton, Virginia

*I*t had been a week since Betsy had sent the young couple in search of the mysterious woman. They never found her. She had disappeared. Caleb did find several of Stokes' friends who were delighted to talk about him: about his success at the factory and his great potential, of his excellent relationship with Walthrope and Mrs. Henderson, how he was indispensable to both of them, how tragic his death was. Eventually his friends confided that Stokes dissipated himself with a convenient woman, a small woman, an odd woman for a man such as Stokes, a dishonorable woman, definitely not to be trusted . . . beneath him really, but you know how those things are. Perhaps she had killed him. Stokes' friends certainly didn't associate with such women and couldn't begin to suggest where Caleb might find her. Caleb and Marie Ann followed other leads, reaping additional information and finally reporting all of it to Betsy. The couple's report, incomplete as it was, resolved Betsy's doubts.

Caleb, Marie Ann, Rebeka and Betsy now visited in quiet tones in the Henderson home's ample library. They were expecting Walthrope to join them for dinner shortly and each straightened and adjusted clothes or posture when John announced him. With happy greetings for each member of the party, Walthrope casually strolled into the room.

Betsy had sent word to Walthrope a day earlier that she hoped he could come by for a visit. She had matters beyond the scope of the factory she wished to discuss with him. She asked that he keep the appointment confidential as she wanted to minimize embarrassment to a particular gentleman. She wrote that she knew he would understand her position. He had immediately sent a reply:

My Love,

Your request that I call upon you tomorrow to discuss certain private affairs has been received by your humble servant. It would be an honor to call upon someone who has become so dear to my heart, and I hope that you will allow me to join you for dinner. Let me certify that this servant would deem it a great privilege to assist you with any matters you may have regarding any of your business enterprises. It need not be said that this servant has and always has had the utmost respect for Mr. Moore, especially when one considers his sacrifice. I understand the trust you had placed in him was more than, most unfortunately, he could bear under his difficult circumstances. This servant has been ready at a moment's notice to step forward to assist you if you had at any time indicated such a need or desire. Your most thoughtful concern for Mr. Moore's feelings does you great credit and will be utmost in this servant's mind as we meet. Be confident that no embarrassment will accrue to Mr. Moore because of the actions of this friend.

If it pleases you, it is hoped that another, most important matter may be discussed during our meeting as well. It has become apparent that it is an appropriate time to discuss a subject that is very dear to my heart. Hopefully, you will share those feelings.

Our meeting tomorrow will be anticipated with great happiness and pleasure. Till then, I remain
Your most faithful servant,
Lucius

Walthrope was pleased with his reply. It showed sensitivity to Betsy and Caleb, but made it clear he anticipated handling the mills and farm. It also sweetened the occasion with the promise of a vague romantic purpose beyond the business discussion. He smiled as he speculated about how excited she would be to read that he had something special to discuss. He took pleasure in visualizing her inability to sleep that night, pacing the floor, waiting for their rendezvous, wanting it to come. He nodded his head knowingly when he received a short note from her later in the afternoon indicating that she looked forward to dinner with him. At an appropriate, discreet time, they could discuss the matters of interest to both of them.

Walthrope was right. The night was long for Betsy. She paced the floor imagining the anticipated discussion. She envisioned possible scenario after scenario in her mind, wondering how it might end, mentally reenacting the scenario she liked best. Then doubts crept back into her mind, and she started through a new set of scenarios. She had discussed the purpose of the meeting with her mother. Rebeka had immediately discouraged her daughter from her intentions. It was foolishness! But Betsy was adamant, and Rebeka reluctantly ceded to her daughter's will.

At breakfast, Betsy, to her mother's surprise, told Caleb and Marie Ann of the intended meeting. Caleb responded quickly. He appealed to Betsy, asking her not to meet with Walthrope, to give Caleb a little more time. He asked that she let him handle it for her; hadn't he handled it well so far? Her course was not right. Marie Ann followed his lead, begging her to listen to Caleb, promising her that Caleb could handle it. Marie Ann pleaded that Betsy give Caleb the opportunity, and he would get the help needed to take care of everything. She thought Betsy was moving too quickly. She pointed out there was danger in moving too fast. Caleb could do it. Let him. Hadn't he proved faithful? His wound, Marie Ann admitted, slowed him down a bit, but he could do it. Rebeka listened quietly, watching her daughter's gracious responses and determination with pride, mingled with dismay. The breakfast concluded with tacit acceptance of Betsy's decision.

Each of them, like Betsy, began to pace the floor in different rooms. Betsy paced in the library. She could hear the sound of Caleb's crutch above in his bedroom as he walked back and forth there. She marveled at his stamina and empathized with his frustration. But she had made her decision. He would not have to worry about it any more. Caleb's pacing eventually stopped, but by that time Betsy didn't notice because she was lost in her own nervous agitation.

As Caleb paced, there had been a knock on his door that brought him up short. He crossed the room, opening the door to Rebeka and Marie Ann. Surprised to find them there, he nonetheless invited both women into the room. They quickly entered, and Marie Ann softly closed the door behind them.

"Caleb, this is madness!" Marie Ann had begun. "We've got to persuade her not to do this . . . to let you do it. You've done so well with it already."

Rebeka said only, "Is there nothing you can say to convince her?"

Caleb laughed, "Mrs. Richman, I suspect you have more influence with her than either of us. I would appreciate it if you approached her."

"I've interfered too often in the past. I can't do it . . . not again. More to the point, she wouldn't listen to me."

Caleb became serious, "Then I don't believe there's anything we can say to deter her. Certainly I would like it to be different, but it's not in the cards."

As Walthrope arrived, each member of the party arose as he rushed to greet them. He approached Rebeka with a greeting she felt was more appropriate for a son to a mother. He approached Marie Ann compassionately and Caleb with undue kindness.

He then turned his attention to Betsy, stepped close to her, greeting her warmly, "My dear Betsy, I am grateful to find you in full health and beauty." Even as he said these words, he noted her pale complexion, her look of exhaustion. The night had passed just as he had imagined it would for her. What a pity she had lost sleep, because he had never slept better. Perhaps she would be able to sleep tonight—perhaps not. She would be wrought-up by their engagement; most likely she would be unable to sleep again. What a pleasurable thought: her sleepless again, thinking . . . dreaming . . . of him.

"Mr. Walthrope, thank you so much for coming," she said.

"Betsy, I think you must call me Lucius now . . . under the circumstances."

She continued without acknowledging his comment. "I wanted to put off our discussion until after dinner, but I can't wait any longer. If it's acceptable to you, let's discuss our business first . . . before dinner."

"If you prefer," he looked nervously at Caleb, uncomfortable that she would bestow management of the mills and farm on him in front of the former, soon-to-be disgraced soldier. "Wouldn't you rather do it in private?" Walthrope's ecstasy overcame his concern for Caleb's feelings. The deed would be done now, immediately, he wouldn't have to play this silly role through dinner. He was so close now to the end of the game.

Seeing him glance at Caleb, Betsy said, "Oh, Caleb's aware of my decision . . . of everything." She smiled sadly, "He'd like it to be handled differently, but understands."

Walthrope turned solicitously to Caleb, "It will work out for you, Caleb . . . very well. I've given it some thought. At the factory, I have something that will be perfect for you."

Caleb looked blankly at Walthrope and didn't respond.

Walthrope turned again to Betsy, his excitement showing from behind his usual calm demeanor. Betsy had never seen him like this and motioned for him to sit. He sat in a chair near the couch on which Betsy sat and looked expectantly at her. The other three took seats at a distance from Betsy and Walthrope, Caleb sitting slightly out of Walthrope's view. Caleb's position made Walthrope slightly nervous as he assumed Caleb was angry with him for taking over responsibility for farm and mills. Walthrope inadvertently glanced to his side to see where Caleb lighted. Why didn't they discuss this privately? This was awkward, awkward for everyone. Walthrope smiled and looked again at Betsy. Betsy leaned back in her chair, consciously attempting to relax.

"Mr. Walthrope . . . Lucius, I don't know where to start."

"Wherever you like, my love."

Betsy waited. "Lucius . . . a while ago, I heard a story I'd like to tell you."

"A story from your lips to me is as honey is to a bee." Walthrope smiled broadly, still unable to conceal his excitement.

Caleb spoke up, "Just don't get stuck in the honey."

Walthrope felt a flash of anger. Why was he here? Maybe there wouldn't be a role for Caleb after all. But then he remembered that this woman and all her possessions would soon be his. He forgot Caleb.

Betsy continued, "Several months ago, a man and a friend were together. They were upstairs in the man's house. There was a knock on the front door . . . a pounding really. It was late at night, and the man went to answer it. The friend stayed upstairs, quietly waiting. This friend heard yelling . . . fighting below. The friend was frightened and hid in a dark corner of the bedroom. The friend heard the fight end, then heard an unfamiliar tread in the back of the house, up the stairs . . . in the same room. A stranger, barely visible, but visible nonetheless in the dark, pulled open drawers . . ."

Walthrope's face was pale. "What has that got to do with your mills and farm, with Caleb . . . with us."

"Hear me out, Lucius. Be patient."

As she spoke the words, she realized why she had brought him here, why she insisted on confronting him personally, why she had not left it to Caleb and the sheriff. It was simple—revenge. She wanted to be the one who unmasked him; wanted to see his face when she exposed him. She wanted him to know she had discovered what he really was. The realization brought her shame, but she hated him. He had used her—even now was still trying to use her, deceive her. She also realized that Lucius Walthrope was not a man to be trusted: violent, cunning, perniciously sophisticated, deceitfully romantic, dangerous, especially to the occupants of the Henderson home who now knew so much about him. Betsy stared at Walthrope. She couldn't go back; she had to finish the confrontation. Thank goodness Caleb was here, but Caleb in his condition could hardly stop a man, an animal like Walthrope.

Walthrope's suspicions passed, and he resigned himself to hear the rest of the story.

"Where was I?"

Caleb volunteered from across the room, "Cluttering rooms."

Walthrope turned his head and directed a hostile glance at Caleb, who looked back without feeling.

"That's right," Betsy said. She ignored the visual exchange between the two men. "That friend watched as the stranger went through the room. The friend was silent, still, unseen, until she heard the soft sound of a window breaking. The friend . . ."

"It's a woman," Walthrope said laughing nervously. He remembered the sheriff saying that a woman had helped in Stokes' murder. He was angry with himself for dismissing the possibility that someone else was in the house that night. He could have easily discovered who she was and ensured she never talked. Then he remembered: The woman who visited Betsy. It was her; it was so obvious. Why hadn't he seen it before? But it was too late to deal with her now. He was getting sloppy . . . much too sloppy.

"Oh, did I say it was a woman? My mistake." Betsy said in feigned innocence. "The friend found the man downstairs . . . dead. The friend ran. They blamed the murder on a woman and a soldier."

Walthrope shifted nervously, "That's just like Stokes' murderer. That's right, it was a woman and a soldier. But I never heard there was anyone else in the house. Are you sure about that? "

"No one knew anyone was in the house, but the friend saw the man who murdered Stokes . . . saw him and remembered his face. She didn't know him, but saw him again and learned who he was."

"This is wonderful then," Walthrope said brightly. "We know who killed Stokes. Let's tell the sheriff. Have the soldier arrested. The woman—she was prob-

ably in on it. You can be sure of that . . . in on it together. She was no friend of Stokes. I know how these
women work. I know. I was his close friend."

Betsy spoke patiently, saying, "We know who killed
Stokes. That friend came to me."

Rebeka and Marie Ann watched in despair. They
feared for Betsy and for themselves.

Walthrope continued to speak. "It was that woman,
wasn't it. I knew she was up to something. Betsy. This
is wonderful news. It won't bring Stokes back, but we
can bring the miscreant to justice! Let's go to the sheriff right now. Is the murderer still in town?"

"We don't need to go to the sheriff," Betsy said firmly.

Emotionally devoid eyes stared at Betsy, giving her
an unintentional glimpse into his character. He said,
"You tell me all this because . . . ?"

"I know who killed Stokes."

He responded with enthusiasm again in his voice, "I
know that. You've said that a dozen times, in a dozen
different ways. If you know, let's tell the sheriff or go
to the army, but let's not just sit here while the culprit
flees. Tell them who did it. Let them arrest the man. It
was a man and that woman wasn't it—or was it two
women?"

"Don't you know?"

"Betsy, what nonsense is this? All I know is they
were looking for a soldier and a woman."

"They were looking for the wrong person. I know
everything."

"Then go to the sheriff, woman! Stop this game! I'll
go! I'll tell them for you. Tell me who it was—I'll han-

dle everything for you. Is that your concern? Is that what you wanted to ask me?"

She didn't take her eyes off him, "Lucius . . . I know you killed Stokes."

"Me? That's absurd! How can you believe such a thing? Don't you know me after all this time? Don't you know I could never do such a thing?"

"I know you killed Stokes."

Walthrope spoke in an accusing tone, "Did that woman tell you that? It doesn't surprise me." His voice softened, "I have a confession to make to you, Betsy. Didn't Emily tell you? I confided it to her many months ago. I thought surely she had told you. It would have made it so much easier for me, less embarrassing. I didn't want to have to tell you. There is a certain humiliation for me associated with it. That woman—the woman who came to visit you, she was no stranger to me. I knew her. She once loved me. I, for charity's sake, was kind to her, but I never loved her! And I never did anything dishonorable! She took my charity for love. When I moved, when I came to Staunton, she followed me, forever harassing me. She demanded that I love her, demanded that I marry her. She said once, 'After all that has happened between the two of us, you must marry me. I am with child.' It was . . . she was pitiful. I reminded her as kindly as I could that we had never been together. I could not be the child's father. The poor woman became hysterical, crying and screaming. She yelled at me and said she would find a way to make me suffer . . . as she suffered; that she wouldn't rest until she destroyed me." His voice became still softer, "I never believed she would go so far—to kill a man, just to dishonor my name. I thought she was harmless. I would have . . . oh . . . it doesn't matter now. It's too late. Stokes is dead. Poor fellow. All of this because a deranged woman seeks to destroy me. Betsy, can you forgive me for not confessing this earlier, warning Stokes, warning you of her? You might have been in harm's way as well. I should have confided in you directly when I found her here with you. I should have known she was poisoning you against me, hoping to destroy the happiness we have together, happiness she coveted but could never have. She might have harmed you had I not interrupted. Can you ever forgive me for this, my dear Betsy?"

Betsy's mind worked frantically. Could she be wrong? Had the woman deceived her? What she had taken as terror in the woman's eyes, could it have come from a burning hatred and her fear at being caught in her lie? She remembered the woman's visit vividly and Walthrope's sudden appearance—his threat. Then it was a threat after all, because he knew her, because he knew what kind of woman she was, because he knew she was trying to destroy him and thus destroy Betsy. When Caleb and Marie Ann had been unable to find the woman, Betsy assumed Walthrope had followed the woman, killed her and hidden her body. But it wasn't that. Betsy now imagined the woman had simply run away to the next town; been found out in her deceit and run to protect herself from public exposure. Walthrope mentioned Emily. She surely would have told her of this if they hadn't had a falling out; but the two women never spoke to each other. Betsy began to relax. It was all a misunderstanding, then. Walthrope had not killed Stokes. It was that woman and a renegade soldier, or that woman alone. She felt relief; the confrontation could end. He had shown her the truth. She sighed and smiled.

Walthrope smiled back warmly. But his smile was in stark contrast to the look she had seen earlier on his face . . . in his eyes . . . and suddenly it discomforted her. When she was ready to accuse him, the foreboding look was there just briefly. It was coldness . . . something she had never seen there before. It held no concern for Stokes . . . or the miserable woman . . . or Betsy, only ice. She knew it now. In the fire of rage, Lucius Walthrope had killed Stokes. Now he turned his ice upon her. Walthrope had coveted all she had: her factory, mills and farm. What would a man do who covets a farm? Would he kill a man? Would he kill them all? Walthrope was a master thief, a master deceiver. Betsy had been vulnerable, eagerly accepting his lies. She had not seen him clearly. It was painfully apparent now—all were lies. She spoke slowly, "I know you killed Stokes."

Walthrope did not discern how close he had come to deceiving her once more. If he had, he would have continued his innocent role, appealing to her emotions, to her desire to see good in everyone. Instead his powerful anger drove him. Its sound chiseled into his voice as he said, "That's unfortunate for you."

They sat silently. Anger was visible on Walthrope's face and in his posture, but he said nothing more. He looked slowly, threateningly at each person, resting his eyes last on Rebeka. He had an impulse to break her neck. It would be so easy. He could do it before anyone could come to her aid. That would be sweet revenge for this disappointing turn of events. He looked at Betsy, thinking of all that was slipping—had slipped—from his fingers. Then he remembered and imagined a dirty Union soldier, the letter writer, a lowly private and Betsy together. He imagined all she had in the hands of the soldier. He hated Betsy.

Marie Ann watched Walthrope's transformation from smooth to coarse. She saw his fury and involuntarily shivered. She wished she were closer to Caleb, who sat motionless, breathing calmly, intently watching Walthrope's hands. Rebeka's only concern was for her daughter, and thought of going to her side to protect her, but she waited.

Walthrope stared at Betsy. She must never be happy. His anger became despair. Trapped! Rage seized him. He said in a quiet, threatening tone, "You should have stayed out of it, Betsy. You should have left it alone. It would have been better for all of you."

Caleb, still watching Walthrope's hands, interjected, "And why would that be?"

Betsy said quickly, "Caleb . . . please!"

Walthrope ignored Betsy's plea to the former cadet and answered Caleb, "Because Betsy's visitor, that odd little woman whoever she was, was right. I did kill Betsy's dear friend, Mr. Stokes, with my bare hands. Betsy, it felt good! Mr. Stokes hated you more than you could ever imagine—our lovely Betsy. But don't think I killed him for you! That's not why I killed him. Do you want to know why I killed him?" He smiled coolly at Betsy. "Because Stokes wasn't good enough at stealing from you, dear fool. Yes, that's right, he and

I . . . stole a fortune from you. Stokes just wasn't quite good enough to cover it up. So you see he really did deserve to die."

He glared at Betsy. He mocked her, saying, "It was you my dear who killed him. You bear that responsibility! Don't look so surprised! It was you who questioned the factory being closed. It shouldn't have been. You were right. It should have been operating as if nothing unusual was happening. It should have been open when you got there, but it wasn't. If you'd investigated, just gone in, looked around, you would have found that money was being made, lots of money, off speculating and smuggling, all in your name. Great patriot Elizabeth Henderson, wife of the late Captain Thaddeus Henderson . . . a speculator . . . a smuggler! Can you imagine that? Shocking, isn't it? I am shocked and ashamed of you, Betsy! How can you ever raise your head again in this town . . . in the Confederacy? You have betrayed your foolish and dead husband, your friends. Tsk . . . tsk. Have you no shame?"

Walthrope paused long enough to catch his breath and to think about the revolver resting in his coat pocket. He would put it to use soon, but not yet. "It would have been safer for you . . . each of you . . . not to know the truth. Oh Betsy, instead of the honor of being Mrs. Lucius Walthrope, you disgraced your husband's name and had the grave misfortune of being killed in your own home by a despicable soldier who you brought in out of the goodness of your heart . . . a cripple . . . half a man . . . not even a man. I have this strange feeling that he will kill you today, Betsy . . . this very hour. Each of you will be killed by this depraved and crippled soldier." He turned his head and looked, laughing, at Caleb.

Caleb sat, still motionless, still breathing calmly, but his anger had burst within him. Only by using every fiber of self-control was he able to hold himself back. Half a man? He would show Walthrope what half a man could do. He wanted to grab and choke him, kill him with his own hands. Pity for Betsy overwhelmed him because of this complete and merciless betrayal. But Caleb would be faithful to her. He would do nothing without her approval, and she had sworn him to do nothing.

Walthrope continued outlining his planned scenario, "I arrived just in time to take Mr. Moore's life for his terrible slaughter of each of these charming ladies. And you . . . my dear, innocent, foolish girl," he looked directly into Betsy's eyes, "you will join your rotting husband in good Virginia soil."

"Are you threatening us, Walthrope?" Caleb snarled.

Lucius' face turned quickly, and he glowered at Caleb. "Are you so stupid, you don't even know a threat? You have to ask if you've been threatened? Did they cut out your brain when they sawed away your leg?" He turned to Betsy again. "Come the end of the war—and this is the most tragic part—your precious little Union soldier will come to find only a gravestone for the honorable Captain's wife who he so kindly wants to love. Think of his sorrow! Tragic . . . tragic."

For the first time, a look of shock crossed Betsy's features. The depth of Walthrope's anger had not surprised Betsy, but she did not anticipate his knowledge of Hank. She was unprepared for this revelation. How did he know? No one knew except Emily. Surely she hadn't told him. Surely she wouldn't, she couldn't. Would she? It didn't matter, not now. He knew! Her face paled.

He smiled when he saw her surprise. "Oh yes, Betsy, I know all about your great love. I read every letter, every . . . precious . . . sweet . . . word he wrote. Does everyone here know you cavort with the enemy?"

Walthrope breathed deeply, "I could strangle you right now and report to Richmond I had to do it—merely stopping a spy. What Confederate secrets have you told your lover? Did you do it for love or for the money he paid you? How much did your soldier pay you? Did he give you silver and gold?" He laughed and looked again at each person in the room. "Yes, our faithful patriot not only makes a fortune speculating but has another little secret. And your secret, your cavorting, will stop here."

Betsy moved from shock to anger to hatred, but she controlled her hatred and slowly regained her composure just as Walthrope stood up and moved menacingly close to her, standing above her. She looked up at him defiantly, her angular jaw set hard. Her challenging stare angered him more. He growled animal-like and slapped her face with the back of his hand. A large ring on his finger gashed her cheek and blood ran freely from the wound. Instantly Caleb pulled a revolver from his coat, anger permeating his features, and trained it on Walthrope.

Betsy saw Caleb and cried out, "No. Caleb! No! You promised."

"Not this!" Caleb yelled at her.

"What a surprise, our leg-less soldier can still hold a gun," Walthrope said, taunting Caleb when he saw that Betsy was restraining him.

Rebeka moved quickly to her daughter and pressed a handkerchief firmly to her cheek, but Betsy ignored her. She sat calmly. She looked directly into Walthrope's face, and without looking at her mother, gently pushed her away. She spoke in an abnormally soft voice, "It doesn't matter, Mr. Walthrope. You are in jeopardy as we sit here. I alerted the sheriff to everything. I told him what happened and he, even now, is looking for you. They are coming . . . coming very soon."

Fear flashed from Walthrope's eyes. Why hadn't he thought of Caleb having a gun? He was getting sloppy. He would like to finish Caleb off . . . but how? In the meantime, he turned again to Betsy. "Why have you called me here then?"

Betsy thought for a moment of her desire for revenge, of the blood on her cheek, of the jeopardy in which she had put them all. "I wish I hadn't, but you'd best leave now. It's your only chance, but I doubt you'll make it, and I hope you don't." Vindictively she added, "And you'll leave on foot . . . as I believe my money bought the horse you ride. You'll leave without transportation. But for the life of me, I don't know why I even let you leave after what you've done. I don't know why."

"Walthrope, you will leave here without your gun as well," Caleb added unexpectedly with his pistol still aimed at the now-exposed rogue. They glared at each other. Caleb continued, "You will not leave this room alive if you do not leave the gun."

Caleb directed Marie Ann, who had been stunned by the interview, to search Walthrope's coat. She hesitated from fear and Caleb commanded Walthrope to drop his coat on the floor and kick it toward Marie Ann. Walthrope slowly removed his coat looking for an opportunity to grab a hostage or throw something at Caleb . . . anything that would distract him and give Walthrope a second to charge the former cadet. But Caleb was too far from him and all three of the women had unconsciously moved farther away. When his coat was on the floor, Caleb demanded again that Walthrope kick it toward Marie Ann. Instead Walthrope attempted to kick it high in the air toward Caleb, quickly following it in a rush for Caleb's gun. Walthrope had misjudged the strength of his kick and the distance to Caleb. The coat fell short and Walthrope could see Caleb's muscles contracting, ready to fire. Walthrope stopped his failed charge, held his hands up to reassure Caleb, but it was too late. Caleb pulled the trigger and the hammer came down on the cylinder with a metallic echo, but no explosion. Caleb looked down nervously at his pistol. Betsy remembered with horror that she had crept into Caleb's room earlier in the day and removed the caps. She had seen him loading it and worried that his discouragement had reached a new low and that he contemplated suicide. In her concern for him, she had removed the caps, never suspecting his true intent.

Walthrope laughed and mocked Caleb, "No wonder you got shot in the army . . . no one ever told you how to load a weapon."

The failed shot brought Marie Ann to action. She flew across the room, past a startled Walthrope and grabbed his coat. Walthrope chased her, but Caleb rose quickly to meet him. Using his crutch as a bat, he smashed it into Walthrope's stomach, bringing the murderer to an instant halt.

Marie Ann by that time had reached the coat and pulled from its pocket a small pistol. She trained it nervously on Walthrope, while Caleb hurriedly hobbled to her side and took the pistol from her. As he did, Marie Ann dropped noisily to the floor. It had been too much for her. Betsy glanced kindly at Marie Ann who lay on the floor and at Caleb whose eyes remained fixed on Walthrope.

Walthrope smiled bitterly. They had clumsily outsmarted him. He felt contempt for the woman who lay pathetically on the floor, for the one-legged soldier who didn't know how to load his gun, for the naive young woman from whom he had stolen so much, for the mother from whom he still wanted to choke life. He hated them all, would still like to kill them . . . end it here. But he remembered Betsy's mention of the sheriff being on his way. It was time to give up the struggle and flee. Without further word, he walked toward the door, paused, turned quickly around. In the motion, he saw Caleb still training the pistol on him. Walthrope smiled and bowed graciously. "Mr. Moore, Miss Allen, Mrs. Richman . . . and my dear Mrs. Henderson, it has been a pleasure. It's disheartening to end it like this on such unfriendly terms . . . such a pity. Perhaps we'll meet again some day. I know I would like that."

With everyone's eyes still on him, and in his shirt sleeves, Walthrope stepped from the room, slamming the door behind him. Caleb immediately lowered himself to Marie Ann's side and Rebeka went to Betsy to treat her wound that continued to bleed and had by now soiled her cheek, neck, dress and chair.

Betsy sighed. He was gone. Gone. She would never have to look at him again. It was over. Her bluff had worked, but not well. At least he didn't know she had never contacted the sheriff. No one—besides her—had been hurt. It hadn't worked as she had expected, but it was over. Betsy wondered why she had let him go. Why hadn't she called the sheriff? Why didn't she let Caleb shoot him with Walthrope's own gun? Then she remembered that too many people were already dead. She just wanted him to go away, for him to know that she knew what he had done, that she had discovered it. She just wanted it to be over.

Chapter 32
January 1864, Near Staunton, Virginia

As Hank approached the farmhouse he had visited once before, he could see its two-story pillars. The land around it was still beautiful but winter quiet. No one was in sight. He climbed the stairs, approached the door, and knocked without pausing to consider how momentous he expected the experience to be. He had thought about this hour continually for more than a year. After fighting on many battlefields, in the boredom and hunger of winter camps, during long, uncomfortable wet marches, he had envisioned this scene and imagined its outcome. Sometimes the images ended in the happiness of a lifetime of love; often when he was downcast, he would dream unhappy endings that fed his passing desire for self-pity. In a real sense, anticipation of this moment at this door had kept him alive.

The same elderly black man with whom he left the letter more than a year earlier opened the door and looked at him vacantly for a moment. He didn't remember Hank and took him, even out of uniform, for a hungry soldier, many of whom passed through the area, stopping at this door on their way home or to some new assignment. They invariably would ask for a bite to eat. Betsy was generous with all who came and had given instructions when she returned to Staunton that her servants were to take care of all soldiers who knocked at the door. John spoke to Hank, "Come around to the back, sir. I'll give you something to eat." The slave began to close the door.

Hank said firmly, extending his hand to stop the door, "I thank you for that kindness, but I'm not here to eat. I've come to see Mrs. Henderson."

Bewildered, John did not invite Hank in as was his usual practice with guests, but said, "Wait. I'll tell Mrs. Henderson you're here." He pushed on the door and Hank lessened his resistance so the door slammed hard in his face. John failed to ask Hank his name in his hurry to close the door.

The servant moved quickly toward the library that faced the back of the house where Mrs. Henderson's confrontation was just concluding. As he approached the library, an unmasked Walthrope rushed from the room, slamming the door behind him. Seeing John enraged Walthrope even more, and he savagely shoved the old slave into the wall. John rebounded from the wall and collapsed, senseless, to the floor.

Hank in the meantime turned, had stepped away from the door and off the porch. He admired the fields, where the grass had turned nearly completely white. He remembered his father's fields and imagined what it would be like to farm these. It wouldn't be so bad. A hill across the road caught his attention and his mind, bent by battle and death, shifted to thoughts of the simplicity of fortifying and holding it. Hank imagined skirmishers at that moment silently waiting in the grass at its pinnacle.

Hank stood by the porch with his back to the house when Walthrope, still raging and in shirt sleeves, swung the door wide open. He approached Hank rapidly from behind, and before Hank could turn around, raised his foot and kicked it hard into the middle of Hank's back. Hank fell to the ground stunned. He immediately wanted to hurl himself at whoever had kicked him, but he remembered the widow and her dead husband. A deep and sudden melancholy descended on him. It was clear to him. George had been right. The widow couldn't love him. She had given instructions: Strike him, kick him, kill him. He was among those who killed my husband. She had corresponded with him only to entice him here for this final humiliation . . . and death. She had probably already sent word to Confederate authorities. He had to escape. He rose quickly, glanced back and recognized his attacker: Lothario! One of the speculators—the worst of his mockers from the stage ride of a year ago. His anger surged. He felt an impulse to attack him. But he restrained himself: His heart was rent. What good would attacking this man do? He moved away from Walthrope and the house.

Walthrope also recognized Hank, and in a leap of comprehension understood this was no Confederate, but a Yankee—the Yankee, the letter writer and not stupid as he had appeared on the stage coach that day. He had deceived Walthrope. He was the Yankee! Walthrope knew it and wanted to kill him. That would crush Betsy's final hopes of love and lifelong joy.

Walthrope felt giddy—perhaps the story could still end happily. He laughed, "It's you. All the stupidity in the world has gathered in one place on the same day. Run, boy, run! You shall not have her!"

Hank didn't run, but he did walk briskly northward. Humiliated again, he wanted to be away from there, to forget the widow, Staunton, Virginia, to forget it all; to get back to the Union, where he belonged.

Walthrope, mocking Hank, called after him, "Did you come to court the widow, you fool? She wants nothing from you, Yankee, but to see you dead. I got her first. I have her. She's mine. You have failed!"

In his mind, Walthrope cursed Caleb. If he only had his gun, this soldier's career would end here. He pulled a concealed knife from his pant leg and charged after Hank.

All the while he was retreating, Hank had listened intently to what was going on behind him. As Walthrope approached, Hank turned to face the man, and side-stepped his charge. Hank saw the knife as Walthrope passed. Walthrope recovered, turning again toward Hank, and lunged at him stabbing the air. Hank grabbed the arm and hand of his assailant, keeping the knife away from him and throwing Walthrope roughly to the ground. Walthrope, disoriented, dropped the knife. He rose unsteadily to his feet. He had lost track of the knife, still he attacked Hank, and the soldier instinctively swung his fist hard and high into Walthrope's gut. Walthrope again fell to the ground, gasping for breath. Hank watched him. Walthrope moaned, gasped for breath and rolled on the ground in panic. Hank wanted to hit him again, but he instead pulled his pistol from beneath his winter coat. Walthrope slowly got himself under control and rose from the ground. He saw the gun. Avoiding Hank's stare, and as quickly as he could, Walthrope stumbled, still bent over from the blow to his gut, away from the farmhouse, Hank and Staunton. Hank continued to watch him, confused. Walthrope seemed to be fleeing the house. Hank remembered the conversation he listened to so intently in the stage coach as Walthrope and his friends plotted against a widow . . . in Staunton . . . a rich woman . . . beautiful. He suddenly feared for Mrs. Henderson; he knew the hearts of these men. But there was nothing he could do for her. They had her under their control, and she hated Hank. Without looking back at the house, Hank slowly made his way for the road to Indiana.

The ferocity of Walthrope's blow and his collision with the wall physically and mentally stunned John. When the old servant had recovered sufficiently to think clearly, he made his way to the library. Caleb was still comforting Marie Ann; Rebeka was still treating Betsy's wound. Betsy sat, emotionally spent. They had heard the commotion in the hall, but hadn't investigated, assuming it was a harmless result of Walthrope's rage at discovery . . . not realizing it was his wrath levied against another human being. John's entrance woke Betsy from her trance. She looked up slowly, saying, "What was that noise, John?"

"Nothing, ma'am, just Mr. Walthrope."

Mrs. Henderson smiled kindly at the servant, in her stupor of thought, not realizing the blow he had suffered.

"Ma'am! You're hurt!"

Betsy smiled at him and replied, "It's nothing, my friend, just Mr. Walthrope."

John stood quietly for a moment, then spoke again. "Ma'am?"

"Yes."

"A man was here. He looked like a soldier. I told him to come around to the back of the house, and I would feed him. But he said he wished to speak with you . . . though I think he's gone."

"Gone?" Betsy questioned as she rose quickly from her seat. Her thoughts were rapid: Could it be Hank? Could he be here? He couldn't leave, not again. She took the handkerchief her mother held to her face and keeping pressure on her cut moved swiftly through the door. Her mother and the couple followed.

Once in the hall, she felt the winter cold through the still-open front door and saw a figure in the distance walking on the road.

The man's anger and words puzzled Hank. Had the widow belittled Hank to him, even as Lothario schemed against her? She must have, otherwise this man would never have known about him. Did she hate Hank that much that she would choose him over Hank? He felt betrayed. Betsy, Daniel, Charlie, Nathaniel, George, Naomi, and now the widow—he had lost them all. He unintentionally moaned as he shuffled his feet forward.

When Betsy reached the door, she carefully studied the man as he moved down the road. His posture and movements were familiar. It could not be! She held her composure, moving slowly and deliberately, in spite of an overwhelming exhilaration. Betsy forgot her battered slave, her mother, Caleb, Marie Ann . . . or Walthrope and the possibility that he was still near. She stepped to the edge of the porch and yelled out as loudly as she could, "Don't leave! Please don't leave!"

He barely heard her call. He stopped. Was this one more trick, another trap? He turned and looked toward the house. He could see several people on the lower porch. They were looking in his direction. One called him again. Without thinking, he straightened to parade-ground posture and marched toward the house, accelerating his pace without ever realizing it. She saw it, smiling to herself. She then remembered her face, the blood on her hands and on her dress and wished again she hadn't confronted Walthrope. It hadn't been worth it. She felt ashamed of her desire for revenge, and now to meet Hank looking like this. She cringed inwardly.

Hope swallowed Hank's despair completely. He felt his heart quicken—not from exertion—but as it did before battle. He wanted to run forward . . . double time . . . to get into the fray . . . get the thing done . . . see if he lived or died . . . just to have it over. He had felt this way before, but had learned self control at schooling near Gainesville, at Second Bull Run, at South Mountain, at Antietam, at Fredericksburg and at Gettysburg. It was as if each battle had prepared him for this one moment. He kept a tight grip on his nearly irresistible desire to get to the woman, as it were, waiting for an order to charge. But this time, there would be no order given, making obedience easy. He was now his own company commander: general of his own army, an army of one. He would have to decide for himself to advance or retreat.

He marched forward, closer to the house and the woman. She was coming in focus now, and she stepped from the porch to the grass. The others remained unmoved on the porch. Naomi was right: She was young, slender, beautiful. Suddenly he felt cold, his body stiffened. He felt an attraction . . . a repulsion. Dismay and a feeling of imminent personal destruction rolled through his members. An emotional wind blew hard against his face, forcing him to lean forward to keep going just as he had when crossing fields in psychological winds created by spinning Minié balls. Images of the war, of the battles overwhelmed him. To have fought to survive for so long; to be destroyed now when he thought he was safe. He stopped, lowered his head, stared at the ground and thought. He couldn't go forward . . . not another step. Like a Minié ball in its last few yards, he was spent. There was no more fight left in him.

The woman of whom he had dreamed, the only dream that had kept him alive, was somewhere in that house. He wanted to see her. He had fallen in love with her in absentia. But one more obstacle loomed colossal before him, larger now than all the others combined. It was like a bad dream, people rising from his past to test him in these final few yards, to test how much he could take and whether he truly loved the widow. How could she stand between him and happiness again, even if it was only happiness imagined?

She watched him, still knew him, understood him, loved him. She wanted to go to him, to reassure him, to explain it all to him, to help him with each step to the house. Horror filled each moment: He might not step forward—but might retrace his march with dignity and pride. She wished she could remove his agony, but she dared not move. It was . . . it had to be his decision now. She had made hers. These last steps were his. A feeling of lost time, so much lost time deluged her. She lowered her hand unknowingly from her wound and squeezed her hands into tight fists. Momentary self-loathing swept away all other feelings. Then she saw his head rise and his posture straighten.

He stepped forward in a proud, rhythmic cadence. He reached the yard, stopped abruptly and said, "I seek Elizabeth Henderson, widow of Captain Thaddeus Henderson. I was told she would be at this house."

Rebeka, Caleb, and Marie Ann watched in disbelief.

Hank stared hard at Betsy, making her uncomfortable. This wasn't at all what she'd expected. He still didn't know she was the widow. He hadn't comprehended it. His eyes betrayed no sign of recognition or reconciliation. She wanted to cry, but was distracted imagining the inner strength that held back the sorrow and disappointment he must have felt seeing her here, imaging that she stood between him and his widow. He looked older than he had in Winchester when she last saw him, when she rejected him. Memories, hardship and sorrows had already left their premature marks and lines on his face. She worried that they might not all be from the war. His skin, roasted under the sun of summer and toughened by winter, was coarse and dark. She could see, even with his slouch hat on, that his hair had receded from his forehead.

He stood without flinching, awaiting her reply. Her mother watched in amazement, sudden understanding and with compassion. Lucius had explained it all inadvertently in his anger. She remembered and mourned Samuel—he looked so much like Samuel.

"I'm Elizabeth Henderson," Betsy replied, her voice choked with emotion.

Hank's face fell with embarrassment, his eyes dropped to the ground, his feet shifted. "I had no idea . . . I didn't know."

"I know you didn't," she responded softly. "But I did."

"Why didn't you tell me?" he stammered. "I had no idea . . . I would not have . . . I could not . . . I had no idea." He paused. All dreams of happiness gone, dreams that had kept him sane as he played his instrument in the Great Orchestra of Death. He felt despair, regret that he had left home, lost this beautiful friend, that she had lost her husband, that he had built his vision of the future on a mirage—something that could never be. Almost begging, he said with eyes closed and directed both at her and himself, "I'm sorry. I am truly sorry."

"So am I," she said gently. Neither of them moved till she added, "But I'm glad you've come." In a pleasant tone, she continued, "You know my mother . . . Mr. Moore . . . Miss Allen."

Hank took Betsy's words and tone as an invitation. Could there be hope then? He ignored the introductions and walked across the yard until he stood directly in front of her. She watched him as he looked down to his side and reached into his pant pocket. He pulled out a battered, dirty, heavily blood-stained envelope and raised it in his hand, with his palm up. With his other hand, he placed a brass button on top of the envelope.

She stared at the button and the blood and remembered her dream of Thaddeus. She ignored the letter and reached for the button. Leaving it in his hand, she touched it and his fingers reverently. He reached up and gently touched the fresh gash on her face.

As Rebeka, Caleb, and Marie Ann watched, each was thinking of a beautiful fall day more than four years earlier in Winchester when friendship, principle, loyalty and duty had seemed so simple.

Epilogue

Not Long Ago, Brawner's Farm at Manassas National Battlefield Park, Virginia

As she finished the story, the young woman reached out to touch the button Reid still held in his hand. He opened his hand for her, and she pressed her fingers against it reverently.

"That's the story of this button, and your great-great-great grandfather."

Reid stared at the woman. There was nothing to say to her. She was beautiful with her large, light green eyes. He hardly noticed now the thin scar that ran across her cheek. He slowly pulled the button toward his face, examined it closely as if looking for other secrets it might still hold back. He abruptly clutched it in his hand and rose from the ground and still in silence, walked toward the dilapidated farmhouse. She watched him.

It would be a family tradition: He would give this button to his children—future sons and daughters. They would bring it here. He would make them promise as his father had made him promise. How else could they understand what they'd been given? If only they could hear the story from this woman: she knew it so well.

Reid never noticed her slip away nor the striking resemblance she bore to an old family photo . . . a daguerreotype . . . passed down through the family. Instead, he was distracted by old sounds around him. They gradually grew to a great crescendo: marching, music, talking, laughing, horses on the Pike. The wood seemed smaller than when he'd come through it, the house different and new. He stood near trees in a cultivated orchard. How beautiful it all seemed. How sad that it would be scarred so soon. Then he saw him . . . a gawky, tattered general riding across the field. He rode past Reid toward hidden Confederate soldiers in the distance. Reid almost called out to him by name, but thought better of it. Reid eagerly turned his head toward the Pike. He searched for a boy from Woodstock among the blue-clad marching men. He saw him! It had to be him. Reid watched him . . . knew what he thought, what he feared, what awaited him beyond the wood they now shared. Reid smiled . . . willingly and completely submerged in 1862.

*B*ut if the cause be not good, the king himself hath a heavy reckoning to make, when all those legs and arms and heads, chopped off in battle, shall join together at the latter day and cry all 'We died at such a place;' some swearing, some crying for a surgeon, some upon their wives left poor behind them, some upon the debts they owe, some upon their children rawly left.

William Shakespeare in King Henry V, Act 4, Scene 1

About the Author

Michael J. Roueche grew up in Northern Virginia and has spent almost all of his adult life in the Old Dominion, where he worked for many years for an international corporation. Always a romantic, only in more recent years did he discover the Civil War that surrounded him, thanks to Bruce Catton books from his father's library and a good friend who gave him a copy of Michael Schaara's "Killer Angels." He and his wife of 34 years now live in Colorado, where they enjoy hiking and exploring the High Plains and Rocky Mountains, with their alpine vistas, aspen groves, evergreen forests and amazing wildlife. They have five children and several grandchildren.

Visit him at <u>www.michaeljroueche.com</u>.

Made in the USA
Charleston, SC
14 May 2013